PENGUIN BOOKS

Conquest

Stewart Binns began his professional life as an academic. He then pursued several adventures, including a stint at the BBC, before settling into a career as a schoolteacher, specializing in history. Later in life, a lucky break took him back to the BBC, which was the beginning of a successful career in television. He has won a BAFTA, a Grierson, an RTS and a Peabody for his documentaries. Stewart's passion is English history, especially its origins and folklore. *Conquest* is his first novel.

Conquest

STEWART BINNS

PENGUIN BOOKS

PENGUIN BOOKS

Published by the Penguin Group
Penguin Books Ltd, 80 Strand, London WC2R ORL, England
Penguin Group (USA) Inc., 375 Hudson Street, New York, New York 10014, USA
Penguin Group (Canada), 90 Eglinton Avenue East, Suite 700, Toronto, Ontario, Canada M4P 2Y3
(a division of Pearson Penguin Canada Inc.)
Penguin Ireland, 25 St Stephen's Green, Dublin 2, Ireland (a division of Penguin Books Ltd)
Penguin Group (Australia), 250 Camberwell Road,
Camberwell, Victoria 3124, Australia (a division of Pearson Australia Group Pty Ltd)
Penguin Books India Pvt Ltd, 11 Community Centre,
Panchsheel Park, New Delhi – 110 017, India
Penguin Group (NZ), 67 Apollo Drive, Rosedale, Auckland 0632, New Zealand
(a division of Pearson New Zealand Ltd)
Penguin Books (South Africa) (Pty) Ltd, 24 Sturdee Avenue,
Rosebank, Johannesburg 2196, South Africa

Penguin Books Ltd, Registered Offices: 80 Strand, London WC2R ORL, England

www.penguin.com

First published 2011

2

Copyright © Stewart Binns, 2011

The moral right of the author has been asserted

Set in 12.5/14.75 pt Garamond
Typeset by Palimpsest Book Production Limited,
Falkirk, Stirlingshire
Printed in Great Britain by Clays Ltd, St Ives plc

ISBN: 978-0-718-15677-0

www.greenpenguin.co.uk

Mixed Sources
Product group from well-managed
forests and other controlled sources
www.fsc.org Cert no. SA-COC-1592
© 1996 Forest Stewardship Council

FSC

Penguin Books is committed to a sustainable future
for our business, our readers and our planet.
The book in your hands is made from paper
certified by the Forest Stewardship Council.

To all those valiant souls who fought for their freedom
in the years 1066 to 1071 – history has not forgotten you.

Here begins a certain work concerned with the exploits of Hereward the renowned Knight . . . We think it will encourage noble deeds and induce liberality to know Hereward, who he was and to hear of his achievement and deeds, and especially to those who are desirous of living the life of a soldier. Wherefore we advise you, give attention and you who the more diligently strive to hear the deeds of brave men, apply your minds to hear diligently the account of so great a man. For he, trusting neither in fornication, nor in garrison, but in himself, alone with his men waged war against Kingdoms and Kings and fought against princes and tyrants.

De Gestis Herwardi Saxonis (The Life of Hereward the Saxon),
a story written by monks early in the twelfth century

And they talked and sang of the Wake and all his doughty deeds, over the hearth in lone farmhouses, or in the outlaws' lodge in the hollins green; and all the burden of the song was, 'Ah that the Wake was alive again!' For they knew not that the Wake was alive for evermore; that only his husk and shell lay mouldering there in Crowland choir; that above them and around them, and in them, destined to raise them out of their bitter bondage and mould them into a great nation, and the parents of still greater nations in lands as yet unknown, brooded the immortal spirit of the Wake, now purged from all earthly dross – save the spirit of freedom, which can never die.

Hereward, the Last of the English, Charles Kingsley, 1877

Contents

Introduction

In the middle of the eleventh century, three men fought for the future of England and the British Isles.

The victor, William the Bastard, Duke of Normandy, became King of England. His ruthlessness, his all-consuming lust for power and his outstanding skill as a leader founded a Norman dynasty that led England to become the most formidable political force in northern Europe.

England was not conquered easily. Its many tribes of Celts, Danes and Saxons had fearsome reputations in battle and strong traditions and cultures. There were many crucial incidents, but the Battle of Senlac Ridge, near Hastings, on the southern coast of England, on 14 October 1066, was the defining moment. Only a few days after he had defeated the Norwegian King, Harald Hardrada, at Stamford Bridge near York, the slaughter of Harold Godwinson, King Harold II of England, in what became known as the Battle of Hastings, changed the course of world history for ever. William's victory cast him as the villain, while Harold came to be seen as the heroic leader of a brave but vanquished people.

However, there was another man of those times whose heroic deeds were almost lost in legend.

This is the story of that man.

He became William's most formidable opponent, a man whose name would become synonymous with the dormant spirit of England under the Normans and all that 'Englishness' eventually came to mean.

Prologue

The hour was growing late but the rapidly descending sun was still strong and the heat of a hot summer's day had yet to subside. The undulating hills of Greece's western Peloponnese gave little hint of human activity except where an occasional shepherds' track cut a path over the high ground. Only in a few places had men made more permanent marks. Lonely chapels — simple stone sanctuaries, topped by Byzantine crosses — were totems of peace and truth in a world mostly bereft of such treasures.

High above the rugged hills, an old man sat on a rocky perch contemplating the far horizon to the north-west. He looked towards his homeland, a distant land he had not seen for over fifty years. His eyes watered as he peered at the waning red orb of the setting sun.

Several hundred feet below, amid the forests of pine, a column of mounted men turned into an open meadow. The stone chapel at the edge of the glade had small round windows, a solid oak door and a simple wooden hut behind the nave for the resident priest. The men dismounted after a long day in the saddle, and stretched their legs. They were an awesome group of men: fifty Varangians and fifty Immortals, supported by a baggage train of servants, cooks and grooms. All were in the service of two of the most important men in the civilized world: the revered Prince John Azoukh, formerly a Turkish slave, now a royal prince, and Prince John Comnenus, the son of Alexius Comnenus I, Emperor of Byzantium, a man on whose shoulders rested the hopes of an ancient lineage and a mighty empire.

Leo of Methone had been listening to the approaching commotion

1

for nearly half an hour. He had been educated in Athens, had worshipped in Rome and had even prayed at the altar of the great church in Constantinople. He knew to fear the tread of advancing armies.

It was late August in the year of Our Lord 1117. Anxiety gripped the Byzantine Empire, an empire begun in pagan Rome over 1,000 years earlier that now stood between Christianity and the heresy of Islam.

Leo had hidden in the undergrowth long before the soldiers arrived at his peaceful clearing. He was greatly relieved to see that they were men of the Emperor's army rather than a band of brigands, but astonished when he recognized them as Imperial Guards and realized who was leading them. He knew from his dress that the man at the head of the group was of the royal house, but the presence of the dark-skinned man next to him confirmed that the two lords were the renowned 'Two Johns of Constantinople'.

Leo's heart was pounding from exertion and anxiety. His mind raced: why is the young heir to the throne of Byzantium here? It is known throughout the Empire that his father is dying and that his sister, Anna Comnenus, will do anything to take the throne and rule with her husband, Bryennius. So why leave Constantinople on a journey of many weeks at a time like this?

Leo's train of thought was broken by the Captain of the Imperial Guard barking his orders: 'Troopers of the Princes' Guard, dismount! We camp here tonight.'

John Comnenus watched with amusement as Leo the priest approached him. His dark-brown cassock was scuffed with dirt from his hasty retreat to the undergrowth, he was covered in thorns and seedlings from his prickly hiding place, and his sandals squelched from the soaking they had received as he waded the stream behind his church.

'Good evening, Father. May we spend this night with you?'

2

Leo had never spoken to a prince before. He summoned all the composure his ecclesiastical education could afford him. 'Your Highness, it would be a great honour. But I have little to offer you other than God's house . . . and . . . ' He hesitated, nervous about his presumptuousness, ' . . . my blessing.'

The young heir smiled broadly, supremely confident in his status and authority.

'That is all a weary man needs. Besides, we travel well with all the trappings of court. Will you join us? The butt is Cypriot, from my father's vineyard; our cook is a Venetian and he can conjure a feast from old leather and the bark of a tree if you give him gentle oil and keen spices.'

Leo recognized immediately that what people said was true: John Comnenus was a man of great charm and humility.

'Sire, you are more than generous. But I am a poor priest of the countryside; I know nothing of the sophistication of towns and cities, and certainly nothing of the manners of a royal table.'

John Azoukh answered for John Comnenus. 'It is we who should be humble. We are guests in your beautiful meadow. Let us eat; the chill of the night air will soon be upon us.'

An hour later, over a hundred men sat in the cooling twilight to enjoy their food and wine. Leo said grace, then sat and gazed at the scene before him. Behind John Comnenus stood his equerry and men-at-arms: three tall men in blue tunics with gilded trim, their burgundy cloaks held by heavy bronze clasps of the royal house of Comnenus. With the light from the campfires flickering across their bearded faces and intricately worked armour, they had the ostentatious trappings of court soldiers, but their rugged demeanour was of men hardened by the ferocity of battle.

Prince John Azoukh sat beside the heir to the Purple of Byzantium. Twenty-eight years old, the same age as his royal companion, his was a remarkable story. As a small child he had been taken as a slave by a general of the Imperial Army, who, charmed by the little boy's humour and intelligence, had given him to the Emperor Alexius as a present.

Leo could see why the Arab slave had endeared himself to the family of Alexius: his soft black curls were the perfect complement to a clear olive skin, gentle dark-brown eyes and a strikingly handsome face. But his most endearing quality was his infectious vitality. The Emperor had recognized his charms but also his intelligence; he grasped numbers and languages quickly, wrote poetry and played the flute beautifully. John Azoukh, the slave, was brought up at court as if he were John Comnenus' brother; they became inseparable.

John Comnenus also had many qualities but was more reticent and considered. He was shorter than his Moorish companion and not the most handsome of men, but wearing his crimson smock, gold wristlets, gleaming bronze breastplate and a ready smile, he had the aura of a benign leader. There was much anticipation that Prince John would continue the wise and honest rule of his father. Byzantium was an empire of many cultures and peoples. Its noble families had intermarried with the aristocracies of the many lands they had conquered, creating a mingling of 'old blood' and 'new blood'. For 500 years, since the fall of the Roman Empire in the west, Byzantium had kept alive the traditions of the Graeco-Roman world, and Christian civilization.

To the right of the Prince were the Immortals. First raised by the Persians centuries before, these men from Byzantium's eastern provinces were renowned for their loyalty and fierceness in battle. Behind them, arranged in neat rows of tripods, were their pointed mail-fringed helmets, long pikes and round shields, and tethered lines of immaculate grey horses, freshly fed and groomed.

Forty years earlier, in 1071, the Byzantine army had been in disarray *after the disaster of the Battle of Manzikert. Muslim armies had besieged Byzantium to the south and east, Asian barbarians had threatened from the north and, in the west, powerful forces from northern Europe were rivals for power in Christendom. However, Alexius I had reorganized the army and reinvigorated the Immortals.*

The Varangians, to the left of the Prince, were no less impressive. Not so uniform in appearance, they carried a terrifying assortment of weapons, including their redoubtable weapon of mayhem, the double-handed battle-axe. Only with years of practice and a massively powerful upper body was it possible to wield it with deadly intent; it struck fear into the hearts of all their enemies. Although these men were foreign mercenaries, they were intensely loyal to their oath of allegiance and had served the throne of Constantinople for over a hundred years. Some were Vikings from Scandinavia; many were Normans from Sicily or North Africa. There were Celts from Europe's northern wilderness. A few were English. Legend had it that, fifty years before, a handful of housecarls from the army of King Harold of England, who had survived the final redoubt at the Battle of Senlac Ridge near Hastings, had fled to Constantinople to join the Varangian Guard rather than submit to the rule of William the Bastard, Duke of Normandy.

The Varangians' hair and beards were longer and wilder than those of the Immortals, whose tight black curls were kept neatly trimmed. Their locks also presented a mix of colours: red, blond and black and every shade in between, including the grey tresses of many gnarled veterans. Their shields came in all shapes and sizes and were decorated with a variety of creatures like an heraldic circus: eagles, boars, rams, bears, serpents and myriad mythical beasts. The royal household never ventured far without a bodyguard of Immortals and Varangians.

Way above Leo's clearing, in an eyrie all of his own, the wizened face of the old man creased into a contemplative smile. He was recalling his own adventures. He too had been a warrior.

'Father, we need your help.' John Azoukh's voice broke through the babble of a hundred men, now seriously engaged with their food, wine and conversation. 'We are here on the Emperor's business. There is an old man who lives in these hills and we need to find him. We mean him no harm; he is a friend of the great Alexius, who speaks very highly of him. He says that he has the wisdom of a man who has lived three lifetimes.'

'I know no such man anywhere.' Leo was startled to hear the description of a man of rare distinction and feared he had been too obvious in his denial.

To the locals the man was a hermit, rarely seen, a foreigner from a northern land. Nobody knew much about him, except that his unwelcoming manner and fearsome appearance led everyone to avoid him. He walked with the bowed back of an old age bedevilled by arthritis. Nevertheless, his frame was formidable, with broad shoulders and powerful arms and hands like those of a blacksmith. He had a shock of grey-blond hair that cascaded down his back and a snow-white beard that contrasted sharply with his deeply wrinkled face, burned chestnut-brown by the Mediterranean sun.

Leo had visited his reclusive parishioner just once and had spent only an hour with him. He had learned nothing of his past, but his manner and bearing gave strong hints of a turbulent life and of a man of rare gifts. He had longed to return and learn more but had promised not to; it seemed neither honourable nor wise to break a promise to such a man.

'Are you sure, Father?' There was a hint of impatience in John Azoukh's question. 'You must understand that all the great work of the Emperor Alexius must now be consolidated by the rightful succession of his beloved son, John.'

'But, my noble Lord, what has that got to do with an old man in the hills of Elis?' Leo responded meekly, but with a firm resolve not to place one of his flock in danger.

'So you do know such a man?'

'I didn't say that, sire. I simply don't understand what anyone from my humble parish could offer the heir to the throne of Constantinople.'

'Wisdom, Father Leo,' John Comnenus interrupted in a gentle tone, sensing his friend's irritation and Leo's discomfort. 'My father says I have all the qualities to follow him, except wisdom. He isn't much longer for this life and he grows anxious. My sister, Anna, is very shrewd; she plots against me and has powerful friends and an ambitious husband. My father doubts that I have the wisdom to deal with her. He has asked me to make this journey, to find this man and hear his story. He says that when I hear the account of his life, I will understand how men find the wisdom to know what they have to do and the courage to act on their judgement. So, Father, that is why we are here.'

Leo was overwhelmed by the Prince's frankness. 'My Prince, this is too much for me. I don't know . . . '

'Let me finish.' John Comnenus understood the embarrassment felt by the priest. He smiled at him and continued his story. As he did so, he pulled an amulet from a pouch around his waist. 'My father gave me this talisman, which he has worn throughout his reign. He said that if I give it to the man I seek, he will know that it comes from my father and represents a sacred trust. We have visited your superior, the Bishop of Corinth, and he told us that you are a good man, a fine priest, and that we could place our trust in you. But he also told us that you wouldn't easily reveal the whereabouts of the man we hope to find. Years ago, my father asked the bishop to find a sanctuary for this man and ordered the local governor to have his garrison keep a discreet but watchful eye on the district.'

Several things suddenly began to make sense to Leo: the bishop's long lectures about the sanctity of the confessional, no matter how disturbing the revelations of a man racked by sin might be; the reminders about the necessity to protect every member of the parish from prying questions, even if one of his flock was a stranger from afar; and the frequent visits from the governor's men-at-arms, asking about the welfare of the locals and whether any armed men had been sighted in the vicinity. All this just to protect a hermit?

John Comnenus continued. 'I know you want to do your duty as a good priest; I don't ask you to do otherwise. Please take this amulet and carry it to the man we seek. You are only the third man to touch it since it was placed around my father's neck thirty years ago.'

Leo looked down at the amulet. Hanging from a heavy silver chain was a translucent stone the size of a quail's egg. It was set in scrolls of silver, each of which was a filigree snake, so finely worked that the oval eyes and forked tongues of the serpents could be seen in detail. The stone itself was yellow in colour and, at first glance, apart from its size and smoothness, seemed unremarkable. But then Leo held it to the light of the campfire and grimaced in horror at the image he saw. Silhouetted in the baleful yellow glow of the stone was the face of Satan, the horned beast that had haunted men from the beginning of time. Close to the hideous face, trapped in the stone like the devil's familiars, were a tiny spider and a group of small winged insects.

'It's an abomination. God help us. Surely all who see it are cursed.'

The young Prince of Byzantium tried to reassure the man of God. 'It is what it is, but it is not to be feared.'

'Sire, I don't understand, it is Lucifer himself.' Leo held it as far away as he could without dropping it.

'Look again, Father.'

With a squint of revulsion, Leo examined the amulet again. As

8

he twisted it in the light he saw something else. Cutting through the stone was a streak of red, like a splash of blood, which, at a certain angle, obscured the face of the Devil.

'My father told me it carries five messages of abiding truth. The first message of the stone is courage: that we must face up to our fears and anxieties. The second message is discipline: it tells us that only through discipline and strength of will are we able to control the darkness within us. The third message is humility: we are reminded that only God can work the miracles that make the world what it is. The fourth message is sacrifice: just as the sacrifice of the Blood of Christ saved our mortal souls, so we should be prepared to sacrifice ourselves for God and for one another. Finally, the fifth message is wisdom: the wisdom not to be afraid of the stone, but to gain truth from it. The amulet reveals the face of the Devil surrounded by his acolytes, but they are trapped – entombed by the Blood of Christ. It is a sacred amulet and the man we seek has been its guardian nearly all his life. Now I am returning it to him, in the hope that he will feel that I am also worthy of it, thus anointing me as a true sovereign, just as he endorsed my father many years ago.'

As Leo clenched his fist around the amulet and thrust it deep into the pocket of his cassock, the Prince could sense his inner turmoil.

Leo turned to the Prince. 'Sire, does this man have a name?'

'My father didn't give me his name.'

Leo suddenly realized that although he had met the man, he too had no idea what his name might be. He referred to him simply as the 'Old Man of the Mountain'.

John Comnenus interrupted his train of thought. 'Go to your altar and pray for us and then get some rest. Rise early and go to this man. You will not be followed, you have my word. Give him the amulet and ask him if he'll see me.'

Leo responded with relief. 'Thank you, sire, for understanding my hardship in not immediately doing your bidding. I do know a man who lives high in the mountains. He may be the one you seek but he has asked me to respect his solitude. I will go to him; it will take a day to get there and to return.'

The Prince smiled at the priest. 'Only a truly honourable man would protect a stranger in such circumstances. The bishop was right: you are a good shepherd to your flock. Come, I will walk with you to your chapel.'

As the pair walked across the clearing, Leo felt uplifted by the Prince's words and honoured to be entrusted with an object so close to the Emperor's heart.

John Azoukh began to play his flute. It was a balmy night in a perfect setting, a rare opportunity for the warriors of Byzantium to enjoy a few moments of quiet reflection and to dream of home and their loved ones.

Several hundred feet above them in his high pasture, with his own vivid reminiscences fresh in his memory, the old man had fallen asleep. He now woke with a jolt, his body aching in parts, numb in others. He managed to pull himself upright and slowly made his way to his humble shelter. He was soon asleep again, but not before his thoughts had once more returned to the turbulent events that long ago engulfed his life.

Early the next morning, the Captain of the Guard and a dozen men took Leo to the beginning of the steep path into the hills before turning back to let him make his long journey alone.

The sun had already started its late afternoon decline as Leo reached the high pastures where he knew the man he sought had his simple home. He approached a crescent of open ground fringed by trees with, at its centre, a small wooden hut set hard against the rocks that rose sharply to the crest of a hill behind. It was an idyllic spot *from where, on a clear day, it was possible to see the distant shimmer of the Mediterranean, a full two days' walk away to the west. The basic wooden shelter was a lean-to jutting from the rocks, its roof covered with animal skins weighted down by large stones. The roof extended a little to cover the doorway where a simple frame of interwoven reeds acted as a door. At the back of the hut a dry-stone chimney and hearth had been built.*

It was a harsh world in the depths of winter, but today, warmed by summer's heat and surrounded by meadows bristling with life, it seemed perfect. Two goats were tethered in the open pasture, poultry ran around in aimless circles, neat rows of vegetables and herbs grew against the edge of the rocky backdrop and, over to the east, a small lake was home to a plentiful supply of fish. The surrounding hills, which seemed to stretch endlessly into the distance, offered good hunting, with boar, deer and rabbit. As Leo surveyed the scene, he could see several animal skins stretched out to dry in the sun and piles of freshly cut firewood.

It was the distant screech of a hawk that made Leo turn round. As he did so, he saw his quarry silhouetted on a large rock no more than ten steps from him. Leo shuddered at the sudden apparition; the man's large frame obscured the sun, the rays of which burst around him.

'This is a surprise visit, Father. You have had a long walk.'

The dark presence spoke firmly and deliberately. Leo averted his eyes as the figure moved away from the line of the sun, allowing its glare to fall on his face.

'Come to my hearth, we'll eat. You must be hungry.'

The voice was deep in tone with the croak of age and, although his Greek was good, it had the harsh edge of a foreign accent. Leo decided he should explain himself straight away.

'I come with a reques—'

Leo was interrupted before he could explain.

'I know.'

There was almost a sigh of resignation in his host's voice as he led the priest towards his simple shelter. Leo felt even more ill at ease. How could the Northerner know he was coming? In what mysteries had he become embroiled?

For a while they drank and ate, exchanging simple pleasantries, before Leo again decided to come to the point.

'I have been given an amulet to return to you. It has been carried here by Prince John Comnenus, the son of Alexius I, and his friend, Prince John Azoukh. They travel with a column of Imperial Guards. It pains me to carry the ungodly thing but it apparently has great meaning—'

Leo was halted in full flow.

'Are there Varangians among them?'

'Yes, and Immortals.'

The man's face creased into a warm smile as Leo handed over the amulet. A large hand clasped it and a pair of deep-blue eyes fixed it in their gaze. The priest noticed the arthritic knuckles, the two broken fingers and the patchwork of scars that disappeared beyond the man's forearm under the sleeve of his smock. The biggest of them was the width of a finger—a pale, jagged gash across a skin wrinkled by age and desiccated by the sun. Even more striking were the scars on his face. His left cheek was sliced from under his eye to the corner of his mouth, and there were several more souvenirs from a long life of mortal combat. Nevertheless, his face retained a rugged dignity which the sun seemed to have cast in bronze. The scars were like illustrations in a manuscript: what stories could they tell? Who had inflicted them?

'I wondered if I would ever see this again.'

Leo's host became quiet as he thought of home, an island kingdom many miles away to the north-west. He could see the chalk cliffs of its south coast. He imagined the verdant swathes of its forests and heathlands and the myriad wildflowers in its glades and clearings. He remembered its pungent odours of burnt ash and fresh manure and the sweet smells of mown hay and woodsmoke. He heard the blether and rush of its brooks and rivers and the din of birdsong and insect life. It had been a much-troubled land but, in his mind's eye, it seemed timelessly peaceful.

'What does the amulet mean?'

Leo's question broke the spell of the old man's reminiscences of home.

'It's called the Talisman of Truth and is said to be as old as time. I first saw it nearly three score years ago. It seems to follow me around.'

'You make it sound like a curse.'

'Maybe it is. Some say it is a guiding light, meant for kings, to allow them to see the wisdom of ages.'

'A prince who will soon be an emperor has travelled here with this Talisman. He asks to speak with you.'

As the Northerner got to his feet, Leo noticed the pain on his face.

'I sensed that if I lived for another summer, this prince would come.'

The old man paused. Leo noticed that his hand was shaking and that he was wincing from the effort of movement.

'May I ask how many summers have come and gone in your life?'

'Eighty-two, Father.'

Leo looked at the man in amazement, not doubting for a moment the truth of the answer, but wondering how a man could live so long, especially a man so heavily scarred by battle. Leo had heard that some men had lived beyond their eightieth year, but he had never met one.

'You had better make your way home now, Father. Let me fill your flagon and pack some bread and cheese for you.' The ancient warrior spoke warmly, concerned for a man who had a difficult descent ahead, especially as the last part would have to be negotiated long after nightfall.

'What will I tell Prince John?' asked Leo.

'Tell him that I am honoured to be asked to speak with him. I will be with him as soon as I can.'

'Will you not travel with me?'

'No, I have much to do here. It will take me some time to make my way down the mountain. Go to the Prince and ask for his patience.'

As Leo prepared to leave, he could not resist a parting question. 'You are obviously a man of some repute. May I ask why you are here, on the top of a remote mountain with only goats and wolves for company?'

The old man stared long and hard towards the distant sea before he answered. 'Father, I have lived a full life and done many things. I have seen most of our world, met all varieties of its feeble humanity and come to understand how weak and inadequate we are. But from here, when I stare into the distance, I am reminded of the strength, wisdom and courage that many people are capable of, especially the most humble. That gives me hope, it keeps me alive. Perhaps it's kept me alive for this day.'

Leo did not respond, but simply followed the old man's gaze towards the western horizon.

After a while, the Northerner continued. 'I came here with the Emperor Alexius many years ago, when he was raising one of the Greek themes for the Imperial Army. Many good men came from these hills and valleys. The old sages told us stories of how the ancients had a sacred temple near here, at a place called Olympia, built in honour of their God, Zeus, where great warriors from the Greek world would compete in contests of war and physical skill. When I retired from the Emperor's service, I could think of no better place to find solace in my old age.'

'I know nothing of such a place and I'm not sure it's part of our Christian tradition.'

'It isn't, Father. Many generations ago, Olympia was destroyed in an earthquake, its location forgotten, and in all my years here, I've never been able to find it.'

'Can you not find our Christian God in these mountains to bring you solace?'

'No, Father. Our "Christian God" has not revealed himself to me too often — not even here, close to Heaven!'

'Your words are a path to Hell and an eternity of suffering.'

'I know, Father, but my cynicism is born of bitter experience, both of men and of God. Aren't we supposed to be in His image? Look into men's hearts, what do you see, good or evil?'

Leo responded with the philosophical certainty of a priest. 'With God's help we can be all the things He wants us to be.'

'Well done, Father, you know all the right answers; I wish I had your faith.' He paused and smiled. 'You should hurry; the sun is making its way towards the west. Go safely. I will see you with the Prince tomorrow.'

His mind racing, intrigued by all that had happened in just a few hours, Leo made his way down the mountain as rapidly as he could.

As he reached the thick forest of the mountain's lower slopes, a dank mist swirled up from the valley. Increasing fatigue and the dark of the night slowed Leo's progress.

He found a sheltered overhang in the rocks to rest.

Leo slept fitfully and, when he woke with a jolt, he was cold and wet. His head and neck ached and his legs, made numb under his weight, tingled as the blood rushed to them. He longed for the soft straw and warm furs of his little hut in the clearing below.

The glow behind the mountain suggested about half an hour before dawn. He got to his feet and turned towards the path. As he did so, he saw, standing at a bend in the track just a few paces below him, the mysterious Northerner he had left only a few hours ago.

As Leo's eyes adjusted to the light, he noticed that the old man had effected a remarkable change in appearance. His long hair was tied back, his beard was neatly trimmed and he had the unmistakable appearance of an officer of the Varangian Guard. He wore a blood-red tunic trimmed with gold and a heavy, ruby-red cloak fastened by an ornate bronze clasp. Over one shoulder, held by a finely tooled leather strap, he carried a large circular shield adorned with the motif of the winged lion of Byzantium. Slung over the other shoulder was a heavy battle sword with a fine gilt handle and delicately worked sheath. Along his heavy belt were leather pouches for two shorter stabbing swords, a small close-quarters axe and a jewelled dagger. Then Leo's eyes focused on the most fearsome weapon he had ever seen. The shaft was the diameter of a man's wrist and its head stood almost at shoulder height. Although all Varangians carried a two-handed battle-axe, this was a double-headed version with two huge crescent-shaped blades. Leo wondered what mayhem it had caused and stared in awe at a man who seemed to have shed thirty years overnight.

'Follow me . . . and try to keep up!'

Leo did his best, but the old man moved more quickly than seemed possible for someone of his age.

Two hours later, they were close to Leo's chapel.

As they approached the perimeter guards, the Northerner stopped, drew himself up to his full height and bellowed in the clear, clipped tones of a man used to giving military commands: 'Be alert in the camp! A former Captain of the Varangian Guard approaches. I am Godwin of Ely.'

He strode into the camp with Leo scurrying in his wake. The

picket guards stood aside, clasped their weapons and snapped to attention. As the two men entered the clearing, with the sun just beginning to crest the hillside behind them, the Princes' men got to their feet. A discernible murmur travelled through the ranks as the older men recognized the gilt and braid of a Captain of the Old Order of the Varangian Guard and saw the double-headed axe, carried effortlessly and balanced halfway down its shaft by a powerful hand.

Leo shuddered as he looked at the faces of the guards when the old man strode past them. Who was this man who could command such instant respect from elite soldiers such as these?

John Comnenus rose as the two approached, but before he could offer a greeting, the visitor addressed him.

'Greetings, sire. I am your humble servant, Godwin of Lily.'

John Azoukh turned as he heard the greeting, his beard dripping with water from the leather bowl in which he had been washing.

The old man bowed and turned to him. 'Greetings, Prince John Azoukh. I am honoured to meet you.'

'Good morning to you. You have surprised us; we did not expect you so soon.'

'I was told the heir to the Purple of Byzantium wished to see me. To delay would have been impolite.'

As the old man spoke, John Comnenus noticed that his breathing was not as controlled as it had first seemed and that sweat was dripping from his forehead and hands.

'Please join us. Stewards, bring a chair.'

'Thank you, sire.'

'Tell me, I am right, am I not, you wear the uniform of a Captain of the Varangians of the Old Order?'

'You are right, my Prince. I was Captain of the Varangians during your father's early campaigns. I am an Englishman and I joined the Guard in 1081, the year your father became Emperor.'

17

'Godwin of Ely, noble Englishman. Please sit with us.'

'Thank you, sire.'

As stewards brought food and water, Godwin sat with the Two Johns of Constantinople and Leo took a place on a rock a few feet away.

'I have come with greetings from my father. He often thinks of you and the many battles you fought together.'

'Your father is a great man; it was an honour to serve him. How is he?'

'I am afraid he is dying. His stomach is putrefied, it is slow and painful, but he hangs on through fear of what will happen next.'

'I am saddened to hear that; it is not a fitting end for a man of valour. The only consolation is that he has the strength to bear it like few men I've ever met.' Godwin looked at the Prince with a sympathetic smile as their eyes acknowledged one another with genuine warmth. 'You have brought the Talisman of Truth. How may I assist you?'

'My father told me to come here, to give you the Talisman and ask you to tell me a story. He said it would help me find the wisdom to know what is right and what is wrong.'

Godwin moved uneasily in his chair, as if a great burden had been placed on his old shoulders. 'I hoped I would never have to tell that story again.' He paused, as if preparing for an ordeal. 'My time should have come at least ten summers ago. Every year, as the autumn winds rushed around my home, I felt death coming, but it passed me by. With each spring, I began to realize that I was being granted the extra years for a purpose. When the good priest clambered up the mountain to see me, I knew what it was he carried.' Godwin spoke quietly, with all the solemnity of his great age, then his eyes brightened a little, as if to ease the tension he had created. 'Sire, would you grant me just two favours in the telling of my story?'

'Of course.'

'I need one of your fine cavalry horses. I can only tell you the story from where I can remember the detail – on the top of my mountain – and I doubt that I can get back up there without the help of a horse. Also, I need Father Leo to hear my story. My time isn't far off and a kindly priest may be useful to me in facing the unknown.'

Leo smiled. 'Godwin, all men need a priest when they face God; only heathens face the unknown.'

'Precisely, Father!'

Now, all four men were smiling.

Prince John Comnenus called to the Captain of his Guard. 'We leave within the hour.'

As he approached, the Captain bowed in turn to the two Johns, and then he turned to Godwin and spoke to him in almost reverential terms. 'Godwin of Ely, I am privileged to salute you.' The Captain clenched the hilt of his sword and nodded his head.

Godwin grasped his sword and nodded back.

Several hours later, the Princes' Guard was camped in the high meadow beside Godwin's mountain home. Ripples on the lake forewarned that the wind would soon rush off the mountain and chase away the setting sun. Although the air was not yet cold, it soon would be.

The stewards did their best to make sure the four men were comfortable. They had made a roaring fire and collected a large supply of wood. Godwin and John Comnenus sat on sacks of straw and leaned back against the rocks which were strewn around the side of the lake, their sharp surfaces softened by furs and bearskins. Prince John Azoukh sat nearby, within earshot, with Father Leo beside him. Leo knew that the story he was about to hear would not only be a saga of kingship for the young prince but also Godwin's private confession.

Godwin had insisted that he tell his story in the open, looking north-west, where he could see the setting sun and, in his mind's eye,

England, the land of his birth. John Comnenus reflected on the scene, and how different it was from Constantinople. Here was tranquillity, without intrigue, mistrust or evil deeds; just nature and its eternal cycle.

'Is it time for me to hear your story now?'

'Yes, sire, I am ready. But understand this: it is not my story. It is the chronicle of another man — a man from a distant country and another age.'

'But you are a legend — an invincible warrior. My father tells me that you carried the Talisman because you embody all that it means.'

'I am merely a participant in the story. The Talisman has belonged to many men, but this is the story of a messenger, a man who carried it in search of a leader worthy of the name. He was an Englishman, who, as guardian of the Talisman, found his own destiny; a destiny that was difficult to live with, but even more difficult to die for.'

'That sounds like a riddle, Godwin.'

'Maybe it is, sire. But every man must find his destiny, live with it and then come to terms with its reckoning. So must kings . . . and so must emperors.'

1. Young Thegn

The year was 1053, the eleventh year of the rule of Edward I, King of England, later to be called 'The Confessor', an accession that had ended a brief dynasty of three Danish kings on the throne of England. Edward was of the royal Cerdician house, a centuries-old Anglo-Saxon lineage from England's heartland in Wessex. However, for twenty-five years before becoming King, Edward had lived in exile in Normandy at the home of his mother, the redoubtable Emma of Normandy.

Edward ruled a kingdom that was far from secure. The ambitious Welsh warlord, Gruffydd ap Llywelyn, controlled most of the land west of Hereford and was attempting to unify the Welsh tribes. To the north, Macbeth, King of the Scots, was a shrewd and resourceful leader. The Danes and Norwegians were always looking for opportunities to plunder England's riches, as they had for centuries. Most significantly of all, the restless Normans lay in wait across the Channel in northern France, on the lookout for an opportunity to strike.

The Norman leader was the ferocious William, Duke of Normandy. The 26-year-old illegitimate son of Robert, sixth Duke of Normandy, and Herleve Fulbert, daughter of a humble tanner of Falaise. Herleve's origins were ordinary, but not so her looks, nor her personality. She was strikingly beautiful and keenly intelligent. Like his mother,

21

William was a remarkable individual. He had gained the dukedom as a minor at the age of eight and had fought hard to keep it. But he was not satisfied with a mere dukedom; he wanted the kingdom of England and to found an enduring dynasty.

The Normans were a strange paradox. Although descended from Vikings, they represented a unique blend of Norse ferocity and southern European sophistication. To the anguish of all they encountered, they loved to fight and ruled their conquered lands with an iron fist. Some were clever and cunning adventurers, or great builders of fortifications and cathedrals; a few were ardent and self-righteous empire makers; others were simple opportunists who lived for the moment as mercenaries and cut-throats. William had all of these traits in a diabolical blend.

Bourne, a small village in Lincolnshire, was a quiet place far removed from the power games of kings. To the west of the village ran the great Roman road to York and beyond it lay the Bruneswald, the great forest at the heart of England. To the east were the Fens, a morass of dangerous marshes covered with dense, often impenetrable undergrowth. The village sat on slightly higher ground where sluices, begun by the Romans, drained off the surplus water, leaving soil rich enough to allow the local farmers to prosper.

The Thegn of Bourne was called Leofric, a descendant of an old Saxon landed family and a man much admired in his community. He married above himself when he became betrothed to Aediva, a woman from a nearby Danish community who was descended from the gentry of North Fresia. There was much mixed Saxon and Danish blood in

England, with several areas of Danish settlement close to Bourne, and a tolerant coexistence had been established.

Bourne was a relatively prosperous village but, even so, life was simple and sometimes harsh. The cycle of the seasons was managed by back-breaking toil, where the only respite from six and a half days of hard labour was a Saturday evening of drinking and feasting in the Thegn's longhouse. This was always followed by a church service on Sunday morning, when the humble parishioners would be reminded of God's mercy for the righteous and of the fires of Hell for those less virtuous.

Built over a hundred years earlier from split oak trunks, the longhouse was over thirty yards from end to end. The food was plentiful and the mead flowed copiously as the old sagas were recited by the senior men of the village. The small wooden church nearby was the ethical anchor of the community and Aidan the Priest its moral helmsman. But even he could do little about the primordial instincts that flowed through the veins of the good people of Bourne.

God-fearing Christian Bourne coexisted with a much older Bourne, where ancient beliefs still thrived. Pagan rituals to ward off the forces of evil, which were thought to lurk deep in the forests or to slink in the black waters of the marshes, were regularly held in the dead of night. The women of the village knew how to mix potent drinks, perform erotic dances and recite haunting incantations. There was a tradition of manly competition; wrestling, archery, hunting and drinking contests were fair game and allowed the men to show their prowess and impress the womenfolk. Beneath its rustic simplicity, the real life of Bourne was earthy and crude.

Hereward, the son of Leofric of Bourne, had been born eighteen years earlier, in the year 1035. The King of England at the time was the Dane Harold Harefoot, the son of Cnut the Great and his wife, Aelfgifu of Northampton. He held the throne as Regent, awaiting the arrival of Hathacnut from Denmark, the son of Cnut's union with Emma of Normandy.

When he was younger, Leofric's status as a village thegn meant that, from time to time, he had been required to serve as a housecarl in the King's army, but he was more of a farmer than a warrior. His son was a very different proposition. Even as a boy, Hereward cast a formidable shadow. He was not born to be a humble farmer, a minor thegn to a small community; he preferred the adventure of open spaces, the challenge of the unknown and the achievement of turning an obstacle into a stepping-stone. He could ride before he could walk, he could run before he could think about where he was going, and he could control others before he understood how to use that supremacy wisely. He was rebellious and troublesome and soon became a lost cause to his parents.

Hereward was a prodigiously tall six feet one inch. His heavily muscled frame carried no fat and his long, athletic legs formed a strong base for a powerful upper body. Even as a teenager he could beat all the men of the village in whatever challenge they threw at him, and as soon as he had hair on his chin several of the more precocious girls of the village were inclined to take him off to the woods to have their way with him.

His behaviour became intolerable to his parents.

Matters came to a head in the spring of 1053, shortly

after Hereward's eighteenth birthday. It was a beautiful day, the sky crystal blue and the air still but enlivened by the cacophony of birdsong. Hereward and his father had been hunting with the village freemen in the Bruneswald. All men feared the seemingly endless Bruneswald. In the deepest parts it was as dark as night, and even the most daring hunters did not venture too far from the main tracks, for fear of what they would find, human or otherwise.

They had had a good hunt. As usual, Hereward, who had seen the deer first and had his arrow in flight before the others could reach for their bows, had bagged the main kill. As the hunting party approached the village, Hereward threw his prize across the neck of his father's horse and rode off to the north, shouting as he went that he had a couple of things to attend to in the fields.

Leofric knew that he would be wasting his time trying to stop his son. He could only bellow into the distance, demanding that he be at his table by sunset. He watched Hereward disappear through the trees; his only son, a man-child he loved deeply, but who was a constant source of pain to him. The boy's sense of fun was infectious but his body had outgrown his mind and he did not know how to control himself. No one had the fortitude to stand up to him, and his behaviour brought dissent and unrest to the village and challenged the authority of the church and its priest. Word had even reached Leofric's distant relative and his namesake, Leofric, Earl of Mercia. In no uncertain terms, the Earl had already told Leofric to control his son, or he would do so.

Leofric had pleaded with the Earl to nominate Hereward for King Edward's housecarls, but the answer was always no; he was too undisciplined to serve with the King's elite corps.

Leofric suspected the worst, listening to the receding thud of hooves as his son rode away. He knew that Hereward was going to see a woman who was not only the most desirable in the district but also the kept woman of Thurstan, Abbot of Ely.

Thurstan was a devious man with powerful friends.

Gythin rushed to Hereward as he approached her small cottage. 'Hereward! I don't think it's safe for you to be here; I'm so frightened.'

A striking woman, several years older than Hereward, Gythin had long auburn hair and bright hazel eyes. She had clear skin and strong features: high cheekbones, a small pouting mouth and a thin beak-like nose. She reminded Hereward of a bird of prey – beautiful but dangerous. He had been sharing her bed for several weeks, an experience very different from the quick trysts with the village girls.

He loved her body: she had strong shoulders, broad hips and a firm flat stomach. Sex with her was a revelation. She had taught him how to be gentle with her, how to touch her, how to tease her and how to control himself. There had been many long nights spent rehearsing these heavenly techniques. Hereward hoped this would be another, but Gythin's cry of alarm had made his heart race.

'What's wrong?'

'I think Thurstan knows about us.' Her words came quickly and breathlessly.

'He hasn't sent for me for three weeks. He always sends for me – or he sends me money – but I haven't seen anyone in days. I have a terrible feeling about this; I must leave

Bourne. Maybe the sisters at Huntingdon will take me.'

Hereward adopted his most mature bearing, galvanized by this sudden cry for help. He grabbed her and held her tightly; she was soft and vulnerable in his arms. As she lifted her eyes to meet his, he saw how terrified she was and he realized how much she risked by letting him bed her. He also realized how much he cared about her.

These were strange feelings for him; he had not cared about anyone before – except himself. His parents had always been there, and he readily took them for granted; his male friends were good company, but their time together was usually spent in a superficial haze of debauchery; his female acquaintances were merely passing fancies, assignations of little consequence – at least for him. Gythin was different; she listened to him – soothed him – but, somehow, was also able to chide him and scold him, without evoking his anger. She often told him how dangerous anger was. How she had seen it all too frequently in men, leading to the most terrifying of consequences.

She had had few opportunities as a child – her origins were too humble to afford her an education or a husband of status   but she had a sharp mind and the body of a seductress, leaving her only two options: to use her mind in a convent, or her body in a rich man's bed. She had chosen the latter; Thurstan was not the first of her 'benefactors'.

'Thurstan will kill you if he finds you here, and I dread to think what he'll do to me . . .'

'Gythin, stop! You have nothing to be frightened of while I'm here. It would take ten men to take you from me.'

'Hereward, you are big and strong but you are a child in

the real world of cut-throats and murderers. I won't let you be hurt.'

'I'm no child. Have I not put to the ground any man who's faced me? No one can better me on a horse, with a sword, or in a grapple.'

'I don't doubt your strength, or your courage. If it's what you choose, one day you will be a great warrior, but you're not yet trained in real combat and you're not skilled in the underhand ways of men who kill for money. Thurstan knows such men.'

Hereward felt sufficiently insulted to want to continue the debate. But he had held Gythin closely for long enough to feel the stirrings of another powerful emotion. His arousal soon provoked a response from Gythin and he forgot all notions of challenging the ominous men she was so certain would find him wanting.

'Let me show you what this "child" can do for you, madam.'

Gythin started to sob uncontrollably, but her spasms of distress gradually lessened and did not quell the intensity of her embrace as her mouth and her tongue began to devour Hereward in a frenzy of fear and passion. She pulled him inside the doorway of her small cottage; in their haste, they were naked in an instant and their forceful lovemaking over quickly before they both fell into a fitful sleep.

Hereward's infatuation with Gythin had blinded him to the risks they were taking. He was both naïve in making light of his lover's vulnerability and arrogant in assuming he would be able to deal with any threat their liaison posed, especially to her. For her part, Gythin had rarely experienced a meaningful relationship and beneath her concubine's cloak was emotionally frail. In Hereward she had found a lion of a man to share her bed; not just a leonine lover, but a man in whom she recognized exceptional qualities.

But Hereward's dalliances with Gythin had not gone unnoticed in Ely. She was right: Thurstan knew where to find men of evil.

Stealth is the assassin's way; he chooses his moment and strikes swiftly and silently. This one had been hired three weeks earlier. An Andalucian by birth, he had learned his two prodigious skills from the Moors: great deftness in cutting stone with a mason's chisel and equal dexterity with an assassin's knife on rather more pliant material – human flesh. He would cut anything for money: a stone cherub to grace the nave of one of God's holy places or the neck of a young woman to exact retribution on behalf of one of God's priests. He and four formidable companions had spent the last week planning their move.

As the pall of a moonless night descended on Gythin's remote dwelling, the first intruder pulled back the crudely woven woollen screen at the single window, climbed in and silently let in the other four through the door. Gythin woke first with a jolt, letting out a piercing scream as her eyes focused on five shadows, half-lit by the flickering bedside candle.

Hereward was on his feet in an instant, but they were ready for him and, before he could take a pace, a heavy hunting net enveloped him. As he stumbled forwards, struggling to free himself, a wooden mace thumped into his neck, toppling him sideways into the hearth. In the same moment, the net was pulled towards the door, tightening itself around him. As Gythin rushed to Hereward's aid, she was struck heavily in her midriff by the dark man from Spain, a blow which cost her her breath and her momentum. She fell to the ground, doubled up in pain and gasping for air. This freed all five men to pull their netted quarry outside the hut, across the small clearing and towards the nearest tree.

A thick rope was tied to the net, thrown over the sturdiest branch and Hereward, barely conscious and unable to put up a struggle, was hauled into the air. His assailants secured the rope to an adjacent tree, leaving Hereward swinging like a trapped animal. After they had pulled his hands through the net and tied them firmly to the rope above him, they threw a pail of cold water over him to bring him back to full consciousness. The leader then spoke to him in stilted English in an accent that Hereward found difficult to understand.

'When I finish woman, I come back. I geld you so you become quiet boy. I not hurt you much, my blade very sharp.' His face contorted in a demonic grin as he reinforced his point with a deep slash to Hereward's cheek.

Hereward found it hard to speak; the net was cutting into his jaw. 'You'd better kill me, foreigner. If you don't, I will hunt you down, as sure as your mother is a whore.'

'You should mind your filthy tongue; I cut this also when I finish woman.'

The impact of several harsh blows from the men's heavy maces and the distant sound of Gythin's cries for help were Hereward's final memories of the brutal encounter. As he drifted in and out of consciousness, Gythin's desperate cries echoed in the recesses of his mind.

He had failed her abysmally.

Leofric worried about Herward all evening. He knew only too well of his son's latest conquest and was aware that the woman was not a simple village girl. He also knew that, despite his command, Hereward would not be at his table for dinner. Encouraged by Aediva, he resolved to teach the boy a lesson – something he had not done since Hereward was eleven, a leniency he now decided had been a mistake.

He took a dozen good men with him, several of whom had scores to settle with Hereward. His intention was to embarrass him in front of Gythin, haul him back to the village and punish him in front of the entire community.

Leofric's men were trained soldiers who accompanied him whenever he did military service. They made a stealthy approach, expecting to find Hereward asleep in his lover's arms.

When Leofric shouted to Hereward to come outside, there were several moments of silence before a human shape suddenly pulled back the woollen window covering and tumbled on to the ground. At the same time, the cottage door was flung open and another shadowy figure made a rapid exit.

It was only when the torches of Leofric's men illuminated the frightened faces of the assasins that the mayhem began.

The initial surprise and the dark of the night aided the escape of the assailants. Although the first two out of the cottage were cut down in a flurry of blows as the men of

Bourne surrounded them, the other three – including their leader – dashed out of the doorway in the confusion and disappeared into the night.

When Leofric entered the cottage, he found Gythin shockingly mutilated. She had been tied up and staked out in front of the hearth. No doubt brutally raped beforehand, her body had been incised with a patchwork of deep cuts. It appeared that the wounds had been carved slowly and carefully to ensure that she remained conscious for as long as possible and suffered the maximum pain and degradation. Her only relief would have been when she finally bled to death.

Leofric bellowed Hereward's name repeatedly, to no avail. It was only when they started to dig Gythin's grave that one of the torches caught Hereward's outline, still hanging from the tree where he had been hoisted by his assailants.

He was gently let down and found, to his father's intense relief, to be alive – if only just.

Hereward did not fully regain consciousness for several days, and even then he could hear only muffled voices and see only vague shapes. He could feel his tongue and utter a few sounds and was able to move his hand just enough to grab his groin. To his immense relief, he seemed intact. His recovery took weeks; there had been many broken bones and the headaches were unbearable, but eventually they subsided and his bones healed. His survival was largely due to his mother's skills as a nurse. Aediva had given Hereward his Danish blood and was typical of her people: self-reliant and independent. She knew how to restore strength to a shattered body.

Hereward appeared to be chastened and subdued during

his long recovery and, as time passed, the feeling grew in the village that some good had come of the terrible events and that the young man would now mend his ways. Aidan used the incident in his sermons almost every Sunday. He was the only man in the village, besides Leofric, who could read and write. He had taught Hereward English and Danish, and even a little Norman French. In one particular sermon, Aidan gave full vent to his oratorical skills.

'The Lord has given us a gift in Hereward, son of Leofric. One day he will be Thegn of Bourne – but only in name, unless he learns the wisdom of the true Lord, our God in Heaven.' Then he looked at Hereward directly. 'Hereward, you are a gift from God with so many talents, but you are flawed: you are not yet a man and far, very far, from being a good man. Only you can overcome your weaknesses and conquer your demons. If you do not, they will drag you into an abyss from which there is no return. We can help you, but only if you will allow us to. If we fail and if you fail, the great strengths that God gave you will become a curse. Be warned! This is your last chance.' He then turned to the congregation. 'Let us pray for him.'

Aidan's words were wise, but Hereward sat impassively, not really listening; words of wisdom did not mix too well with his hot blood. Despite outward appearances, Hereward was not subdued. As his body healed, his anger grew. His right arm had been broken in three places but his left had escaped any fractures. And so, as soon as he could walk, he had taken himself off into the forest every day, ostensibly to exercise his weakened body and clear his addled head, but his real purpose was to visit his secret training ground. It was a small clearing where he had hidden his sword and his battle-axe, where, hour after hour until an exhausted body would not let him go on, he taught himself to use his weapons with his left hand until he was as proficient with it as he had been with his right.

He spent most of the time with his axe, which, harnessed to his powerful frame and natural athleticism, had always been a fearsome instrument in his hands. But now he had a new purpose, fired by anger, which seemed to give him superhuman strength and the axe even more malicious power. The scarred trees in the clearing were testament to the many thousands of blows he had hacked into the oaks of the forest. He repeated, over and over again, the killing routines he had seen practised by the King's housecarls on military training days: thrust and parry, cut and slash, chop and slice.

When he could cut and hack no more, he would sit and sharpen his weapons, survey the results of his toil and contemplate the terrible vengeance he would soon exact.

2. Vengeance

It was almost the end of 1053 before Hereward was ready to venture beyond his village again. His body had healed; his right arm had regained its strength and now matched the power of his newly trained left hand.

He often thought about Gythin's words, and now realized that she had been right. He had been taught the most brutal of lessons: the difference between the competitive playfulness of a manly contest and the mortal challenge of men intent on killing. The months of brooding in isolation had not diminished his anger, but he had learned how to channel it for a deliberate purpose: the pursuit of four men – the three surviving assassins who had mercilessly murdered Gythin and the coward who had sent them, Thurstan, Abbot of Ely.

There were no goodbyes in the village; he spoke to no one, not even his father. The gratitude he should have felt towards his family and his community was not there; such virtues needed a mind much more mature than Hereward's, especially now that his was clouded by hatred and pain. He had learned a salutary lesson about fighting, but nothing about respect and humility.

Ely was a day's ride from Bourne. He took his time; there was no need to hurry. He announced himself to everyone he met on the road. He wanted his prey to know he was coming, hoping they would feel the dread that Gythin must have experienced. He cut an impressive figure, riding tall in the saddle, dressed in the finery of a man of his station and carrying his weapons of war.

The abbey church of Ely was visible for miles around, the centrepiece of a burgh that stood but a few feet above the Great Fen which surrounded it. Its precious elevation gave it a solid footing, making it an island in an inland sea of marsh and bog. The church formed the heart of the precincts of a vast and wealthy abbey. By contrast, the burgh was a small cluster of thatched hovels with only a few grander two-storey houses for the rich merchants. It was a quiet place, enlivened only on market days when the farmers and the villagers from the surrounding countryside brought their wares.

Hereward entered the Isle of Ely across the single ancient causeway from the west. So focused was his purpose, he was oblivious to the bleakness around him. The Fens were frozen and had been for weeks in a winter that had been unusually harsh, with little respite from the hard frosts and strong gales. The desolate scene was empty and monotonous, except for a few clumps of trees on patches of high ground where snow had collected in drifts like the plumes of waves at sea. Punctuated only by black holes cut by the locals, who fished them for their larders, the smooth ice of the Fens reflected the gull-grey sky like a mirror.

Leaning into the harsh east wind, their faces covered against the chill, the few people who crossed the causeway were wrapped in heavy cloaks. Most people noticed Hereward as he passed. The deep scar on his face suggested he was a man of violence. People sensed trouble and many shied away from his pointed questions: had they seen three men, one of them a dark foreigner with a heavily studded dagger? Was the Abbot in residence?

Eventually, a wool merchant told him what he wanted to know. The three men had spent the summer carving a baptismal font for the Abbot. They were highly regarded masons from Spain and travelled the length and breadth of the country serving the great churches. They spent most of their wages visiting Edgar the Tanner, who, besides preparing hides and brewing mead and beer, ran the local whorehouse.

A strong stomach was required to visit Edgar's establishment: the heat of the fire and the stench of humanity engulfed Hereward as he strode into the small thatched building. It was late afternoon, too early for most drinkers and for Edgar's whores, who were still sleeping off their exertions from the night before. Only half a dozen men sat at the long oak tables. They stiffened as the visitor removed his cloak, revealing his sword and battle-axe. Hereward's weapons gleamed as he stood in readiness.

Edgar, who had been preparing a new brew, broke the silence. 'You're welcome, young sir. Sit and drink with us.'

'Thank you, sir. I seek three men. I will know them when I see them, and they will know me. I am Hereward of Bourne.'

Edgar was not a man to be awed by an eighteen-year-old boy, even one as formidable as Hereward. 'Aren't you a bit young to be about the Earl's business?'

'This is not the Earl's business, this is my business.'

'Sir, we live by the law here. If you have a score to settle, you should go to Earl Leofric –'

Before Edgar could finish, a dark man, whom Hereward

had last seen all those months ago, stepped forward. 'You are lucky boy, a few minutes more with me and you would be pretty gelding, but I see I leave my mark on your face. I thought I would meet you again. Now I finish what I start . . .'

Hereward sensed movement in the room; his two other quarries had slipped in behind him. With a quick glance over his shoulder, he saw the blades of their swords, poised ready to strike.

'Woman was very beautiful, but she was harlot. She didn't want to die, she beg us, took us all, but the whore didn't make us forget our duty – we kill her anyway. We gave you beating but you heal good. It is shame your recovery has been waste of time. Are you ready to die, boy?'

There must have been a signal between the three of them, but Hereward did not see it. His two foes to the rear had each taken a full pace before he sensed their movement. He turned quickly and instinctively sank to his knees as both their swords flashed over his head. As he made his turn, he sank his axe deep into the midriff of the attacker to his left, inflicting a mortal wound, and then rose and thrust his shoulder into the side of the second man, knocking him over a nearby table. But his main adversary was already at his back, about to strike. Hereward had just enough time to halt the foreigner in his final stride by jamming the point of his blade into his throat.

His foe held only a dagger but, instead of submitting, he smiled. 'You are quick boy . . . and good with axe. I hope you are also good with sword.'

The second man had regained his feet and started to circle towards Hereward, stepping over the body of his friend, now in his death throes on the floor in an ever-widening pool of blood. He had picked up a burning log from the fire and threw it at Hereward, hitting him hard on the forehead, the hot embers scorching his face. At that moment, both his foes struck: the first slashed him across his upper arm with his sword, but he parried the thrust of the leader's dagger with his sword. Hereward turned away from danger and dropped his axe so that he could take a firm grip of the wrist of the leader, using his great strength to neutralize the danger of his dagger.

Hereward's sword arm, although wounded, was free and he quickly put it to lethal use by plunging his blade through the chest of the second man, shocking the life out of him. He released his grip of his sword, allowing the victim – still impaled on the end of it – to fall backwards into the fire. But Hereward did not loosen his grip on the wrist of the man he most wanted to kill; now he had him at his mercy. He used his right elbow as a bludgeon to batter the Spaniard's face, shattering his cheekbone. Then, with one hand, he held him around the neck in an unbreakable headlock and, with the other, slammed his hand relentlessly on the table until his dagger dropped to the floor.

He started to squeeze the life out of his victim, as the all-powerful adrenalin of vengeance pumped through his veins. The Spaniard was a strong man with the hands of a mason, but he could not break Hereward's grip. Edgar the Tanner looked on in shock: Hereward's first victim lay on the floor, his lungs slowly filling, drowning him in his own blood; the second's lifeless body was beginning to be consumed by the open fire; and the third, the leader, was being slowly and agonizingly strangled to death.

Hereward did not look at the man, nor speak to him; he just stared into the distance, thinking of Gythin. The man struggled at first, but then his movements subsided, his face swelled and his eyes bulged as if they were going to burst. Finally, the puce of the man's gorged face paled, his lids closed over his blood-filled eyes and his body went limp.

Hereward held on, savouring the act of retribution.

The only sounds were the spit and crackle of the fire and the gentle dribble from the man's leggings as his bodily fluids drained away for the last time.

It took Hereward only a few minutes to walk from Edgar's tannery to the abbey. Blood flowed down his arm, and his face was blackened by soot and etched with scarlet burns, but he did not falter. He almost ran across the cloister of the abbey, avoiding the beautifully decorated stone crucifix in the centre of the crosswalk. It was deserted except for a few benches lining the quadrangle to facilitate prayer and contemplation.

Hereward threw open the heavy wooden door of the Great Hall. At one end, a huge fire spat flames towards the blackened roof timbers high above and filled the air with woodsmoke. There were several armed monks in the shadows, two more stood by the Abbot, along with his man-at-arms. They looked like Normans, with their distinctive chain-mail armour and nose-guard helmets.

The Abbot was a man to behold: his robes were a rich fawn, like chamois leather, and around his neck a heavy chain held a glistening gold crucifix, encrusted at its four corners by large rubies. He did not move, nor even look up, as Hereward made his dramatic entrance; he seemed to be in meditation, staring at the Scriptures that lay before him on the pages of a beautifully decorated Bible. Apart from his ostentatious garb, he had the appearance of a devout man of God: he was clean-shaven, had tonsured, cropped hair and the stern face of an ascetic. His left hand rested on the Holy Book, his right was hidden from view beneath the table; Hereward assumed it held a dagger. Silence reigned for a moment as the young thegn of Bourne surveyed the scene.

'Do close the door; Ely's winter chills me to the bone.' The Abbot spoke in the clear, precise tone of an educated cleric practised in speaking down to congregations. 'The usual arrangement is to make an appointment with my clerk.'

Hereward did not respond.

The Abbot still did not move his head, nor glance up from the page. 'Do you read the Holy Scriptures?'

Again, Hereward said nothing.

'You should. Let me read to you from the Book of Revelation of St John the Divine: *And when he had opened the fourth seal, I heard the voice of the fourth beast say, Come and see. And I looked, and behold a pale horse: and his name that sat on him was Death, and Hell followed with him.*' Finally, the Abbot looked up.

This brought an instant response from Hereward. 'You are right; I bring Hell with me, Thurstan, Abbot of Ely. I intend to take you to Leofric, Earl of Mercia. There I will ask that you be tried for murder before the King. If you resist, I will kill you.'

Thurstan smiled. He looked down at the Scriptures once

41

more. 'You misunderstand. Let me continue: *And power was given unto them over the fourth part of the earth, to kill with sword, and with hunger, and with death, and with the beasts of the earth.* You see, I am Death. I have the power of the sword and the beasts of the earth are mine . . . I think you have already felt my power . . . and met my beasts.'

'Your beasts are no more. They have felt *my* power.'

Thurstan's face turned to anger for the first time. His demeanour suddenly became vicious, contorted and cruel.

Now Hereward recognized his enemy, the kind of man who could, without a hint of remorse, order the murder of a woman in cold blood.

'You are a naïve boy. The Beast is legion; however many you kill, there will be multitudes more. Look around you.'

With that, Thurstan's men stepped forward from the gloomy shadows of the hall and drew their swords. More than ten yards and the formidable obstacle of a large refectory table separated Hereward from Thurstan. However, without hesitation or regard for the impossibility of the odds, Hereward leapt on to the end of the table and raised his battle-axe. Almost immediately, the blades of the nearest swords slashed at his legs and he had little choice but to hurl his axe in an attempt to impale his quarry.

Hereward had practised the technique for many months. It was a close call, but Thurstan moved just enough to his left so that the wide blade of the axe missed his head and smashed into the back of the ornate oak chair he was sitting on. Nevertheless, his evasive movement, downwards and to the left, had raised his right shoulder enough for the blade to tear into his flesh and shatter his collarbone. As soon as Hereward realized that his axe had made a mark, he somersaulted from the table in an attempt to find a space within which to defend himself. But his legs were weak from the lacerations they had already received and, as soon as he hit the ground, he collapsed into a heap.

Thurstan's men rushed towards him, poised to hack him to death.

'Hold!' Thurstan bellowed with as much volume as the deep gash to his shoulder would allow. The whole of the upper right-hand part of his robe was already dyed crimson from his wound. He sat motionless; even the slightest movement, in an attempt to extricate himself from the axe, cut deeper into his flesh. 'Remove this confounded axe before it cuts me in two!'

Without hesitation, two of the Abbot's warrior priests stepped forward. While one held Thurstan's upper body, the other levered the axe upwards out of the deep gouge it had made in both the flesh and bone of its target and in the solid oak of the chair. The wood screeched as the blade was prised from it, but could not mask Thurstan's howls.

'This petulant son of Bourne is dripping blood all over my floor. Bring him here, hang him from the roof.'

Hereward was bound by the wrists and hoisted off the ground by a rope cast over the bracing piece of the roof's massive cruck beam. He had numerous sword wounds to his legs and buttocks; he could not feel some of the toes on his left foot, and blood was rapidly draining out of him. He was left to hang like a carcass in a smokehouse, and a large spit pan was placed under his feet to catch the blood that seeped from his legs.

One of the priests made an all-too-apparent observation to Thurstan. 'My Lord, your wound is deep. You too are losing much blood; I'm afraid you will have to bear the hot iron.'

'I know that, you fool! Prepare me.'

A hot poker was thrust deep into the fire. As they waited for it to attain the deep-red glow of a branding iron, Thurstan was stripped to the waist and placed on the table. Two men held a leg each; two more stood on either side, holding his arms with their weight on his chest, while a fifth knelt on the table behind him and pulled his face away from his stricken shoulder. The deed was quickly done. As the iron sank deep into the Abbot's shoulder, the wound sizzled and a cloud of pungent smoke carried the stink of burning flesh into the air.

After a while, unconsciousness spared Thurstan any further suffering and he was carried away to his bedchamber.

It was late evening before the Abbot reappeared in the hall. He was ashen-faced, grimacing with pain and able to stand only with the support of two men.

'Is he alive?'

'I'm not sure, my Lord. I think his blood is all but drained from him.'

'Let's see if a hot iron can rouse him.'

Hereward had lost consciousness some hours earlier, but now he could feel a dull pain. He did not have much feeling in his legs, and his head was jammed backwards by his arms. He could see only the dark beams of the roof and the flicker of firelight in its rafters. He could hear muffled shouts echoing in the distance and felt as if he were floating.

His strongest sensation was the smell of roasting meat; he could remember the hot iron on Thurstan's wound and the sickening scent of scorched human flesh. Then he realized where he was and what was causing the pain: this time, the flesh being seared was his.

Thurstan had just enough strength to lift his left arm and prod the glowing red poker into Hereward's wounds. As soon as the steam of the blistering flesh carried away the iron's potency, Thurstan ordered that it be quickly reheated.

Hereward was now fully conscious and would have cried out if he could, but there was no air in his lungs to carry a sound.

He thought about his short life – remembering Gythin, his village and his parents – and, for the first time, he was frightened. He had always thought of himself as invincible; now he was helpless, lonely and minutes from death. Tears stung his eyes and rolled down his face.

He now understood why other boys cried; he remembered the fear and loathing in their eyes as he bested them in their countless contests. He was suddenly overwhelmed by an immense sense of guilt. He knew that it was his reckless pursuit of Gythin that had caused her death, and he felt ashamed.

Never was a man less ready to meet his Maker; surely these were the fires of Hell already consuming his flesh.

Leofric knew instantly where his son had gone when he disappeared from the village.

The same loyal group of men who had accompanied him on the fateful journey to Gythin's cottage once more travelled with him to seek the aid of Earl Leofric. The Earl helped him formulate a plan to save his son's life.

With the Captain of the Earl's Guard, a dozen of his men and a warrant for Hereward's arrest, Leofric burst into Abbot Thurstan's hall just after midnight.

The men stopped dead in their tracks at the scene before them. Hereward's limp body, silhouetted by the dying embers of the fire, twisted slowly as it hung from the roof. The faces of his torturers glistened with sweat; the room was dark, more like a dungeon than a place of worship. Thurstan, again in a state of unconsciousness, was slumped in his chair with his men standing around him, not knowing what to do.

Hereward seemed lifeless, almost beyond hope.

For a few moments, a stand-off ensued between clerical law and the Earl's secular domain.

Leofric spoke with the authority of a thegn of England, trained as one of Edward's elite housecarls. 'Who here speaks for Thurstan?'

A tall monk stepped forward. 'I do.'

'I have a warrant for the arrest of Hereward of Bourne. It is signed by Leofric, Earl of Mercia. I will take him now.'

'This is a matter for the Church. It will be resolved when Abbot Thurstan recovers.'

'You address a thegn of the realm, priest. This matter will be judged by the King at Winchester; he rules on all matters, temporal and ecclesiastical. I suggest you make a quick decision, or you will be held to account for what has happened here.'

The monk glanced at his colleagues and surveyed the Earl's Guard with Leofric.

'We will require guarantees that this young thug –'

Sensing the priest's capitulation, Leofric pushed past him before he could finish his sentence.

Hereward was cut down.

He seemed lifeless, his skin the pallor of limewash. Leofric rushed to him, pulled him up by his shoulders and searched for signs of life. His body was cool and stiff, as if rigor mortis had begun.

Leofric's head sank in despair as he gently rested his son's head on the stone floor.

'He's alive.' The Captain of the Earl's Guard spoke quietly but confidently. 'He's breathing.'

The Captain knelt, then pushed down hard on Hereward's chest. As he released the pressure, the injured man's lungs filled with air and the faintest of breaths could be felt across his lips.

Leofric leapt to his feet. 'Get him on to the cart. Let's get him to Peterborough.'

3. Outlaw in the Wildwood

In a petition that both fired his imagination and taxed his intellect, it was many months later that King Edward heard the plea of Leofric, Thegn of Bourne, concerning his son, Hereward. The evidence had taken the whole of a morning session and it was now well into the afternoon, and still the King had not passed judgement. No one at the King's Council at Winchester could think of a precedent. Edward had withdrawn from the Great Hall and was pacing his cloisters deep in thought; the formidable Harold Godwinson, Earl of Wessex and England's senior earl, who also happened to be Edward's brother-in-law, strode a few feet behind.

Life in England under the saintly King Edward was peaceful, but there were great anxieties about the future. His formidable mother, Emma, was the daughter of Richard I, Duke of Normandy and, during the reign of the Danish kings, Edward had spent his early life exiled in Normandy. Much more comfortable with Normans, he had appointed many of them to powerful positions in the realm. Also, despite his marriage to Edith, the daughter of Earl Godwin – who, until his recent death, had been England's most powerful earl – he had spent most of his reign at odds with the Anglo-Saxon aristocracy, especially the Godwin clan, now led by Edith's brother, Harold Godwinson, the eldest of Earl Godwin's five sons.

Thought by many to be far too effete and intellectual to

be king amid the much more robust Anglo-Saxon earls, Edward had nevertheless brought the rule of law to his kingdom and had earned the grudging respect of his people. The anxiety was now about who would succeed him: Edward's marriage to Edith was childless and there was no direct heir to the throne.

Harold Godwinson broke the silence of the cloisters. 'Sire, under law, the boy should be executed. He is the son of a thegn and we cannot allow our local dignitaries to behave like cut-throats.'

The King did not respond.

'The boy is uncontrollable.'

'He intrigues me.'

'Sire, he killed three men and almost cut in half one of your clerics!'

'Thurstan is not one of *my* clerics; he was preffered by the Church hierarchy against my judgement. He is corrupt and conniving, and probably deserved what the boy did to him. If I had my way, I'd execute him, not the boy.'

'Sire, it is your duty to uphold the law.'

'I know my duty; I don't need to be reminded of it by the Earl of Wessex. Bring the boy and his father. I will speak to them before I pass judgement.'

Leofric of Bourne and his son entered Edward's cloisters as meekly as their station demanded and bowed in unison. The King of England was an impressive figure. He had the kindly features of a devout man of God, his hair was greying auburn and he wore a full, well-cut beard. His smock and leggings were of finely woven wool and his cloak, a rich burgundy, was elaborately embroidered in fine thread and gathered over his left shoulder by a large circular clasp in gold filigree decorated with garnets and amethysts. Hereward could also see the gilded pommel of the King's sword, its engraved design of serpents and dragons representing England's fierce Anglo-Saxon origins. Even though Edward, a man of letters, had never drawn it in anger, it was the ancient weapon of the Cerdician Kings of Wessex and England, a proud lineage going back hundreds of years to the time of Alfred the Great and beyond.

The King spoke to Leofric first. 'How are you, Leofric?'

'I am well in body, sire, but my heart is heavy with regret. I have caused you great turmoil and my son is lost to me. I have brought him before you because I want him to salvage his life. If you grant me my claim, there is just a chance that he can find a way to redeem himself.'

'You have served me well many times, Leofric; I will try to help you.'

'I am grateful, Sire.'

The King turned to Hereward. 'You are a troublesome young man who vexes me greatly.'

'Sire –' Hereward tried to speak.

The King cut him short. 'Your father has saved your life twice. He is a brave and loving father; you have wronged him beyond belief. I am about to pass judgement on you but, before I do, I want you to know that your father is also very wise. You should die for the appalling crime you have committed, but by going to the Earl of Mercia and seeking a father's ancient right of retribution against a son, he has saved your life for a third time.'

He paused to take a deep breath. 'Because you despatched them before they could answer the charge, there is only indirect evidence to support your accusation that the men you killed had murdered the woman Gythin. The crime against her was a heinous offence, but I have not been asked to rule on that and thus it is not within my jurisdiction here. I can act only on evidence, and there is nothing substantial to link the woman's murder to Abbot Thurstan. You descended upon Ely with murder in your heart, when, if you felt a crime had been committed, the appropriate recourse would have been the good offices of Earl Leofric at Peterborough. You killed three men in the premises of Edgar the Tanner, before attacking one of my abbots and maiming him for life. You should thank God Almighty that your father's application means I do not have to order your execution; there has been enough killing. I shall accept the argument of Leofric, Earl of Mercia, on behalf of your father, and confirm that the punishment they seek against you is appropriate.'

The King paused again and stared at Hereward intently. 'I am going to cast you out from everything that you have known and all those things that bring a man comfort and warmth. You will be denied the sight of God and His priests' confessionals. May God have mercy on your soul.'

The King continued to stare at Hereward for a long time, contemplating the traumas the boy had already lived through in his short life.

Perhaps Edward could also sense something of what might become of the young man, because he suddenly broke the silence and, beyond anyone else's hearing, whispered to the Earl of Wessex, 'Why do I sense that this may not be the last I see of him?'

The Great Hall of Winchester was full as Harold Godwinson, Earl of Wessex, rose to read King Edward's judgement.

Abbot Thurstan sat solemnly, his right arm limp and withered, while Leofric, sitting opposite him, looked like a broken man.

It had taken many months of care by the nuns of Peterborough before Hereward was fit enough to stand trial. During this time, his father wrestled with the dilemma which his son had created for him. After seeking the advice of Earl Leofric, he had to face a dreadful decision. The only certain way to save the life of his son and forestall his execution was to disown him and claim the ancient right to have him banished as an outlaw.

'Let all here understand that on this fifteenth day of April, 1054, King Edward of England has issued a proclamation granting judgement to Leofric, Thegn of Bourne, in the matter of his son, Hereward, as petitioned by Leofric, Earl of Mercia.'

Harold spoke solemnly, with all the authority of the Earl Marshal of England. He stood tall, his flaxen hair resting on the collar of his ceremonial cloak, his right hand clasping his sword of office and his left hand holding the proclamation that condemned Hereward as an outcast.

'From this day forward, Hereward of Bourne will be banished from his lands and his people and will be placed beyond the law and the sight of God. All his rights to taxes, titles and service are confiscated forthwith, as are his lands, holdings and possessions. Anyone granting succour, solace or having anything to do with this man will, in turn, also be banished. This proclamation will be heard across the land by order of our sovereign lord, King Edward.'

As the Earl finished speaking, the entire assembly rose and the King's housecarls presented arms. Edward remained seated, slightly slumped on his throne, saddened by the finality of the act of banishment. In his thirteen-year reign, he could remember only four occasions when he had ordered that a man be made an outlaw.

Hereward knew what he had to do: he bowed to the King, turned, and made his way towards the huge double doors of the Great Hall of Winchester.

His father watched him go with tears in his eyes.

No one else looked at Hereward as he limped into the streets of Winchester. Only the blacksmith approached him, to snap around his neck an iron collar and daub his head with pig's blood – the symbols of an outlaw. A mounted housecarl then rode in front of him to the city walls and closed the gates behind him. Now, no burgh would open its gates to him; no village would give him food or water; no man, woman or child would speak to him; even priests were required to shun him. The heavy collar of the outlaw, inscribed with the chilling word 'condemned', ensured that no one could mistake his status. Although a blacksmith would have the tools and skill to remove the collar, the clasp bore the King's seal and breaking it was punishable by banishment.

Hereward's fate was to be a living death.

As Hereward walked away from Winchester, he attempted to walk with the proud, upright gait of a dashing young thegn, but it was futile. There was no semblance of pride left in his heart; he was a broken man. For the second time he had come close to death and once again endured a long and painful recovery from wounds so severe that they would have killed most men. This time, however, his rehabilitation had been a period of deep introspection and regret, not one of simmering rage. Gone was the festering anger brought about by his first encounter with mortality; he had thought only of his stupidity and selfishness. He now realized he had been stupid in believing in his own invincibility, in thinking only of his own pain and revenge, and in failing to bring Thurstan to justice by legitimate means.

The torment of being hoisted like a defenceless animal, and tortured for several hours, had been a purgatory in which an entire childhood of fears and nightmares had been visited upon him. Now, many months later, the memories still haunted him.

Throughout Hereward's recovery, he had longed to be able to return to Bourne – to seek forgiveness for a lifetime of conceit and bullying, and to see Gythin again in a time before the whole tragic business had begun – but he knew these thoughts were no more than daydreams. He knew that he would never see his family again and he knew that Gythin had gone for ever.

Hereward's melancholy was suddenly jolted by the distinct sound of a horse snorting. It was only a few yards away, but its rider was difficult to discern; he wore a dark hooded cape and neither horse nor rider bore any distinguishing features. As soon as the mounted figure spoke, Hereward realized it was his nemesis, Thurstan.

'You should have killed me.' Thurstan paused, assuming Hereward would answer.

But no response came. No anger rose in Hereward's heart and he resumed his journey, turning his gaze to the track ahead.

'Make sure the forest hides you well; you will need its

every leaf and branch to conceal you and its darkest corners to prevent you casting shadows. Look behind every tree and bush and in the tall grass in every clearing, because if I ever hear word of you, I will hunt you down and, when I'm ready, I will strike, be sure of that.'

Hereward did not turn round, and seemed oblivious to everything that had been said to him.

Thurstan did not move for several minutes, nor did he blink, but fixed his eyes on Hereward's back as he disappeared into the gloom of the forest.

The distraught figure walked for the rest of that day and slept for only three or four hours before continuing on his aimless route deep into the forest. At every turn, he took the lesser track and was soon walking a path barely wide enough for a man's shoulders. By the end of the second day, he was marooned in the vast wildwood of southern England.

Hereward's biggest challenge in his banishment was not the well-being of his body, but of his mind. He had hunted in the Bruneswald almost every day of his life and survival was second nature to him. Days passed into weeks. He drank from streams and took a bird or a hare when he needed one; he fashioned traps and snares, even without a sharp blade; he collected flints of stone or shale whenever he saw them. He spent countless days roaming deeper into the hinterland and, knowing that the power of the King's law diminished the further west he went, he moved in the direction of the sunset. As the days grew shorter and the air colder, he prepared for winter and chose a clearing high on a hillside facing south-west to build a refuge. There he spent the long, cold winter in total isolation with only his own thoughts for company.

The teachings of the Church of Rome, repeated over and over again by Aidan the Priest from his pulpit at Bourne, had never meant much to Hereward, but his encounter with Thurstan had led him to reflect on the meaning of everything, especially his own flawed existence. He had always taken so many things for granted. He had had little regard for his village life and his family, their ways and virtues born of centuries of tradition; now he realized how much he missed them. He had never contemplated the importance of the land itself – rivers, forests, heaths and fens – and he had dismissed the wildlife of his ancient land – its infinite variety and complexity – as merely a source of sustenance; now he appreciated their true significance in the cycle of life.

From childhood he had witnessed life and death, decay and renewal, but had never fully appreciated the wonders of nature and the inestimable quality of human life; now, in his enforced solitude, he marvelled at them. He could not wait for summer and all the colour and flurry of life it would bring.

Just as nature had lain dormant during the winter, so had Hereward's need for companionship, but with the first hints of spring came the first stirrings of his desire to live normally again. From the length of the days and the burgeoning of nature around him, he guessed it was Eastertide of the year 1055. He was twenty years old, a notorious outlaw and had been all but dead twice. His bones had been smashed in several places, his flesh was scarred all over his body and his will had nearly been broken by a mortal enemy. But he had survived. He resolved to find solace in a life of simplicity, far from the land which had banished him.

Hereward spent the rest of the spring and summer moving slowly west and north. His native Bourne was only a few feet above sea level and his ancestors had dug the ditches, channels and canals that drained the land and kept the water at bay, so he could follow a watercourse easily. He also knew how to read directions from the position of the sun and how to navigate from the stars.

Game was plentiful and bows and arrows were easily made from the natural resources of wood, bone and flint. He found a piece of crude iron in the ruins of an abandoned village and, after many days of grinding and polishing, had fashioned a sharp metal blade to perform the cutting, slicing and scraping of his daily routine.

He continued to avoid direct contact with his fellow human beings, afraid to compromise either them or himself. Under cover of darkness, he had negotiated two important thoroughfares. Hidden in the undergrowth, he had overheard passing conversations that told him that he had crossed two ancient arteries to the south-west of England and was only ten miles from the burgh of Gloucester, a name he recognized. He knew it to be an important place, close to a river that flowed to the Great Western Sea.

The adrenalin began to course in his veins as he sensed the opportunity to begin a new life; he was lean and fit and his great strength had begun to return. He retreated to higher ground, and found a commanding position from where he could survey the vale beneath him and formulate a plan of escape into the wilderness beyond England's borders.

It was a late summer evening when Hereward witnessed the most violent storm he had ever seen. The day had been hot and humid and, as night drew in, the sky grew black and ominous, although the air remained warm and cloying. He found a high promontory, which brought the relief of a cooling wind, but it was the turbulent air of a brewing storm.

As he sat there for what must have been several hours, he witnessed nature at its most awesome. Vicious winds ripped branches from sturdy oaks heavy with the leaves of summer; the sky exploded in every direction with brilliant flashes of lightning, and eerie silhouettes of trees and hillsides were suddenly illuminated before disappearing as quickly as they had appeared.

Hereward wondered if storms really were God's work, as the village folk believed. He preferred to think that the magnificent display before his eyes was nature's work; why and how it could unleash such menace was a mystery to him but his instincts told him it was a tangible mystery, not a supernatural one. He was reminded of one of the insights that had become so important to him during his long isolation: that the only thing to fear was the dread created in one's own imagination.

Then, as he felt the first splashes of rain, his eye glimpsed movement through the trees in the valley below. He stiffened, but nothing stirred again and he assumed that it had been a deer or a boar. A few minutes later, an enormous bolt of lightning exploded close to him and he saw, no more than ten paces away, the silhouette of a figure.

Hereward leapt to his feet and yelled above the storm, 'Name yourself, stranger!'

There was no reply. Hereward looked into the darkness, but could see nothing. Then, as the first heavy rain of the storm lashed his face, there was another vicious crack of blinding light and the man was barely ten feet away, his shock of white hair and beard bathed in momentary daylight.

Hereward yelled again, 'Who are you?'

'Stop shouting, boy! I'm not deaf.'

The intermittent illumination of the storm was sufficient to reveal the wrinkled face of a man who had lived a very long life. Torrents of rain soaked his silvery locks, his piercing dark eyes squinted against the lashing gale; but he stood proudly, unbent in the howling wind.

'You have chosen a wild night on which to lose your way, old man.'

'I am not lost; I have come to talk to you, Hereward of Bourne.'

'How do you know my name?'

'It is hardly a mystery; you are, after all, a notorious outlaw.'

'What do you want from me? You know you put yourself at peril by speaking to me.'

'I want to hear your story; the little I've heard intrigues me. As for peril, I doubt anyone would trouble to shorten my meagre life; there is so little of it left.'

'I hate to disappoint you, sir, but my story is not one I wish to share with strangers.'

'I know you better than you realize. You have been alone for a long time and carry a great burden in your heart.' The old man looked at Hereward and smiled. 'I can help you. I understand loneliness and shame; I have lived with those two companions most of my life. I have a simple shelter near here, which you are welcome to share for a while, and I have an excellent flitch of bacon hanging by my fire.'

Hereward was intrigued by the stranger. Curious to know how his notoriety could have reached an old man deep in the forest, he agreed to his offer.

The old man's home took several hours to reach, deep in the wildwood.

When they arrived, just before dawn, his shelter was little more than a large lean-to against the cold winds of the north and west. He had chosen an exposed rock facing a natural meadow, close to a fast-flowing stream, and built a roof with two supporting sides from a framework of trimmed branches, lashed together and covered in skins. At the maw of the structure was a fire that provided warmth and a hearth for cooking. All around were the home-made accoutrements of an experienced man of the woods: traps, cooking pots, weapons and tools. The primitive shelter, although spartan, was festooned with drying skins, hanging meat and sacks of herbs and vegetables. He wanted for nothing, took little from his environment and, were he to die in his sleep one night, a few seasons of nature's cycle of decay and renewal would all but obliterate his presence.

That evening, after a bellyful of rabbit stew and several horns of mead, Hereward spoke directly to the old man. 'What is your name?'

'I am called the Old Man of the Wildwood. That is my name now and that is how it will remain.'

'But you haven't always lived here?'

'I have been here most of my life, but I was born a long way from here, close to the burgh of Winchester, where, as a young man, I was ordained.'

Hereward settled back, sensing that a long story was about to unfold.

The old man described how the life of a priest had, at first, been perfect. He had absorbed knowledge like a sponge and soon became renowned for his intellect and grasp of ancient texts and languages. But he eventually lost his way and his faith. His drinking increased and an affair with a lady-in-waiting at court led him to be defrocked, banished from Winchester and, like Hereward, cast out into the forest.

'Life is so short. I worry about how many more seasons I'm destined to see. The priests tell us we will go on to a better life in the blessed company of God, but I have my doubts. I fear my likely eternity is right here, in the earth of my own wood, rotting in the mulch like the leaves of my trees. But where will my deepest thoughts and fanciful dreams go?'

'Isn't that why we should all leave a legacy?'

The old man smiled.

'Spoken like a sage, young Hereward! But you are right; if our legacy is wholesome and true, we can face death with equanimity.'

There was a long silence as both men contemplated the forbidding prospect of death without the comfort of God and his Heaven.

The old man broke the silence. 'It takes a brave man to consider a world without God to relieve its burdens, and an even braver one to contemplate eternity without Him.'

'I don't know that it's brave; I think it's got more to do with the way a man feels about his own frailties and those of his fellow men.' Hereward paused and looked at the old man for some time before continuing. 'Why do you choose to be a hermit when you could have found a woman and raised a family, or joined a band of forest people?'

'I don't have much time for other people; they were the source of my problems. I found the frivolities of women too superficial and the friendship of men too unreliable.'

Over the coming days, the two men talked for many hours. As time passed, Hereward realized that the old man's cynicism disguised a highly intelligent mind that had discovered profound contentment through an ascetic existence.

Late one night, as their fire subsided and the first chill wind of autumn rushed through their clearing, the Old Man of the Wildwood seemed reluctant to sleep and sat staring into the distance for some time before speaking. 'I fear for this land, it is very precious to me.'

'But Edward is a good king and people prosper. Harold of Wessex leads his armies and there is peace.'

'Yes, I know. It is the future I worry about. Edward has no heir and England is the greatest prize in northern Europe; it is rich, its people industrious, its land bountiful. There are many envious eyes: the Scandinavians, of course, but it is the Normans who concern me most. Edward is fond of them, but I know them only too well. They are ruthless and will bring the avarice and deceit of Europe with them.'

'Surely the English thegns and their housecarls would never let that happen?'

'Perhaps not, but there would be great bloodshed in the reckoning of it. England could be overrun, our way of life destroyed. I see it in my dreams: burning, rape, death. An everlasting hell where England and the English are cleansed from their homeland like lice from a dog.'

'Those are the visions of a seer. Is that what you are, old man?'

'Perhaps that's what I've become, Hereward. It is of no importance; what matters is the future, and our destiny as a people. In my many years here, deep in the forest, I have come to understand the importance of our way of life and our traditions. We have to preserve them. They are what makes us who we are. Our ancestors have lived in the forests and heathlands of England for generations. They have crossed its downs and hills and built their temples and shrines there.'

'But there are many peoples on this island. There are many tribes of Celts, and the Danish clans – including my own ancestors through my mother.'

'Yes, but they share the traditions. We all know the legend of Wodewose; he sees only men, not their language nor their race. He lives here, in these woods; he lives throughout our ancient land. He is the Green Man of our childhood and reminds us of the eternal cycle of life and death and the need to live with nature, not to fight it. These Normans, with their homage to the sophistry of the Church of Rome, dismiss our ways as pagan and destroy them. We must never let that happen.'

'But Wodewose is a mythical creature to frighten children.'

'Not so, my young friend. He is deep in our memories.

The Celts call him Myrddin Wyllt – the sire of Mother Earth. Don't ever forget him.'

Their conversations about the ancient ways of England continued over many days.

The Old Man of the Wildwood told Hereward many stories that he had never heard before. He talked about the old ways of the Saxons; the Norse sagas of gods and heroes; the ancient beliefs of the Romans and the cults of pagan Rome; and the rituals of the Druids, who believed in the power of the sun, the moon and the earth itself.

After a while, Hereward came to realize that it mattered little whether these stories were true or simply myths. What was more important was that England's heritage should survive the trauma it was soon to endure.

Then, one evening without warning, the old man brought their time together to a sudden close. 'You should leave in the morning and go to Gloucester. It is only three days' walk. You will find a new path there. Follow it to your destiny, which lies far from here.'

'Is that the seer speaking?'

'Yes it is. You should listen.'

'What will you do?'

'If you are asking whether I will miss you, the answer is, yes, I will miss you. I have come to like you, Hereward of Bourne. But I am not sad, for I now know what my legacy will be.'

'Will you share it with me?'

'It is you.'

'Me? I don't understand; I have no future.'

'You are mistaken.'

The Old Man of the Wildwood looked towards the east

and the encroaching darkness. 'You will help shape the destiny of many. Hopefully, through you, much we have spoken about will be remembered and will survive. You will see many things, visit many places and live a long life. But I must warn you, you will face great turmoil and despair, with little respite, except in great old age, when you will find solace in a small measure of wisdom, as I do.'

Hereward was shocked. 'How will all this come to pass, I am an outlaw?'

'I sense it in you. You must do two things. First, you must find my daughter –'

Hereward interrupted him. 'You have a daughter!'

'Yes, her mother died in childbirth; the child is my illegitimate daughter. Her mother was a lady-in-waiting to Queen Emma at Winchester, the mother of King Edward. I was chaplain to Queen Emma and she took pity on me, despite my failings, and helped me get away with my daughter.'

'You raised her in these woods?'

'Until she was fourteen. Then she went to the nuns at Hereford, where I knew she would be safe and could continue her education. I raised her as well as I could. I taught her Greek and Latin, English and French, how to make medicine from the herbs of the forest, and as much of the sciences and philosophies of the ancients as I could remember. She took my books and manuscripts with her; they were her safe passage for the future.'

'And the second thing I must do?'

'Ask her to give you the Talisman.'

'What is the Talisman?'

'She will tell you.'

'What is her name?'

'She is called Torfida.'

'How will I find her?'

'You will find her.'

The old man started to chant the plainsong of the great cathedrals, something Hereward had first heard while waiting to be judged by the King at Winchester. Now it signalled his departure from a remarkable man and took on a haunting quality, making him think of the legend of Wodewose and the many other stories he had heard.

The old seer said only one more thing before continuing his mantra long into the night. 'Go well, young Hereward; give my love to Torfida. You will help her to fulfil her destiny, and she will be your guide in finding yours.'

4. Gruffydd ap Llywelyn

It did not take Hereward long to make a complete reconnaissance of Gloucester. He secreted himself close to its wooden walls and meticulously observed its daily routines until he could remember all the merchants and farmers who used its gates. He learned to recognize each of its men-at-arms, and studied the habits of the gatekeeper who barred the entrance every night.

Hereward soon devised his escape route. The river was wide and navigable, and there was a small harbour to handle the busy trade between the rich hinterland and the sea to the south-west. He knew that Normandy and Brittany lay to the south of England and that a renegade Englishman might find a warm welcome there. He had also heard that the influence of King Edward did not extend to the wild Celtic lands far to the west, nor to the Danish settlement in Ireland. Perhaps now that he had sullied his Anglo-Saxon blood, he could find a new home with his Norse mother's kith and kin.

The execution of his plan did not take long. There were several small boats on the quayside that had not been used in all the time he had been paying his frequent visits. So he waited until the dark of the moon and the dead of an overcast October night, slipped a boat from its moorings, clambered into it and let it drift downstream. He used a broken branch from the forest as a paddle and, despite the river's gentle flow, made good progress. It was the next part of the journey that concerned him, when the river became much wider to merge with the open sea.

He was no seafarer, had no cloak to hide his outlaw's collar, possessed neither weapons nor tools and had the daunting appearance of a wild man of the forest. Soon, the modest waterway became an ever-broadening, faster-running river and its banks receded further into the distance. He decided to stay close to the right bank, the northern side. Although he did not know where the lands of the Celtic people of Wales began, he guessed it must be close to the northern edge of the river. The Welsh had been fighting the English for decades; perhaps they would give him passage to Ireland.

Hereward spent over eighteen hours in the boat, slowly working his way to what he hoped would be another kingdom and the possibility of freedom. It was dusk and high tide when he finally chose his landing ground, a gently sloping sandy bank, surrounded by thick woodland and lacking any sign of habitation. For many days he walked deeper and deeper into the forest. The ground rose before him as he ventured further from the coast, moving with caution, knowing that he was almost certainly treading on foreign soil.

The many Celtic tribes of western Britain had lived there since the beginning of time. Through centuries of bitter struggle, they had fought the Romans and prevented them from settling the west and the far north. Later, when the Saxon tribes came, they resisted them too, so that they were able to settle only in the former Roman provinces in the south and east. Many Celts were thought to retain their pagan beliefs or, if they professed to be Christian, still practised the secret ways of their old religion under the veneer of the Church of Rome. When the storytellers came to Bourne, they told gruesome tales of Celtic warriors painted in woad and of their princes, who decapitated their conquered victims and ate their children. From childhood Hereward had been taught to avoid the Celts at all costs.

As he moved further inland the ground became very different from the English territory with which he was familiar. This new ground was much more rugged and seemed greener and wetter than his homeland. The scattered human settlements were fewer in number and further apart, and the wildlife was far more abundant. He had heard that at the end of the earth there was a great wilderness; perhaps this was it, a place capable of consuming men without trace.

Eventually, Hereward's progress was halted by the wide bend of a fast-flowing river. On the opposite bank, standing impressively on ancient fortifications, were the ramparts of a major burgh. He could see the bustle of hundreds of soldiers and row upon row of horses tethered on picket lines. Drifting on the wind, he could hear the din of hectic activity and the thud of drums; not the ominously measured throb of the drums of battle, but the light timpani of celebration. There were skirls from pipes of different timbres and shrieks of excited laughter, while countless flags and banners rippled in the wind, lending flashes of crimson, green and yellow to the monotony of a darkening sky. The lofty oak walls of the settlement were surrounded by the shelters of a temporary military encampment; it looked like a victory was being celebrated and, from the look of the flags, these men were not English. They were Celts – the wild men of Wales.

Then, inexorably, he became aware of the unmistakable stench of death and the harrowing cries of men in agony. Although he dreaded what he would find, he moved towards the tortured sounds and sickening smell.

Soon, he came to a clearing in the forest and beheld a sight he would never forget.

Lying before him was a mass of humanity: men twisted and tangled together, contorted between shields and axes, spears and swords, steam rising from their bodies, blood seeping from their wounds and the rattle of death rasping in their throats. He turned away, but a morbid fascination made him look again. Arms and legs were severed, sometimes a head; torsos were impaled, guts spilled from bellies. The air was still warm, the frenzied heat of men striving to kill one another still hanging in the air.

The human scavengers, who would soon come and desecrate the bodies of the dead and dying, had not yet arrived. Hereward was alone amid the stench.

What had all these men died for?

Surely nothing could justify carnage like this?

Suddenly a hand grasped his leg. It was the blood-soaked hand of a warrior slashed across the face by a sword and impaled by a spear. His scant beard was matted with dried blood, almost obscuring his features, but Hereward could see that he was a handsome young man, probably still a teenager, with dark eyes and a flowing mane of black hair. In between the streaks of blood, he could see the intricate arcs and swirls of tribal warpaint, the unmistakable blue of Celtic woad. The boy tried to speak but managed only a few gurgled sounds. His lungs were awash with blood; he was slowly drowning in his own life force. As Hereward bent down towards him, the youth's taut grip relaxed and his heaving torso stilled, his anguish over.

Hereward turned away and moved quickly towards the river. He tried to suppress what he had seen and to focus instead on planning how he might cross the river. He was pondering how to get closer to the encampment and burgh when he heard rapidly approaching footsteps and spun round to see the bobbing head and shoulders of a young, dark-haired man running methodically along the path behind him. He appeared to have no armour, no companions and, except for a seax, no weapons.

In an instant, Hereward decided to waylay the youthful runner. He ducked into the undergrowth and threw his shoulder into the lad's knees as he passed, propelling him, headlong, into a blackthorn bush.

The cursing began immediately, but not in a language Hereward understood. The boy looked around, saw Hereward, who was by now smiling broadly, and cursed even more.

'Are you Welsh?' asked Hereward.

'Of course I'm Welsh.' The reply came in English from the now deeply entangled, much scratched and severely irritated youngster. 'You sound like an Englishman. If you are, you're either a fool or a very brave man to be this far from home.'

He spoke in perfect English, and almost without accent, as he slowly and painfully pulled himself from the undergrowth. His woollen smock and leggings were torn in several places and blood already seeped from the scratches to his skin beneath.

'When my Lord hears of this, he'll cut you in half!'

'Who is your Lord?'

Before the young man could spit out his answer with all the venom his rage could muster, he noticed the collar on Hereward's neck.

He hesitated. 'That's the seal of Edward, that limp-wristed English King. No wonder you look like you've been living in a pigsty.'

'What's your name, boy?'

'Don't call me "boy". You're not much older than I am; you're a long way from home and wear the collar of an outlaw. I'm the one who should be asking the questions.'

Hereward smiled again. 'I am Hereward of Bourne. I was outlawed by Edward, King of England, at Winchester. That was over a year ago, and now I am making my way to Ireland.'

'Why were you outlawed?'

'That is no business of yours. Let me help you up.' Hereward held out his hand.

The young man grabbed it but, as he did so, he moved his right foot behind Hereward's legs and kicked him hard behind the knees to unbalance him. As Hereward fell, the boy twisted the hand that had been offered to him and neatly locked it behind the bigger man's back.

'Very good, boy.'

With his chin resting firmly on Hereward's shoulder, his breath quickened by the sudden exertion, the young man hissed, 'My name is Martin Lightfoot, messenger of my Lord, Gruffydd ap Llywelyn, King of the Welsh.' With his free hand, Martin pulled his seax from his belt and held it at Hereward's throat. 'You smell, you filthy

Englishman. I think I should kill you to rid our country of your foreign stink. If I throw you into the river just here, you should wash up on the English shore where you belong.'

Using his free hand, Hereward grabbed his adversary's wrist firmly, then slowly pulled the seax away from his throat. Try as he might, Martin could not resist the Englishman's considerable strength. With his arm still locked behind his back, Hereward got to his feet, leaving the Welshman dangling forlornly from his shoulders. It took only a moment for Martin to realize that his Saxon foe was more than a match for him.

He released his grip and catapulted himself to the ground well away from Hereward's grasp. 'You are a big son of an English pig, that's for sure.'

Hereward ignored the insult but was curious about Martin's lord. 'I thought the Welsh were ruled by different princes, each the lord of his clan.'

'It has taken my Lord Gruffydd five years of campaigning to bring Wales under one banner. We defeated the tribes of Morgannwg and Gwent here only yesterday, and now the whole of Wales is united for the first time in our history.'

'Will you take me to your King?'

'Why would you want to see my Lord — he'll kill you for sure.'

'Perhaps, but it was a king who outlawed me from my homeland; maybe this king will free me so that I can find a new home.'

'Why would you trust me?'

'You have an honest face; and besides, I have the parchment that you're supposed to give to your king.'

Martin had not noticed that, in the struggle, Hereward had grabbed a parchment from the young man's belt.

'You filthy Englishman! Give it back to me. My Lord will have my head on a pole.'

'I've heard that such delightful punishments are favoured by your Celtic princes. We'd better hurry so that you can complete your mission.'

Martin, rapidly calculating his predicament, realized that he had little to lose by doing as the stranger asked, so he turned and resumed his steady pace towards his original destination. 'You'd better keep up, and remember to give me the parchment when we get to the gates.'

Hereward followed as quickly as he could, but the young Celt ran like a deer. By the time Martin reached the ferry, Hereward was almost fifty yards in his wake.

Martin yelled to the guards well before he arrived at the riverbank, but in Welsh, so Hereward had no idea whether he was sounding the alarm or just announcing his arrival. The guards drew their weapons but looked more curious than threatening as Hereward approached.

'Come quickly!' signalled Martin. 'I mustn't delay.'

The four oarsmen were pulling hard before Hereward had sat down. A rope had been stretched across the fast-flowing river to keep the boat on line but, even so, it was a struggle to get across.

As the boat approached the opposite bank, it was obvious that some in the camp were still celebrating. Drunken shrieks, both male and female, filled the air; clear notes from flutes and horns occasionally cut through the repetitive thud of drums; a few sporadic words from songs of victory rose above the piercing laughter. This army had clearly won a great victory and was celebrating long and hard.

But it was also a disciplined army. As others rejoiced, sentries, sober and sombre with their backs to the proceedings, stared intently across the river or into the surrounding forest, alert to any danger or intruder.

It was also a brutal army. All around the perimeter of the camp were the spreadeagled bodies of its enemies. They were also Celts, but Welshmen from different tribes, who had been tied to wooden frames and hoisted from the ground. Most had had their eyes cut out, some also their tongues, noses and ears; several were still alive.

Hereward had not seen war before. His father and the men of Bourne had told him endless stories of battles won and lost, of heroic deeds and daring adventures in pursuit of worthy causes, but nothing of the kind of cruelty now before his eyes.

On reaching the opposite bank, Hereward gave Martin his precious parchment and, accompanied by two guards, they made their way to the centre of the camp. There, in the midst of the celebrations, sat the man Hereward hoped would offer him the chance of a new life.

This was the second king he had seen, but this monarch was not a sophisticated aesthete like Edward. Gruffydd ap Llywelyn was a warrior; his dark-blue smock covered a barrel-like chest and his thick woollen cloak only added to his significant presence. His armour and weapons were neatly arranged beside him: the sword and mace of a warlord, a beautifully decorated shield with a brightly polished iron boss, a heavy mail jacket and an ornate helmet, etched with swirls of serpents and dragons. Next to the

King was a large group of heavily armed hearthtroops – menacing, battle-hardened veterans – the finest of his warriors.

Martin Lightfoot stepped forward with his parchment clasped in his right hand, bowed deeply and handed his document to the King. 'My Lord King, I bring news that Aelfgar has landed with eighteen ships. He brings his finest warriors from Northumbria, and Danish allies from Ireland. He will be with you at first light tomorrow.'

The King studied the document closely before shouting to everyone within earshot: 'Aelfgar, Earl of Northumbria, declares his loyalty to me. Our new kingdom already has powerful allies!'

Roars of approval and warlike chanting echoed around the camp.

Gruffydd turned to Hereward and scowled. 'Who is this stranger you bring into my camp?'

'Sire, a notorious outlaw from the English, who asks to be placed at your mercy. I thought he might be useful.'

'You think too much, Martin Lightfoot. Unfortunately, you don't think as well as you run.'

The King's retinue laughed loudly.

Hereward seized the moment, bowed deferentially and addressed him. 'My Lord King, I am an outcast from my own people. I am Hereward of Bourne, of honest blood from my Saxon father and my Danish mother. I seek passage through your lands on my journey to Ireland and a new life.'

'You are an outlaw – and an English one at that – so tell me: why shouldn't I order your immediate execution for having the audacity to approach my camp?'

'Forgive my impudence, sire. I am being rightly punished for my actions, but my own folly created a heinous crime that I thought I had the right to punish. My banishment has helped me see things more clearly. Now, if I do not assert myself and find a way into exile, I will die in the forest.'

Gruffydd rose from his campaign chair, approached Hereward and slowly circled him. He examined his iron collar, recognized King Edward's seal, looked closely at his scars and then returned to his seat.

'The celebrations stop in two hours. No drinking tonight. The men must rest, clean their weapons, their armour and themselves. We begin our training to challenge King Edward tomorrow. I don't want the Saxons to think we're savages – at least, not until we kill them! Make sure the outlaw is washed and cuts his beard. The blacksmiths can remove his collar. Perhaps I'll keep it to put around Edward's Norman neck when we reach Winchester! I like the look of this Saxon; he has the stance of a warrior and the bearing of a noble. By the cut of him, I wager he can fight as well.' Gruffydd then turned to Hereward. 'You will sit at my table tonight and tell me your story, and bring that scamp Martin Lightfoot with you.'

That evening, after months of solitude, Hereward shared food with more people than he had ever seen before, and did so in the presence of a king. Several times he reached for his iron collar, his constant companion for more than a year, but each time, instead of pig iron, he found flesh and felt the elation of his new freedom.

At the King's command there was no alcohol on the table. Nevertheless, Hereward began to glow from the

conviviality of conversation and laughter. He looked fit
and healthy; a long summer in the open had bronzed his
skin and bleached his hair; his scars had healed and he could
easily have passed as one of Gruffydd's Norse mercenaries.
When, at the King's instruction, he rose to tell his story
wearing a bright blue smock and new woollen leggings
given to him by one of Gruffydd's chieftains, he cut a handsome figure.

It took Hereward nearly twenty minutes to tell his tale.
Fortunately, almost all the Welsh nobles understood
English; he told his story lucidly and with authority and,
by the end, the entire gathering was hanging on his every
word.

'You tell a good story, young Hereward of Bourne, well
done. Tomorrow we will see if you can fight.'

'Sire, I have not come here to fight.'

'That may be so, but tomorrow you will fight . . . or die.'

Martin beckoned Hereward away from the scene. 'We
meet our Northumbrian and Norse comrades tomorrow.
The King will make you fight one of his finest warriors to
amuse the army and our guests from across the water. You
must be ready; it will be a fight to the death.'

'I have done enough fighting, Martin. It is not the life I
seek.'

'Hereward, it is obvious from your story that, like me,
you find it difficult to avoid a fight. No matter what we do,
even if we don't go to the fight, the fight will always come
to us.'

That night Hereward and Martin spent several hours
discussing the wayward and dangerous paths that they
seemed destined to follow. The young Welshman was as

quick-witted and humorous as he was fleet of foot. Born in the wild mountains of North Wales, he had spent his childhood chasing lost sheep for his father before being recruited as a messenger for the army. At the time, Gruffydd was the Prince of Gwynedd, but he was building a strong military base to support his ambition to unite all the tribes of Wales. Martin, soon to be christened 'Lightfoot' by Gruffydd's men, became the Prince's principal messenger and, with his long dark locks and wraith-like body, became recognized all over the country. It was said that he was swifter than the wind, with a step so light he left no footprint.

Hereward spent most of the rest of the night thinking about his new dilemma.

He sensed that he was being drawn towards a life he had resolved to reject, but that Martin was right: his future would be a long saga of mortal combat, his destiny determined in battle.

The sun had barely risen when Hereward awoke to the sound of the horns and drums of Aelfgar's approaching column. He counted over 700 men, half behind the ram's head banner of the Earldom of Northumbria and half behind the dragon's head of the Irish Norse of Dublin. They were a formidable sight and, when drawn up with Gruffydd's battle-hardened army of over 2,000, would form a significant fighting force. The two leaders greeted one another to the sound of piercing cries and cheering from both armies.

Gruffydd addressed his visitors in standard Anglo-Saxon, a lingua franca most of the gathering understood. 'Aelfgar,

Earl of Northumbria, welcome to my camp. You are a loyal and trusted friend. Everything is prepared for your army, let them rest.'

'I thank you, Gruffydd ap Llywelyn, King of the Welsh. The omens are good for our alliance.'

At dusk that evening, Hereward was brought before the King, his guest, Earl Aelfgar, and the assembled nobility of the alliance. Gruffydd had chosen as Hereward's opponent one of his hearthtroop, a heavily set man, who looked as though he could wield his axe and sword to murderous effect.

'I hear you refuse to fight, Hereward of Bourne. You foolishly refuse a king!'

'I prefer to say "decline", my Lord.'

'Don't play games with me!'

Aelfgar intervened. 'I have heard about this young man. His disrespect has all but got him killed before; now he insults you, my Lord King.'

'He does, but at least his answer is honest and brave. I think he'll fight if he has to.' Gruffydd turned to his chosen man. 'Kill him.'

The warrior stepped forward and immediately swung his axe at Hereward's neck but, with a gentle sway of his hips, he easily moved his upper body out of range of the blow. The attacker quickly thrust forward with his sword, only to see Hereward move quickly to the side to avoid the danger. Now that his opponent was off balance, it was easy for Hereward to step in, grab the warrior's wrist, pull him forward and aim a heavy kick to his midriff, bringing him to his knees. In retaliation, Gruffydd's man swung wildly with his battle-axe, but Hereward sprang high into the air, well above the arc of the blade, and stepped out of harm's way. Further attacks ended in the same way, until it was obvious that Hereward was far too agile for his adversary.

The audience was impressed; none had seen a man as big as Hereward move so nimbly.

As Gruffydd's man stumbled with exhaustion, Aelfgar asked the King if the captain of his housecarls could mount an attack.

Gruffydd reluctantly agreed and signalled his man to withdraw.

'My Lord, this is Einar, the finest of my warriors, he will despatch the outlaw.'

'We'll see, my friend, let him try.'

Einar was a giant of a man with a flowing red beard, perhaps the most imposing man Hereward had ever seen. He walked up to Hereward, who stood his ground.

When they were nose to nose, Einar growled, 'So you won't fight, Saxon?' Almost before he had finished, he head-butted Hereward full on the nose, knocking him backwards, blood spurting from his nostrils. 'Perhaps that will persuade you!'

Hoots of laughter echoed around the gathering as Hereward hit the ground, dazed and in great pain. In an instant, the big man's sword was drawn, ready to strike a mortal blow, but Hereward grabbed a fistful of earth and threw it into his adversary's eyes. This bought him a vital moment to jump into a crouching position and propel himself into his foe's stomach, knocking him to the ground. Maddened by the pain of a broken nose, Hereward kicked the fallen man several times, winding him badly, before jumping on his sword hand with one foot while kicking him in the face with the other. Einar rolled away, spitting blood through his smashed teeth, but in doing so left his sword behind. Seizing it, Hereward was able to parry the first blow from Einar's battle-axe.

As it was now obvious that Hereward had decided to fight, the King beckoned to one of his hearthtroop to throw the Englishman a shield. A ferocious duel ensued with neither man giving ground. Every blow was blocked, every thrust parried, until Hereward's youth and strength began to tell and Einar tired. Hereward was able to grab the shaft of Einar's axe and use it to turn him into a headlock which immobilized the big man.

As soon as the fight had gone out of the giant redhead, Hereward released him and stepped away, declining the custom to despatch his beaten opponent.

'My Lord King, I have killed too many men in my life already; I have no desire to kill another.'

'Agreed. You have made your point well. Tomorrow you ride with me.'

Martin began to lead Hereward away, but not before Einar offered him his hand. He had never been bested in a contest before and was full of admiration for the young Englishman.

The two men embraced as a murmur of appreciation rippled around the assembly of warriors; none had ever seen a stranger so quickly win over a crowd, or so readily gain the respect of a king.

5. Battle of Hereford

Hereward shivered with emotion as he watched four huge columns of heavily armed infantry, each led by a cohort of cavalry, weave their way through the forest. His pulse raced with excitement, but he was also troubled that this army of Celts, Danes and Norsemen, allied with treacherous Northumbrians, was about to attack his homeland.

Despite the fact that his own people had outlawed him, he felt guilty that he was experiencing the primordial thrill of impending battle.

He looked around at his companions, who were grim-faced and determined. It excited Hereward to be with seasoned warriors like Einar, men to stand with in a fight, men with whom it would be an honour to die.

He had spent several weeks with Gruffydd's Welsh army, enduring their training regimes and helping them replenish their supplies of weapons, food and horses for a new wave of military campaigns. It was late October 1055 and over the long weeks of preparation he had decided that, if it came to a battle with King Edward's army, he would fight. It had been a difficult decision, but he was now riding with Celts and Norsemen; he was wearing their armour and carrying their weapons.

He looked at Martin and Einar, riding at his side, and acknowledged them with a nod of respect. Hereward knew that in moments like these, lives change for ever.

The Welsh had prepared for months to attack Hereford, one of England's most strategically important burghs. Ralph, Earl of Hereford, was the Norman nephew of King Edward, who had made him Warden of the Welsh Marches. He had brought many Norman knights, clerics and administrators to his earldom, much to the consternation of the locals.

As Gruffydd's columns made open ground in a wide valley, some two miles west of Hereford, Ralph's cavalry were skulking on the wooded hillsides. The Earl had determined that Gruffydd's combined force of Welsh, Northumbrians and Irish-Norse was an ill-disciplined rabble, weakened by mercenaries of dubious loyalty. Also, because many of the Celts were on foot, he thought it would be vulnerable to a swift and decisive cavalry attack. His horsemen broke cover and bore down on the invaders. The Earl's thegns carried the red and yellow banners of his lands in Worcestershire, Herefordshire and Gloucestershire, but most of his senior commanders were Normans, recognizable by their full-length mail coats and heavy continental horses.

At first their attack, with the advantage of surprise and higher ground, looked like it might be decisive as there was little more than 200 yards between the leading horses of the Earl's cavalry and Gruffydd's infantry. But Ralph's strategy was naïve. The Welsh army and its allies were elite warriors who had fought many battles during years of campaigning. Within moments of the surprise attack, Gruffydd's hearthtroop began to circle to protect him, while the body of his force re-formed to charge the oncoming cavalry. Supported by the Northumbrians on their right and the Irish on their left, they surged forwards in a V-shaped formation towards the heart of Ralph's phalanx of horses.

The Earl's cavalry had not expected such a bold response. They were in loose formation, expecting easy pickings among infantry exposed on open ground, but Gruffydd's column was tightly packed, rigidly disciplined and had gained significant momentum. As the two armies collided, the carnage began in the front ranks: men screamed, trying to inflict blows or avoid them; horses reared, struggling to free themselves.

Gruffydd's infantry held its shape. The lances and shields of its front ranks, reinforced by its collective discipline, formed a solid, surging wall that was far too strong for the Earl's cavalry. The horses behind the first wave of the attack streamed down the sides of the solid phalanx of foot soldiers and made easy targets for the spirited infantrymen of Wales, wielding swords and battle-axes. Many riders turned and fled but a small group, perhaps no more than thirty, were more determined. From their distinctive shield designs and the human skulls tied to their saddles, Hereward guessed they were Welsh chieftains, defeated by Gruffydd, who had thrown in their lot with the Earl of Hereford. Despite the catastrophe of Ralph's reckless attack, this small group fought on, moving ever closer to Gruffydd's position.

Although they were small in number, the ferocity of their onslaught soon saw them engaging the King's hearthtroop. Their leader, distinguished by a magnificent bronze helmet with a boar's head crest, suddenly burst through the line of defending guards and made open ground within a few yards of the King. Several of his followers poured through the gap and, in a blind fury of revenge, began cutting down Gruffydd's housecarls in swathes. Hereward was only a few feet from the King and, supported by Einar and Martin, moved forward to protect the royal cordon. The three men put themselves between the King and his assailants and unleashed a fury of blows that cut down several of the attackers.

Hereward was at the forefront, tall in his saddle and using his axe to murderous effect. He moved purposefully towards the boars' head chieftain and made eye contact with him. They clashed immediately, with Hereward ducking under a huge swing of the Welshman's axe. It gave Hereward the split second he needed as he thrust his lance deep into his opponent's ribcage, somersaulting him over the rear of his horse. He then turned to the back of the melee, grabbed Gruffydd's reins and pulled his mount around.

As he did so, he shouted at the King's housecarls: 'Hold your ground, protect the King!'

He pulled the King's steed away from the assault, and shouted again: 'Make way for the King! Make way for the King.'

The wall of royal hearthtroops parted and Hereward escorted Gruffydd over to Earl Aelfgar's cavalry, which had been holding firm in reserve.

'I don't normally flee in battle, especially from one I'm winning!' spluttered the breathless King.

'With you removed, my Lord, their fury will soon be spent. Your housecarls will easily cut them down.'

As Gruffydd thought about Hereward's answer, Aelfgar spoke for both of them. 'The young Saxon thinks as well as he fights.'

Hereward was soon proved right. Encircled by Gruffydd's elite warriors, and with their quarry safe with Aelfgar's cavalry, the Welsh chieftains were quickly overwhelmed and ruthlessly massacred.

Gruffydd's thoughts quickly returned to the main battle. 'Earl Aelfgar, you must commit the cavalry. Before the day is ours, we need to find the Earl's infantry.'

After witnessing the bloody failure of the Earl's cavalry, his infantry were retreating through the trees at full pelt. As Aelfgar's cavalry bore down on them, Ralph and his surviving mounted thegns tried to persuade his infantry to hold, but the howling invaders put the fear of God into them. The rash move to commit his horses in a surprise attack had been a disastrous miscalculation by the Earl of Hereford. Many good men had already paid with their lives; many more would be caught in the open in a chaotic retreat, and a trail of death that would lead all the way to the walls of Hereford.

As his loyal troops died in their hundreds, Ralph abandoned his burgh to its fate and fled towards Winchester and the protection of King Edward.

The first of the victors poured into Hereford at dusk and the mayhem of war continued as the rape and murder of the innocent began.

Hereward and the leaders arrived in the burgh shortly after the advanced guard. Houses were being torched and male inhabitants were being put to the sword; booty was being loaded into carts; larders and grain stores were being emptied and the screams of women and children could be heard everywhere.

As Hereward, Martin Lightfoot, Einar and the Captain

of the King's housecarls arrived at the nunnery of Hereford, the great wooden cathedral, adjacent to the nunnery, was already in flames. Warriors were stacking books, church plate, altar crosses and tapestries on to carts, while several clerics lay in pools of blood in the doorway. At the entrance to the nuns' quarters, the sight of men surging forward, fighting one another to get in, abruptly reminded Hereward that the Old Man of the Wildwood had sent his daughter to the nuns at Hereford.

He turned to the Captain of his housecarls. 'Captain, there may be a woman in there I need to find.'

'Stand aside!'

At the Captain's bellowed order, the men grudgingly parted, allowing access to the refectory.

The Mother Superior and the older nuns had attempted to form a circle of sanctuary at the high table, protecting the younger women. One of Aelfgar's Northumbrians reached into the cowering group, dragged out a struggling girl, no more than sixteen years old, and threw her at the Captain. As he did so, he yanked her crude woollen habit, ripping it apart, to render her naked at his feet.

She immediately crawled into a ball to hide herself.

'This one is yours, Captain! Do you want her?'

The Captain nodded at his sergeant-at-arms, who immediately cut the man down with his sword.

'Take him out and throw him in the midden! The rest of you, out, now! Mother Superior, my men will escort you as close to Gloucester as is safe for them. Take whatever you need, but you must leave immediately.'

She and the other nuns suppressed their sobs as Hereward called out, 'Is there a woman here named Torfida?'

'I am Torfida.'

The voice came from the naked figure still coiled on the floor. Hereward offered her his cloak and, as she wrapped it around herself, he could not fail to notice how beautiful she was. He also saw a large amulet around her neck and assumed it was the object her father had told him about.

Hereward spoke gently to her. 'Your father told me that I would meet you. He sends you his love.'

Although the young woman was still heaving with the fear and anxiety of what had just happened, she composed herself quickly. 'He was a great man.'

'What do you mean by "was"? Have you heard of his death?'

'No, but I'm sure he's dead. The forest has taken him; I can feel it.'

She spoke with such conviction, Hereward saw little point in challenging her. 'He said that I must ask you for a talisman.'

She paused for a few moments and stared at him with a rare intensity. 'So you are the one.'

With that, Torfida walked towards her Mother Superior and whispered to her for several seconds. Then they kissed and parted and the matriarch ushered her flock away.

'I must come with you now.'

Hereward was shocked at the firmness of Torfida's words. 'You don't know where I'm going.'

'Wherever it is, I must come with you.'

Despite her tender years, she had regained her composure remarkably quickly. 'And what of the amulet?'

'That comes with us. We will talk about it when I think it is time. Until then, we will not speak of it again.'

They arrived at the King's camp, some distance from the ravaged burgh, where Gruffydd was celebrating in earnest. He had a drinking horn in his hand and it was obvious that he had been using it liberally.

'Hereward, I see you have found yourself a beautiful young girl. Bring her to me.'

'Sire, she is a virgin and a Sister of the Church.'

'I realize that, boy! I just want to look at her.'

Torfida did not wait for a response from Hereward; she removed the cloak he had given her and let it fall to the ground, not attempting to cover herself. Hereward moved towards her but, with a slight movement of her hand, she gestured to him to stay away. Then, with a jutting of her jaw and a deep intake of breath, she stood proudly in front of Gruffydd and several hundred of his warriors.

Her boldness shocked them into silence.

Torfida was striking: her jet-black hair, dark eyes and olive skin made her resemble a Mediterranean princess more than a fair maid of England. Although not much older than a child, her breasts were full, with nipples firm and dark; her hips were broad and there was a muscular tone to her limbs, a product of a healthy life in the forest. Her sexuality, emanating from her self-confidence and bearing, was arresting and way beyond her years.

The silence lasted for several seconds.

Torfida stared defiantly at the King. He stared back at her, equally resolute. Eventually, the King relented with a shake of his head, as if breaking a spell.

'Madam, you are beautiful.' The King spoke for every man there. 'Hereward of Bourne, cover her. Take her to the women, have them dress her; I place her under your protection.'

Hereward hesitated for a second, feeling the strength of her will, before her smile signalled that he could proceed. As he draped his cloak over her shoulders a second time, for a fleeting moment he enjoyed the excitement of touching her warm skin.

The King spoke again. 'Hereward of Bourne, I grant you safe passage in your journey to the west. Take young Lightfoot with you and, with Earl Aelfgar's permission, the big man too.'

Aelfgar nodded his approval.

'As for the young woman . . . Before you go, madam, I will see the object you wear around your neck.'

'My Lord King, it is only a trinket, a gift from my father.'

'Don't deny me. I would like to know what object of intrigue adorns such a desirable creature. Step forward.'

Hereward shuddered, fearing that the King's mood might darken. As Torfida strode the five yards that separated her from Gruffydd, his instincts cried out to him to rush to her aid.

The King stood as she approached; that in itself was unusual, but his whispered question was bizarre. 'Do you understand the old ways?'

'Sire?'

The King leaned closer to her. 'Do you know the ways of the Druids, practised under the moon, and the hidden truths from the time before the new faith came to us?'

He put his hand on her shoulder and gripped her flesh. Torfida stood firm, but did not respond.

'Do you understand the lore of the forest, the mythical

beasts and the rituals of our ancestors?' He moved his hand to Torfida's waist, then towards her buttocks.

She still did not respond.

'I sense you understand these things.'

'My father taught me many things, both old and new.'

The King gave her a long, suggestive stare as he slowly moved his hand over the mound of her backside. 'Did you practise the black arts during the long dark nights alone in your cell?'

'I practise many things. But when I'm alone, I think only of how to overcome evil and the wicked things that men do.'

'You talk like a seer.'

'My father was a seer.'

'What did he tell you about the amulet you wear?'

'He told me to respect it, to understand it and to learn from it.'

The King released his grip on Torfida and sat down. 'My family have lived in the mountains of Gwynedd for centuries. As children we were told a story passed down to us from ancient times. It tells of a great journey, undertaken by a flaxen-haired hero. He was seduced by a dark temptress who held the secret of his destiny. She carried an amulet which was so old that no one could remember its origins, but it was a powerful talisman which entranced all who saw it.' He paused, peering into Torfida's eyes, trying to bend her to his will. 'Show me your amulet.'

Torfida leaned forward so that the amulet swung freely.

Gruffydd could see it clearly, but he could also see her breasts, even her nipples, which she made no attempt to hide. He wallowed in her sexuality and breathed deeply, preparing to devour her, there and then, in front of the entire army. The King's blood rose as he thought how easy it would be to take her. No one could stop him.

Torfida spoke to Gruffydd in hushed tones, but her gaze was steely; only those close by could hear the words.

'The Talisman tells me the truth about men. It shows me their hidden weaknesses, exposes their worst sins and reveals their greatest fears.'

Torfida's chilling words broke the spell of the King's manipulative game. She continued to stare at him intently, as if peering into his soul. He looked at the Talisman, saw the grotesque face of evil captured in its stone and pulled away, trying not to appear shocked.

He was silent for several seconds.

'What do you see in me?' His question was asked meekly, like a boy seeking reassurance from a mother.

'You are a great warrior, a hero to your people. Your life is a constant war, a perpetual struggle for supremacy against your enemies. Gruffydd ap Llywelyn the man is Gruffydd ap Llywelyn the King; it is as it is.'

'Am I condemned to Hell because a king has to do what he has to do?'

'I do not know the answer to that; but never underestimate the power of the Anglo-Saxons. One day, they will come for you in overwhelming numbers, and then you will have to decide whether to stand and fight, or to submit. After that, your destiny is hidden from me. Only you can determine that, but you will be long remembered by your people.'

The tension had subsided. Torfida put out her hand and

touched Gruffydd gently on his cheek, as if she were anointing him.

It was an astonishing gesture, both because Torfida had the presence to do it, but mainly because the King accepted it so meekly.

Gruffydd turned to Hereward. 'Hereward, if you ever pass this way again, I would like to know what this beautiful creature makes of you. Take care of her.'

The four companions left camp the next morning and travelled west. Hereward was mindful of his good fortune: he had won his freedom, been given horses and supplies, a few pieces of Welsh silver and had found three companions. The Old Man of the Wildwood had described for him a daunting and challenging destiny, the first part of which had already come to pass.

No one spoke for over an hour; Torfida and Hereward were a few yards behind Martin and Einar when her words broke the silence.

'I doubted my father yesterday. When the soldiers came, I thought my life was over. My father had said that my destiny was with one man – a great man – that I would bear his children and that we would face our destinies together. But I doubted my father, and I'm ashamed.'

'But you don't doubt him any more?'

'No, because he sent you to me. He knew what your future would be.'

'Why is the Talisman so important?'

Torfida kicked on to join the other two. 'All in good time.'

As Hereward watched his three new companions move through the forest ahead of him, he knew his life was about

94

to begin in earnest and that his previous escapades were no more than a prelude for what was to come. He knew that Martin and Einar would be his comrades for life and that Torfida would be his companion, his wife and his mentor.

They travelled west for many days, meeting almost no one on their route. They kept away from the high mountains to the north, but progress was still slow because of the many valleys they crossed. It was a desolated land, its tracks overgrown and its villages abandoned; Gruffydd's wars had extracted a heavy price.

At times on their long journey, Hereward and Torfida would hang back or kick on until out of earshot of their companions. During these private moments, they told each other the contrasting stories of their lives.

Hers was a tale of a girl of the forest who knew no one other than her father, but who, nevertheless, had lived a childhood full of wonder and imagination under the wise tutelage of an inspirational man. His was a saga about a boy who had managed to spurn every opportunity available to him and take the wrong route at every crossroads in his life.

Eventually, from high on the side of a valley, they saw a busy thoroughfare below. Carts loaded with wood and wool and baggage trains of donkeys, oxen and horses confirmed that they had found a major trading route. They met fellow-travellers who told them that they were west of the settlement at Carmarthen and well on the way to the monastery at St David's, from where safe passage to Ireland would be easy to arrange.

Hereward was elated: they could be in Dublin ahead of the cold December winds.

Two more days in the saddle got them to St David's, where Hereward saw the Great Western Sea for the first time, which he knew would carry him far away to another land and a new life.

As they descended the hill towards the shore and the neat rectangular shapes of the houses of the monks of St David's, Torfida's manner changed.

'You can make love to me tonight.'

Hereward was shocked. Because Torfida was barely sixteen, he had tried to put her beauty out of his mind. He had often felt aroused by her, but had suppressed the feeling, deliberately replacing it with a strong commitment to protect her.

'Torfida, you are very beautiful, but you are so young. We should wait.'

'Do you not desire me? I want to leave these shores as a woman, not as a girl. Although I am a virgin, I know what has to happen. My father told me that it is important for a woman to enjoy a man; he also explained that we make love face to face, unlike the beasts, because our pleasure should derive from love, not our animal instincts. I've been thinking about it a lot recently. I know what the King was trying to do, and I enjoyed playing his game. It made me aroused.'

She looked at him with a knowing, suggestive smile. He found her provocation irresistible and remembered her standing naked in full view of Gruffydd and his warriors, proudly displaying her extraordinary beauty.

'Why do I have the feeling that I am going to spend the rest of my life entranced by your spell?' With that, he slapped her horse's hindquarters, making it gallop away.

Hereward's heart was pounding with the joy of youthful

passion. His feelings were true and pure; it was an exhilarating sensation. Twenty yards ahead of him, Torfida laughed aloud, her raven hair streaming in the wind behind her.

As Hereward and Torfida raced along the shoreline, they became distant specks to Martin and Einar. Even at a distance, the intimate playfulness of their encounter was plain to see.

After a while, Einar, a man of few words, observed, 'I suppose we should busy ourselves and organize our passage to Ireland. It looks like young Herry is thinking of other things.'

Hereward and Torfida found a quiet cove several miles along the coast and made camp. They started a large fire and, despite the chill of autumn, took off their clothes and bathed in the sea. They dried one another by the fire, and combed each other's hair, before preparing a meal of fresh hare and root vegetables.

After their food, they made garlands from what they could find in the pastures around them and began an ancient ritual of marriage from the days of their pagan ancestors.

With a horn of mead in their left hand, they grasped each other's right hand and slowly circled the fire, skipping every third stride and gulping a swig of potent mead after each circuit. Gradually they increased their pace and the height of their skip, until it became a leap.

The ritual's gentle eroticism was well crafted. Each could see every detail of the other's body, and the simple rhythms of the dance and the warming effect of the mead aroused them both intensely.

Their lovemaking was gentle and tender at first, but

became more and more passionate as time passed. For Hereward, it was a gradual reawakening after a very long abstinence and the trauma created by his wild infatuation with Gythin. For Torfida, it was all she dreamed it would be, and she warmed to it with increasing relish.

They had only two needs: wood for the fire and sustenance for their bodies.

And wanted only one thing: each other.

6. Amulet of the Ancients

Einar had been right about the extended tryst between Hereward and Torfida. They returned to St David's at dusk on the next evening, both glowing contentedly. Martin and Einar said nothing to them, other than to impart the important news that the monks had agreed to buy their horses and that passage to Ireland had been arranged on the ship of a Breton trader. Its captain, Vulgrin of Brest, spoke little English, but had a reasonable grasp of Irish Danish, a tongue close enough to Einar's Anglo-Norse to allow arrangements to be reasonably straightforward.

The Great Western Sea to Ireland could be treacherous, and the cold westerly winds of autumn made progress slow on the long crossing. Late into the second night on board, Hereward and Torfida found themselves alone at the prow of the ship. At the stern, with Captain Vulgrin at his side keeping a watchful eye on the skies, the helmsman held the huge tiller hard into the wind as he tacked against it. The waning moon was bright enough to throw silver flashes across the undulating water, while the few clouds that did appear dashed across the night sky. The lunar glow kept most stars at bay, but Venus shone through like a sentinel. Vulgrin was watching its position in the sky and knew where it had risen against the Pole Star, making navigation on such a night relatively easy for an experienced sailor. It was on nights when the elements closed in that seafaring became a challenging, often frightening, experience, when the precious lodestone, which by some miracle always pointed north, became essential in averting disaster.

Vulgrin's ship sat broad and deep in the water. Like the Viking ships of legend, its elegantly sweeping boarded sides came to powerful points fore and aft in the form of mythical beasts. Its large single sail could be tilted if the wind was against, but there were also rowlocks along the timber-heads where oarsmen could lend their strength and skill in difficult conditions. With its ruby-red sail fully set and the wind behind from the south-west, it was a fine sight, prompting Hereward to imagine the terror that must have been struck into Anglo-Saxon hearts as, generations ago, the 'dragon ships' of his Danish ancestors suddenly appeared off England's coast.

Hereward felt that he and his companions were safe in the hands of their confident and experienced Breton captain. He was a small but sturdy man who reminded Hereward of the Welsh, a similarity that made him think about the mix of blood on board their craft. The captain and his helmsman were both Bretons, but the four oarsmen were taller and fairer men from Caen, in the heart of neighbouring Normandy, and were typical of its Viking ancestry. Despite her dark hair and complexion, which was more a Celtic characteristic, Torfida was an Anglo-Saxon of pure blood on both her father's and mother's side, while Martin was a small, dark native Celt from one of the North Wales tribes. Einar was Northumbrian Danish, a true Norseman, like a Viking of legend, whose large ruddy appearance matched perfectly the image of his ancestors who had sailed through the Skagerrak generations ago to maraud the British coastline. Hereward was the only one on board who was of mixed blood; he was equally proud of both his Anglo-Saxon and Danish origins.

He remembered the stories Aidan the Priest had told him as a child of the many historic battles between the Saxons and the Danes. It struck him again how unsettled his native land had been, as its many different peoples vied for supremacy. That struggle continued. The great battle at Hereford had shown only too clearly that, under Gruff-ydd's forceful leadership, the Welsh tribes were a formidable force. The Scandinavian kings in Norway and Denmark still had designs on the throne of England, which was also drifting ever closer to Normandy, a dukedom with which King Edward had strong ties.

As a boy, Hereward had assumed that life in the England he knew would always be stable and settled. Now he realized that many forces were at work; his homeland had a precarious future. As the ship sailed on, he occasionally looked back towards his native soil.

Would he ever return?

Was it his destiny to play a part in the turmoil to come?

Torfida suddenly put an end to Hereward's introspection by handing him the Talisman. 'You should take this now.'

'So this is what your father talked of – the thing that made Gruffydd tremble and contemplate his future.'

'My father told me that it has made many men question not only their future, but also their past.'

'Is it supposed to frighten me?'

'Does it?'

'No.'

'Then you have your answer.'

101

'Gruffydd said it had special powers.'

'Its power lies in what men think of it.'

Hereward examined it, slowly turning it against the light of the moon. 'It is the face of the Devil, in what looks like amber. But how can it have the Devil's face in it, with those little creatures? And is that a splash of blood?'

'I don't know. My father said that the ancients believed it to be the blood of the Saviour, spilled by him on the cross, and that it holds the Devil at bay by trapping him in the stone.'

'But why did your father think it important for us?'

'He believed that the Talisman was like a key to wisdom, and that only great men could understand its message.'

'That still doesn't explain its importance for us.'

'The Talisman has always had a messenger. You are now the envoy; you must carry the Talisman until you find the leader who should wear it.'

'How do you know all this?'

'When I was young, my father told me that I was destined to meet the man who would be the messenger of the Talisman and that he would stand at the right hand of kings, be their chosen warrior and lead their armies in battle. The Talisman would become a symbol of trust between the messenger and his lord, a private bond of companionship. You are that man. I know this as my father did; that's why he sent you to me. He told me that I would need to guide the messenger, that we would complement one another and that together we would succeed in fulfilling our destinies. I understand that now. You know my strengths and my weaknesses, and I know yours. My love for you grows every day. I will be at your side for ever – in spirit, if not in flesh.'

'Your father has been right about everything so far. I would be foolish to doubt him, but all I want for us at the moment is a settled and peaceful life in Ireland.'

'A peaceful life is not your destiny. You will become a great warrior; everyone can see it in you. A peaceful life is not my destiny either. I am the guide to a man whose strength and skill will allow us to carry the Talisman to a leader who is worthy of it.'

'Did your father know where the Talisman came from and why he was entrusted with it?'

'It was given to him by Queen Emma, the mother of King Edward. Even during his long years in the forest, the Queen found ways of getting messages to him. Early one morning, when I was eleven years old, we heard a mounted housecarl from her private retinue in the distance. He had been sent to summon my father to Queen Emma's death-bed at the monastery of Glastonbury. That's when she gave him the Talisman. She said that England would soon face a great turning point in its history, when men would fight for the kingdom. Although a Norman herself, she loved her adopted home and its mixed blood and hoped the future king, whoever he might be, would rule England with wisdom and kindness and be a worthy bearer of the ancient Talisman.

'She said that it had been passed to her by her father, Richard I, Duke of Normandy, who had inherited it from her grandfather, William Longsword, and her great-grand-father, Rolf, the first Viking Duke of Normandy. Before that, its pedigree was illustrious. The story among the Norman aristocracy claims that it had been passed through the old Frankish kings and that it had even been worn by the great Emperor Charlemagne. Legend says that Charlemagne had been given it when he married Theodora, the daughter of Desiderio, King of Lombardy, whose family claimed descent from the emperors of Rome.'

'And now it's in our lowly hands on a ship bound for the edge of the world!'

'Let me finish, Hereward. Queen Emma married two kings of England and was mother to two more, but she either decided that her husbands and sons were not worthy of the Talisman, or perhaps they refused it, so she asked my father, the only man she could trust, to find a way for it to continue its journey to its rightful inheritor. She believed in its power and that it was important for the future of the realm. My father promised to try but said that he preferred the contemplative life of the forest to a search for wisdom among future kings. "Then it must be Torfida's task," was her response. "If she is as beautiful as her mother was and as wise as her father, she will be worthy. Trust in the Talisman; it will find a way." They were her final words to him.'

Hereward thought about what Torfida had said and what it might mean for their future.

He held the Talisman at arm's length. 'Given its illustrious history, I suppose we should take great care of it.' Then he placed it around his neck, tucked it into his smock and turned to look out to sea. 'One more thing, Torfida. Your father talked about the Wodewose, and not just as a figment of the imagination of our ancestors, or a myth told by the fire on long winter nights. Your father seemed certain that he was real.'

'My father often thought about the mysteries that exist

between the real world of today and the world of our memories and our imagination. As he got older, he talked more and more about the land, the forests and the traditions of our ancestors. He knew a lot about the religion of the Celtic Druids; I think he had great respect for their ways. He saw Wodewose as a symbol – like our Talisman – something to remind us of things we might otherwise forget.'

'I think I am beginning to understand.'

Torfida looked at him contentedly; their great journey together had begun.

By the middle of the next day, the Irish coast was in sight and, by holding tight to the shoreline, the long traverse northwards to the port of Dublin was soon at an end.

As they tied up on the newly extended wooden quay, they were struck by the bustle of life there. They lost count of the number of ships loading and unloading their wares. Cases of pottery were being carried into warehouses by men as dark in complexion as they had ever seen. Rolls of linen and woollen garments were being piled into the bowels of waiting ships, and a large group of armed men appeared to be embarking on a military campaign. Einar and Martin were well travelled and had witnessed the life of a major city before, but for Hereward and Torfida this was an experience they had only heard about from others. They both stared in wonder as new sights, sounds and smells assailed them from every direction.

Dublin was a well organized city, governed by Irish chieftains under Danish laws and customs. It was a trading settlement, run under firm military rules, and offered few opportunities for permanent work, except as part of the local garrison, for whom the only excitement was settling local quarrels or quelling drunken brawls.

There were better opportunities in the Irish interior, which was not under Danish control, and where rival chieftains fought for supremacy. Here it would be relatively easy for the three men to find work as a chieftain's men-at-arms.

However, recent events in a land far to the north presented a more appealing prospect.

The year before the great battle of Hereford between the English and the Welsh, civil war had broken out in Scotland. With the enthusiastic support of the English Earl Siward of Northumbria, the Scottish king of many years, the proud and much-respected Macbeth, had been usurped by his rival, Malcolm Canmore. A great battle had taken place on the plains of Gowrie, west of Dundee, where Macbeth had been heavily defeated in battle. He had fled to the wild and desolate north, from where he was now looking for good men to rebuild his army. Macbeth's cause seemed to be a just one: kings who were respected by their people were a rare breed and worthy of help.

The quartet discussed their options and agreed to spend the winter of 1055 in Dublin and to set sail for Scotland in the spring of 1056. Torfida found employment as a tutor to the children of a wealthy local merchant and the men joined the militia of a Gaelic trader who made frequent visits to Cork to collect wool and linen.

The time passed quickly as the prospect of an adventure in a new land grew closer. The men practised their fighting skills every day in a gruelling series of drills and exercises, while Torfida's charm and personality endeared her to the wealthy of Dublin and prompted many conversations with visitors to her employer's home, one of the finest in Dublin. Guests came from many lands, and with news of turmoil throughout Europe. Henry of France had invaded Normandy, but had been defeated by the formidable Duke William. The Viking King of the Rus, Jaroslav I, had died early in 1055 and his lands, stretching from the Baltic to the Black Sea, had been split between his five sons. The predictable civil war had soon followed.

Torfida absorbed everything she could from everyone she met: new languages and dialects; information about trade and prices; stories of pilgrimages and miracles; news about the building of new churches and castles; and confirmation that the schism between the churches of Rome and Byzantium, begun by a papal bull in 1054, had become permanent.

This last piece of news greatly saddened her: if men could not agree on God's word, on what could they agree?

Hereward and his companions were ready to leave their temporary home in Dublin in March 1056.

Their captain on the journey to the west of Scotland was a Norseman. Captain Thorkeld's trade was weapons – the finest a warrior could want. His home port of Göteborg, in the land of the Swedes, was a place renowned for forging the swords and axes of war. There was an ancient art to the folding and working of hot iron to make it both tensile enough to take a sharp edge and malleable enough not to break. The furnaces of Göteborg were known throughout Europe for the skill of their weaponsmiths.

Thorkeld had learned of Macbeth's plans to raise a new army. Originally, his consignment of weapons was destined for a chieftain in Cork, whom he knew would pay well, but not as well as Macbeth. So Thorkeld had decided to turn tail and return northwards. He offered Hereward and his companions free passage to Scotland in exchange for service as men-at-arms on the treacherous journey to Macbeth's garrison in the Scottish Highlands.

They made landfall at the head of Loch Linnhe, where they bought horses for the long journey into the mountains of the north. Thorkeld left his four sailors with his ship and set off with Hereward and his companions, accompanied by six fearsome henchmen. His cargo was very valuable and these men provided escort in exchange for a share of the profits. The cargo of weapons was carefully hidden within rolls of wool and flax and the group agreed that, if challenged, Torfida would purport to be a lady of the Earldom of Northumberland with her escort.

Hereward and Torfida had never seen a land like Scotland before. The further they travelled, the bigger the mountains became; snow still lay on the highest peaks; the streams and rivers were torrents from the melting snow of a long winter and, in the great forests of pine, the wildlife was beginning to stir again after its long hibernation.

The group finally arrived at Glenmore, a huge valley protected by the tallest of mountains. Here the locals confirmed that Macbeth was camped between two vast lochs, at the site of an ancient Roman fort dedicated to the Emperor Augustus. It was a place secure from attack, where Macbeth could be supplied from both the western and the northern seas. It took most of the next day to reach the first outpost of Macbeth's camp. As they approached, guards stationed high in the rocks hurried towards them.

Communication with the guards was not difficult: their native language was a Celtic tongue that Martin could understand. When the Sergeant of the Guard was shown what the packhorses were carrying, he insisted that they wait for a mounted escort into the camp. When it arrived thirty minutes later, it numbered more than twenty heavily armed horsemen.

Hereward's first impression of these men was that they were seasoned warriors but ill disciplined and dispirited. Their appearance was shabby, their weapons dull, their horses neglected. If these mounted men were from Macbeth's elite housecarls, then the King had a dire military problem.

His initial assessment was not changed by the state of the King's camp as they rode in. Few sentries could be seen, and men sat about idly poking their fires or snoozing on their sacks. Some looked up as the new arrivals passed by, but with a nonchalance not typical of a king's army. Most disturbingly, a quick count by Hereward tallied no more than 400 men and perhaps 250 non-combatants; it was hardly an army to recapture a stolen crown.

As they dismounted, the King emerged from his hall. Macbeth was less than impressive: his eyes were sunken into his gaunt face; his skin was pale and lifeless; his dark-red hair and beard were lank and tangled; and he stooped as if his hulking bearskin cloak was too heavy for him. His men spoke to him in their Celtic language; he responded in English.

'I hear you bring weapons to trade.'

Hereward spoke first. 'My Lord King, our good friend Thorkeld will sell you his fine weapons. My companions and I have come to fight for your cause. We hear you are a rightful king and that your rival, Malcolm Canmore, has taken your throne by force of arms.'

'Isn't it more usual for men like you to fight for money and spoils, rather than a good cause?'

'It is, sire. We would expect to be rewarded, of course, but our main purpose is to help your cause and to pursue our destinies, which have led us to you.'

'Well, it is an unusual introduction. Perhaps you are a good omen.'

Torfida interrupted before Hereward could answer. To Macbeth's astonishment, she spoke in North Gaelic, the language of the local people.

'We are, my Lord King.'

'Who are you?'

'I am Torfida of Winchester, and I pursue the same destiny as these men. Hereward of Bourne is my betrothed.' Torfida reverted to English, not wanting to stumble with her limited Gaelic. 'He is a great warrior, as are his companions. They can help prepare your men for battle.'

Colour began to return to Macbeth's face, but it was a flush of anger, not of ruddy good health. 'Can they now? I think you are impudent, madam.'

'I do not mean to be, sire. Hereward fought with Gruffydd ap Llywelyn at the Battle of Hereford and saved his life. Einar was Aelfgar of Northumbria's Champion, and Martin Lightfoot was King Gruffydd's swiftest messenger. They will testify to Hereward's courage and strength. Hereward –'

110

Realizing that the King was losing patience, Hereward interrupted. 'Let us work with your Captain, under his command . . . but, rest assured, we can help you.'

'I will summon my Captain. He will be the judge of that. If he doesn't take to you, he will run you out of these mountains on the point of his sword.' The King turned and disappeared into his hall.

Hereward turned to Torfida, clearly displeased. 'Torfida, you spoke too soon and said too much.'

'This King needs your help; there is no time to waste on niceties.'

'I have no experience of leading armies.'

'Well, now's the time to learn. Talk to Einar and Martin. They've been in armies; they can help us work out how we can impress the King and his Captain with our military prowess.'

Hereward interrupted forcefully. 'When you say "we", you mean "me". Don't ever speak out again on my behalf, or on behalf of Martin and Einar, without talking to us first.'

Just as Hereward had finished speaking, a tall man, accompanied by his men-at-arms, loomed behind him. His Sergeant announced him.

'This is Duncan, Earl of Ross, Captain of the King's hearthtroop.'

'My Lord Earl, I am Hereward of Bourne, the outlawed son of Leofric, Thegn of Bourne.'

'You have strong nerves to walk into this camp and presume to speak to the King.'

Einar rarely spoke but, when he did, everyone listened. 'My Lord, he can match any man here. I am Einar, Champion to

111

Earl Aelfgar of Northumbria, the son of the late Earl Siward.'

'Not a good recommendation my friend, coming from the Champion of a house that colludes with our enemies.'

'I was the Earl's Champion, my Lord; I didn't decide his alliances. Test Hereward in combat. He will prove his worth against any of your men.'

'I think I'll just kill the upstart.'

The Earl drew his sword and threw back his cloak. He was a powerful, dark-haired man who carried the scars of many years of combat. Hereward stepped back, withdrew his sword and adopted a defensive posture.

The fight did not last long. The Earl struck out furiously, but Hereward was able to parry every attack with ease and without striking a single aggressive blow. The Earl was impressed and, breathing heavily and none too pleased with his inability to despatch Hereward, relented.

'You fight well, Hereward of Bourne. Find a place in our camp for the night. I will speak to the King and we will discuss this again tomorrow.'

The Earl marched away, muttering to his men. Thorkeld, who had watched Hereward's display of swordsmanship with astonishment, stepped forward to shake his hand.

'I have never seen a man handle a sword so well. What can you do with other weapons?'

'The axe is my favourite. My arms are strong, and I can use both my left and my right; necessity forced it upon me a few years ago.'

'Are you strong enough to use this?'

From under a woollen blanket, Thorkeld pulled an enormous axe, the like of which Hereward had never seen before. Freshly forged and ground, it gleamed with the blue tinge of the finest weapons. Most remarkably, it had not one blade, but two; it was a double-headed, two-handed axe. Hereward had heard from the Norse sagas that Viking gods could wield such weapons, but had assumed that they were no more than fantasies.

'My father is the finest weaponsmith in Göteborg.' Thorkeld held the axe out as if it were an altar offering. 'He has only ever made two of these: one for Svein Beartooth, High Champion of Magnus the Good, Lord King of Norway and Denmark, which was buried with him when he died several years ago, and this, an exact replica. Let me see you swing it.'

It was heavier than anything Hereward had ever held before, but finely balanced. Both blades had been worked with intricately tooled etchings in the shape of serpents and dragons, and the ash shaft had been stained with russet-brown dye and deeply patterned on its shoulder and heel with geometrical designs.

He began to swing it smoothly and easily with two hands and, in short bursts, with one.

'I've never seen anyone who can swing such an axe with one hand.'

Then Hereward lifted the mighty weapon in his left hand, tilted it behind his head and hurled it at a tree fifteen yards away. It tumbled in the air before embedding itself with an impact that made the tree shudder and the axe quiver. 'I tried that once before and missed. It nearly cost me my life.'

There was a stunned silence for several moments.

Einar spoke first. 'I didn't think I would ever meet a man stronger than I am, but you are such a man.'

Thorkeld tried to wrench the axe from the tree, but only succeeded with the help of one of his men-at-arms.

'The weapon is yours, Hereward of Bourne. I have been looking for a man worthy of it for many years. Use it well.'

'I cannot accept such a gift; it is the finest axe I have ever seen.'

'You must accept. It was made for a man like you, a man who can unleash its power.' Thorkeld handed him a sword and seax of the same quality and design. 'You must take these as well. I know that in years to come the chroniclers will write sagas about your exploits with these weapons.'

Hereward was overwhelmed. 'How can I thank you?'

'I have a feeling that in your hands, Hereward of Bourne, these weapons will become part of legend. There is something about you, I sense it . . . One day you will become a leader of men.'

7. Duel at Lumphanan

A long night of planning had borne fruit by the morning. Hereward and his companions had talked all night, trying to devise training routines and military tactics that would transform Macbeth's soldiers from a rabble into an army. Martin and Einar had been involved in serious military training all their lives, and Hereward had an intuitive sense of physical conditioning and martial discipline. Torfida was able to commit to memory all the complicated routines they devised. She had no experience of military tactics, but took to the planning of them with her usual enthusiasm and intelligence.

Torfida thought it prudent to watch from a distance as Hereward, Martin and Einar marched down the side of the glen towards Macbeth's camp. The entire army, assembled on Earl Duncan's orders, greeted them.

Hereward was a sight to behold with his new weapons shimmering in the sun and his broad shoulders almost hiding his war shield, painted in alternating colours of crimson, black and gold to resemble the curved spokes of the wheels of a chariot. Einar had given him a Viking helmet, which had belonged to his brother. Made in quarter plates of iron, joined by reinforced bronze bands, it had a domed top and nose and eyepieces shaped to fit tightly to the face. On its front, from the tip of the nose guard to the dome, ran a piece of highly polished bronze, elegantly chased with runic swirls. He could have been a royal prince of Scandinavia rather than an Anglo-Saxon outlaw.

Formed up as an army, Macbeth's men were even less impressive than they had appeared the day before. Few knights were present and Earl Duncan appeared to be the only man of any rank. Macbeth was nowhere to be seen. Most of the men looked bored; some were carrying injuries and a few had badly infected wounds. The Earl, one of the few men who still had the bearing of a warrior, stepped forward and addressed his men in Norse, a language all understood.

'Men of the King's army, we have a guest with us today, a knight from the land of the Saxons.'

A snigger of contempt rippled through the ranks.

'He is a fine warrior, granted recognition by King Gruff-ydd of Wales. His companions, Einar and Martin Lightfoot, are experienced soldiers. We will listen to what they have to say.'

The Earl acknowledged Hereward and stepped aside. Hereward walked slowly along the front rank of men. This was his moment. There was no training that could prepare a man for an occasion like this.

Either his instincts would get him through it, or the cause was lost.

'Who speaks for you?'

There was silence.

'Every army has a man with a loud voice. Who speaks for this one?'

'I can speak my mind. I am Donald of Moray, from the home of my King, Macbeth of Moray.'

A sturdy man with sharp blue eyes and greying hair

stepped forward. He had obviously fought many battles: his face and hands were scarred, his mail coat had been repaired many times, and his shield bore the marks of many fierce blows.

'You will call me "sir" when you address me, Donald of Moray.'

'Not yet I won't, laddie.'

'Then how do I earn the title?'

'You're not man enough, young Saxon.'

Roars of laughter came from the Scottish ranks.

'What is the military challenge a man should fear most?'

'Combat training, four to one. We use it in the King's hearthtroop; it sharpens our senses! We use wooden training swords, one weapon each and a shield. Nothing else permitted.'

'Agreed.'

'But as you boast that you are a great warrior, we'll use real swords!'

Without hesitation, Hereward agreed once more.

The army hooted uproariously; Macbeth's men meant to humiliate an impudent intruder . . . then kill him.

Hereward took off his helmet and threw it to Einar. Then he turned to face Donald of Moray.

'I hope you will be one of the four.'

'Don't worry about that, laddie!'

Hereward removed his cloak and axe and the rest of his weapons.

Leaving Donald and three of his comrades, Macbeth's men dispersed to sit on the hillside to get a better vantage point for the entertainment to come.

Two of Hereward's opponents could have been brothers,

the similarities were so strong; the third was a small dark man with a slightly crazed look in his eye. All were trained killers, but this one looked deranged.

Rapid movement and the precise coordination of sword and shield were the keys to survival in an uneven contest of this sort. Although Hereward was a man equal in size to his opponents, he was much younger and quicker on his feet.

In a contest that did not take long, what followed brought gasps of admiration from the army.

Hereward's four opponents tried to encircle him, but he always moved to a point where he could see at least three and catch any thrust from the fourth in the corner of his eye. They attacked in unison to reduce Hereward's freedom of movement, but he kept moving and parried his way between them. He was soon able to grab the crazed-looking one and put him in an arm lock against his elbow joint to persuade him to release his sword. He then let him go and struck him hard with the edge of his shield, knocking the sense out of him.

Three to one was much easier to deal with, as they found it much more difficult to encircle him. A slash to the thigh of one, and a heavy blow from Hereward's shield to the head of another, brought the contest to an abrupt end. In between, he had playfully tripped them, tapped them on their backsides and ducked away from all their blows. None of the four men had been able to put a scratch on the young Englishman.

Donald of Moray fell to his knees, exhausted. He took some large gulps of air, then slowly regained his feet.

'You are a fine swordsman; I salute you. You have earned our respect . . . sir.'

The army cheered. They had enjoyed a dazzling exhibition of swordplay.

Earl Duncan stepped forward. 'Well, young man, it appears you have won the respect of the men; they seem to like you. Do you have anything else to say to them?'

Hereward bowed to Duncan. 'My Lord Earl, with your permission . . .' He then turned to address the army. 'Men, go back to your tents and make ready! There will be a full inspection in one hour; every man to be in battle order.'

Earl Duncan was stony faced. 'Very well, we will see how the men respond.' His expression remained severe for a few moments, but then softened. 'You have my authority to take in hand the preparation of the army. I will need a daily report.'

'Thank you, my Lord.'

On Hereward's signal, Einar took over.

'Move! You heard what he said. Move!'

On time and in good order, the army assembled once more. They already had a more purposeful air about them: faces had been swilled, beards trimmed and knots dragged from hair. Weapons had been cleaned, as had mail and leather coats, and mud had been shaken from wolfskins and woollen cloaks.

Hereward stepped forward once more. 'I have pledged my loyalty to your lord, Macbeth of Moray, King of all Scotland, Lord of the Isles. Does any man here not do the same?'

There was silence.

'As I inspect your ranks, any man temporarily unfit will be excused training until he is fit for duty; any man no longer able to fight will be sent home to his family with a piece of the King's silver in his pouch; the rest will work hard every day. You will long for battle as a welcome relief from the hard work of training, but no man will do more than I do. I will do everything I ask of you and more. We will eat together twice a day – first, two hours after sunrise, then again at dusk. There will be no personal cooking pots and no private expeditions for game. I will organize hunting parties and the King's stewards will organize the food for all of us. There will be two hours of training at dawn, before food, and then rest. We will resume at midday and finish one hour before dusk. Everyone will use that hour to wash and prepare for food; I will have no filthy warriors at our tables.'

He paused and looked along the ranks. 'In an army worth fighting for, every man has the right to speak his mind. Does any man here have a question, or anything to say?'

'Who is the pretty English lassie, sir? They say she's bewitched you and the King.'

A chorus of laughter erupted from the men. The voice was impossible to identify, hidden deep in the ranks.

Hereward replied with a grin. 'I cannot speak for the King, but she has certainly bewitched me; we are to be married.'

A peal of cheers rang out.

'We want to be married in Scone, by the Bishop, with the good Macbeth sitting on the Stone of Kings, in his rightful place!'

Another, louder clangour swept over the glen as the men waved their battle-axes and swords in a gesture of approval. They had first taken to Hereward, not only because of his display with a sword, but also because he treated them with openness and honesty.

For the rest of the morning he brought each rank forward and inspected every man in turn. There were many fine warriors in the army, and Hereward chose almost sixty whom he decided would become the King's new hearthtroop. He intended to take personal control of it, reorganize it and train it as befitted an elite corps.

At the end of the long inspection, during which Hereward had allowed the men to sit, he spoke to them once more. As he turned to face them, they all jumped up as one and the ground shook. Armour and weapons clanked and clattered, creating echoes down the glen. Hereward felt a shiver down his spine.

Torfida, watching from a perch above the glen, glowed with pride. She saw Hereward, a 22-year-old former outlaw, striding around in front of his new army.

'There will be only three parts to your training: speed, with Martin Lightfoot, the swiftest man I have ever seen; strength, which Einar will lead, the strongest man in the armies of the North of England; and skill, which I will oversee personally. We start tomorrow at dawn. The men I spoke to about the King's hearthtroop, I will see you in two hours. Hail, Macbeth! Hail, the King!'

The men echoed Hereward's clarion call for several minutes.

Afterwards, Donald of Moray spoke to Hereward. 'No one has ever addressed them like that before, the men respect you and so do I . . . sir.'

Hereward shook the Celt firmly by the hand, grateful for his words of support.

He spent the rest of the afternoon talking to his selected band of men for the new hearthtroop. Hereward surprised himself: he was not sure how or why, but he seemed to have an instinctive grasp of military techniques and disciplines.

He was in his element, and he knew this would be his calling for the rest of his life.

When Hereward arrived at the High Steward's tent just before dusk, he was met by Earl Duncan, who told him that the King demanded his presence in his Great Hall. When they arrived, Macbeth was pacing up and down.

'I hear you intend to give away my silver?'

'Yes, sire.'

'Not even Earl Duncan gives away my money without my permission.'

'Sire, you must allow me to make decisions about military matters.'

'I must! I must! I must not do anything of the sort! Don't you dare tell me what I *must* do!'

'Sire, I earned the right to perform this role for your army.'

Macbeth rose, puce with anger. 'By God, I will strike you down myself!'

'That decision needed to be taken today. I couldn't send those men home with nothing in their pouches. They have no spoils of victory; they will be destitute.'

'Let them starve!' the King bellowed.

'My Lord King, your army will not serve you if they know that is what you think of them.'

'They will serve me, whether they like it or not!'

'Sire, I had heard that you were a wise and good king. Those are not the words of such a king.'

Macbeth jumped up and made towards Hereward with rage in his eyes.

Earl Duncan stepped between them. 'Kneel before the King, Hereward of Bourne. Beg his forgiveness!'

'I will not!'

In the few dreadful moments that followed, Hereward's future – indeed, his life and the lives of his companions – hung by a thread. He thought about the Talisman around his neck. Was it speaking through him, giving him the courage to defy a king? Macbeth glowered at him, poised with his hand grasping his sword, until his fury slowly subsided.

A long silence ensued.

The King's eyes softened and he began to look vulnerable and sad. 'I should have you killed.' Then he paused again and looked down. 'The truth is, I am a king in name only; in that, you are right. As for the rest of it, we'll talk again when I am calm. In the meantime, my stewards will issue the men with their silver. Now leave me.'

'It would be better if you did it, sire.'

Yet again, Hereward had trusted his instincts – but he feared that he may have taken a step too far.

Macbeth resumed his pacing of the length and breadth of his hall, muttering as he did so. Each time he reached his hearth he threw another log on to the fire and peered into its flames. After several minutes of brooding, he returned to stand face-to-face with Hereward.

He adopted a more forthright demeanour. 'I will give them their silver, thank them for their loyal service and send them home to their families.' He turned to Earl

Duncan. 'Tell the High Steward to summon the men Hereward has dismissed. Then call my servants; I will go to the river to bathe. Tomorrow, Earl Duncan and I will join the army for training.'

Hereward had gambled that beneath Macbeth's irascible, disheartened facade was a decent man and a good king.

Macbeth offered Hereward his hand, an honour rarely given to a man of modest birth. 'It took great courage to speak as you did. Now make my army as strong as you are.'

The training of the army went on through 1056 and into the early months of 1057; only the deepest snows of winter brought a temporary halt.

Macbeth and Earl Duncan did exactly the same training as their men, and word spread throughout Scotland that the army had regained its pride, and that the discipline, though hard, was fair. Men started to arrive almost daily. By the beginning of March 1057, the army numbered six cohorts of highly trained men, plus seventy recent arrivals, who were still undergoing training. There was an entire cohort of cavalry, every soldier had a full complement of weapons and two of the cohorts were trained archers.

But Macbeth's army was still relatively small. If he was to face Malcolm Canmore in a full-scale battle, he would need several hundred more men. Word arrived that Malcolm Canmore was moving north with a large force. Once again, he had the support of King Edward and the English, this time in the guise of Tostig, the new Earl of Northumbria and the brother of Harold Godwinson.

Hereward advised caution, but Macbeth was impatient to regain the throne.

After many months of peaceful preparation, Macbeth began the march south to meet his enemy.

Events began to take on a sudden momentum when messengers arrived with news that a large force of allies of Malcolm Canmore had sailed up the Firth of Cromarty and landed on the Black Isle, near Dingwall. This was in the heart of Macbeth's homeland, where his people were largely unprotected. Canmore knew that Macbeth would have to turn back towards the north-east and fight. It was an attempt to outflank Macbeth's army, which duly turned and began the long march northwards up the Great Glen of Mor.

They made a fine sight: the cavalry rode the flanks with small reconnaissance parties of horsemen peeling off on scouting missions; the infantry marched in closed ranks in double-time, occasionally breaking into a trot when the ground allowed it. The rhythmic din of feet and hooves and the clatter of the baggage train reverberated for miles around the peaks and troughs of the mountains.

After three days of marching, scouts returned with news of the strength of Canmore's forces. The northern contingent included over 100 English light cavalry, almost 200 housecarls sent by Tostig, an assortment of Celtic archers, mercenaries from Ireland and several squadrons, at least 80 men, from Denmark. Canmore's main force in the south was a large army of lowland Scots, well in excess of 1,000 men, which was moving north to rendezvous with his allies.

Macbeth knew he could not defeat both armies; his only chance was to strike at the head of the beast and confront Canmore and his main force.

He spent several hours in private, mulling over his strategy, before announcing the audacious plan to turn east, traverse the Mountains of Monadhliath and cross into the Grampians. Canmore would not believe anyone would attempt such a bold move, especially with the remnants of winter still making the mountains treacherous. The baggage train was sent the long way round and told to meet in two weeks' time at Inverurie on the Don.

As the days passed and Hereward became familiar with the terrain, he realized how daring Macbeth's route was. Some of the passes were lethal, with progress only possible in single file. There were steep and precarious climbs and descents and exposed crags and ridges where footholds were difficult to find. Nevertheless, late in the afternoon, after five days of hard marching unique in the history of Scottish warfare, they found Canmore's main army making its way north towards the Howe of Alford along a small tributary of the River Dee near the settlement of Lumphanan.

Macbeth's army appeared from the mountains, to the amazement of Canmore and his men.

Canmore's force was stretched out over a wide area and it would take them some time to become organized. Macbeth ordered Hereward and Earl Duncan to lead his cavalry in a lightning attack. The tactic worked: the well-disciplined horsemen, riding in tight formations, inflicted heavy casualties on scattered groups of Lowlanders.

Hereward was at the vanguard, creating a maelstrom with his axe and driving large gaps in Canmore's infantry. Macbeth looked on in wonder as Hereward's exploits became more and more prominent. Men were drawn to him like a magnet as he drove deeper into the enemy ranks.

His great axe, and the massive arc he could scythe with it, created a devastating killing ground around him.

Eventually, as nightfall approached, Macbeth signalled to his cavalry to disengage. Both armies made camp in the forests above Lumphanan, Macbeth to savour a victory in the initial skirmish, Canmore to lick his wounds.

Before first light the next morning, Hereward pleaded with Macbeth not to launch a frontal attack. He had barely 700 men and was outnumbered almost two to one, but Macbeth had rediscovered his conviction, was flushed with the success of his march through the mountains and euphoric from victory in the previous evening's cavalry charge.

'You have trained the army well; they are ready to fight, and so am I. No more talk! Today I will wear my crown again.'

By dawn, the two armies had formed up on either side of the narrow vale of Lumphanan. The scene was set for a formal pitched battle, but events took a surprising turn.

When Canmore surveyed his opponents, he saw a royal army that looked like a force to be reckoned with. Its march across the mountains had impressed him, and last night's bloody nose had unnerved him. He was also conscious that the forces of his allies were a long way away.

Canmore strode out more than fifty yards into the no-man's-land between the two armies. For several minutes, he paced up and down, peering at the ranks of Macbeth's forces. He could see how uniform and steadfast they were; this was an army ready to fight. His own force was ill prepared, having expected to trap Macbeth much further north. He feared that his numerical superiority might not be enough to ensure victory.

He needed a new plan and, within minutes, had decided on a bold gamble for the throne of Scotland.

He sent an envoy galloping across the open ground with a message for Macbeth. It offered a personal duel – a fight to the death for the crown – in front of their armies.

It was an extraordinary move, but there were precedents for it in the traditions of conflict in northern Europe. Canmore's reasoning was sound: he was young and virile; Macbeth was much older and the best of his fighting days were long gone.

The odds were heavily in Canmore's favour.

Macbeth thought long and hard about the challenge and turned to Hereward for advice.

He was forthright. 'Sire, let us stand our ground here. It will be many days before Duncan's army of cut-throats arrives from the north. We've grasped the initiative; that's why Canmore has issued the challenge.'

'But I have a chance to resolve this here and now. It is my throne; I can win it back myself and prevent more bloodshed. Remember, I need to keep my army intact. King Edward has greedy eyes for Scotland and has been plotting my downfall for years. If too many Scots kill one another here at Lumphanan, who will stop Harold Godwinson's housecarls when Edward orders them to cross our borders?'

The King had made up his mind. He rode along the ranks of his men as word of the challenge filtered through to them.

At first, there was silence, then a cry went up: 'Hail, Macbeth, King of the Scots.'

A retort soon came from the opposing army standing 500 yards away: 'Hail, King Malcolm.'

As the competing chants echoed around the glens, Macbeth turned to the messenger. 'Tell Malcolm Canmore that I accept his challenge for the Throne of Scone. All weapons, treasure and the loyalty of their men go to the victor to unite Scotland under a strong king. We will meet in fifteen minutes.'

Macbeth chose Earl Duncan and Hereward as his seconds, while Canmore chose two Lowland earls from the English borders.

Macbeth was almost forty years of age; Canmore was fifteen years his junior and a much more powerful man.

The preparations for the contest were meticulous. Tridents were placed in the open ground, midway between the armies, to receive the combatants' cloaks and weapons. The duel would begin with swords and shields, but axes and spears were placed in the tridents and could be used at any time.

When everything was ready, the two men faced each other.

As the seconds retreated, Hereward placed the Talisman around Macbeth's neck.

'What is this?'

'It is an amulet of kings from many generations and many lands. It is said that it has been worn since the days of Rome. You should wear it as the true king.'

Macbeth looked at it. 'Not the most attractive of charms!'

'No, but a very powerful one.'

'Thank you, Hereward, for all you have done for my army . . . and for me.'

Earl Duncan spoke the final words before stepping away. 'For Scotland, my Lord King, for the Throne of Scone.'

Canmore and Macbeth eyed one another warily.

Macbeth spoke first. 'For the throne of Scotland, Malcolm Canmore.'

'For the throne of Scotland, Macbeth of Moray.'

A long and gruelling struggle followed.

Canmore began impetuously, and Macbeth was able to parry his attacks with ease. After a while, some blows began to land on both men, but their mail coats prevented deep wounds. There was a passage when each held the other's sword arm and cuts and bruises were inflicted in a scuffle of shields and sword hilts. Both men became soaked in perspiration, the steam from which rose in a haze around them. They discarded their helmets, revealing their sweat-soaked hair and matted beards. Both armies roared and hollered for their leader as they witnessed a fight fit for legend by two kings battling for the throne of their domain.

As Macbeth began to tire, he found it hard to fend off the blows. Suddenly, Canmore's sword glanced off the King's shield and made a deep gash in Macbeth's forehead. Blood flowed down his face, making it difficult for him to see.

Canmore attacked ferociously as Macbeth wilted, until, unable to defend and parry any more, he was struck through the midriff by the full thrust of Canmore's lunging sword. He sank to his knees, the sword still embedded in him, his blood spewing through his mail coat and cascading on to the ground. He could not speak and had only moments to live. His rival, not satisfied with his opponent's imminent death, went for his axe and, as he knelt before him, decapitated Macbeth in one mighty blow.

A great cheer swept across the valley from Canmore's army.

In a final act of cruelty, Canmore picked up Macbeth's head by its hair and raised it to his army.

'This is the head of Macbeth, once King of Scotland. I am Malcolm Canmore, King of Scotland, Lord of the Isles!'

His army began to run towards him in a frenzy of excitement; the spoils were theirs, without having to spill any of their own blood. Canmore threw Macbeth's head on the ground, where it left a trail of blood as it rolled away. The soldiers laid down their weapons as Canmore's stewards rushed to unload Macbeth's gold and silver. A horse was brought for his body and his head was placed in a hemp sack.

Hereward was bereft.

There was nothing he could have done to help Macbeth: the rules of combat were unbreakable; no one might intervene, no matter what happened between the two men.

He collected the Talisman from the ground where it had fallen. It was covered in blood, which he chose not to remove. Nor did he place it around his neck, but carefully folded its chain and slowly pushed it into his belt pouch. He resolved to give it back to Torfida.

He was sorry that he had given it to the King – whatever its powers, it had not been of much help to Macbeth.

Following the tragedy at Lumphanan, the four companions accompanied Macbeth's family and Earl Duncan to the distant island of Iona for his burial.

It was a moving and solemn occasion, as the mourners sang the ancient melodies of the Scottish kings and the horn players sounded the final lament. The island was a lonely, windswept land, a holy place for the Scots and a mystical sanctuary that held the remains of many generations of their nobility.

As the horns sounded their final notes, the wind swirled around the mourners and rain started to lash their faces, mingling their warm tears with the cold outpouring of the western skies. The assembly stood in silence for several minutes until the squall subsided. Then a small fissure opened in the black clouds of the horizon and the setting sun paid its homage to a dead king.

Earl Duncan, Lord of Ross, raised the King's sword in salute and then passed it to Queen Gruoch, who laid it gently on his body. Six of his hearthtroop, led by Donald of Moray, lowered the elaborately carved lid of his stone sarcophagus on to his tomb.

Then there was silence.

Macbeth's widow, a woman of beauty and charm, bade them farewell. She granted Hereward a parchment endorsing his bravery, as well as a significant gratuity from her estates.

Hereward had given the Talisman back to Torfida after Macbeth's death, saying that he never wanted to see it again.

Torfida had quickly become very animated. 'You gave it to him as a lucky charm, an amulet to ward off evil. That's not what it is. You still don't understand, do you? It's a symbol of wisdom and kingship, not a lucky charm. The wisdom must come first, then the warrior may wear it and harness its power – because he understands its meaning.'

'You talk in riddles. The damned thing is just a lump of amber. The only mystery is how it hoodwinks apparently intelligent people like you.'

132

Torfida had stormed off in a fury, leaving Hereward to look back on the sad events in Scotland.

It was something he would do many times in the months and years that followed, as they travelled far from Scottish shores.

As Godwin of Ely completed his story of the demise of Macbeth, King of the Scots, he breathed a prolonged and mournful sigh.

There seemed to be tears in his eyes, but he soon closed them. Within moments, he had fallen into a deep sleep.

It had been a long night; dawn would soon be bringing a new day to the old man's precious haven.

Prince John Comnenus got to his feet and stretched himself. He ordered that an extra bearskin be placed over their ancient storyteller and that the fire be replenished. Leo the priest had also fallen asleep.

As the two princes walked towards the east and the rising sun, John Azoukh smiled to himself. 'He tells the story as if it happened yesterday. But it was sixty years ago!'

'I suppose he has had plenty of time to remember everything in detail; there's not much else to do up here in the mountains. I suspect that's part of the reason he's here, so that he can remember.'

'Our storyteller is obviously Hereward of Bourne. Why do you think he has assumed the identity of Godwin of Ely?'

'I'm sure that will become clear as the story unfolds. We're still only in 1057. My father was just a nine-year-old boy then. This man has lived a very long time.'

'Isn't it interesting how his life has moved in a great circle? Now, he's a wild hermit, living out his days in isolation.'

'*Exactly as the Old Man of the Wildwood foretold.*'

The two princes strolled for a while, deep in thought. After several minutes of reflection, it was John Comnenus who ended the quiet introspection.

'The Talisman hasn't yet revealed itself as an object worthy of the respect my father gives it. The King of the Welsh seemed wary of it, while its influence on Macbeth didn't seem to help his cause!'

John Azoukh looked at his friend and smiled. 'I suspect the importance of the Talisman is also part of the story to come. It would not have ended up adorning the neck of the Emperor of Byzantium if it didn't have some significance.' He paused, seeming concerned for his friend. 'Would you risk a fight to the death for the Purple of Byzantium, as Macbeth did for his throne?'

'That is a good question, my friend. I have been thinking about that. Would I have the courage? Would I be prepared to lose everything to fight for what I thought was right?

'I'd like to think so, but it's easier to say than to do. Macbeth must have known he had little chance against a stronger, younger man. Perhaps it was his way of regaining his self-esteem after the crushing blow of losing his crown and his sad personal decline. Now, at least, he will be remembered for his courage, not for his defeat.

'I hope I'm never in the same position and that I never have to make that choice.'

John Azoukh placed his arm around the heir to the throne. 'I hope so too. Let's get some sleep.'

It was well past noon before Godwin of Ely was ready to continue his story.

The day had become typically hot. There was no need for bearskins and log fires. Instead, the stewards built shades from leafy branches and drew fresh cool water from the lake.

After a long and relaxed lunch, with much good humour and a little wine, the four men settled themselves for the continuation of the saga of the life of Hereward, Thegn of Bourne.

8. Ancient Wonders

Although Hereward had the trappings and demeanour of a nobleman, he still used the simple title Hereward of Bourne. Even so, wherever they went, they were in demand; everyone wanted to know what sort of man carried such mighty weapons, to meet the beautiful woman at his side and admire their formidable companions.

They journeyed to Göteborg to visit Thorkeld and his father. The old man was delighted to meet the owner of his lethal masterpiece – the Great Axe of Göteborg, as it had come to be known – and thrilled to hear that it had already drawn blood in battle. In Scandinavia, they wandered to most of its major settlements, all the while absorbing Norse culture. Einar and Hereward, in particular, felt a great affinity with the lands of their ancestors.

They then travelled, via the Baltic port of Riga, to the Viking city of Novgorod, where Norse craftsmen were building a new cathedral, a project which captured Torfida's imagination. She spent countless hours with the master carpenters, learning the many intricate joints they used in their magnificent timber structures.

Martin and Einar both found Viking wives during their extended stay in Novgorod. Martin's spouse, Ingigerd, was short and slim with flaxen hair and bright blue eyes. Einar had married Maria, a buxom redhead, who treated Ingigerd like a younger sister. And so, the quartet that had left Scotland became a sextet.

They moved on, travelling down the mighty rivers of Russia to Kiev, the southern capital of the Viking Rus. Viking rule was firm in the Rus, a territory that extended from the Baltic to the Black Sea, and the native Slavs had long since given up their armed resistance against the colonizers from the north. Kiev was the seat of the kingdom; it was a bustling, lively city at a crossroads of routes that stretched from the ancient lands of the Mediterranean to the military powerhouse of Scandinavia.

The Rus was still enjoying the benefits of the benign rule of King Jaroslav the Wise, whose long reign had only just ended. Through astute alliances and marriages, as well as skilful military campaigns, Jaroslav had created a powerful empire across a vast tract of territory. Trade from there to the south, to Constantinople – the celebrated capital city of the Empire of Byzantium – was constant, and they saw furnishings, jewellery and clothes of breathtaking finery being carried by caravans of traders.

Torfida longed to continue to Constantinople and then into the Mediterranean to see the cities of the ancient world, especially Rome. There, she could learn more languages, refine her Greek and Latin and hear of new advances in medicine, astronomy and mathematics.

Hereward preferred to return to Scandinavia. In Göteborg, they had heard of the famous exploits of Harald Hardrada, King of Norway, a great warrior, said to be six and a half feet tall. Hereward had been intrigued to learn that while still in his early twenties, Hardrada had been Captain of the Varangian Guard of the Emperor of

Constantinople. Hardrada was waging a long-term campaign for supremacy in Denmark against Svein Estrithson, King of the Danes. If ever there was a man worth fighting for, it was surely Hardrada. He might also be a man whose qualities of leadership were such that he would be a worthy recipient of the Talisman, fulfilling Hereward's mission as a messenger.

Torfida tried to force a decision. 'We must go south; our destiny leads us to the Mediterranean. I must see Constantinople.'

Hereward was rarely short-tempered with Torfida, but he had yet to come to terms with the death of Macbeth. 'And what of the rest of us? What of our destinies?'

'All our destinies are the same; we have already made that choice. My destiny is your destiny.'

'I would rather fight with Hardrada. He is a Norseman, a man with the blood of my Danish ancestors.'

'I sense that your quest lies to the south, not to the north. I have heard of a man like Harald Hardrada. He is a Norman called Robert Guiscard. He fights in the Mediterranean from a city called Melfi, in the south of Italy. He has just been proclaimed Count of Apulia following the death of his brother.'

'Torfida, removing the burden of this Talisman is more important than the direction of our journey.'

'We have to be patient until we find the man who should wear it. It is not yet time to part with it; your journey still has many twists and turns. A great battle is coming, Europe is in turmoil, I have been listening to all the accounts. Strong leaders are emerging and one of them will bring our mission to an end. One of them will be the right man; you will know.'

'Macbeth was a great king and a brave man. What he did that day at Lumphanan, in saving all those lives, and accepting a challenge he had little chance of winning, was surely worthy of the Talisman.'

'Yes, it was.'

'I don't understand; you said it wasn't the right time.'

'I'm not suggesting Macbeth didn't have the right to wear the Talisman; I'm sure he did. But you gave it to him to help him win, and it couldn't do that for him. His life had run its course; he had all the wisdom he needed and the courage to do the right thing.'

'I should have given it to him earlier, when he paid off his men and began to act like a king again.'

'It still wouldn't have altered his destiny. You would still have been with him at the end to retrieve it from the battlefield. Its journey, and ours, goes on.'

Torfida smiled at him with a warmth he had not seen in a long time. He reflected on what she had said before getting to his feet.

'Give me the Talisman; it is time for me to wear it again.' He pulled Torfida into a tight embrace. 'Isn't it time we got married? I think the Talisman of Truth has just imparted an important message: it's time I made an honest woman of you!'

They laughed together and swung one another round in a whirl of joy.

At long last, the pain of the events in Scotland could begin to recede. Kiev in the spring presented itself as the ideal place for their union. April was on the fulcrum between the formidable winters of the heartlands of Asia and its equally prodigious summers. And so, as the temperate air of the Levant began to exert its influence, they decided that the time was right to marry in the eyes of God.

Hereward and Torfida were married in April 1059, in the historic wooden cathedral of Kiev by Theodore, Archbishop of the Rus. The cathedral was a towering masterpiece in elaborately carved oak, and the wedding was a glorious occasion. Martin and Einar stood either side of Hereward; Ingergerd and Maria flanked Torfida.

When it came to the time for the two principals to step forward and proclaim their vows, Torfida lost her composure and began to sob. With Hereward holding her firmly and whispering sympathetically, she eventually gathered herself a little. The spontaneous joy of Torfida's outburst brought tears to the eyes of her female companions.

Hereward had never seen Torfida so unable to control herself, and he realized how vulnerable she was under her veneer of wisdom and self-confidence.

Although she had said her destiny was to be his guide to the intangible mysteries of the Talisman, Hereward knew he would need to be Torfida's constant guardian in the much more corporeal challenges they would face on their journey together.

Hereward, Torfida and their extended family set sail from Kiev two days after their wedding. It was a week before the festival of Easter and the Dnieper was hectic, with merchants, soldiers and pilgrims hoping to reach their destinations before the festivities began. After a short stay in the bustling Black Sea port of Odessa, they sailed through the Bosporus, the gateway between two worlds, and were soon staring at the immense walls of the golden city of Constantinople.

They remained wide-eyed for days afterwards, overwhelmed by the incomparable sites before them: the Emperor's Palace and the Hagia Sophia; monasteries, schools of learning, great houses and luxuriant gardens; huge warehouses of traders' goods and street upon street of shops, selling everything they could think of and much else besides. None of them had ever seen anything like it, and they decided to stay for several weeks.

Torfida spent hours talking to the learned and the devout pilgrims who thronged the Hagia, the greatest church in Christendom. There were travellers from as far away as Baghdad, Jerusalem and Alexandria, all with tales of Arab learning and achievements in mathematics, astronomy and architecture.

When it was time to move on, they bought passage on a Greek merchant ship bound for Brindisi via Athens. As they sailed further and further from Constantinople, Hereward's admiration for the scale of the Byzantine Empire grew and grew. Even several days out from Athens, and hugging the Greek coastline west of the island of Corfu, they were still within the realm of the Emperor of Constantinople. After finally disembarking at Brindisi, they began their journey across the flat plains and into the rugged hills of southern Italy. They were now at the limit of the Byzantine Empire and on the border of lands under the hegemony of the Norman lords of southern Italy.

Torfida felt invigorated by the warmth of the land and its exotic atmosphere. It was May; everything was in full bloom and the countryside was alive with insects, birds and wildflowers.

Late one evening, as they relaxed in their camp after dinner, Torfida nestled close to Hereward and whispered, 'I told you we should come south, the warm air obviously agrees with me . . .' She paused. '. . . I'm pregnant.'

'My darling Torfida! I'm so happy. Let's hope this man, Robert Guiscard, is a man worth fighting for and that we can find a position with him. We are going to need to work for our living . . . and for our baby.'

'We will find useful work, worry not.'

They told the others immediately and there was much celebrating that night. Einar, who had grown to like Byzantine wine and always seemed to have a flask somewhere in his baggage, quickly made one appear to ensure that the merriment carried on well into the night. Martin sang his Celtic verses about maidens and heroes, love and comradeship.

Hereward looked at Torfida. He loved her very much, and now she had his child growing inside her. He turned to look out over the hills to the Adriatic Sea in the distance, radiant in the moonlight. What a strange journey theirs was: where would their adventure end?

And what would be their fate when they got there?

The bastion of Robert Guiscard stood menacingly on a strategic hilltop, some way back from the fertile plain of the Adriatic.

A stone keep was under construction within its palisaded walls, and large groups of people seemed to be making their way towards the city. Every building flew a flag or banner of some kind and from the pinnacle of the keep flew the striking red and gold emblem of the Count himself. Robert was the sixth of the nine sons of Tancred de Hauteville, an adventurer of humble birth from Normandy, who had fought his way to success and power. He was like many Normans of his time: brave and daring with an overpowering desire for conquest.

Hereward and his companions soon discovered the cause of the commotion. In three days' time, Pope Nicholas II would arrive in Melfi to invest Robert as ruler of not only Apulia, but also of neighbouring Calabria and Sicily. The Normans did not yet hold Sicily and Calabria, but there was method in the Pope's beneficence. Nicholas had been Pope for only five months and faced two rival powers who challenged Rome's authority. The Saracens, who were men of Islam and a great menace to Christianity, held Sicily, while Calabria was held by the Byzantine Emperor, Rome's great rival for control of Christendom. By granting Robert Guiscard sovereignty over these lands, even if only in name, the Pope was giving him an open invitation to venture out and conquer them.

Nicholas II also had an internal squabble, which required a solution. He had a rival, Benedict X, who claimed the Holy See, and had declared himself Pope on the death of the previous incumbent. Although he had been forced to flee Rome by Nicholas, Benedict still represented a threat. Nicholas needed Norman martial prowess to make Benedict come to heel. By allying himself with the Normans, and giving holy purpose to their private ambitions, Nicholas hoped to extend his influence to the whole of Italy.

Torfida was beside herself with excitement at the prospect of seeing the Pope, the one called 'Holiness', the man who had the ear of God himself. Once again, Torfida took on the guise of a noble lady. She would act as if she were on a pilgrimage to Rome and had decided to make a detour on the occasion of the Pope's visit.

When the Pope arrived, he brought an entourage of over 250 people: 200 elite guards from his own private army, plus several cardinals, bishops and advisers, as well as myriad bureaucrats, servants and cooks. Not many looked like clerics; save for a few monks in their cassocks, most looked like soldiers, for in those troubled times, most men of the cloth were also men of the sword.

Pope Nicholas was younger than Torfida had imagined. She stared intently at the great gold crucifix around his neck, gleaming in the sun, rubies and emeralds at each corner. More like a weapon of war than an instrument of a disciple of Christ, his mace, embossed with the crossed keys of the Vatican, rested across his right elbow. He wore a short red cape, edged in ermine, and a tall conical cap encrusted with yet more precious stones. As he passed in his open carriage, he opened his palms in a gesture of peace to the adoring crowds.

Two powerful men from Rome accompanied the Pope. The first was the wise old Abbot Desiderius of Monte Cassino, whom Nicholas had just appointed Cardinal Priest and Papal Legate to Campania, Benevento, Apulia and Calabria. The second was the Benedictine monk Hildebrand, Papal Ambassador at Large and thought to be the most astute man in Europe. The Pope needed these two men at his side if his reign was to have any meaning. Not only did he have military and political problems, he was also faced with deep-seated moral issues within the Church.

First of all, he wanted to reform the process of elections to the papacy, to avoid schisms and the emergence of rival popes. Secondly, simony, the sale of ecclesiastical positions, encouraged widespread corruption throughout Christendom. Thirdly, concubinage, the taking of wives by members of the Church, was common throughout Europe and led to widespread criticism of the hypocrisy of its priesthood. These issues led to frequent revolts within the clergy and the growth of radical reform groups.

In short, the Church of Rome was in tumult and Nicholas was planning a series of synods to cure it of its ills.

It would not be easy.

The investiture at Melfi was a grand affair. Robert Guiscard knelt before the Pontiff and kissed his ring before the Pope placed three crowns on his head in succession, to symbolize his lordship of the three domains. Each crowning was accompanied by loud cheering and a fanfare from Melfi's walls by three sets of trumpeters: one from the Vatican, one from the local Italian nobility and one from Guiscard's Norman army.

It had been announced that, following the ceremonial rites, the Pope would say mass in the open air, after which the congregation could file past for a blessing. Einar and the three women were in position early, to be close to the front, but Martin and Hereward watched from a distance, feeling rather more cynical about the sanctity of Rome.

The worshippers were brought forward in large groups and knelt before the Pope, heads bowed, to receive the papal anointing. When it came to the turn of Torfida's group, instead of moving on after the blessing, she stood, genuflected, and spoke directly to the Pontiff.

It was unheard of for anyone to speak to the Pope without being spoken to first. The papal guards moved forward to apprehend Torfida; Einar, who was just behind her, looked back towards Hereward and Martin with an anxious glance. Pope Nicholas looked bemused and turned to his companions, Desiderius and Hildebrand, both of whom were smiling wryly. He also began to smile and signalled to his guards to relent. Torfida had spoken in impeccable Latin and had asked him, in the most humble of ways, if he had ever read the writings of the Venerable Bede, the Anglo-Saxon scholar-monk, especially *The Martyrology of the Birthdays of the Holy Martyrs*.

There were a few moments of agonizing silence, as Torfida waited to hear if the Pope would respond. She kept her head bowed as far as it would go, her eyes firmly closed. Hereward shifted uneasily. He was desperate to be by her side and thought back to his moment of truth in front of Macbeth's army.

This was Torfida's moment.

Pope Nicholas spoke clearly and confessed that although he had heard of Bede, he had never studied his works.

'But I have,' interrupted Hildebrand.

'And so have I,' said Cardinal Desiderius. He turned to Torfida. 'How do you know the writings of Bede, my child?'

Torfida was at least ten yards from the three holy men and had to project in a clear and loud voice. 'My father read them to me when I was a little girl, your Eminence, I know them by heart.'

'But there are hundreds of pages.'

'His words are wise and easy to remember, and my father was an excellent teacher.'

The Pope, now charmed by Torfida's exemplary Latin and, no doubt, her beauty, spoke again. 'Who was your father?'

'A priest of Winchester, your Holiness, a scholar and confessor to Queen Emma, mother of Edward, King of England.'

'What became of your father?'

'That is a long story, your Holiness. One which would delay you unnecessarily and prevent these good people from receiving your blessing.'

'Yes, indeed. Thank you for reminding me about the works of Bede; I will be sure to read them.'

Torfida bowed deeply and moved on.

Einar, Ingigerd and Maria rushed her away from the crowds and they later rendezvoused with Hereward and Martin in a quiet part of the city. Little was said between them; they were shocked that Torfida had been so foolhardy in a strange world so far from home.

Hereward thought he understood – Torfida felt she needed to grasp every opportunity, no matter how intimidating, to find the path that would reveal their destiny.

That evening, Robert Guiscard presided over a grand feast in the Great Hall of Melfi. It was an evening of much merriment, with an inebriated Duke doing most of the talking; minstrels played and there was a clever display of juggling and trickery by a troupe from Venice.

As soon as it was polite to do so, the Pope withdrew to his rooms. He had already made inquiries about the bold young woman who had spoken to him during the day and had sent word to her that he would grant her an audience.

Hereward had insisted that he accompany her. He looked around now at the ostentatious trappings of the Pope's quarters in wonder; he had not seen such treasures since he had had his private audience with King Edward at Winchester. Only five years had passed in what was becoming an ever more eventful life. He was still only twenty-four, Torfida just twenty. The young English couple knelt as the Pope and his companions entered the room.

For over an hour, they conversed with three of the wisest men in Europe. The men were intrigued by the story of Hereward's turbulent life, and enchanted by Torfida as she recited from the Gospels and talked at length about Bede. She asked them about dogma, probed them about morality within the Church and queried the lack of separation between Church and State. They seemed not to be in the slightest offended or discomforted and treated her as an equal. Hildebrand, in particular, seemed to admire her broad knowledge and her grasp of theology.

Finally, with some trepidation, she raised the subject of the Talisman and, as she began to describe it, saw the benign look on the face of Cardinal Desiderius turn to consternation.

'If the Talisman you speak of is the one I think it is, you should be careful what you say to us here. Not only that, you should hand it to us immediately, so that it can be locked away deep in the crypt of the Vatican.'

'Why, your Eminence?'

'The Devil's Amulet, if that's what it is, was hidden in the tomb of a heretic in the vaults of my monastery at

149

Monte Cassino for many centuries. Legend says that it was a pagan amulet worn by the high priestess of a satanic cult in Ancient Rome. It was stolen in the sixth century, when the Lombards sacked the monastery, and was never seen again.'

'But I know it as the Talisman of Truth.'

'That may be so, but it is dangerous for you to dabble with such things. Perhaps you are a witch, come to beguile us with your sweet smile and clever words, and this husband of yours sent by Lucifer to protect you.'

Hereward stiffened at the sudden change in the mood of the Cardinal.

Torfida was shocked at the ferocity of the tirade and took a deep breath.

The Pope looked concerned. 'Calm yourself, Desiderius. Let us hear what the young woman has to say.'

'Thank you, Holiness. The Talisman was given to me by my father. He interpreted it differently and thought it represented the ultimate dilemma in men's hearts: the struggle between good and evil.'

Desiderius still looked scornful, but Hildebrand cocked his head as if he knew what was coming next. The Pope saw the change of expression and listened carefully as Torfida described the Talisman in detail.

'There is no doubt that it is the face of the Devil, surrounded by his acolytes, but it also contains the blood of our Saviour, Jesus of Nazareth. His blood entombs the Devil in stone through his ultimate sacrifice in giving his life for us. And so, the Talisman tells us how we can defeat our weaknesses by controlling our evil thoughts and deeds, thus allowing our goodness to triumph.'

'That is very astute, Torfida.'

'Thank you, Father Hildebrand.'

'But dangerous! Do you believe it to be a metaphorical totem, the symbolism of which is meant to lead men to truth and wisdom?'

'Exactly, Father Hildebrand! That is why it is so intriguing.' Torfida smiled in admiration; Hildebrand understood her thoughts about the power of the amulet and had described its mystery far better than she could ever have done.

'In which case, it denies that role to the Church and is thus heretical.' Now Hildebrand, like Desiderius, looked concerned. 'You are being naïve, Torfida. Cardinal Desiderius is right to warn you. These conundrums are not a game; they involve articles of faith, and question the very nature of our existence. There are many in the Church who would recoil in horror if they heard this conversation.'

The Pope intervened. 'Where does it come from?'

'I don't know, Holy Father. Other pieces of amber have insects trapped inside them, and ancient folklore says that they are the trapped spirits of tortured souls. But the face of Lucifer and the streak of blood are a mystery. I have been talking to wise men all over Europe in the hope of finding out.'

Hildebrand interrupted with a question of his own. 'Do you suppose it could be a freak of nature?'

'In what way, Father?'

'Nature plays many tricks on us; there is much we don't understand. But if it is just a freak of nature, then there is another solution.'

151

'That it is a harmless trinket?'

'Well done, Torfida. It would have no significance at all, except in our imaginations!'

The Pope intervened again. 'Now you are straying into the dark corners of heresy, Hildebrand. Thc things in nature that we don't understand are God's business. If he wanted us to know about them, he would tell us; or rather, he would tell me, as I'm his messenger on earth.'

The Pope smiled mischievously, which broke the tension. Then they all smiled, even Desiderius, and with that, the Pope brought the conversation to an end.

'To our chambers; it is late. Come back and see us in the morning, and we will talk again. For now, let us sleep on your conundrum.'

Hereward was alarmed and spent a restless night.

He knew only too well that many parts of Christendom still observed the practices of the old pagan religions, often running in parallel with their Christian beliefs. He also knew that the Church could be fanatical in rooting out heresy.

Now that he had learned that the Talisman was once called the Devil's Amulet, nagging doubts surfaced about the coincidence of meeting Torfida in Hereford, and her father's wild predictions about their joint destiny.

Perhaps the Talisman brought death, not wisdom?

Perhaps the Old Man of the Wildwood was a sorcerer, and Torfida a witch sent to seduce him for some nefarious purpose?

He stopped himself and tried to put such thoughts out

of his head, but the next morning, Hereward accompanied Torfida to the Pope's quarters with some trepidation.

The Pontiff tried to put them at their ease. 'Please sit and relax. You are here as children of God; this is not an inquisition.'

'Perhaps it should be.' Cardinal Desiderius could not resist the caustic remark.

'Torfida, following our conversation last night, the three of us have spoken at some length over breakfast. Hereward, let us see the amulet.'

Hereward removed it from his neck and placed it, cautiously, in the Pope's outstretched hands.

'It is remarkable. I have seen many things in the crypt of the Vatican, but this is truly amazing.'

He passed it to the others. Hildebrand took it with the inquisitive look of the curious intellectual; Desiderius, clearly ill at ease, glared at it with contempt.

'Hildebrand has persuaded us that your quest for the meaning of the amulet is laudable – dangerous, but laudable. Desiderius would have me lock it away and have you two do penance in Rome, but I don't think that is necessary. Your quest together, in search of wisdom for yourselves and for the ultimate recipient of what you call the Talisman of Truth, is commendable. Your remarkable journey so far has persuaded me that we should let you continue.

'Hereward of Bourne, take good care of your wife. You should be careful and constantly seek the guidance of God in what you do. I cannot bless the amulet because I am mindful of Cardinal Desiderius' dire warnings, but I will bless you two and the new life that Torfida carries. Kneel, my children.'

The Pope replaced the Talisman around Hereward's neck, who quickly tucked it under his smock, as the Pontiff placed a hand on their heads and blessed them.

'Go in peace.'

9. Robert Guiscard

A few days after the Pope and his entourage had left for Rome, Hereward and Torfida presented themselves and their companions to Robert Guiscard, the new lord of southern Italy. The Duke was keen to meet the people about whom he had heard so much over the last few days, especially 'the woman', as he put it, 'who dares to speak to popes'.

He exchanged courtesies, then turned to Hereward. 'What brings such noble and important Northerners to our humble dukedom?'

The sarcasm in the Duke's voice prompted Hereward to speak up. After Torfida's insistence that they should travel south to serve with Robert Guiscard, she had been helping Hereward improve the simple Norman French he had been taught as a child by Aidan, Priest of Bourne.

'My Lord Duke, we are soldiers committed to fighting for the cause of the righteous. It is said that you are charged with uniting Italy by removing from its foothold here the Empire of Byzantium, a distant realm that no longer recognizes the Church of Rome. You also plan to rid Sicily of the Saracens, an alien people with a strange religion. We can think of no better cause than yours in the two duties you have been given by his Holiness. We offer our services as senior commanders in your garrison, particularly in the preparation and training of your men.'

'That is an elegant introduction, Hereward of Bourne. So, not only do you presume to know the details of my arrangements with the Pontiff, you have the gall to suggest that you can teach us how to fight!'

The Duke guffawed heartily and turned to his court, all of whom laughed with him. A solid, round-faced man with ruddy cheeks and a thin patchy beard, he could easily have been a butcher or a blacksmith, had not his and his family's notorious cunning and strength of arm elevated him to the lofty perch of a dukedom.

'I carry with me parchments testifying to our standing from Queen Gruoch of Scotland, widow of Macbeth, and Iziaslav I, Grand Prince of Kiev and King of the Rus. We would not presume to teach Norman warlords how to fight. Your reputation and that of your kin goes before you, but we wish to join you as highly skilled and experienced soldiers who can help your cause. I would like to serve at the level of knight, my companions, the mighty Einar and the brave Martin Lightfoot, as sergeants-at-arms.

'Anything else: a pension, lands in Normandy, one of my daughters as a concubine?' He chortled loudly again.

As before, his court joined with him, enjoying the Duke's sardonic repartee.

'Just to serve, my Lord Duke.' Hereward was solemn and calm, trying not to rise to the Duke's baiting.

Guiscard turned to his younger brother, Roger, who had recently arrived from Normandy for the celebrations and would soon begin campaigning in Sicily. He lowered his voice to a whisper. For what seemed an eternity the two spoke in hushed but animated tones, their conversation private.

Hereward glanced at his companions, who looked around uneasily, assessing the odds in what could be a very difficult situation. Guiscard was clearly a brute of a man; an adventurer successful enough to enlist the blessing of popes but, nonetheless, an ogre. Einar counted a dozen heavily armed men in the room. Then, from another chamber, the Duchess Adela appeared, a stout and maternal figure, and approached Torfida.

'I hear you are a philosopher and speaker of many tongues. I see you are also with child. The women in the town say you are a witch powerful enough to seduce popes, and that the child is the Devil's progeny.'

Torfida bowed to the Duchess. 'Your Grace, the child is my husband's, Hereward of Bourne, a great knight of England. I am his obedient wife and your Grace's humble servant.'

'But you speak privately to popes.'

'I am just a woman on a journey with her husband. It led me to a pope; I did not seek it.'

The Duchess seemed only to be teasing Torfida. Her questions were delivered gently and with a wry smile, suggesting she realized that the gossip she had heard from her ladies-in-waiting was nothing but idle talk. She turned to her husband and hissed into his ear like a scolding matron.

His brother added words of caution, this time for all to hear. 'Robert, look at the battle-axe on the Englishman's shoulder; I have never seen a weapon like it. Look at him, his scars, the scale of him. This is a formidable man; let me take him to Sicily to fight the Saracens.'

Guiscard turned to his visitors. He looked Torfida in the

eye, clearly intent on intimidating her, but it was as if he were looking into a mirror: the more intensely he stared, the more resolute Torfida appeared.

Seconds later, the Duke threw back his chair and charged towards the doors of the Great Hall. 'I am made Duke, but I'm no longer master in my own house! Where's my damned steward? We go hunting! Bring that new butt of Cypriot wine . . . and that new servant girl from Bari. She will string my bow of an evening and fill my quiver for the chase!'

This parting boast, a cruel insult for his wife, made no impression on the Duchess Adela, who was busy talking to Torfida about the work to be done in Melfi.

Roger Guiscard walked over to Hereward and offered his hand.

As Hereward left the great hall, Torfida at his side, he spoke to her about Duke Robert.

'I hope the Pope is right in trusting this enterprise to such a man. He is without virtue of any kind.'

'Except as a warrior.'

'But surely the Pope expects more from someone he makes a duke.'

'Sometimes popes and kings make choices born of necessity rather than moral virtue.'

'Then who takes care of virtue?'

'Hereward of Bourne, that is a very good question. You are becoming quite a philosopher!'

Hereward looked out across the busy square of Melfi and the scores of people resuming their lives after the previous week's excitement.

'In times like these, with virtuous people hard to find, who protects these innocent souls?'

'Perhaps we do, Hereward.'

Hereward looked at his wife, soon to be the mother of his child, with a sudden seriousness. He knew her statement was not an idle boast.

'Torfida, is what we do worthy, or do we fool ourselves that our purpose is just?'

'You do what you must because you are a warrior. Einar and Martin follow you because they admire you. Men look to you for leadership; they always will. I am with you because I love you and because I know that something of great importance lies at the end of your quest.'

'Will there ever be a time when we can rest, when there is peace in the world?'

'I have read that many centuries ago, under the rule of Ancient Rome and, protected by the legions of the Caesars, the world lived in peace. Many kings and warlords have striven for that ever since – a peace by force of arms – but I often wonder if there could be another kind of peace: a peace born of the common agreement of men; observed by all, enjoyed by all, enforced by justice, not by war.'

'What would men like me do in such a world?'

'You would lock your weapons in a chest and find other ways to become heroes.'

'How?'

'You would test yourself: swim rivers, climb mountains, discover new lands, compete in trials of strength and speed like the Ancient Greeks, or even play chess – something you could do in your old age.'

'What is chess?'

'A game of war played on a board with figures for kings

and queens and armies. One day, I will teach you how to play.'

'You are such a dreamer, Torfida. I can't imagine a world where men would resolve their disputes with trials of strength and games of strategy.'

'I know it's a dream, but it's a good dream. What a world that would be for our child.'

They kissed and embraced, inspired by Torfida's speculations, before Hereward brought the conversation back to reality.

'Do you think Roger, the Duke's brother, is a good man?'

Torfida thought about the question for a moment. 'I think so. He looks fierce, but he has gentle eyes.'

'I hope you're right.'

Torfida gave birth at the end of 1059. Duchess Adela insisted that the delivery be at the new hospital in Melfi, an institution she was determined would become the finest south of Rome. It was run by an order of nuns from Ghent, in Flanders, devoted to the care of the sick. One of the sisters, Adeliza, a large woman with big red hands and fat hairy forearms, specialized in childbirth and was assigned to Torfida as her midwife. When the time came and Torfida took off her dress to squat at the birthing stool, Adeliza had a surprise for her.

'You're going to have twins, my Lady. You're not as big as some, but, mark my words, you're going to have two little creatures!' She proceeded to run her stubby fingers across Torfida's belly. 'Here's one . . . and there's the other. You can always tell, the shape of the belly is different. The important thing is to get the second little mite out; the first is easy, but the second often hides.'

In the end, Adeliza's skills were barely required and both babies popped out like peas from a pod; they were twin girls – Gunnhild and Estrith. These were happy times. Ingigerd and Martin also produced a child, called Gwyneth. Einar and Maria had a little girl they named Wulfhild, and thus the family of six became a tribe of ten.

Torfida was indeed right about Roger Guiscard.

For the next three years, Hereward, Einar and Martin campaigned with him in Sicily and throughout the heel and toe of Italy. Torfida stayed in Melfi and the surrounding area, working with the Duchess Adela in establishing hospitals and almshouses, and supporting the monasteries in their work with the poor. Hereward and Torfida saw one another at the end of each of Roger's campaigns. During these furloughs, Torfida fulfilled her promise to teach Hereward the nuances of chess. He took to the game well, enjoying its affinity with the tactics of the battlefield.

When the men came home from their campaigns, they returned largely unscathed. Hereward put the Great Axe of Göteborg to fearsome use, and there were only minor setbacks in a year of successes, the greatest of which took place near Taranto in the summer of 1061.

Guiscard's Normans had come across a large Byzantine column and forced it to retreat. It was the major part of a Greek theme of good quality, but was slowed by the cumbersome baggage train of the local Byzantine governor and several Greek merchants and their families. As the Normans closed in, the Greeks' reluctance to abandon their bulky possessions put them in great peril. Either noble duty or foolish miscalculation led the Byzantine general to leave it too late before insisting that the baggage be left behind. Even then, there were acrimonious arguments and widespread confusion, and many of the merchants were still digging makeshift hiding places for their possessions when the Norman force crested the hill behind them.

Within minutes, Hereward and his companions were in the vanguard of a cavalry charge that swept into the valley below with fearsome momentum. The men of the Greek theme hastily formed a reasonable redoubt, but the Normans had too much impetus to be repulsed. The battle lasted less than an hour. The first wave of Norman cavalry easily breached the Greek lines, and it was only a matter of time before the infantrymen, exposed in isolated pockets, sought surrender.

Hereward cut an impressive figure in battle. Sitting tall in his saddle, with his golden hair flowing below the rim of his helmet, the great sweeps of his war axe cleared wide arcs of ground around him. The Normans suffered few casualties, but many in the Greek ranks were cut down, as the Norman horsemen ploughed through them.

It was Hereward himself who reached the Byzantine General first. He and a few of his bodyguards had become detached from the bulk of his theme. On seeing this, Hereward pulled up his mount and signalled his companions to halt. Faced with the choice between a valiant but futile fight, and a less than glorious surrender, the General chose the noble death of a warrior.

He summoned his guards to his side, perhaps fifteen men, and with the cry, 'For the Emperor!' kicked his horse into a gallop towards the Normans. Hereward immediately ordered a charge in response. As the General closed, he saw him nod to his men on either side to acknowledge their comradeship and bravery. They had attacked an overwhelming force without hesitation, just as they had been ordered to do.

Hereward felt enormous admiration for his foes. Beneath the face-guard of the General's ornate plumed helmet, a full grey beard was plain to see. He was a soldier of many years' experience. He would have fought many battles and killed many men; now it was his turn to die. The brutal truth was that these would be his final moments on earth. He made straight for Hereward, his eyes fixed on the Englishman.

He was dead before he hit the ground. Hereward caught him full in the chest with his great axe, catapulting him out of his saddle and over the back of his horse, leaving him spreadeagled on the ground. The weapon protruded from where it had been plunged: clean through the General's armour and deep in the breast of a noble soldier of Byzantium.

Only four men survived the courageous charge, and they were soon rounded up. Hereward learned from the Byzantine prisoners that his foe was General Michael Andronicus from Rhodes, a man with nearly thirty years' service, who had risen from the junior ranks of an army he had joined as a boy of fifteen. He was given an interment worthy of his rank and distinguished service, in a ceremony that Hereward supervised personally and with all the respect due to a fellow warrior.

Calabria was cleared of the Byzantine army by the end of the year; Roger Guiscard returned to Melfi a hero, and southern Italy became a Norman stronghold. Duchess Adela was determined that Norman rule would be at least palatable to the local Italian population, if not embraced by them. She worked tirelessly to ameliorate the usual Norman brutalities, and life in Apulia became peaceful and prosperous.

Hereward and his loyal group, flourishing in the warm Mediterranean climate, became assimilated into the Norman community, speaking their language and enjoying their zest for life. There was much for Torfida to do and, while Ingigerd and Maria looked after the farmhouse that the three couples shared, she became, in essence, the steward of Adela's domain. She learned much from the locals about Greek and Arab healing and had already acquired a good grounding in the Arabic language.

Hereward's military knowledge was expanding at a pace, as was his understanding of the strengths and frailties of men in battle. Being at war suited him; he needed to fight, to satisfy his martial instincts. But he needed a reason to fight – not just wantonly and savagely, as most men did, but for a purpose that he felt was just.

Even though Robert Guiscard was a tyrant whose family ethic was founded on aggression and conquest, the Normans had brought much to their previously troubled domain. Hereward had a love of tolerance and justice that was shared by Roger Guiscard and the Duchess Adela, and thus found moral justification for fighting on behalf of his hosts.

The campaigns in Calabria and Sicily were a new kind of warfare for Hereward. This involved much more mobile battles than were usual in northern Europe. The rapid deployment of cavalry was vital, as was the need to move supplies at great speed. Naval warfare was also on a larger scale than in northern Europe. Hereward encountered 'Greek fire', spewed forth from the telltale dragon's mouth mounted on the bow of Byzantine triremes. It was said that only the Emperor of Byzantium himself knew the secret ingredients of 'the fire'. Once ignited in wooden cylinders lined with lead and catapulted into the opposing fleet, it would spew its deadly contents everywhere. Its main ingredient was pitch, which meant it adhered to anything it hit, including sails, ships' timbers and, of course, men. It would even continue to burn on and under water.

The Normans recruited many mercenaries from North Africa, Spain and the Adriatic, men whose families had fought Saracens for generations. From them Hereward learned of warfare by stealth – techniques little known in the north – where men stood and faced one another in open conflict. He was fascinated by the tactics of infiltration, disruption and deception. He learned how, under cover of darkness or by the use of camouflage, a small group of men, or even a single man, could burn tents, poison wells, scatter horses, steal weapons, or assassinate leaders.

During the Sicilian campaigns, Hereward would often lead incursions into Saracen camps to create havoc. One of his companions, Alphonso of Granada, a man with a good deal of Arab blood in him, became Hereward's most trusted accomplice and a close friend. Eventually, the small but immensely agile and robust young man became accepted by Martin and Einar as the fourth member of their brotherhood-in-arms.

Hereward became the most respected man in Roger's army. He was a trusted knight and friend to his Norman employer, who was himself a noble warrior. There was even a reconciliation of sorts between Hereward and Duke Robert.

After a particularly gruelling but successful campaign in Sicily, the Duke invested Hereward into the chivalrous Order of the Knights of the Cotentin, an honour normally given only to Normans.

As 1062 turned into 1063, Hereward began to sense that Norman success in Sicily was only a matter of time; although a vast and mountainous island, the Saracens were being rooted out of its rugged terrain village by village, and their total expulsion was inevitable.

As winter set in, Torfida noticed Hereward increasingly looking north. He could see the dark, brooding clouds over the high Apennines, imagery which reminded him of home. She knew that it was time for their journey to resume.

Throughout the previous two years, they had heard many reports from the Norman heartland in northern France and, in particular, tales of the exploits of William the Bastard, Duke of that land. Almost six feet tall, and distinctive by his bright red hair, he was several years older than Hereward, with an impressive reputation. He had inherited his dukedom at the age of eight, and had held on to it, despite the attentions of many who plotted to wrest it from him. He had a wily grasp of European affairs and an eye for new territorial opportunities.

Early in 1063, news reached Melfi that William had invaded the neighbouring state of Maine, following the death of its ruler. Hereward's focus was now increasingly fixed on the northern horizon. It was becoming apparent that the great territorial prize to be had in northern Europe was England. Great warriors watched it like hawks: not only Duke William in Normandy, but also the equally ferocious Harald Hardrada, King of Norway, and Svein Estrithson, King of the Danes.

As Hereward speculated about the future of his homeland, Torfida's love for him deepened. He had become the pride of the Norman army of Apulia but, more importantly, had found a measure of humility to diminish his conceit. He now used judgement to control his instincts and had developed a thoughtfulness to counterbalance his volatility.

Torfida knew that the north beckoned, and it was not lost on her that their journey was beginning to scribe the arc of a great circle, leading Hereward back towards England.

10. The Omen

Everyone was saddened to leave Melfi. Roger granted Hereward his heavy Norman horse, complete with armour, and
from the Duke there was a parchment describing his valour
in the service of Apulia and Christendom. Lord Roger had
asked Hereward to take the title 'Sir Hereward Great Axe',
as this was how the men of the army referred to him, but
he declined, saying that he had been christened Hereward
of Bourne and that he would prefer to keep his unadorned
family title.

They had all earned considerable sums in the service of
Apulia, especially Hereward in his capacity as a knight. For
their journey north, they were able to hire six retainers.
They were all Normans who had welcomed the opportunity
to return home: a sturdy sergeant and two crossbowmen,
a groom, and two servant girls. Hereward and Torfida had
risen in the world and now had the distinctive bearing of
the sophisticated nobility of Europe.

They stayed a week in Rome. However, the Papal See
was rife with intrigue and plots and not a place in which to
linger. However, the rest of the Italian peninsular became
an ever-increasing source of wonder for them as they took
the opportunity to visit Pisa, Siena, Florence, Bologna and
Padua, before completing their sojourn in the magical city
of Venice. The great church of St Mark, in the final stages
of being rebuilt, was a haven not only for worship, but also

for learning and philosophy. Everything on the Italian peninsular seemed to be built on such a vast scale; the churches, roads, palaces, monasteries and castles dwarfed anything they had seen in their homelands.

Torfida was like a human sponge in collecting knowledge and like a magpie in collecting artefacts. She bought a richly illustrated parchment map of the known world. When she showed the map to the others, they looked on in awe as she tracked their journey around its fringes.

The map also offered a stark reminder of the next phase of their travels: the Alps. They were grateful that it was high summer; it was not a journey they would have wanted to make in winter. Their passage took them past huge walls of white peaks stretching as far as the eye could see. Hundreds of feet beneath them, like a world in miniature, lay a wide valley of forests, lakes and pastures. At one point, Torfida jumped off her horse and walked into the distance on a tapestry of wild flowers to admire a sight more beautiful than anything she had ever seen.

After several minutes had passed, Hereward walked over to join her. She was motionless; her eyes were open wide, tears running down her cheeks.

She looked at him and began to sob. 'How can anything be so beautiful? I have seen many wonders in many places, but how can this be? This is how Heaven should be.'

'Perhaps it is Heaven.'

'Oh, Hereward, let's go down into the valley and stay awhile. The children can swim in the lakes; we can catch fish for dinner and collect wild berries. It is so magical.'

'Of course we can stay – as long as you like.'

He held her tightly, rocking her like a baby. As she buried

her head in his chest, he looked out across the vast expanse before them.

Torfida was right: how could anything be so astonishing?

They made camp in a wide meadow by a lake, sheltered by a huge wall of rock towering above. Fish were plentiful; there were numerous varieties of berries, as well as mushrooms of all kinds, and the forests teemed with game.

Gunnhild and Estrith were identical twins and resembled their mother. Although their hair and eyes were not as dark as Torfida's, they were unmistakably her daughters. They had also inherited her curiosity, picking up anything that moved, and poking, prodding, pulling and plucking anything that did not.

They were learning to talk in the many languages of their extended family. Knowing only too well that ability with languages was one of the few ways in which a woman could gain a modicum of respect in a world dominated by war and trade, Torfida insisted that everyone in the group spoke to the girls in their native tongue. Not satisfied with that, Torfida was also determined to teach them Greek and Latin.

From their father, they had inherited boundless energy. They walked very early and were well coordinated and athletic but, unlike their father – whose restlessness and truculence had started as a toddler – Gunnhild and Estrith were well behaved. Indeed, Torfida would not have it any other way.

The idyllic setting of the Alps put Torfida into a contemplative mood. She did not want to leave, and spent hours weaving fantasies about how they could build a life for themselves high in the mountains and raise their children in peace. Late one afternoon, Torfida was deep in such a reverie when she was suddenly and cruelly reminded of reality.

She was clambering among the crags, high above their camp, on one of her frequent expeditions to collect specimens of the myriad alpine flowers she used in her medicines. The air suddenly turned foul like the stench of a blacksmith's furnace and her hair stuck out from her head at right angles. There was a faint but audible crackling in the atmosphere around her and she suddenly felt very cold. Then came an ear-piercing crash, as if the earth were rending itself open, and Torfida was thrown at least ten yards down the crags, landing on her back on a grassy slope. Her whole body ached as if every part of her had been kicked and punched, and she could smell the sickly odours of singed hair and scorched flesh.

She opened her eyes a few moments later, as a booming echo of thunder rumbled round the mountains. Torrential rain began to fall and, as it did, steam rose from the ground around her, the sky was as black as pitch and the wind began to howl.

She knew she had been struck by lightning and, by some miracle, had survived. She lay motionless, as if petrified, drenched by the storm's downpour. Aware only of the continuous screeching in her ears, she was unable to hear Hereward's desperate calls.

Martin reached her first, closely followed by Hereward, Alphonso and Einar; all feared she was dead. Martin had seen the lightning go to ground only a few feet from her. Knowing the mountains well, he had sensed the sudden change of atmosphere and the drop in temperature and, realizing that Torfida was high up, had scanned the slopes to locate her.

Just as he saw her, the bolt struck.

They carried her down the mountain as her body began to convulse. The skin on her face, legs and hands looked as if it had been hung in a smokehouse; tiny vessels had burst in her eyes, there were trickles of blood from both nostrils and her hair looked as if it had been frizzled in an oven. They could feel how hot her body was, and they noticed that her clothes were smouldering.

It took Torfida several days to recover. Her bloodshot eyes cleared and oil of lanolin helped restore her hair, but her mood remained sombre. The weather had continued to assail the mountains, even though it was late August. For Torfida, a place that in one moment had been a paradise had, in an instant, presented a glimpse of Hell that would give her nightmares for the rest of her life.

She spoke to Hereward alone. 'I had begun to forget our purpose. This is an omen, a warning not to forget again. We must leave tomorrow; time is moving on and God only knows what is happening in England.'

Torfida began to cry. She looked as bereft as Hereward had ever seen her.

'The King is old now, perhaps he is dead already. War may have started.'

'Torfida, calm yourself.'

'I am frightened, Hereward. We think we have the ability to make things happen, to change things, but compared to God and the world of nature he created, we are insignificant. That knowledge shakes me to my very core.'

'Torfida, don't talk like that, I need you. Whatever it is

that we're supposed to be doing with this cursed thing around my neck, I need you.'

She began to fight back the tears. 'Hereward, get me out of these mountains. Let's make haste for Normandy.'

'Get some rest. We'll break camp in the morning and sleep on lower ground tomorrow night.'

Hereward kissed her and held her tightly until she finally fell asleep. As he listened to the wind wail around the mountains, he too felt a quiver of anxiety. He had never believed in prophecies and omens, but now he felt a primordial shudder of instinctive fear and, desperate for the reassurance they would bring, he longed to wake the others.

He fought his demons and held Torfida even tighter. Whether it was an omen or not, Hereward knew that mountains were dangerous places and he feared that lightning could indeed strike twice. He resolved to get as far away as possible, as quickly as Torfida's recovery would allow.

Everyone remained subdued for the next few days; they all wanted the mountains to be out of sight and for Torfida to regain her vitality.

Eventually, after several weeks and a detour to avoid the French strongholds of Paris and Chartres, they entered the Norman province of Evreux. They had not been so far north in a very long time and everyone shivered in the fresh autumnal winds. But, more importantly, Torfida was happier. Hereward stayed close to her. She seemed to be back to her alert, purposeful self. She had cut away all her singed hair, leaving a boyish bob that made her look much younger. Her eyes had regained their brightness and her skin its clarity.

Torfida's decisiveness was also back, and she advised

Hereward that they should head for Rouen, the seat of Duke William's power.

They arrived in Rouen three days later.

It was a bustling city with new buildings being erected everywhere. The markets were busy and the people seemed affluent. Normandy was thriving. Duke William was on his way home from the cathedral at Jumièges, after giving thanks for victory over the Province of Maine. His invasion earlier in the year had been successful and he now held sway over the whole of northern France above the Loire. Not only that: the King of France, Philip II, was still a minor and the Duke's only other serious rival, Geoffrey of Anjou, had recently died, leaving little threat from the south.

After finding lodgings in the city and bidding farewell to their retinue from Melfi, they prepared to watch the Duke on his triumphant return.

The streets were bursting with people and hundreds of sentries were deployed to keep clear the processional route. The Bishop of Rouen, flanked by the entire hierarchy of the Norman Church, and the newly appointed Bishop of Le Mans, the capital of the conquered Province of Maine, waited at the great door of the cathedral to anoint the conquering hero. Fanning out from the bishops, on both sides, were the abbots from Normandy's monasteries, the sheriffs from its provinces and the great and the good of the city of Rouen.

At the centre of the group, and a pace or two ahead, was a woman who, at first glance, could easily have been mistaken for a child. At not much more than four and a half feet tall, she was dwarfed by everyone around her. Matilda, Duchess of Normandy, daughter of Baldwin V, Count of Flanders – William's most important ally and guardian of the young King Philip of France – was a direct descendent of Alfred the Great of England and had a personality which belied her diminutive stature. It was known throughout Normandy that her marriage to Duke William was happy and that she was quite capable of standing up for herself, even in the presence of her formidable husband. Her tiny frame did not prevent her from enjoying robust health, producing three sons, five daughters and being now heavily pregnant with a ninth child.

Hereward and Torfida found the mood of excitement in the city infectious. As the horns sounded in front of the cathedral to signal the Duke's entry into the square, they cheered along with everyone else. The Duke's archers and crossbowmen came first, followed by a column of infantry, all marching four abreast in excellent order. The bowmen wore leather jerkins with brown woollen leggings, small leather skullcaps and, in addition to their bows, carried seaxs. Wearing mail hauberks and distinctive pointed helmets with long nose-guards, several columns of infantry and cavalry came next, carrying both sword and spear and holding the famous Norman conical shield. Then came the Duke, in the midst of at least a hundred colourfully dressed knights, many of them lords in their own right. With their huge destriers strutting beneath them, most carried a small pennon on their lance to affirm their chevalier status, but some carried much bigger and more elaborately designed gonfalons, which asserted their nobility as barons. The crowd could recognize where each knight came from by the local colours of his pennon or gonfalon; those from towns close to Rouen, such as Fécamp and Yvetot, were greeted by particularly fervent cheers.

The Duke finally came into Hereward's view. His ducal coronet covered a mane of thick red hair and his ruddy complexion was framed by a neatly trimmed beard, slightly darker than the hair on his head. He wore an unexceptional woollen cloak over his mail coat and had the same armour and weapons as his knights. However, resting on the pommel of his saddle was the legendary 'Baculus', his formidable wooden war club. A weapon of war dating back generations to the Normans' Viking ancestors, all previous Dukes of Normandy had carried it as an icon of authority and virility.

Sitting upright on his mount, William did not smile at his subjects, only giving a perfunctory nod to a particularly loud greeting, or to a face that seemed familiar. The crowd was impressed by his physical presence; he was clearly someone born to rule and rule firmly.

William was not his father's legitimate son. The old Duke, Robert I, had fallen for a beauty called Herleve, the daughter of a humble tanner from Falaise. No one had been surprised that he had bedded her, but his long-term affection for her and the acceptance of their son, William, as his heir, had caused outrage.

Following the death of his father, Duke Robert, on the way home from a holy pilgrimage to Jerusalem, William became the Duke of Normandy in July 1035, at the tender age of eight. He was placed in the care of disciplinarian tutors and even harsher martial instructors, watched over day and night by knights loyal to his father, and he was

176

denied any female or maternal presence in his life. His mother died when he was still a teenager, leaving William with few memories of a woman who had shown him little affection. Most boys would have wilted under the pressure, or snapped, but William was strong of body and resolute of mind. He increasingly developed into the role of powerful warrior and leader that had been ordained for him. He became uncompromising, like his tutors, and durable, like his instructors.

His life had been a long and bitter struggle against internal intrigue and external threats. As he struggled to forge Normandy into the most powerful presence in Europe, he was aided by his two half-brothers: Odo, Bishop of Bayeux, one of his most loyal and trusted confidants, and Robert, Count of Mortain, another close ally.

When the Duke reached the Bishop of Rouen for his anointing, he surveyed the most powerful subjects in his realm with the air of a man totally at ease with his position as their lord and master.

The Norman warrior tradition was potent and remorseless, and he was its apotheosis.

Duke William went hunting immediately after his anointment as Lord of Maine, and it took Hereward and his male companions almost two weeks to gain an audience with him.

The Duke read Hereward's parchment of recommendation with a stony face. It was going to be a difficult audience.

'This is an outstanding recommendation, Hereward of Bourne. I know of Guiscard; he is a man not renowned for his excessive generosity, so his testament bears much

177

weight. I see you refused to be dubbed knight, but carry the Order of the Cotentin.'

'I choose to carry my name by birth, your Grace. I like to live a modest life.'

'So do I. I like that in a man. Modesty and discipline are vital to a long life as a warrior. Would you expect to serve me as a knight?'

'I would, your Grace.'

'But without the title?'

'Yes, your Grace.'

'You answer directly; I like that. And what of these men?'

While the Duke looked them up and down, Hereward introduced Einar, Martin and Alphonso, outlining in detail their various martial talents. Hereward was impressed to see that William was looking at their weapons, checking their appearance, assessing the condition of their clothes and armour and even checking the trim of their hair and beards. The Duke understood soldiers well, and knew how to tell the difference between good and bad.

'They would be my men-at-arms. I would pay them out of my allowance from you, my Lord Duke.'

William of Normandy smiled for the first time. 'You amuse me, Englishman. I don't usually pay my knights; their service comes to me as a tithe through the obligation owed from the grant of their lands and titles.'

'But they are your kinsmen, your Grace. I would serve you as a mercenary.'

'Mercenaries usually serve as infantry or levies, not as knights.'

'But I am an exceptional soldier.'

'Perhaps you are; you certainly don't lack confidence.'

The Duke rose from his ornately carved chair and stood directly in front of Hereward. He carried his Baculus with him, resting it in the bend of his right arm, and Hereward realized immediately that the Duke was left-handed.

'There aren't many men who can look me in the eye, Hereward of Bourne. I like my warriors to be big men; it puts the fear of God into the enemy. Do you see this? It has been carried by my family for many generations. Our Viking ancestors carried it on their conquests across the northern seas and it is spoken of in their sagas. It never leaves my side and is now the ducal mace of Normandy. My son will carry it, as will his son and grandson. By then, it will be the mace of England, the mace of a king.'

'Your Grace?'

'Yes, Hereward of Bourne, very soon, your England will be mine.'

'You intend to invade?'

William paused a moment to caress the Baculus, as if it were a holy relic. 'No need, although it would be a thrilling campaign. No, I am promised it. King Edward is half Norman, he was brought up here. We are cousins: his mother, Emma, was my great-aunt, sister of Duke Richard II. Edward has no children and my blood gives me primogeniture; Edward accepts this.'

The Duke rocked on his heels and he lifted himself a little so that he was slightly taller than Hereward. 'It is in the record. Several years ago, Edward sent Robert of Jumièges, a fellow Norman whom he had made Archbishop of Canterbury, to inform me in person that he had nominated me as his heir.'

'Yes, your Grace, but Harold Godwinson, Earl of

Wessex, is now the King's Earl Marshal. The Godwin family is very powerful, and they would not welcome a Norman on the throne of England.'

The Duke's guttural voice boomed around his Great Hall. 'They won't have any choice! I have sent word to the King, insisting that he sends the Earl of Wessex to me in Rouen, to confirm the succession and his acceptance of it. Edward has agreed and, when the time is right, the Earl will come to my court and swear his loyalty.'

Hereward was astonished. Was this known in England? Many Englishmen disliked Edward's Norman upbringing. If they knew he planned to hand the throne to the Duke of Normandy, there would be a rebellion among the thegns. After the years of struggle by the Saxons to rid themselves of Scandinavian rulers, they would not give up their land to a Norman without a fight.

'So, Hereward of Bourne, to the matter in hand. You give good answers; I like you. It is agreed. You will join me, and your companions will be your men-at-arms. I have many excursions planned and, if you prove your worth, your reward will be land in England when I am king. Until then, I will pay you modestly from my exchequer, but I expect you to earn it.'

'Thank you, your Grace. I should also tell you that I was an outlaw in England, banished by King Edward for an act of vengeance.'

'A deed done in anger?'

'No, my Lord, in cold blood.'

'That is the best kind of revenge; it gives you time to savour it. Worry not; I will set aside your banishment when I am king.' With that, he slapped Hereward on the back and asked him to sit with him. 'You will travel with me. In two days, I go on a tour of the provinces to inspect my army. While we travel, you can tell me more about your act of revenge.'

The Duke's tour of Normandy lasted until Christmas 1063, when tradition required him to be on his ducal throne in Rouen on Christmas Day to receive gifts from his loyal subjects.

Long days in the saddle with his men, in the wind, rain and snow of a Normandy winter, did not seem to discomfort William in the slightest. In fact, he seemed to thrive on it. Generally, he was in good humour, especially when he took a day off to go hunting. He was respected by his men and was usually excellent company. But there was a dark side to his character, which would emerge quickly and uncontrollably. His reactions to indiscipline or misdemeanours of any sort were always severe, usually violent and sometimes bestial. His face would redden to the colour of spilled blood, his eyes would protrude and his voice, harsh at the best of times, would thunder in anger. Everyone knew not to get in his way or catch his eye in such moments. Miscreants would be beaten or flogged; sometimes, he would assault them himself.

In one such incident, witnessed by Hereward, the Duke had to deal with a case of rape and murder committed by a young groom. When the man was brought before the Duke, he made the mistake of trying to excuse his crimes by saying that the girl was very pretty and had smiled at him. The Duke rose in fury and beat him to death with the Baculus, bellowing obscenities at him as he did so. It was the most violent attack on a man Hereward had ever witnessed, even on a battlefield.

He learned that it was not the first time the Duke had personally administered such a punishment.

When they returned to Rouen to celebrate Christmas, Hereward shared his concerns with the others. In particular, he sought their advice on the wisdom of continuing in William's service.

Martin was usually very talkative, but his mood had become morose in the last few days following news from England of the defeat and slaughter of his King, Gruffydd ap Llywelyn. It was a gruesome story.

At the beginning of 1063, King Edward ordered Harold, Earl of Wessex, to deal with the recalcitrant Welshman once and for all. He led a small band of mounted housecarls on a surprise winter raid on Gruffydd's royal enclosure on the River Clywd in Rhuddlan. Gruffydd escaped by the skin of his teeth, but Harold destroyed everything in sight, including his entire fleet.

In the summer, Harold went back to Wales with a much bigger army, moving up from the south, while his brother Tostig, Earl of Northumbria, attacked in the north. Three months of bloody clashes ensued, with Gruffydd trying to fight a guerrilla campaign with an ever-dwindling force. Eventually, Gruffydd had to go to ground, but not before a final act of defiance, when, tied to a hinny and suspended by their hair, he returned to Harold the severed heads of eight of his housecarls.

The English were even more vindictive in response, roaming the countryside and carrying out summary executions. The Welsh princes capitulated and sued for peace.

Harold, with brutal irony, asked for the head of Gruffydd as a condition of the settlement. His own people relentlessly pursued the King into the wild and desolate mountains of Snowdonia. When he was finally cornered, alone and defenceless, he was bound like a wild boar, hung upside down and beheaded.

Harold had been conciliatory in victory. Gruffydd's brothers were made earls in Wales as vassals of King Edward. He persuaded the King to revoke the law banning intermarriage between the English and the Welsh and, as an example to all, agreed to take Gruffydd's widow, Ealdgyth, as his wife.

Martin had much to reflect on in the passing of his king. However, he was firm in his views about the Duke: he did not like him and argued that they should find another employer.

Alphonso was also clear on the subject of service to the Duke. It was cold in Normandy and he wanted to return to the south. For him it was simply a matter of climate.

Einar was level-headed and considered, as usual. He pointed out that there was no finer army in the whole of Europe. The pay was good; Rouen was a fine city and – if Edward had nominated him as his successor – then, one day, William would be the rightful King of England. Ingigerd and Maria agreed with their men, but Torfida was strangely quiet. For her, the months since their arrival in Normandy had passed quickly. She was busy during the week, tutoring the offspring of the rich of Rouen, and on Saturdays she helped the nuns with the poor children at the alms house of Rouen Abbey.

Unusually, Torfida spoke last about the Duke. 'If William

becomes king after Edward's death, there will be a war, because the English nobles will not accept it. Then there are the Scandinavians; Harald Hardrada and Svein Estrithson, King of the Danes, both have envious eyes on England. We could easily have another Scandinavian ruling at Winchester. England could become an unholy battleground between three ferocious armies –'

Maria interrupted Torfida in full flow. 'You paint a frightening picture, Torfida, but what of us? What do we do?'

Torfida's reply was succinct. 'As for us, Maria, we follow a path that has been pointing towards England ever since we left Melfi.'

Hereward had been thinking carefully about all that had been said. 'Maria, it is always your choice whether you continue with us on our journey. Torfida and I have chosen our path and we will follow it. The rest of you must find your destinies. If you think they are with us, we will always be in your debt; if you choose another path, we will understand and you will go with our blessing.'

Ingigerd responded without hesitation. 'I think I can speak for all of us. Where you go, we go; it's as simple as that.'

Torfida embraced each of them in turn and thanked them for their loyalty.

Hereward returned to the vexing subject of the English succession. 'It is not Edith who has failed to provide an heir; it's the other way round. Edward likes boys, it's well known. They say Edith is a virgin and that the King only married her to cement the alliance with her father, Earl Godwin. A queen can't sprout an heir if her king doesn't plant his royal seed.'

Torfida responded, repeating her catechism about destiny. 'Perhaps you're right. But my point is, a great war is coming and, somehow, we are going to be a part of it. I am certain that our journey has been leading us to it, so we must continue what we are doing and wait to see what our destiny brings us.'

'I cannot fight for the Normans against the English – they are my people.'

'And mine, Hereward. I am not suggesting that we fight our own people. We should continue as we are for now; we can make our decision about what to do when the time comes. This Duke is a fearsome man, but we have been delivered here for a reason. That reason will soon become clear, I know it.'

Hereward looked around the table.

They all nodded, even Martin.

They would stay.

William returned to his relentless quest for military excellence in early January 1064, ensuring that Hereward and the men spent several more months with the Duke in training throughout Normandy. Torfida and the family stayed in Rouen.

As time passed, it occurred to Hereward that since they had arrived in Normandy, Torfida had rarely talked about the Talisman.

It was as if she knew it had brought them to where they needed to be and that it would lie dormant until the next phase of their lives came to pass.

11. The Oath

The next crucial phase in the lives of Hereward and Torfida began, like many important happenings, without warning.

It was early May 1064, a warm spring day with nature in full bud. The Duke was mounted on his destrier in the middle of a Norman conroi, a powerful squadron of twenty-five mounted warriors led by a knight. They were practising an attack with their spears pointed downwards like lances, a devastatingly effective cavalry technique if carried out in a disciplined formation. The Duke knew that if ever it came to a fight against the English housecarls, his mounted conroi would have to break their legendary shield wall.

Riders cresting the horizon with messages for the Duke were commonplace, but these three had an urgency about them that was immediately apparent. When they reached William, they and their horses were sweating profusely and the men relayed their message breathlessly.

An important English earl had been shipwrecked on the coast, near the mouth of the River Somme, in the lands of Guy, Count of Ponthieu, William's brother-in-law and his vassal. Guy had seized the earl under the Lagan Law of shipwrecks and was holding him in Montreuil, from where he would be ransomed for a sum befitting his status. One of the ship's English crew had escaped and fled to Rouen – to seek Duke William's help, and with news that the shipwrecked mariner was none other than the Earl Marshal of England, Harold Godwinson, Earl of Wessex.

William bellowed at his messenger almost before he had finished his report. 'Go to my brother, Odo, and tell him that he must take fifty men to that fool Ponthieu and have Earl Harold delivered to me immediately. I will welcome him into Normandy at Eu, six days from now. Go! Go quickly!'

William was riding hard to Rouen within the hour.

Harold Godwinson must have been both relieved and impressed as he crossed the wooden pontoon on the River Bresle at Eu. On the opposite bank was the substantial presence of the Duke, surrounded by a grandiose assortment of counts, bishops, sheriffs, knights and 250 of his finest warriors. Not only that: as a mark of his beneficence, the Duke had paid Guy of Ponthieu a preposterous sum for the Earl's ransom.

The show of respect between the two men, as they hailed one another with their swords and then shook hands, was sincere. Here were the two most important warlords in north-western Europe – one already called 'sub-regulus' to King Edward, the other a king in all but name, lord of the most powerful province in the region.

As William and Harold rode off together towards Rouen, Hereward could not help but notice their similarities rather than their differences. Both were exceptionally tall, although Harold was slightly shorter; both were fair, one very blond, the other a distinct redhead, and both were proud and self-confident. They were talking animatedly in Norman French, and seemed in good humour.

For the next few days, the Duke and the Earl were rarely seen. Their discussions were held behind closed doors in William's palace at Rouen. Nevertheless, the rumour soon spread around the city that, indeed, this was the visit William had said would happen and that the Earl of Wessex had come to pay his respects and acknowledge the Duke of Normandy as his future king.

Rouen was alive with excitement. The English King was already sixty years of age; it could not be long before William's accession came to pass. England was known to be a rich land with prodigous harvests and sturdy beasts, a treasure trove waiting to be plundered by every opportunist in Normandy.

As Hereward and Torfida sat by their hearth and discussed the dramatic arrival, their thoughts moved quickly to the motives of Harold Godwinson. Surely, the Earl felt great unease in bowing to Duke William? He must also know of the reputation of the Normans? If William became king, Normans would rapidly fill the bishoprics and supplant the earls and thegns.

There would be war.

Perhaps he was striking a bargain with William and they were planning England's future together, with Harold negotiating guarantees about his own position?

Or would he simply take the throne himself after King Edward's death?

The next morning, the Captain of the Duke's personal squadron and two sergeants-at-arms arrived at the farmhouse and summoned Hereward to the Duke's palace.

On hearing the news, Torfida jumped to her feet and

grabbed Hereward excitedly. 'This is the moment we've been waiting for; you are going to meet the Earl. By the time he leaves Normandy, we will know what we must do. But, be careful, there are great forces at work here; these are powerful and dangerous men.'

When Hereward reached the ducal palace, he marched up to the richly carved throne with the brisk step of a confident man. Queen Matilda sat to the Duke's left, Harold was on his right.

Hereward bowed as the Duke introduced him.

'My Lord Earl, this is Hereward of Bourne, a man you may know.'

'I do, your Grace. I proclaimed him banished at Winchester some years ago.'

'Indeed, he told me all about it; he has led an interesting life since then. Tell the Earl of Wessex your story, but spare us the details.'

Hereward bowed again and gave a short account of his chance meeting with Gruffydd, King of the Welsh, and of the Battle of Hereford. He described his involvement in the affairs of Macbeth, then recounted his long journey to Italy and his experiences in the service of Robert Guiscard in Apulia and Sicily.

Harold listened impassively before responding. 'A great adventure, your Grace, but there is little in it to commend him to me. Although he nobly served your kin in Apulia, he has spent the rest of his time fighting for our enemies.'

'Ah, but in fairness, my Lord Earl, he was an outlaw, cast out by his people. Besides, the two enemies you speak of are both dead, and Scotland and Wales now bow to Edward at Winchester.'

'They will soon owe fealty to Westminster, on the Thames near London, your Grace. The King is building a fine new palace and cathedral there.'

'So that is where I shall be crowned?'

Harold looked discomforted at the Duke's provocative question. 'Quite so, your Grace.'

Hereward scrutinized Harold as he answered. He spoke softly and submissively, as if he did not want to agree, but had to. Hereward sensed that Harold was cornered – not fearful, but trapped. He was not a man to be easily frightened; nevertheless, he seemed conspicuously uncomfortable.

'Well, what do you say, my Lord Earl? Will you take him? He is a fine warrior and one of your own.'

Harold looked at Hereward again, this time with a hint of the warmth of kinship in his eyes. 'His Grace, the Duke, has recommended that you accompany me on his new campaign against the Bretons, an expedition in which he has generously asked me to be at his side. I have listened carefully to Duke William. I accept that you left England without help or favour and within the terms of your banishment. I also agree that, apart from your choice of employer, your service in Wales and Scotland does you credit. I am told that you are a fine soldier; I am happy to have you in my hearthtroop, Hereward of Bourne.'

Hereward knew instantly that the die was cast, as Torfida had predicted.

Brittany was ruled by Count Conan II, but his rule was precarious. The Bretons had fierce tribal loyalties, and Conan had difficulty holding the tribal fiefdoms together. William had formed an alliance with Rivallon of Dol, a rogue Breton whose domain was in the border region. He had recently come under attack from Conan's army and had appealed to William for help.

This gave the Duke the opportunity to invade Brittany and make his western border secure all the way to the Atlantic.

Ten days later, William's army was in the field, in battle order, and approaching Normandy's border with Brittany. The Duke's army was ready to flex its muscles and demonstrate to Harold the power of Normandy's military machine.

With the towering citadel of Mont St Michel in the distance, Harold was impressed by the army of Normandy as it marched across in full battle regalia. There were over 2,500 men, the elite of William's forces. Harold headed a contingent of forty Englishmen. Just behind him, carried by two of his housecarls, were the Earl's war banners: the Dragon of Wessex and his own personal ensign, the Fighting Man. The English standards were flying as part of the colours of a Norman army, which, if events were to unfold as seemed likely, might soon be an occupying army in England.

They crossed the border with Brittany at the River Couesnon. Barely ten miles further on, Lord Rivallon was besieged behind the walls of Dol by Conan's army. Duke William ordered a halt and then gave instructions to make ready a forward camp so that they could move off before dawn and attack on the cusp of daylight.

That evening, the strategy was agreed: with the infantry in reserve, William would advance with his cavalry and mount an immediate attack. The Earl of Wessex, his knights, his housecarls and Hereward, with his three men-at-arms, would form their own conroi, and would attack second in line of precedence. They would be to the right of William's personal conroi, the Matilda Squadron, each of whom carried on their lances a sky-blue riband, the favours of Duchess Matilda.

The attack the next day was swift and decisive. The Bretons were caught in the open, largely unprepared; they had expected a traditional pitched battle and were surprised by a cavalry attack in semi-darkness. Most of their cavalrymen were mounted, but not drawn up sufficiently well to rebuff a full-frontal charge. William's attack at full gallop was an awesome sight: 300 horses sweeping across the contours of the countryside in twelve tightly formed conroi, in three waves, four conroi abreast.

It was futile for the Bretons to try to engage. Count Conan, realizing that the day was lost before it had begun, joined his men in flight. When the horn sounded for lances to be couched, a great roar went up from the walls of Dol to match the thunder of the hooves of the Norman horde, and the slaughter began. For the Norman cavalry it was like sticking pigs in the forest, as they cut the Bretons down one by one.

Eventually, some pockets of resistance did form, as a few men decided to turn and fight. In one incident, a large group of Bretons managed to unseat three Norman knights by luring them into soft ground. The Normans were obviously in peril and Harold, leading the nearest conroi, went to their aid. He ordered his men to dismount and attack on foot, to avoid the same fate that had befallen the heavy Norman horses. With his housecarls behind him and Hereward and his companions in the midst of them, he set about the enemy.

It was an impressive onslaught, conducted in William's full view. Harold, advancing at the point of a wedge of flailing yet precisely choreographed English battle-axes, cut his way through the melee. Using their shields as a solid defensive wall, and striking either side of them with their axes, the Anglo-Saxon housecarls demonstrated to William their renowned battle technique at its best. Hereward was in his element, not only because it was hand-to-hand combat, but because the men he was fighting with were his kith and kin and he was but a yard from Harold, the Earl Marshal of England. Supported by Martin, Einar and Alphonso, he kept a close eye on Harold, constantly protecting his flanks and rear.

It did not take long to rescue the beleaguered Normans and get them mounted on their destriers. William was doubly delighted: the Bretons had been routed and taught a lesson they would never forget; and his English guest had not only witnessed the victory, but had also played a heroic part in it.

The Duke decided that he liked the Earl of Wessex; he was a brave warrior and a man worthy of standing with Normans in battle. He hoped that, following his succession, Harold Godwinson would agree to be his Earl Marshal and thus avert a revolt by the English earls.

William's dreams of wealth and power were becoming more and more tangible by the day.

Harold talked at great length to Hereward on the march back from Dol. The Earl was impressed by the carnage wrought by Hereward's Great Axe during the skirmish and thanked him for staying so close to him. Harold described himself as a soldier at heart, a man who felt more comfortable on the battlefield than at court. Nevertheless, he had gradually grown to respect King Edward, whose effete manner and Norman sympathies he had initially despised. At first, he had refused to travel to Normandy for a meeting with William, but the King had finally convinced him. He was a persuasive man and a shrewd and clever ruler who had done much to bring stability and prosperity to England. Now that his long reign was in its twilight years, Edward feared the uncouth barbarians from Scandinavia, especially Harald Hardrada, the King of Norway.

Edward was convinced that to secure England's future, he had to forge an alliance with the Normans. Hemmed in by the French to the south, and the Holy Roman Empire to the east, the Normans needed land and a kingdom to call their own. In exchange, England would get what it needed: a bridge to mainland Europe and its sophistication; the Norman spirit of adventure and conquest; and their rigid system of social discipline. To achieve this, Edward knew that William would have to be his successor; there was no other choice.

Hereward was appalled to hear Harold's account of Edward's reasoning. It would mean the end of everything he cared for as an Englishman. England's traditional Anglo-Saxon culture would be transformed from its pastoral simplicity into the harsh efficiency of a Norman state.

He decided to say what was on his mind. 'But, my Lord, you could be King.'

Harold smiled at him warmly. 'Most people think that I

want the throne, but I'm a soldier, not a king. Edward says the days of warrior kings will soon be over, that there are far more important things for a king to do than rampage across the country fighting battles.'

'I'm not sure, my Lord. The Duke of Normandy is a warrior; he fights his own battles and rules his domain as firmly as any in Europe.'

'The King says men like the Duke of Normandy and Harald Hardrada are a dying breed; that England must be ready to change from its ancient customs and practices and become a land with an ordered system of government like the empires of Europe.'

'Perhaps, but I still believe you could guide England's future just as forcefully as William.'

'The King doesn't think I have a good enough claim. Although my Anglo-Saxon pedigree is noble, I have no claim to the Cerdician line of Edward's family; that honour rests with Edgar the Atheling. Both the Duke and Hardrada have blood much closer to the King's.'

'But you would be the choice of the Witan; all the earls would support you.'

'Edward doesn't believe kings should be chosen by the earls and the thegns; he thinks that it leads to intrigue and anarchy. He says that monarchs should rule by dint of their bloodline, so that succession is beyond argument.'

'My Lord, I can't begin to think of England under Norman rule. All Anglo-Saxons will fight to the last man to prevent that.'

'I think you're right; our people will fight and thousands will die. Edward knows that if I support the Duke and he gives me and my fellow earls appropriate concessions, we might create an alliance that most of England could be persuaded to accept and war would be averted. However, what no one knows is whether William would make such a bargain and, if he did, whether he would keep it.'

Sensing that these matters would be talked of many times before a decision was made, Harold abruptly changed the subject of the conversation to a preoccupation more typical of soldiers on campaign. He reminisced about the seductive qualities of Edith Swan-Neck, who had given him five children, before moving on to the merits of Norman women. Few had impressed him, but there was a young girl at William's court to whom he had taken a particular liking. If William would agree, he intended to bed her as soon as they reached Rouen. He had been away for many weeks and a romp with a soft and slender young beauty was long overdue, especially one as sweet as the girl he had in mind.

Hereward smiled inwardly at Harold's earthy manner. There was nothing devious or complicated about him; he had simple virtues and easy vices, just like his soldiers. The more Hereward thought about it, the more he was convinced that, after Edward's death, England had to be ruled by Harold. Plain man or not, Harold would do what was right according to the old ways: merciless in battle, magnanimous in victory; harsh with wrongdoers, kind to the righteous.

Hereward looked at the Earl of Wessex riding beside him and, in that moment, resolved that he would do all in his power to persuade him to become king, and that if he took power, he would stand at his side and fight to the death for him and his kingdom. He reached for the Talisman, grasped it under his smock and added another personal conviction: should Harold be crowned King of England, he would place the Talisman around his neck and bring to an end his odyssey as its envoy.

On the evening of the triumphant return to Rouen, William hosted a celebratory banquet in the Great Hall of his palace. William retained control throughout the proceedings, while most around him became more and more inebriated and raucous.

Harold was no exception. William had granted him his young concubine, and he had eyes only for her during the feast. But William had devised a trap which he was about to spring.

The Duke had taken care to invite the Bishops of Cluny, Paris and Rheims to the great celebration to bear non-partisan witness to the devastating coup de grâce he was about to deliver.

The Duke rose with a solemnity of purpose and addressed Harold directly. There was an instantaneous silence among the gathering, abrupt enough to suggest a rehearsed event.

'My Lord Earl, Harold Godwinson, Earl of Wessex, Eatl Marshal to King Edward of England, our noble and esteemed friend from the north, I invite you to join me in an oath.'

Harold shook himself out of his drunken and lustful euphoria. Hereward looked at him anxiously. As in a game of chess, a disguised gambit was about to be revealed, a move that would seal the fate of a kingdom. Harold, swaying a little, joined William at the head of his great oak dining table.

'In the presence of our revered guests, my Lords temporal

and ecclesiastical, I do swear, when God determines it should be so, to place myself at the service of England as its King in succession to Edward, that most wise and noble of monarchs. I hereby further swear that I entrust the command of my army in England to my gracious and worthy friend, the noble Lord, the Earl of Wessex, who will serve as my Earl Marshal, answering to no one in England or Normandy save me.'

William beckoned Harold closer to him, smiling benignly as he did so. 'My lord Earl, place your hands on mine on this ancient Bible, carried here by the monks of Mont St Michel, the most holy relic in our land, and swear with me this oath.'

William had called 'check' but Harold knew it was 'mate'; there was nothing for him to do but to swear. Harold pulled himself up, found some clarity of thought and voice through the fog of inebriation, placed his hands on William's on the Holy Book and uttered the fateful words.

'I do swear.'

Even before Harold sat down, the Norman scribes had begun to commit the proceedings to parchment.

History's course was set.

William looked triumphant, but Harold's jaw was set, his face stern and his fury barely disguised. The future of England, the destiny of the Anglo-Saxons, and of all the peoples of Britain, had turned in a trice.

It was a moment that would seal the fate of the British Isles for generations to come.

12. Return to England

There was great excitement in Rouen and throughout Normandy at the news of Harold's acknowledgement of William's right of succession. To the Normans, it was the penultimate step on the road to vast new wealth and power. Now, it was only a matter of waiting for the ageing English King to die.

Four days after he had sworn his calamitous oath to William, Harold agreed to take food with Hereward and Torfida at their farmhouse outside the city.

Harold was very subdued when he arrived. Since the banquet, he had taken too much solace in flasks of the Duke's wine; he looked worn out, with bloodshot eyes and swollen eyelids.

At first he played with the four young daughters of the household, who were then sent off to bed before the eight adults sat down to eat. The Earl obviously enjoyed the boisterousness of the children. Torfida was impressed, noticing how gentle he was with them and how they warmed to him, despite his imposing size and all the finery of his office. Harold began to relax as the adults shared a horn of wine, some pleasantries and good food. When Harold began to talk about the spider's web of political intrigue in which he was trapped, the other members of the family excused themselves, realizing that sensitive issues were about to be raised, leaving Hereward and Torfida to their discussions with Earl Harold.

'Torfida, I have talked with Hereward about the unfortunate circumstances I find myself in, and he has offered me firm words of advice. I hear your knowledge and wisdom extend to many things. What would your counsel be?'

In response, Torfida gave a lucid account of her time with Hereward.

She then talked about her father and how he had predicted her destiny and that of Hereward. 'He could predict the climate in the affairs of men. He knew from where the political wind blew and sensed when a storm was brewing in a kingdom's skies.'

'He sounds like the old seers at the court of the Danish kings, in the days before King Edward.'

'Seers are wise men, my Lord. My father was the wisest of them all, I believe.'

'What would he have said to me?'

Torfida looked solemn. 'Forgive my forthright answer, my Lord, but you have asked me a direct question. You are a man of noble spirit. You know right from wrong by second nature, because your heart is good and true. You hold the future of England in your hands. William's avarice knows no bounds and he has been promised the throne of England. No one can stop him taking it – except you.'

'I have sworn a holy oath in front of many witnesses. Word will already be on its way to Rome. I cannot renege on an oath.'

'But if King Edward were to change his mind about the succession, the oath would be null and void. No matter how reluctant you were, you acted only in good faith, as your King had asked.'

'But the King will not be swayed.'

'My Lord, you must tell him what Duke William is like and of the cruelty he will mete out to the people of England.'

Hereward reinforced Torfida's view with his opinion of William. It was a view that Harold had been reluctant to hear during their march back from Brittany.

This time Hereward did not seek permission. 'I have seen many acts of ruthlessness in war and many atrocious things done in the pursuit of vengeance, but this man is like no other. There is a sinister darkness in him. Not only is he driven by perverted passions, he is also a master of intrigue and deceit. It is a frightening combination.'

Harold thought for several minutes about what had been said to him, before rising to stand by the fire, kicking at its ashes. 'I miss the fire in my hall at Glastonbury. I pine for England and a people I care about so much, but it is hard for me to accept your argument, no matter how forcefully you put it.

'I may be the Earl Marshal of England and the Earl of Wessex, but my family is not of royal descent. Godwin, my father, was an exceptional man who elevated our family from obscurity to be the most powerful in England. His father, Wulfnoth, was like you, Hereward. He was a local thegn, from Compton, a small village in Sussex. Godwin was a splendid warrior, became a favourite of King Cnut and rose rapidly. Cnut made him Earl of Wessex. Now, four of my brothers are earls of England and my sister, Edith, is King Edward's queen; all thanks to my father's prowess.

But, despite our positions, we are new blood and there is much barely concealed resentment among some of the old English families. So imagine my anxiety at now contemplating becoming King.'

He paused, not moving, or even blinking; he just stared, wide-eyed, as the reflections of the flames flickered across his face.

Then, he stirred from his musing. 'I mustn't tarry any longer with idle thoughts. I have stayed long enough here in the land of the Normans. I have done my worst. I wish it were otherwise, but the deed is done.' He turned to Hereward and Torfida with a new resolve. 'England beckons, my friends. I must speak with the King about all that has happened here. Hereward, if I seek your release from the Duke, will you return to England with me? I will gladly have you in my service as a captain in my housecarls. Torfida, you can bring your wisdom and fill our heads with knowledge and ideas.'

'My Lord, Hereward is banished from England. There are many who would not welcome his presence.'

'It is ten years since he was made an outlaw. I will recommend him to the King as part of my retinue. His banishment will be revoked; you have my word on that.'

Hereward answered for both of them. 'My Lord, we will be honoured to serve you and return to England. We pledge ourselves to you and to the people of England with all our hearts.'

It took only a day for word to reach Hereward that Harold had secured his release from Duke William. In two days' time they would ride north to Fécamp, where Harold's ship was at anchor, to embark for England.

Before their departure, Hereward was summoned by William for an audience.

'You have obviously made a good impression on the Earl of Wessex. He was most insistent that you accompany him to England.'

'The Earl has told me that my banishment will be revoked. It is a very important opportunity for me, and I thank you for releasing me from your service.'

'Is Normandy not to your liking? I thought I had found a warrior who would be in my service for many years to come.'

'My Lord Duke, I hope I have served you well, but I never imagined that one day I might have the chance to return to my home.' Hereward found himself employing a subtle feint, knowing full well that William was weighing his position and manoeuvring himself to his best advantage. 'But I am not entirely lost to you, your Grace. If I now go into the service of the Earl of Wessex, then, in accordance with the oath you have both sworn, I will soon be returned to you. When you are made King of England, the Earl of Wessex will be your Earl Marshal. He will answer to you, as I will to him, and we will both do your bidding.'

'I wonder about you, Hereward of Bourne. Are you far shrewder than your muscle-bound frame might suggest, or are you just well rehearsed by that clever wife of yours? You have served me well enough, but there is a reticence about you that makes me think you are not truly loyal.'

'Your Grace, I hope that I have been diligent in my service to you. My desire to serve the Earl of Wessex is not meant to be disrespectful to you in any way, quite the opposite. I have learned much about Norman ways that will be of great benefit to the English army.'

Hereward was becoming adept at the diplomatic language of dukes and kings and hoped that William did not notice the irony of his answer.

'Train them well; I will need a strong army to protect my northern borders against the Scandinavians. Fair winds to England; I will see you there in due course. You will be at my coronation in Westminster.'

'Thank you, your Grace.'

As Hereward turned and reached the door of the Great Hall for the last time, he congratulated himself on the successful outcome of his verbal sparring with William. He thought he had done well in responding to William's doubts about his sudden desire to throw in his lot with the Earl of Wessex.

However, just as he was about to step through the doorway, he was suddenly robbed of his moment of satisfaction.

'Hereward, remember, when we meet again, I will be your King and you will be my subject. You would be wise to remember that.'

With eleven extra bodies in the Earl of Wessex's flagship, conditions were cramped for the crossing to England.

For the children, it was their first experience under sail and a daunting one as, mid-Channel, the ship began to heave in a heavy sea. Torfida told them some of her exotic stories and Martin sang their favourite lullabies; as he sang, the entire ship's company listened in silence. The only other sounds were the cracking of the great sail and the creaking of the vessel's timbers as they were tossed and twisted by the waves.

For Hereward and Torfida it was a poignant moment. They had been away for a long time and were returning to a land they thought they would never see again.

For Harold, with every league they travelled, he was getting closer to a kingdom, the fate of which would soon be his to determine.

They made landfall close to the mouth of the river Rother in Sussex and, within an hour, were tying up at the small settlement of Rye in the manor of Rameslie. Men were despatched to find horses for their long journey along the Downs to Winchester, which, as it was mid-November and the wind from the west was likely to be raw, would be a demanding ride.

Traversing the Downs at speed was an exhilarating experience; even Alphonso, who did not care much for northern climes, appreciated the sense of vitality it brought. It had been agreed that Hereward and his party would stay in Bosham, the harbour settlement of Chichester, where Harold had lands and from where he had set sail for Normandy. Harold would see the King privately at Winchester, to gauge his mood and to hear his current thoughts about the succession. If the King could be persuaded to see him, Harold would send for Hereward, whose first-hand experience might persuade Edward to reconsider his nomination of William as his heir.

The two parties went their separate ways at Arundel. Harold took twelve men north-west towards Winchester, while Hereward and the rest of the retinue headed directly west on the old road to Chichester and Bosham.

To everyone's dismay, several months passed, during which little was heard from Harold.

The inference was obvious: all was not well with the King. The winter of 1064 turned to the spring of 1065, and Hereward and his loyal band busied themselves to help the people of Bosham. Although they were guests of the Lord of the Manor, they were still a burden on the resources of the area and its people, so they dutifully bent their backs to the mundanity of agriculture and the tedium of domesticity.

To everyone's relief, word eventually came from Harold in May. The King was to travel to London to see his new abbey church at Westminster. After many years of toil, Edward's masterpiece, the epitome of his ambition to build a new England, was finished. The most impressive structure in his realm, it was built in the Romanesque style of his Norman kin.

Harold's message told them to meet him in London on the first day of June. The fact that they had been summoned to London must mean that there had been a development of some kind. Hereward and Torfida travelled alone, while the others went west to Glastonbury, Harold's seat in Wessex.

London was a thriving community within the old Roman fortress, and an important strategic stronghold. Under Edward's influence, new houses and wharves were being built all around the old Roman city – to the east at Wapping, across the River Thames at Southwark and Lambeth, and to the west around his new cathedral at Westminster.

They had been told to meet at a large house on Ludgate Hill, the home of Edith Swan-Neck, who enjoyed the bustle of London much more than she did the sedate atmosphere of Glastonbury. Her house was a sight to behold, decorated with fine furniture, silks, tapestries and silver plate more fitting for a queen than a concubine. As her name suggested, she was statuesquely tall with a long, willowy neck. Her blonde hair was tied tightly and cascaded down the length of her back. Her svelte frame was draped in a beautiful crimson silk dress, embroidered with a fine gold border and topped by an upright collar. She had slim hips, a taut stomach – remarkable for a woman who had produced five children – and, to the fascination of everyone who saw her, prodigious breasts, accentuated by her slender build.

Edith was not self-conscious about her womanly assets. She did not try to disguise her femaleness, but was proud of her sexuality. Her face was not beautiful, but it had strikingly sensual features that struck Hereward immediately: strong cheekbones and jaw, an aquiline nose, large emerald-green eyes and full lips.

Harold greeted Hereward and Torfida, before making the introductions. Edith displayed the same flirtatiousness with Torfida as she did towards men, but Torfida responded warmly. She recognized that Edith was a woman who commanded respect and was able to hold her own in a man's world.

'I'm afraid I have few intellectual gifts, Torfida, but I try to make the best of the generous assets God has given me. How I wish I had been granted your marvellous blend of beauty and brains. Hereward is a lucky man . . .' She grabbed both Hereward and Torfida. 'And you're a lucky woman; look at him, what a beast he is.' She laughed aloud, and pulled them over to sit with her.

The four of them talked for several hours as they enjoyed

good English fare and copious amounts of mead. It had been a long excursion in Normandy for Harold, and an even longer exile for Hereward and Torfida. There was much to talk about and, for the most part, it was domestic and mundane chatter.

There would be ample opportunity only too soon for a debate about the perils facing Harold and England.

On the second evening at Ludgate Hill, the conversation finally turned to the pressing issue of the succession to the English throne.

Edward's health was beginning to decline and he was becoming more and more sullen and cantankerous. Harold did not think he had much more than a few months to live, perhaps less. He had spoken to the King many times on the subject of the succession, but Edward remained steadfast in his view that England needed a new future and that it had to come from Normandy.

Hereward came to the point quickly. 'My Lord, did you suggest yourself to the King as his successor?'

'Now is not the time. Edward will talk of only one other candidate besides William: Edgar, the true Atheling, a Saxon of the ancient Cerdic bloodline of the West Saxons, and the grandson of Edward's half-brother, Edmund Ironside, who was King of England fifty years ago.'

The Cerdician kings could trace their ancestry back many generations through Alfred the Great to Egbert, King of the West Saxons, and, beyond him, to the original Saxon settlers of England, a lineage spanning hundreds of years. Except for the recent rule of the Scandinavians, every King of England had been of Cerdician blood.

'Unfortunately, Edgar is only a boy of fourteen, and the King doesn't think he will be strong enough to keep the Scandinavians at bay. He remains convinced that only William can do that.'

Hereward saw an opportunity for a compromise position. 'But what if you were to be the Atheling's Regent? With your army behind him, England could repel Hardrada and anyone else, even William.'

'Sadly, Edward remains preoccupied with moving England closer to Europe. Nominating Edgar to succeed him would, in his mind, move England further away from his ambition for its future.'

'When we spoke in Normandy, you said that Edward believed that kings should be born, not chosen by the Witan or by popular acclaim. Surely he contradicts himself by avoiding a successor who is of true royal blood?'

'There are many contradictions in the character of our King. As for the right to rule through blood, if he thought Edgar would support Norman ways and bring more Normans to his realm, he might agree. But Edgar is a Saxon, part of a hidebound tradition the King is determined to break. And remember, Edgar was born in the home of the Magyars, in the land of Hungary. His father sought protection from their king after he had been exiled to Sweden when Cnut the Dane became our king. He had never set foot in England until a few years ago, and there are even doubts about how loyal the Saxon earls would be to him.'

Harold continued his discourse, outlining a story in which he himself played a controversial role. 'Edgar's father, Edward, was announced as the Atheling, Edward's chosen successor, in 1054. Two years later, I was charged with bringing the young Edward from Hungary and escorting him and his family to England. He arrived laden with treasure and to much excitement. Here was the son of Edmund Ironside, grandson of Athelred, great-grandson of the good King Edgar, the perfect Saxon solution to the dilemma of the childless King Edward. Not a warrior by any means, but an astute and honourable young prince. Most importantly for the King's long-term plan for his realm, he had been raised in the heart of sophisticated Europe, amid the heritage of Charlemagne's noble tradition, a legacy that the King much admired. Edward was thrilled: his prayers for an heir, whom he could nurture and mould, had been answered.

'Then, within days of the Prince's arrival, there was a catastrophe. He fell seriously ill at Rochester and, to this day, no one knows why. He wasn't even well enough to travel to Winchester to see the King. He couldn't eat, his bowels emptied like a torrent and he died in just four days. The physicians suspected an assassin had poisoned him.'

'It could only have been at William the Bastard's bidding!' Hereward spat out his instantaneous condemnation, remembering the gleam in the Duke's eye as he contemplated the prospect of the English throne.

Edith joined the conversation animatedly. 'Many said it was Harold who had planned it, as he had most to gain, and that I, a wicked temptress, had given the boy a deadly potion.'

Harold remembered the events with evident irritation. 'Of course, the King knew I wasn't responsible. Why would I travel all the way to the banks of the Danube to rescue the lad and then have him poisoned in Rochester?' Harold paused and looked at his companions with a forlorn expression, seemingly tired of the intrigues of emperors, kings and princes. 'So there you have it. Edgar is now the true Atheling of the Saxon line.'

Torfida, like Hereward, could see the potential for Edgar to succeed in his minority, with Harold as Regent. 'What is young Edgar like? Could he be King?'

'He is like any fourteen-year-old boy: a callow youth with not even a hint of fluff on his face. He has lived a soft life at court and was born into a culture very different from our own. When they arrived here, he and his sisters spoke almost no English, although they speak it well now. Anyway, regardless of his merits, the King won't hear of it. He was stubborn enough before; now he is impossible. I told him that I travelled back to England with you, an Englishman who had been close to William, who could give him a true and accurate account of the Duke's character and his credentials as the next King of England, but he flew into a rage. He still refuses to see you under any circumstances. We are at an impasse.'

'Perhaps he would listen to me.' Torfida was not averse to making bold statements, but this was one of her most audacious. 'I would not be overawed. I know it is unlikely that the King would listen, but if Earl Harold introduces me, and I have a brief moment with him, there is a small stone I could cast to see if it will make a ripple in the affairs of England.'

Harold and Edith were intrigued, but Hereward realized immediately what Torfida was alluding to.

'Hereward, give me the Talisman.'

'But Torfida, your father guessed that Queen Emma may well have offered the Talisman to Edward and he rejected it. On the other hand, she may never even have considered giving it to him. In either case, the King will not recognize its power.'

'You're right, Hereward, but we have to go where the Talisman leads us. I feel its power is directing our destiny once again.'

Harold and Edith spoke almost as one. 'Torfida, you must explain.'

Torfida described how Queen Emma had given the Talisman to Torfida's father, the Old Man of the Wildwood. She then chronicled its legendary pedigree.

Harold was sceptical, but Edith had heard stories about it as a girl.

'I thought it was a myth. Your father must have been a very special man for the Queen to entrust him with it.'

Torfida's vivid account, with Edith's support, convinced Harold that there was some merit in her suggestion that she should try to meet the King.

'It is possible I could introduce you. Your credentials as a scholar are impeccable, and the King is an intellectual and a philosopher; he might just warm to you. Hereward, you should go to Glastonbury immediately and join your companions. It is you who sends the King into a rage. He knows about your service with Gruffydd and Macbeth; he never forgets an enemy and never forgives one. As your guarantor, I have assured the King that you will do nothing and go nowhere, except under my strict authority. I will tell him I've sent you well away from London to train with my housecarls at Glastonbury; that will placate him a little.

'As for Torfida, the ideal moment will be shortly after the King's architect has handed over the key to the great oak door of the new abbey, while his choir sings for him and he is admiring his new creation. I will tell him of your wisdom and knowledge of the great buildings of the ancient world, and that you have come to admire his new work.'

Torfida seemed enthused, but looked to Hereward for reassurance.

He responded uncertainly. 'I am reluctant to leave you here in London while I sit in Glastonbury with the fate of the throne hanging in the balance. It is a plan worth trying, but how will you switch the conversation from the wonders and intricacies of his abbey to the succession of the throne of England?'

Harold responded to Hereward's question. 'That will be my responsibility. I will remind him that Torfida was in the service of the Duke. Then, if he is prepared to listen, you must tell him about the Duke's wild temper and about the personal beatings and executions.'

Torfida hesitated and took a deep breath. 'I must trust that he doesn't realize I never actually met the Duke, and that it is Hereward who witnessed these things.'

Edith nodded at Torfida's words, and smiled. 'So, my Lord, you agree.'

'I do.'

Hereward was ready to leave for Wessex early the next morning. Torfida would stay with Edith in London, to be ready for her meeting with the King. After Hereward had kissed Torfida goodbye and mounted his horse, Harold took leave of him.

'This is our final throw of the dice. Torfida is a brilliant and striking woman, but I'm afraid the chances of the King agreeing to talk to her are slim. Then, even if she gets beyond that obstacle, there is little chance that he will hear ill of his chosen successor, especially from a woman.'

'But Torfida is remarkable, my Lord. Let us not give up hope just yet. The Talisman could be the key.'

'I do not give up hope, Hereward, but I must prepare for the inevitability that William will still be the named successor upon the King's death. Then, to have any chance of defeating the Duke, I will have to seize power before he arrives on these shores; and I will need the whole of England behind me. Although the main army is mine, I need the housecarls of all the earls and the support of the Fyrd. The Godwin family has many enemies in England and it is a far from foregone conclusion that all the earls and thegns will support me.'

Hereward was encouraged by the direction of Harold's thinking. 'So you will take the throne if Edward does not bestow it upon you or nominate Edgar?'

'Edgar the Atheling remains the right choice; I still hope for that. In the meantime, Hereward, you can be of great service to me. Go to Glastonbury with this parchment. It is for my brother Gyrth, Earl of East Anglia. He is there in training with a large force of my housecarls. It tells him you are a most trusted knight and that you are to have the freedom to inspect my men, wherever they might be. Go to Salisbury, Exeter, Gloucester and Oxford, where I also have men in training. I am strengthening the army as quickly as I can and I want your opinion of them. You know how good William's men are. I need to know how my men compare with Europe's finest, especially Hardrada's and William's. Be totally frank; if it comes to a fight, as it almost certainly will, I need to know what our chances are.'

'By the time we meet again, my Lord, I will know your men and their talents like the back of my hand.' Hereward paused and looked at Harold with firm resolve. 'My Lord, I want you to know that in this fight I will always be at your side. If you fall, I fall; if you triumph, I will be the first to lift you on to my shoulders as the rightful King of England.'

'Thank you, Hereward of Bourne. Go well, my friend.'

As Hereward rode off, Harold's horse was brought to him. His Captain and his personal guards were already mounted as he bade farewell to Edith.

'There are many important men in London and along the Thames that I must talk to. I will leave four of my best men here; I don't want any of the King's eavesdroppers hiding in dark corners. The King will be given the key to his abbey and take communion there on Sunday next. I will be back no later than twilight on Saturday.'

He kissed Edith fondly. 'Take good care of Torfida; she has a miracle to perform on the Sabbath hence.'

'I will, my darling. We have much idle women's talk to keep us occupied.'

Edith's words reflected the two women's firm friendship, grounded in a shared commitment to finding a solution for England's predicament.

As Harold rode off to canvas opinion about the dark days ahead, he knew that whatever Edith and Torfida talked of, it would not be 'idle'.

13. Revolt in the North

Many hundreds of people were waiting outside the King's new abbey church at Westminster for the ceremony of the keys. People had been streaming across the meadows of Chelsea and Holborn all morning. Ludgate was a sight to behold, as the wealthy city burghers, merchants and guildsmen, resplendent in their livery, filed across the old Roman bridge over the River Fleet and made their way through the thriving settlements of the Strand towards the lush green fields of Westminster. There, gleaming in the sun, was the King's symbol of a new England, the finest church in northern Europe.

Edith and Torfida had met Harold earlier and he had described precisely the route Edward would take that day. As Earl Marshal, Harold was responsible for all of the King's public appearances, his itinerary and when and where he would meet people. Harold and Torfida had chosen the exact place within the abbey where she would stand, waiting for the King to pass. Edith would stay hidden among the King's retinue. He was not in favour of Harold displaying his mistress at court, especially since his recent political marriage to Ealdgyth, widow of Gruffydd ap Llywelyn.

There were loud cheers when the King arrived, but Torfida was shocked to see how old and frail he was. He walked with a stoop, his gait more of a shuffle than a stride, his beard and hair silver grey and his eyes red-rimmed and sunken.

With a deep bow, Teinfrith the Churchwright handed the King the huge key to the heavy oak door. This ceremony was intended merely to mark the passing of the keys, as King Edward planned to have the ceremony of consecration at Christmas. The key, the length of a man's arm from fingertip to elbow, was so cumbersome the King had to use both hands to insert it into the lock. When he turned it, a distinctive clang could be heard as the mechanism opened.

More loud cheers went up as the King entered the tall and elegant interior. The public followed their monarch into the nave, as far as its halfway point, while the monks began the sacred melody of plainchant, sending waves of sound echoing around the massive Romanesque columns and arches. It was the first sight that the King's subjects had had of the wonder of the age. All stood and marvelled at it, their necks straining as they peered upwards. Torfida had made her way to her designated position, close to the altar. She had several minutes to wait while the King, guided by Teinfrith and his master masons, made his procession. Harold, with Edward's hearthtroops, stewards and physicians, followed closely behind. The King listened intently to everything that was said to him and took a particular interest in the carving, especially the finely decorated capitals of the arches.

The fine building was a credit to Teinfrith and his masons. The roof was over 150 feet from the ground, a triumph of engineering, and the smooth cream stonework and graceful carving were as well worked as any in Christendom.

King Edward was by now quite near.

As he moved closer, Harold stepped forward. 'Sire, may I introduce Torfida, a woman in my service. She may interest you.'

Torfida curtsied elegantly, and the King nodded in acknowledgement.

'She has travelled extensively, including Constantinople and Rome, and has studied the ancient texts in mathematics. One of her many interests is church architecture, sire.'

'Indeed.' Edward's manner was at first dismissive, then, with a jolt, his face contorted into a scowl. 'Is this the wife of that scoundrel, Hereward?'

Harold was not perturbed by the King's bluntness. 'It is, sire, but she is here in her own right. Hereward is with my housecarls at Glastonbury, as I know his presence in London displeases you.'

'Don't patronize me, Earl Godwinson. You do as you see fit, whether it displeases me or not.'

Torfida was shocked to hear the King speak to Harold so sharply. Edward made to move on and Harold, his face suffused with anger, stepped aside. Torfida decided to take a risk and speak to the King without being spoken to first. She used her impeccable Norman French.

'My Lord King, Master Teinfrith is to be congratulated; the great abbey church of Jumièges pales in comparison with your achievement here. I can see the resemblance to the Abbey of Bernay, but you have improved the vaulting in an extraordinary way, and I can see the influence of Philip of Poitiers in the design.'

Torfida gulped a little; Harold stiffened, expecting the worst.

The King looked at his architect.

Teinfrith looked back, his eyebrows slightly raised. 'Do you know these churches, young woman?'

'Sire, I know a little of the work of Maître Thiebault at Jumièges. It is a fine church and will soon be finished.'

'Indeed it will. But you are not a mason. How do you know so much about the architecture of cathedrals?'

'I have studied the work of the architect Isidor of Miletus, and the mathematician Arthamius of Thralles; I have seen their magnificent legacy, the Hagia Sofia. Mathematics is one of my specialities.'

Teinfrith was astonished; the King looked at him and he nodded, confirming the accuracy of Torfida's information.

Edward turned back to Torfida. 'And your other "specialities", besides mathematics?'

'Sire, theology, languages, metaphysics and philosophy, natural sciences and, of course, history, especially English history.' Torfida looked at the floor uncomfortably, realizing her immodesty.

The King stepped towards her and looked at her with obvious curiosity. 'What is the Latin genus of the great elm?'

'*Ulmus*, sire.'

The King's second question was delivered in Latin. 'Who was Emperor of the Romans after Trajan the Great?'

'Hadrian, sire.'

The King then asked in Greek. 'Who wrote the tragedy *Prometheus Bound*?'

'Aeschylus, sire, sometime after 460 BC.'

'Remarkable. There are only a handful of men in England who could answer those questions. Where did you acquire your knowledge?'

'My father was a very learned man. He was priest to your mother, Queen Emma.'

'How intriguing. If you are referring to the man I think you are, then I knew your father very well; until, of course, he was excommunicated. You must be his bastard child.'

'I am, sire. He took me into the forest and raised me there until I was a grown woman. Then he sent me to the nuns at Hereford.'

'I often wondered what became of Father Waltheof; he was a very good friend. He was fluent in Norman and helped me to improve my English and my Norse. We spoke about many things . . . until his dalliance with one of the ladies-in-waiting caused a furore at court.'

Torfida was hearing her father's real name for the first time. 'Queen Emma was good to my father. She let him have books, and she sent him regular messages.'

The entourage around the King began to shuffle uncomfortably; time was passing and this was an unexpected delay to the schedule.

Harold took a gamble. 'Sire, would you like to retire to the Chapter House? You can sit there and talk a little more with Torfida.'

The King seemed to recognize the Earl of Wessex's ploy, but agreed anyway. Leaving his entourage, the King withdrew to the Chapter House with Torfida a pace behind. Harold kept the King's retinue at a distance, so that Torfida could speak to him in private. Edward's sour demeanour sweetened a little; his deathly pallor became brighter.

'Your father had such wisdom and knowledge, he inspired me. I could have prevented his banishment, but he bore a huge burden of guilt about his fall from grace and refused all help from me or the Queen.' Edward looked at Torfida with a hint of a smile. 'Your mother was very beautiful, you know. I'm sorry she died bringing you into the world.'

'My father raised me and gave me his knowledge. My Lord King, I have been blessed; I may even have acquired a little of his wisdom.'

'Perhaps, but your choice of husband, this renegade Hereward, says little for your wisdom.'

'My King, I do not wish to vex you.'

'That is a risk you will have to take if we are to continue our discourse.'

'Sire, my father spent a long time with Hereward in the wildwood. My father helped him come to terms with his past and to find his destiny. Knowing that Hereward and I were destined to meet, he asked Hereward to be the bearer of a talisman and sent him to me. We now carry that talisman together on a journey to find the man who is destined to wear it.' Torfida reached into the pocket of her dress and pulled out the Talisman.

'I wondered if that trinket might reappear some day. Your father was always fond of the mysterious ways of the past. My mother told me she had given it to Walthoef. She recounted its legends many times and tried to convince me of its power.'

'Sire, it has guided me to you.'

'Madam, it is a pagan amulet of no consequence.'

'Sire, I beg you to let me contradict you. It will be of no consequence only when men understand how to govern themselves without resort to violence. Whether it be a holy relic, an amulet or a cross, as a symbol of faith and truth it can help people make decisions about right and wrong. When we know how to make those decisions without symbols, we will discard them; until then, we need them.'

The King's voice rose. 'You sound like your father. His views came close to heresy; so do yours.'

'My words do not deny God. They reinforce the teaching of the Church, but place the onus of responsibility on our actions and our choices.'

Edward stared up at the ceiling of his Chapter House. 'As my reign was about to begin, my mother asked me to wear your Talisman. She said it would help me understand myself and give me the wisdom to solve the problems I would confront.'

'But you chose not to, Sire?'

'Yes. For me it was very simple; I knew what I wanted to do. My life in Normandy taught me many things. The Saxons are brave and noble people; I am one of them, of Cerdician blood, but they can be brutish and insular and I am determined to direct their future towards Europe. I am also of Norman blood and I can see how the two traditions can complement one another.'

'Sire, I too have lived with the Normans; there is much about them that is brutal.'

'Certainly. They were Vikings once, but they have lived on the European mainland for several generations and they have changed, as the Saxons must change.'

This was Torfida's moment. 'Is that why you want Duke William to succeed you, my Lord King?'

'Yes.'

'Do you know what kind of man he is, sire?'

'I remember him when he was a boy in Normandy. He

was a strong and forceful child and had all the makings of a leader of men.'

'Oh, he is that, sire. You talk of Saxon brutes, but he is a brute beyond mercy; a tyrant beyond all others in a tyrannical world.'

'I have heard all the accounts, and I know he has a dark side; as do we all. But there is much Saxon propaganda about William that emanates from the Godwinsons. You are now in the lien of the Earl of Wessex, and Harold is ambitious to be king. Do you speak for him now?'

'I do not, sire; I speak for England. I plead for a tradition and a way of life. You speak of the value of European culture, but is that what the Saxons want?'

The King's mood darkened. 'What the Saxons want is what I say they ought to have!'

Torfida was alarmed by the King's sudden change of mood. His considered and balanced tone had been replaced by the ferocity of a tyrant.

'Does that shock you, Torfida? My conviction explains why I don't need amulets to help me decide what to do.' Edward glanced towards his retinue. 'I will not favour Harold. He is neither a Saxon of the royal blood, nor a man who would move England into a new age. He is a fine warrior who would have been a magnificent king of an ancient tribe. But I do not want England to be a tribal kingdom; I want it to be a part of the new order of Europe.'

'I don't think the Earl of Wessex wants to be king. He would prefer you to name Edgar the Atheling. Harold would pledge himself as his Regent until he gained his majority.'

The King's tone darkened once again. 'Edgar is a boy.

Hardrada sits in Norway, William in Normandy. If Edgar becomes king, both will invade – and possibly the Dane, Estrithson. If Harold defeats them by force of arms he will be persuaded by popular acclaim to supplant Edgar, and the boy will be lost. If Hardrada wins, we will become Scandinavian again, something that would put me in Purgatory for time immemorial. If William wins, we will have the outcome I prefer, but many thousands will have died in achieving it. So, the answer is clear: nominate William, force Harold and the earls to accept it, and pray for the future.'

The King nodded to Torfida before summoning his servants. She curtsied back and watched him shuffle out of the Chapter House.

As he left, she turned to Harold. 'My Lord Godwinson, your cause is lost. The King will not be swayed.'

Later that day, when Harold joined Edith and Torfida at Ludgate Hill, he expressed his bitter disappointment that William remained the King's nominated successor.

'Well, that's an end to it. I'll tell the King that I am returning to Glastonbury to be with my men. He won't like it, but he will have little choice in the matter. We will join Hereward at Glastonbury. There is much to be done.

'Edith, you should not stay in London. Close the house, pack anything of value and bring your household with you. We may be gone for some time.'

Two days later, the Earl of Wessex, with a large contingent behind him, was heading west. When they arrived in Glastonbury, the burgh and the surrounding countryside resembled an armed camp. Hereward and Earl Gyrth had almost a thousand men in readiness, new weapons were being forged, armour was being made, supply carts were being loaded and the oxen to pull them were grazing in the fields nearby.

Harold called an assembly of his thegns in the Great Hall of Glastonbury. He proclaimed an end to their hope of the King accepting Edgar the Atheling as his successor, or of him revoking his nomination of the Duke of Normandy as the next king. Everyone, to a man, said that they would reject William as successor and accepted Harold's view that unless William brought an army of unheralded size and materiel, it was unlikely that he could secure the throne by force of arms.

The Earl of Wessex was an imposing figure as he stood before the assembled throng of warriors. He was candid about the personal dilemma he would face upon the King's death, but asked them to believe that he was not engaged in a devious plot to claim the throne for himself. However, he was firm in saying that circumstances were conspiring to put England in great danger,

'Whatever perils come our way, I will face them. With you at my side, you noble men of England, we will repel any invader, whether he is Scandinavian or Norman – and even if both hordes fall upon us at once!'

A huge roar rose into the roof of the hall, a cry that turned to a thunderous echo as the warriors thumped their shields with their battle-axes and swords.

Later that day, Hereward offered Harold his assessment of the qualities of England's fighting men. The general level of discipline and fighting skills, both among the levies of the Fyrd and among the housecarls, was on a par with any he had seen, including Byzantines, Saracens and even Scandinavians and Normans. However, there was one area where the Saxon housecarl was beyond comparison. Their close-quarters, highly coordinated battle techniques, especially their shield wall, were without equal. Hereward's only area of concern was the cavalry. The Saxons were adept horsemen, but they eschewed the use of horses in major set-piece battles. On the other hand, Normandy's cavalry with its heavy destriers was the Norman equivalent of the Saxon shield wall: it was their greatest asset.

Hereward put it very plainly for Harold. 'If it comes to a major battle against the Normans, it will be the Saxon shield wall against the Norman destrier.'

Harold thought about Hereward's report for a while. 'What of their bowmen? They have both longbow and crossbow.'

'It is an added advantage for them, and one that we need to combat. While I was in the service of the Duke, I saw some of the finest bowmen in Europe; they could be dangerous for us.'

During the searingly hot summer of 1065 Harold drove his housecarls hard. The messages coming from London told of a King who was becoming more and more irascible and who suffered from frequent 'maladies', where he would temporarily lose consciousness. His speech had become slurred and his balance unsure.

Despite the tension created by the unfolding of great events, time passed slowly.

Harold completed the summer of training with his men, but in early September had to stand down the greater part of his army so that they could return to their homes to gather the harvest.

Then, in October of 1065, just when it needed to be stable, England was thrown into turmoil, and by Harold's own brother, Tostig.

The King had made Tostig Earl of Northumbria in 1055, in acknowledgement of the growing influence of the sons of Earl Godwin. However, Northumbria had been the domain of the Bamburgh family for many generations and Tostig's arrival was not welcome; nor did his punitive rule and high taxes endear him to his vassals.

After ten years of resentment, the Northumbrian thegns eventually rose in revolt against Tostig's rule and called a gemot at York. There, after pledging their loyalty to King Edward, they repudiated Tostig's rule and declared him an outlaw. Mayhem ensued. Tostig's hearth-troop were slaughtered and his treasury plundered until it was bare. The rebels chose a Mercian, Morcar, as their new earl. Anyone within Northumbria loyal to Tostig was ruthlessly purged before the rebels moved south, with Morcar and his followers marauding across the English heartland. Lincoln, Nottingham, and Derby were sacked and the rebellion descended into a rampage of murder, rape and looting. When they arrived at Northampton, they joined a large force of allies led by Morcar's brother, Edwin, Earl of Mercia; hundreds were killed, the burgh was destroyed, the crops in store for the winter were burned and the livestock stolen.

The King sent the rebels a royal command to lay down their weapons and submit their grievances to a Witan of the whole of England. Their response was defiant: they would agree only if the King confirmed the banishment of Tostig and recognized Morcar as Earl of Northumbria.

England was on the brink of civil war.

Edward chose to ignore the ultimatum and called a Witan to meet at Oxford on 28 October 1065. Harold travelled to Oxford without Hereward or Torfida. The issue of the succession was, as things stood, an irrelevance. If a successful outcome was not reached at the Witan, there would not be much of a kingdom left to rule. Edward's authority was ebbing away as quickly as his life, and he knew he could only bring the rebels to heel with Harold at the head of the army.

But Harold needed to keep his soldiers away from the battlefield until it was time to repulse England's external enemies. He knew that civil war would deal a mortal blow to English defences, especially if the King were to die in the middle of it.

The King was in a rage throughout the Witan because none of the earls would support any attempt to crush the rebels by force without Harold's leadership and his house-carls. Tostig was in a similar rage because he had been usurped and neither the King nor his Godwin clan had rushed to his aid. Tostig was so forceful in the Witan in accusing Harold of plotting against him that Harold eventually took an oath in front of the entire nobility of England, swearing that he had played no part in the rebellion.

Tostig's cause was lost and Morcar was confirmed as Earl of Northumbria. Tostig, with his wife, Judith, retreated to Bruges to seek refuge with her father, Count Baldwin of Flanders. Edward was so angry at the outcome that he suffered another succession of 'maladies' and was rushed back to London.

Harold returned to Glastonbury, relieved that the crisis had been averted and that civil war had been avoided, but concerned that England's almost insurmountable problems were now compounded by internal rivalries. In alienating Tostig, England had created yet another enemy – one of its own sons and one of Harold's own kin.

Harold's mind raced as he rode across Salisbury Plain, pondering one potential outcome after another. He made camp at the Great Henge of stones at Amesbury, a place he often visited when he needed to think. Many people feared the Great Henge, particularly at night. There were many legends about the ancient peoples who had built the giant stone circles, especially the rituals of the Celtic Druids, whose influence was still strong in many parts of the country. However, for Harold it was a place of eternal peace and serenity.

Tostig's father-in-law, Baldwin, was one of the most powerful men in Europe and an ally of the Duke of Normandy. Was it possible that Tostig, bitter and angry, could throw in his lot with Duke William and support his succession in return for being reinstalled as Earl of Northumbria, or even as Earl Marshal?

Every new thought made Harold more and more anxious. He broke camp before dawn the next morning and kicked hard into the Blackmore Vale, in the bosom of his beloved Wessex, and on to Glastonbury.

Harold recalled the army in early November of 1065, but heavy snows later in the month made it difficult for the housecarls to train. With over 3,000 men in camp, Harold's coffers were depleting rapidly. Reluctantly, as November became December, he issued the order that all but his hearthtroop were to return home; at least during the dark days of winter, there was little chance of rebellion or invasion.

Braving one of the coldest winters in living memory, the great and good of the land travelled to London for the celebration of Christmastide 1065 in the new abbey church of Westminster. The entire English nobility, both secular and clerical, was summoned, and Harold and Edith decided to open Edith's house at Ludgate Hill for the celebration.

The King, increasingly incapacitated, held on to life and continued his plans for his Christmas consecration.

14. Circling Vultures

It was a minor miracle that King Edward arrived at his church for his Christmastide Court on Christmas Day, 1065.

He had suffered yet another malady on Christmas Eve and had collapsed into his bed in a state of semi-consciousness. However, the next morning he was there on his throne, sceptre in hand, to preside over the proceedings. The occasion had all the ostentation appropriate for a gathering of England's finest, yet it was a sombre affair. All eyes darted from a stricken King, barely coherent and unable to stand, to a sturdy Earl of Wessex, the anticipated successor and putative saviour of a threatened land.

The ceremony was conducted quickly, so that Edward could return to his bed. Three days later, Edward rose one last time – a tribute to the King's obstinate determination to see his emblematic creation consecrated.

As Edward, King of England, looked around his abbey on the twenty-eighth day of December 1065, he declared himself satisfied. The power of God had been reaffirmed throughout the land; the Celts of the west and the Scandinavians of the north were held at bay by the most powerful army in northern Europe; the throne of England was respected by all nations; and scholarship flourished in the abbeys and monasteries in every part of the realm. Most importantly of all, despite not having a direct heir, he had identified a man who would continue his legacy and that man was waiting patiently in Normandy. It had been a difficult task, but his life's work was done.

The consecration, splendid, pompous and protracted, took a heavy toll on Edward and within moments of its end, he had to be rushed from the church straight to his bed.

It would prove to be his deathbed.

Stigand, Archbishop of Canterbury, Queen Edith, Earl Harold and several senior courtiers assembled as the King lapsed into a deep coma, from which it seemed he would not recover. However, unexpectedly, he suddenly sat bolt upright with a look of torment on his face. In a rasping but clear voice, he called for pillows to keep him upright and demanded that the room be cleared, except for Stigand, Edith and Harold.

With eyes staring wildly into the distance, he spoke in a trembling and menacing tone. 'I have seen the apocalypse! The Lord in His mercy has granted me a vision of a terrible fate that awaits the good people of this land.'

He paused for some time, shook his head and gave little whimpers of anguish, as if reliving the vision.

He then took a deep breath. 'They rejected Duke William as King! God punished them by sword and pestilence; they perished in their thousands. My Lord of Wessex, come close to me.'

Harold stepped forward and the King grasped him firmly by his sleeve, his bony knuckles made white by the powerful grip of a frightened man.

'Harold, you are the strongest man in England, the people need you.' He pulled Harold even closer and stared at him like a man possessed. 'I make you their protector.

You must do this for me. Convince the earls and the thegns, the burghers and the townspeople and the peasants of the land; tell them that their future lies with the Duke of Normandy. He is strong; he will keep Hardrada at bay and put the fear of God into the Scots and the Welsh. He respects you and will let you lead his army as Earl Marshal.'

'My Lord King, you ask too much. Don't ask this of me.'

The King continued, undaunted. 'You must do this for England.'

Harold made one final attempt to dissuade him. 'Sire, it is the Atheling, Edgar, who should be King, not William.'

Edward bellowed so loudly in reply, it echoed throughout Westminster. 'I will not hear of it! Do you heed me? I will not have it!' He then turned to Stigand. 'You have heard my testament, Archbishop, it is my verba novissima. Mark my words well, as God is my witness.'

They were his final words.

He fell into a deep coma and died seven days later, on 5 January 1066.

In that tortured week between the King's last words and his death, Stigand, Edith and Harold spoke many times about his verba novissima. They decided to take his words literally: Harold would be declared Protector of England and, as all the earls were still in London, a Witan would be called immediately upon the King's death, to decide who should succeed.

Edward's wishes would be made clear to the nobles but, in accordance with hundreds of years of Anglo-Saxon tradition, the assembled nobility would take the decision.

*

Every man who spoke at the Witan understood the gravity of the proceedings and the importance of his contribution. Some spoke for Edgar the Atheling, mainly out of a sense of loyalty to the Cerdician line, but most were firmly for Harold, despite Edward's wishes. Harold was questioned directly about the oath in Rouen. He acknowledged the question, but asked that his answer be deferred until the Witan was ready to vote on the succession.

By the time Harold spoke, he was King in all but name. Almost to a man, Harold was their choice. They all knew that England faced a perilous future, and that the only man who could lead England was the Earl of Wessex. When Harold got to his feet, there was a hush of expectation.

'My Lords of England, leaders of our noble race, I stand before you humbled by the circumstances of this gathering. A good and learned King has died. He was a Saxon of the royal blood, who did many great things for his realm, and he deserves our gratitude and respect.' He paused as ripples of concurrence went around the gathering. 'But there is a part of his legacy which we should reject without hesitation. He believed that our Saxon ways will hinder our future and said many times that our future lies with, in the King's words, "Europe's empires and kingdoms of learning and sophistication". But do we not have our own ways?'

Harold's rhetorical question was met by yells of agreement.

'Europe is beset by bitter rivalries and dominated by the vagaries of Rome and its henchmen, the Normans. And I will have no part of it!'

A great roar exploded from the Witan as Harold paused for breath.

'Almost two years ago, I swore an oath before papal

witnesses affirming that I would serve as Earl Marshal of this land for its future King, William, Duke of Normandy. I swore that oath at King Edward's bidding in a moment of weakness.'

Harold was interrupted by several cries of 'No!'

'I will not be weak again. On his deathbed, King Edward made me Protector of England and his final testament surpasses my oath to William. He said that God had shown him what we all fear: the destruction of this land in a terrible fight, as the people resisted the rule of Normandy. I am now the guardian of this ancient kingdom and its people. They face the gravest of threats to their safety and prosperity. I now ask you to make your choice. The late King's request was that I ask you, the wise men of England, to accept William as your King. How do you say?'

'No! No! No!' was the unanimous response, as the Witan, to a man, rose to its feet.

'So be it. Therefore, will you permit me to fulfil my duty to England and confirm me, Harold, Earl of Wessex, as your King?'

A great chorus of 'Aye!' filled the hall.

'I am not of royal Cerdician blood. My pedigree is that of a warrior, descended from ancient Saxon and Danish champions of arms. I will serve as your loyal King for one purpose only – to protect this country from those who would destroy our way of life, lay waste our lands and murder our people. If you will lend me your strength, together we can defeat Hardrada and William. So help me God!'

At this, the earls rushed to Harold and raised him on to their shoulders.

The doors of the Great Hall at Westminster were flung open and King Harold II of England was carried into the midst of the rapturous crowd gathered outside.

The old King was buried the next day and Harold was crowned within hours.

Time was of the essence, for Harold had inherited many problems. Not only did he have William and Hardrada's looming presence, but he also had a disgruntled brother festering in Flanders. In addition, the whole of the northern aristocracy, led by the earls Morcar and Edwin, were plotting to secede their provinces from the English realm.

Harold had no hesitation in making Hereward Senior Captain of his personal hearthtroop of housecarls. He and Torfida journeyed to Glastonbury to plan the quartering of the army, which would be called to arms as soon as the grip of winter had loosened.

Duke William was out hunting when news of Harold's succession and coronation arrived. He flew into a terrible rage and demanded the presence of the entire nobility of Normandy at an assembly in Rouen within two days. Apart from the thwarting of his own ambitions, the news nullified the promises he had made to a large group of avaricious relatives and supporters, all of whom wanted one thing: land. Hemmed in by the English Channel on their northern flank and the lands of the French to the south, Normans had been leaving their homeland for decades in search of territory to conquer. Now, the English prey that had been whetting their voracious appetites for years had been snatched from their jaws.

Throughout history, there can have been few gatherings

of men as fearsome as the group that stood before Duke William at his noble conclave. Robert of Mortain, William Fitzborn, Odo of Bayeux, Richard of Evreux, Roger of Beaumont, Hugh of Grandmesnil, Roger of Montgomery, Walter Gifford, Hugh of Montfort and William of Warrene were the most prominent members of a warrior elite based on rigid rules of hierarchy and military prowess. The mood was as solemn as the faces of the assembled warlords. They listened, seething, as William spat out his disdain for Harold – a usurper who had defied the wishes of his predecessor, a liar who had broken his holy oath and a fraud who had misled a weak and frightened people.

As William described his plan for an audacious invasion of England and outlined the massive resources he needed, some murmurings of dismay could be heard.

William identified the doubters and addressed them directly. 'My noble friend, Richard, Count of Evreux, you seem disconcerted by the task.' His sarcasm was not in any way disguised.

'My Lord Duke, I fear no man, nor do I flinch in the face of any army, but Harold is not a weakling and his army is a match for any in Europe. We would need to put many thousands of men on to the battlefield to best him. More importantly, we have no fleet to carry such a force to England.'

William could see that the Count of Evreux's doubts were shared by many.

'Your battle-axe is across your shoulder, my friend. Sharpen it; many mighty oaks shall soon fall across this land. We shall build a grand fleet, the like of which has never been seen before!'

Cheering replaced whispers of discontent, as William's single-mindedness began to rouse his nobles.

'Helmsmen are easily bought, as are ship's constables for our war horses. I need two thousand vessels by Midsummer's Day. We shall sail with eight thousand infantry and bowmen, and two thousand knights and their destriers.'

There were looks of amazement around the room at the scale of William's ambition.

'Remember our Viking ancestors – they feared nothing, least of all the sea. They crossed oceans far bigger than the Sleeve to win legendary victories and vast wealth. Glorious conquest and hordes of treasure await us in England. Go to your lands and prepare for war! Prepare for victory!'

The proposed size of William's armada astonished everyone, but they all knew that such a force would be necessary to defeat Harold. They also knew that nothing on earth would thwart the Duke's determination.

The cry 'Hail William, rightful King of England and Duke of Normandy' rose in unison from the nobles.

Across the Channel, England stood alone. Previous forays into the lands of its Celtic neighbours had created anger and bitterness. It also had long-standing enemies in Scandinavia, in both Norway and Denmark. Other European powers were either allies of Normandy or were embroiled in their own local disputes. The Pope, Alexander II, who had succeeded Nicholas II in 1061, needed Norman support in southern Italy and readily sanctified William's claim to the English throne.

Harold had only one significant bulwark: the English Channel, which could be capriciously dangerous for even the most experienced seafarer. If nothing else, it would buy him crucial time to prepare while the Normans built their fleet. If the Channel could not keep William at bay, it would fall to the sturdiness of England's backbone to save the day – the redoubtable English housecarls.

Day after day and long into the nights of early spring 1066, Hereward and Harold talked tactics and strategy. They concluded that a dual invasion was possible, even a triple one, especially after news arrived that Tostig was travelling from his base in Flanders to court favour not only with William in Normandy, but also with Hardrada in Norway and even Svein Estrithson, King of Denmark.

Much of their discussions focused on the use of cavalry in battle and whether, if attacked on different fronts, the army should use horses to move around the country. They decided to eschew the use of horses, concluding that the great strength of the housecarl was his ability as an infantryman and that the powerful bulwark of the army was its shield wall. Speed would be of the essence to confront a two-pronged or three-pronged attack, and therefore the army should travel as lightly as possible. Horses needed much more care than men, and their fodder was more onerous to transport.

With Hereward setting their tasks and the King at their head, the English housecarls spent the long months of spring 1066 crossing vast tracks of southern England on forced marches, each one culminating in the army assembling in full battle order. Special lightweight baggage trains were prepared, which would keep pace with the rapid movement of the infantry and offer rest and treatment for any stragglers.

With careful planning and preparation, the English infantry could be made all but indestructible.

Harold applied himself to the task like a man possessed.

Harold's recalcitrant brother Tostig moved on from his missions to Duke William in Normandy and Svein Estrithson in Denmark, to attend a gathering at the court of Harald Hardrada, King of the Norwegians.

Hardrada had assembled the entire aristocracy of Norway in his Great Hall in the Viken. He knew what Tostig wanted, and he knew he would need the full support of his warriors if Tostig's wish was to be fulfilled. Hardrada recognized that Tostig had the potential to be the power-broker in the unfolding drama, so the full panoply of the Norwegian royal court was unveiled for the English lord.

Tostig's opening address was eloquent and succinct. It needed to be, as Hardrada was a ferocious character who did not suffer fools easily.

Hardrada had fought his first battle at the age of fifteen, barely escaping with his life. Immensely tall at six and a half feet, he was strong of arm like his adversaries, Harold of England and William of Normandy, and had lived his life as a warrior. He had fought with great distinction for Yaroslav, Prince of Kiev, in his campaigns against the Poles, before journeying south to Byzantium to join the Emperor's fabled Varangian Guard. Manned by formidable Scandinavians, the Varangians were known throughout the civilized world for their military prowess and loyalty. He served the Guard with great distinction, both as a marine in the Imperial Fleet and as an infantryman in Palestine, North Africa, Armenia and Sicily. He emerged as Captain of the Varangians, before leaving Byzantium with a fortune in gold and silver from the booty of war. Still only twenty-eight years of age, he returned to Norway as the most illustrious warrior of his day.

As Tostig stood before Hardrada, he was staring into the face of a legend. Not only was he the subject of the great sagas, he was often their author, rightfully acknowledged as an epic poet on a par with his reputation as an exceptional warrior. Now over fifty years of age, he still had the bearing of a mythical hero.

'My lord King, I come to Viken to pay homage to a great tradition. This land has given birth to famous warriors whose descendents hold sovereignty over vast lands in the north, in Russia and in the Mediterranean. Vikings are feared wherever they tread. In my own country, the Viking tradition is strong. I am of Norse blood through my Danish mother, Gytha, daughter of Earl Thorkils, and proud of it. Sire, England is in turmoil. The North is in revolt and William, Duke of Normandy, is building a fleet with all speed to mount an invasion. England will soon be lost to the Normans.'

Tostig was interrupted by Vik Ospakson, Hardrada's loyal Earl Marshal, who had fought with him in the Varangian Guard. Ospakson rose and stood in silence, waiting in the Viking tradition for Tostig to yield the floor, which he did with a bow.

'Earl Tostig, you speak well. It is to your credit that you address this gathering with such composure. But you failed to mention that Vikings also hold sway over much of Europe as well. Is not William of Normandy a Viking, directly descended from William Longsword, son of Rolf?'

'He is, my Lord. But he is no longer a Scandinavian. He, like King Edward, has been seduced by the trappings of Rome and the soft life of the learned cloister. The Normandy he governs is turning to Paris, to Rome and to Aachen for its wisdom; it has forgotten its northern roots.'

This time a younger warrior stood up, Skule Konfrostre, a close friend of the King's son, Olaf.

'Earl Tostig, noble lord of the English, if you are contemptuous of the Normans, why were you at William's court recently? Were you not also at the court of Estrithson? How many allies do you seek?'

There were hoots of derision in support of the young warrior's caustic remarks.

He continued his barracking. 'Also, is it not true that your own wife, Judith, is kinswoman of the midget Matilda, Duke William's wife?'

More laughter ensued, amid derisory yells from the warriors. Tostig seemed to be losing his audience.

He turned squarely to Hardrada. 'I was at William's court in January to ask him his intentions. He told me he would invade as soon as his fleet was ready. I told him that the Saxons would fight him to the death until Edgar the Atheling, the true Cerdician King of England, was on the throne and I was reinstalled to my Earldom in Northumbria. My brother Harold has made himself King, but Harold is a general of armies, not a king. He has seen an opportunity and taken it; it is an ignoble act. I asked William to support the Atheling as King, and to act as guarantor against any threat to Edgar from my brother, but the Duke rejected my suggestion.'

Hardrada spoke for the first time. 'Tell me of your brother, the new King Harold. Is he liked?'

'He has support, especially in the South, and the army is loyal to him. It is well trained, but it numbers only a few thousand. In the North he is weak; that is where fealty is shown to me.'

Whether or not Hardrada realized Tostig was being disingenuous about loyalty to him in the North, it seemed not to matter. The King, who had listened carefully to all that had been said, stood and regarded the grand gathering of his kinsmen. He made eye contact with many, trying to gauge their mood.

'Since the treaty of the Goda River with King Svein of the Danes, we have been at peace. Our battles with Denmark are over, but the years of peace have blunted our axes. England is rich; its maidens are fair. Are we not Vikings?'

He was carefully manipulating his audience, rekindling the fire in the hearts of his warriors. They began to shout their approval, stamp their feet and thump their shields with their fists.

'I am now fifty-two years old, but my thirst for battle has not been quenched. This noble English earl has brought us word of a great opportunity. He is right, England is weak. Viking rule can be restored to York, to Winchester, to London. Send out messengers, raise your men, bring your ships. We invade England in the summer!'

A great chorus of approval reverberated around the hall as Tostig looked on in awe at the Norsemen in full cry. His wily plotting was paying off: to the south, the Normans were building their fleet; in the north the Norwegians would soon be gathering theirs; in the east his own force was being prepared in Flanders by his loyal deputy, Copsig.

Tostig seemed to have Harold exactly where he wanted him – outnumbered and surrounded.

15. Comet in the Heavens

'The days are growing longer, Hereward.'

'Yes, sire. It will soon be May Day; the Duke's ships must be ready by now.'

Hereward was with King Harold on the south coast, at Dover, inspecting the local defences. Small garrisons had been commissioned along the entire coast, from the Tees in the north to the Severn in the west. News of a landing of any sort, be it Scandinavian or Norman, would be with the King within hours.

Harold had recently presided over his Easter Gemot at Westminster, which began on Easter Day, 16 April 1066. In an unprecedented session of law-making lasting ten days, Harold had instituted wholesale changes to England's institutions: he had altered the tax structure to help those struggling to meet the demands of their lords; ordered the opening of new mints for the production of extra coinage to boost commerce; devolved back to the earls and thegns powers which had been garnered by King Edward; and, to the exclusion of Edward's Norman placements, promoted prominent Saxons to senior positions in the Church and local administration.

Neither man had seen his woman in months. Edith Swan-Neck was in Winchester keeping a wary eye on Harold's sister, Edith, King Edward's widow, so that she could warn him of any scheming between her and Tostig.

Torfida and the twins were in Glastonbury with the rest of Hereward's entourage, helping Harold's quartermasters with the onerous task of maintaining his standing army of housecarls. It was fortunate for Harold that England was rich in taxes from its productive farmers and the foreign merchants who came with gold and silver to buy the products of England's thriving economy.

Hereward had sent Alphonso to Normandy to assess the strength of the Duke's forces and gauge the preparedness of his fleet. He was due to return any day.

'We need Alphonso's report, sire. Your spies give us contradictory stories; I fear they tell us what they think we want to hear, or just repeat the local gossip from Normandy's taverns.'

The King looked up at the rapidly darkening late evening sky above the towering white cliffs of Dover's natural defences. The sea was dark and sombre with no moon to cast its reflection on the heaving waves. Hereward looked at the King's silhouetted profile; here was a man balancing precariously on the fulcrum of history. In the coming months, the destinies of several kingdoms would be determined by his judgement, his sword arm, and his kingship.

As Hereward pondered Harold's heavy burden, he suddenly became aware of agitated murmurings in the camp. Men were getting to their feet and pointing to the eastern sky. The King's quiet contemplation was also disturbed by the commotion.

He looked at Hereward. 'What is troubling the men?'

'I don't know, sire. I have never seen such a thing before.'

Low on the horizon, towards the darkest part of the sky in the south-east, blazed a star no one had seen before. It was as bright as Venus, but had a tail, like the wake of a ball of heavenly fire.

'The men are scared, my Lord King. They are saying it is an omen of doom.'

'Calm them, Hereward. It is a comet, an object a long way away among the stars. The ancients saw them and recorded their movements. Remind the men that there was a comet to herald the birth of Jesus, so it is a portent of our victory to come.'

He smiled at Hereward with a self-belief that was infectious. Hereward went to rally the men. It did not take him long, nor did they need much reassurance. They had fought many campaigns with Harold; as long as the King was in good spirits, they were too. Wisdom was a great comfort in difficult times.

Harold's coastal inspection had reached Chichester by the time Alphonso returned. He reported that he had attached himself to the preparations being made by Robert, Count of Mortain, who was required by Duke William to provide 100 ships for the invasion. Adept with rope and leather, Alphonso had helped prepare the ships for the hundreds of horses that would have to make the perilous crossing to England.

'My Lord King, an almighty host is gathering for the invasion. Two thousand ships have been built. Sea captains, farriers, carpenters, blacksmiths, armourers, tanners and saddle-smiths have come from all over Europe, and every adventurer, outlaw, mercenary and cut-throat from lands far and wide is joining the Duke's war band. There are Hungarians, Bohemians, Bavarians, Frenchmen and Flems. I saw crossbowmen and archers practising every day, and over two thousand knights in full armour have gathered with their war horses.' Alphonso, conscious that he was describing a terrifyingly potent enemy, tried to offer some words of comfort for Harold. 'But you have time, my Lord King; the fleet will not begin to assemble until August, when it will gather at the port of Dives. There it will wait until the Duke is certain that all is adequately prepared before he moves the ships to the mouth of the Somme at St Valéry. The veteran sailors I spoke to said it would not be wise to set sail for at least a month after that because the horses will need to be settled.'

The King queried the delay. 'Why a month?'

'Sire, they will stable the horses on the ships while they are still in dock, to get them used to the movement and the surroundings. With such a large number to transport, they must be tethered very closely together, so must stay calm. My estimate is that the Normans cannot sail until September at the earliest, by which time the autumn tides and winds may bring havoc to their plans.'

'Alphonso, your report is excellent. What do you make of the Normans' morale?'

'My Lord King, their morale is excellent. Early fears about the crossing have lessened, as everyone has seen the painstaking care being taken with the preparations. The farmers are being well paid for their produce; every town and village is flush with the Duke's gold and silver and they are working night and day to provide everything that is needed. The fighting men have only one concern – the English housecarls. But every day of training makes them stronger and their confidence grows. The popular view is that the destriers will break the English shield wall.

'Thank you, Alphonso, we are indebted to you.'

'There is one more thing, sire.'

Alphonso looked at Hereward for reassurance. What he was about to tell the King would not please him.

'Alphonso, the King needs to be apprised of everything, no matter how bleak.'

'I have seen many exceptional armies prepare for war, but these Normans are impressive. Roger of Montgomery is quartering the men, horses and supplies like a Roman general, and families that have feuded for decades are standing shoulder-to-shoulder. They have the smell of conquest in their nostrils; they believe a kingdom which is theirs by right has been snatched from their grasp, so they mean to prevail by force of arms.'

The King stood solemnly. 'I thank you for your honest account; it is invaluable to us. When you are rested, go to your comrades and family at Glastonbury. Regain your strength there; we are going to need you.'

'Thank you, sire.' Alphonso bowed and left the tent.

The King sat down with a sigh. 'Hereward, you have found a good man in Alphonso. There was little in his account to comfort me, but he gave it lucidly and without hesitation. I feared that William's threat would be grave, but he is not only bold, he is also careful and meticulous. Few men would attempt what he is planning; I never expected he would bring such a large force across the Channel.'

Hereward felt certain that Harold would have much preferred to have been Earl Marshal to a wise and generous liege, rather than carry the burden of kingship himself.

With every day that passed, Hereward's admiration for

the King grew. As Harold continued along the coastline into his lands in Wessex, Hereward knew that the time had come to entrust the Talisman to the man for whom he was sure it was destined.

After dinner one warm evening, Hereward reminded the King of its pedigree, and of Torfida's interpretation of its meaning.

'I will wear it with honour. Pray that it brings me the wisdom I shall need.'

It was early May when the first skirmish of the calamitous events of 1066 occurred.

Tostig appeared on the Isle of Wight with a modest force of 60 ships and 600 foreign mercenaries. It was a scouting mission, and an opportunity to fill his coffers for bigger expeditions to come. Having plundered as much as he could find in the south, he sailed eastwards to Sandwich in Kent. King Harold's fleet-footed army was there to meet him and Tostig withdrew, to land later in his old earldom in the north. Again, he was given short shrift, this time by the earls Edwin and Morcar. Tostig's mercenaries were soon disillusioned by the resolute defenders and withdrew, leaving him to seek refuge with King Malcolm of Scotland and await the arrival of his main ally, Harald Hardrada of Norway.

Fearing it was a feint to a bigger invasion, Tostig's foray caused Harold to raise the Fyrd, a mobilization not undertaken lightly, given the cost to the Exchequer. The King's problems were growing: although his rapid-reaction strategy had worked to repel Tostig's invasion, keeping his elite housecarls and the general fyrd in the field for several months risked exhausting his granaries and emptying his treasury. Even more worryingly, if Alphonso was right, and the invasion did not come until September, or later, he would have to stand the army down so that the harvest could be collected.

By 8 September, no invaders had arrived and another long hot summer of training had passed, leaving the men tense and lethargic. Harold had no choice but to let the Fyrd go home. He released all but 1,500 of his housecarls and, so that they would not be caught in any autumnal gales in the Channel, ordered his fleet to anchor in the Thames.

It was what William had been waiting for. As soon as he received word of Harold's decision to stand down his army, he made ready to strike. Within four days, the entire fleet set sail from Dives to St Valéry. At almost the same time as news reached Harold that the Duke's grand army and great armada were on the move, intelligence confirmed that Hardrada's horde had also set sail from Norway. The worst possible scenario was unfolding for Harold and England: both of their enemies were gathering on opposite fronts.

Harold called a Council of War at Oxford for all the nobility of southern England. The earls Edwin and Morcar and the northern thegns did not attend because of the imminence of Hardrada's invasion in the North.

There was a grave silence in the Great Hall at Oxford, as the King read a full and detailed report of Hardrada's progress. He had called a general muster of his forces on the Isle of Askøy in the Byfjord at Bergen. His fleet had successfully navigated the North Sea and gathered in the Orkneys, where they had been joined by allies from Iceland,

Ireland and all corners of the Norse world. This was to be an invasion of Norsemen reminiscent of the great sagas of old, and Harold's estimate of the numbers involved made his earls shudder with alarm. It was thought that Hardrada had brought over 300 ships and at least 15,000 men. As the disquiet grew, Harold raised his voice to try to calm the earls. He was in the midst of describing the extent and quality of his preparations over the summer when a herald rushed into the hall, distressed and exhausted, and asked the King for permission to speak.

Harold nodded.

The man drew a deep breath and, in the clear and precise tones of his calling, made his announcement.

'Sire, I come from the garrison at Nottingham. Yesterday, on the twentieth day of September, there was a great battle at Gate Fulford in Yorkshire. The armies of Edwin, Earl of Mercia and Morcar, Earl of Northumbria, have fallen to the Norwegians, commanded by their King, Harald, known as Hardrada. His royal standard, the Raven Land-Ravager, flies from the Great Hall of York.'

The King bellowed in anger at the herald. 'Why did I have no reports of the Norwegian ships approaching, or of the landing of their army?'

'Sire, it appears that the coastal lookouts reported directly to Earl Morcar, and he chose not to inform you. The first news we had in Nottingham was late last night when riders arrived from Tadcaster.' He then paused and looked directly at the King, knowing that what he was about to add would be particularly hurtful to him. 'Sire, your brother, the Earl Tostig, is with Hardrada in York.'

Harold was incandescent with anger, but he declined to

comment on his brother's treachery. He asked a vital military question. 'What of the housecarls of Earls Edwin and Morcar, how many have survived?'

The herald hesitated for a moment. 'The battle was fierce and many men died in the bogs and marshes of the river Ouse. Hardrada himself led the main attack. Edwin and Morcar survived and made peace with him, but his berserkers cut down hundreds of their housecarls. Survivors said the Ouse ran red with blood all the way to the sea.'

Harold took a deep breath, thanked the messenger and turned to address the Council. As he spoke, he mostly looked to Hereward for reassurance, especially as he was about to abandon the central tenet of his carefully planned summer strategy.

'Command your constables to bring horses; we ride to the North immediately. I will take only the fifteen hundred men currently under arms and as many as I can gather on the way. We will revert to the cavalry tactics of my campaigns in Wales and cut down the Norwegians before they know we are among them. We must be there by the twenty-fourth. My brother Gyrth will ride with me, as will the Captain of my Hearthtroop, Hereward of Bourne. Go! Go quickly!'

The Saxon military machine sprang to life with remarkable efficiency. Almost 800 horses were in Oxford within twenty-four hours. A thousand more were gathered on the way north, to put a force of almost 2,000 men in the saddle by the time the Saxon army mustered at Tadcaster at midday on Sunday 24 September. It was a small force, significantly outnumbered by the Norwegians, but they were England's finest, the embodiment of 200 years of Saxon military tradition.

Harold's force had covered a huge distance in just three days. No other army in the world could have been assembled with such speed, covered such ground and been in such prime condition to fight. The months of training had paid off handsomely.

Harold called for mass to be celebrated and, as the shadows lengthened from a setting sun at the end of a fine English day, he addressed his men from horseback. Hereward watched from afar as the King spoke, but could clearly see the Talisman around his neck. He felt relieved that his long journey seemed to have had a purpose after all.

As Harold's voice rose, so did the hearts of every man there. His horse circled and stomped its feet, its gyrations adding emphasis to his message. He sat tall in his saddle, looking every inch a king in England's gravest hour.

'Tomorrow we ride into battle. There will be no shield wall to protect us; our defence will be our speed and our guile. If there is a pitched battle, we will engage at pace and withdraw quickly to regroup and strike again. Those of you who have served with me for many years will remember our campaigns in Wales. Surprise will be the key to our victory. Tomorrow we will annihilate the Norwegians, who threaten our families and our future. The chronicles will tell of the day for generations to come. Fight for England! Fight to protect our Saxon blood! Long live our cherished people!'

Beyond the King and his army, the sun was setting behind the trees of the forest, its leaves the vibrant colours of an English autumn.

Hereward looked at Einar, Martin and Alphonso, who had just arrived from Glastonbury.

'Tomorrow we stay close to the King.'

At that moment, Hereward's pride in his homeland knew no bounds.

A pivotal chapter in the history of England was about to be written, and these men would determine the outcome.

16. Hardrada

The morning of 25 September dawned bright and clear. The meadows were dank from heavy dew as the rising sun drew swirls of mist from rivers and streams made cool by the chill of night. A warm day beckoned.

Hardrada had been uncharacteristically careless. That morning, buoyed by his reception at York, confident from his comfortable victory over the forces of Edwin and Morcar and feeling certain that King Harold's army could not be within 100 miles of him, he was in a complacent mood. He had made camp at a small bridge on a tributary of the Great Ouse and was overseeing the taking of hostages from the people of Northumbria. The crossing was called Stamford Bridge, on the River Derwent, a few miles due east of York.

The Norwegians had spent the days since their victory filling their ships with the spoils of war and celebrating their success; they were in no state to fight an elite force of Saxon housecarls. Hardrada had advanced from his main camp to Stamford Bridge with only about a third of his force, perhaps 5,000 men. More significantly, he had allowed them to leave behind their mail coats, shields, helmets and spears. They carried only their swords and axes and their only protection was their leather jerkins.

It was a bedraggled body of men.

Harold's army could not have offered more of a contrast.

It had left Tadcaster under darkness and in barely three hours was in York, where the locals were shocked to see a Saxon army enter their city so quickly after the defeat at Gate Fulford.

Harold's housecarls had grown in number. A further contingent of 500 had arrived in the early hours of the morning and swelled his force to close to 3,000 men. Unlike the Norwegians, they were fully armed and well prepared. Harold's advance had been so rapid that no word had reached the North that the Saxons had even left the Midlands. He halted his men just outside York to wait for his scouts to report on the Norwegians' position. When he heard of Hardrada's disposition, he ordered an immediate attack.

This time there would be no final rallying speech.

The first the Norwegians knew of the advancing army of Saxon housecarls was the low rumble of their horses travelling on the wind from the west. At first, they thought it must be more hostages from York. Then, they suspected a double-cross manoeuvre from Edwin and Morcar, surmising that, somehow, the defeated Northumbrians and Mercians had raised a force of cavalry. Only when they saw how many horses were streaming over the hill from Gate Helmsley and heard the rising thunder of thousands of hooves, did they realize that Harold's army was about to descend on them.

Recognizing the gravity of the situation and knowing how effective his brother's surprise attacks could be, Tostig shouted at Hardrada, imploring him to organize a rolling retreat, fighting as they went.

The old warrior would have none of it and bellowed

back, 'We stand and fight. Send messengers to the ships and summon Prince Olaf to come at speed. Raise the Land-Ravager standard; form a shield wall around it. Berserkers come to my side. Men of Norway, stand your ground!'

Harold watched the rapid Norwegian deployment, counted their numbers and, seeing that they had no horses, no armour and few weapons, called a halt to his advance. He summoned a company from his personal bodyguard, twenty-five men in all, and asked Hereward and his three companions to join him. They rode down to the river and sought to parley with Hardrada.

The famous warrior appeared, accompanied by Tostig and a small retinue of berserkers.

'You sit tall in the saddle for a man of modest height, Harold of England.'

Hereward could not help but be amused by Hardrada's comment. Although the legendary Norwegian was at least six and a half feet tall, Harold was also a tall man, standing well over six feet.

'Greetings to you also, Harald of Norway. I will try to observe noble courtesies, despite your presence in my kingdom and your treatment of my people.'

'My Lord Earl, your occupation of the throne of this land is not legitimate. You are not of royal blood. This land was part of Scandinavia until recently; it will be so again.'

'We will settle that argument in due course. First, I would like to speak with my brother Tostig.' He turned to Tostig with a look of contempt. 'You have invaded your own land seeking vengeance, and in defiance of a decision made by the Witan. Few would forgive your actions.' Then the King's face softened. 'But I will do so. Return with me; bring your men. England needs you. There is a foe far mightier than these Norwegians approaching our shores. I will restore you to your earldom and increase your lands in the North. After we despatch the Normans, we will campaign in Scotland against Malcolm, your erstwhile ally. When he is defeated you can add Scotland to your domain. We are still brothers and we can be comrades once again to protect our homeland.'

'It is an interesting offer, my brother, but your brotherly love was absent when I was hounded from my earldom. Today you propose terms because you need my support, but I fight with King Harald and the Norsemen now and I did not bring them all the way to Northumbria to desert them.'

Harold looked sad at his brother's response, but his expression quickly became stern again. 'So be it, Tostig, once my brother, once an earl of England. You will die for your treachery. As for you, Harald of Norway, you are ill prepared and caught in the open on English soil. If you withdraw and return to your ships and leave the plunder and hostages you have taken, I will spare you and your men.'

'You are bluffing, Earl Harold. My force is far superior to yours. I stand on Scandinavian soil. This land is mine through the heritage of my ancestors. If you desire to take it from me, you will have to win it in battle.'

Harold breathed deeply, knowing that many were about to die, and gestured to his men to turn and ride back to the army.

He addressed Tostig one last time, deliberately ignoring his Norwegian foe. 'If Hardrada insists on his patch of English soil, he'd better start digging his grave. As he stands so tall, he will need a big hole.'

As Hardrada watched Harold ride away, he turned to Tostig. 'Your brother has a sharp tongue. I'm going to enjoy cutting it out of him.'

There was only a narrow bridge between the two forces, so Harold decided to abandon the horses and mount an immediate infantry attack. His army advanced on foot in squadrons of fifty, but found their way across blocked by a huge Norse berserker, who despatched the Saxon house-carls in groups of three and four at a time with the wide arcs of his flailing axe. The Saxon squadrons tried to wade across the river but could not do so in shield formation and were easy targets for the Norwegian archers. Hereward looked at the situation and quickly gave instructions to Alphonso, who melted into the crowd of housecarls massing to reach the bridge.

Within moments, the berserker's stubborn defence came to an abrupt end. With a scream of agony, he was impaled through the groin by a spear thrust from beneath the bridge between the planks of its footway. Alphonso had slipped under the water upstream, floated down and positioned himself directly beneath the Norwegian before delivering his fatal thrust. With an almighty splash the berserker hit the water, and the Saxons streamed over the bridge en masse.

The ensuing hand-to-hand fighting continued well into the afternoon. Hardrada had kept his hearthtroop of axemen in reserve, but eventually, they too were encircled. In a bloody encounter that would be recounted reverentially in the chronicles of both sides, English housecarl met Norwegian berserker in a prolonged fight to the death. As his loyal comrades began to die in droves, some of whom had fought with him in his youth in the Varangian Guard, Hardrada broke into the open, grounding any Saxon who came close in a frenzy of blows from his war axe. His fury was only abated by an arrow to his throat, which brought him to his knees, struggling for breath. His warriors attempted to save him with a desperate last redoubt, but it was futile.

Within moments, in a muddy field in the featureless countryside of the lowlands of York, the last great Viking died, in search of one final conquest.

Harold, mindful of the battles to come against the Normans and seeing the toll the hand-to-hand fighting was taking on his men, offered the Norwegians the chance to surrender. Tostig led the defiant refusals as Hardrada's faithful hearthtroop pulled the stricken King back under the shadow of the Raven Land-Ravager. A cry went up.

'Rally to the standard! Fight for the Hardrada! Prince Olaf is on his way with ten thousand comrades.'

The next phase of the slaughter commenced immediately. At King Harold's command, the Saxon housecarls cut swathes into the Norwegian redoubt. The defenders were soon isolated in small groups and cut to pieces. Many drowned in the nearby Derwent as they tried to flee to their ships. Tostig was killed, as were the leaders of Hardrada's Norse allies from the Orkneys, Ireland and Iceland.

At the end, an eerie calm descended on the battlefield, but within minutes yet another murderous episode beckoned. Messengers had reached Prince Olaf at midday, telling of the fighting at Stamford Bridge. Eystein Orri, Hardrada's senior son-in-law, and Prince Olaf's men immediately collected their weapons and armour and set off for the battle-field. It took them over four hours to reach Stamford Bridge. Although it was early evening, the day was still warm as the Norwegian force, numbering more than 8,000 men, roaring for vengeance, sprinted towards the right flank of the exhausted Saxons in a ferocious charge that became known in Norse folklore as the 'Storm of Orri'.

Harold had to think quickly. He estimated that he had lost well over 1,000 men and now faced a superior force that outnumbered his surviving army by four to one.

He called to Hereward. 'Take the remains of the Eagle Cohort back over the river and get them mounted. You must get them back across upstream and attack from the rear. I will hold our ground here with my two Wessex cohorts.'

As Hereward led his men away to the sound of the retreat horn, the front ranks of Orri's Norwegians were already cascading into a Saxon shield wall, hurriedly prepared by Harold's captains. The wall swayed and buck-led and in places was breached, requiring Harold and his hearthtroop to act as reinforcements. The King became anxious as he looked at the Norwegian massed ranks in front of him, three times deeper than his own.

It was only a matter of time before they would be over-whelmed. He looked across the Derwent to the south-east, just as the setting sun touched the horizon, but there was no sign of Hereward and his cavalry. Within minutes, his wall would break under weight of numbers and his cause would be lost. Then he heard the rumble of horses on the move.

Hereward had drawn up the Eagle Cohort in squadrons

of ten abreast, five ranks deep, fifty men in all. Harold counted four squadrons in line of attack, supported by four waves. He quickly calculated: eight hundred men in support; enough, he thought.

As soon as the Norwegians saw the dark cloud of mounted attackers behind them, their rear ranks turned to create their own shield wall; the Norwegians were outflanked, something they hated. By the time they reached the Norwegian shields, Hereward's huge phalanx of horsemen were at full gallop and, by staying close and keeping their discipline, cut through the line of defenders with ease. Hereward was at the centre of everything, often standing high in his stirrups and using the Great Axe of Göteborg to direct the point of attack. Not only was he able to wield his fearsome weapon on either side of his mount, but he was also able to lean out at perilous angles to create even wider arcs of mayhem. His progress was like that of a reaper in a field of barley as he cut swathes through the Norwegians beneath him. His was indeed a grim harvest.

The charge soon began to carve the Norse infantry into isolated pockets. The fleeing Norwegians were pursued all the way to their ships at Riccall on the Ouse. The fleet was torched and with it any chance of escape for the majority of the survivors. Harold's two-pronged attack, committing his cavalry in the rear while his shield wall held its ground, had saved the day.

Hereward had arrived in Harold's service with an unparalleled reputation. Now word of his prominence in the charge, and his bravery at the vanguard of the attack, spread through the ranks of the English army. His exploits and those of his Lord, Harold of England, would be carried back to the Norse lands by the survivors of Hardrada's army to become part of Scandinavian legend for generations to come.

At sunrise, only Prince Olaf had survived of the entire Norwegian aristocracy; the whole of its military elite and most of its seasoned warriors had perished.

It was carnage on a brutal scale.

Harold knew that Norway would not be a force in Europe for at least a lifetime and he let Olaf leave with the twenty-four ships that remained afloat. Earl Tostig's body was retrieved from the battlefield and he was buried at York. The Norwegians were allowed to remove Hardrada's body, which was laid to rest in St Mary's Church, Trondheim, a resting place that became a shrine to his poetry and his heroics.

It had been a remarkable victory for King Harold. After a gruelling march from Oxford, a force of barely 3,000 men, outnumbered by more than four to one, had beaten a Norse army led by the greatest warrior of his age.

The next morning, after they had both had a few hours' sleep, Hereward and the King gathered their thoughts.

The King had won a great victory, but was in a sombre mood. 'My friend, although the first battle is won, the greater one is still to come . . . and I have lost half my housecarls.'

'Yes, sire, but every man who remains is worth two Normans.'

'Perhaps, but it's not just my housecarls I worry about, it is the number of Norman knights. I suspect they outnumber our Saxon thegns almost four to one.'

'That is probably so, my Lord King. But they fight weighed down with armour, which on their heavy destriers makes them awkward and cumbersome. If we choose our ground well, we should be able to unseat them. By waiting for you to call in the harvest, the Duke has left it late in the year. Autumn is a two-edged sword; soon the ground will be sodden with the October rains. His big horses will sink to their bellies.'

'You are a good man, Hereward; you always have a strategic answer. Stay close to me in these coming weeks.'

In a gesture rare for a king, Harold embraced Hereward like a brother. England's two greatest warriors had become the closest of friends.

Harold and his army were on the move again within thirty-six hours. He knew that Duke William was either still in transit in the Channel or had already landed on the south coast. Harold had 1,500 mounted housecarls with him, but to ensure that his baggage train could keep pace, he travelled south much more slowly than he had in his dash northwards. His baggage was laden with Norse armour, shields and weapons, a vital cache of materiel for the forthcoming battle with the Normans – an encounter that could be only a matter of days away.

Messengers were despatched to all parts of the realm. Harold had estimated that he needed at least 4,000 housecarls for the clash against William and possibly as many as 6,000 fyrdmen. He prayed that the annual harvesting had been completed and that such a force could be assembled. Most of his brothers' housecarls – those of Gyrth, Earl of East Anglia, and of Leofwine, Earl of the South West Midlands – were still in reserve and were among England's

265

finest. His biggest concern was the availability of the men of Edwin, Earl of Mercia, and Morcar, Earl of Northumbria. Between them, they had well over 1,000 housecarls of the highest quality but, despite the fact that both men had promised Harold their support, he knew their commitment was questionable. Fiercely expressed separatism had always been a part of northern politics and Harold suspected that Edwin's and Morcar's real purpose was independence for the North.

At the end of the third day of the march south, the advanced party of the army was approaching the River Trent at Newark. News had reached the locals of the great victory at Stamford Bridge, and the King was greeted with loud cheers as he approached the walls of the burgh. He acknowledged the gifts of food from the local burghers, but passed straight through, hoping to camp further south on the road to London.

'These Mercians seem genuine in their affection for you, sire.'

'It is never the people who make life difficult for kings, Hereward. It is their leaders who plot and scheme; it is their ambitions that are at the root of mischief. All the people want is peace and food in their bellies.'

Hereward's admiration for his king, a monarch not of royal blood but nevertheless a great leader, grew by the day. 'Sire, do you think that a kingdom can ever be stronger than the tribal loyalties of its people?'

'Yes, I hope so. As in Roman times, or under Alfred, people will readily lend their allegiance to something far greater than their tribe. If their leaders bring them peace and prosperity, they will follow them.'

'Torfida and I often talk about the Greeks and the Romans and how they believed that people could govern themselves according to principles enshrined in laws and codes of honour.'

'That is my dream for England, Hereward. We are a new people, mere infants compared to the civilizations of antiquity. But England is a rich land with strong people of many races; perhaps we can create a way of life that will be admired like those of Greece and Rome.'

'That is a laudable ambition, my Lord, but it needs men like you to achieve it.'

'But it also needs men like you, Hereward, and women like Torfida. Great civilizations are built by people of intelligence, wisdom and courage, not just by kings.'

Hereward longed to tell Torfida about the King's leadership and how well he carried the Talisman. Soon he would have the opportunity he craved; the King had sent word to Glastonbury that their families should join them in London. He had also sent a messenger to Winchester to summon Edith Swan-Neck. Harold knew that it would be an opportunity for them to say farewell to those who would face the impending challenge from Duke William.

Dusk was fast approaching when Harold's scouts returned with news that there was a suitable clearing ahead for a night camp. The scouts were not alone. A captain of the housecarls of Earl Gyrth, accompanied by two sergeants-at-arms, had met them on the road. Their horses had been ridden hard for many hours and Harold and his entourage guessed immediately what their news would be.

'Sire . . . William, Duke of Normandy, landed a large invasion force at Pevensey two days ago. There was no

267

resistance and they are already on the rampage, looting, burning and desecrating wherever they go. They are executing the priests; whole villages of menfolk are being murdered, the women raped, even boys as young as twelve are being cut down.'

The King visibly flinched at the news. 'Thank you for your report, Captain. How many are there in William's force?'

'Sire, Lord Gyrth's scouts are counting now, but an elderly local man, who served with King Edward's house-carls, estimated about ten thousand: at least three thousand cavalry and six thousand infantry.'

There was a stunned silence at the size of the Duke's invasion force. It confirmed the King's most pessimistic prediction.

'Captain, rest your horses and get some sleep. Hereward, send Martin Lightfoot to see what he can tell us of the Normans' plans.'

Hereward gave Martin detailed instructions about what was needed. The King ordered fresh horses to be brought up so that he and his personal bodyguard of two squadrons could push on to London. He left instructions for his force from Stamford Bridge to come on as quickly as it could and for the entire army to assemble in London in five days' time, six at the most.

Before Harold arrived in London, he went to Waltham Abbey to pray; it was a special place for the King. It contained the Holy Rood, a flint cross, found, it was rumoured, in an ancient ruin by a tenant of Harold's in the Somerset village of Montacute. Two teams of oxen were sent to take the cross to Glastonbury Abbey but – again, according to local legend – the oxen refused to travel north and carried the cross eastwards across the whole of southern England to the ancient Saxon settlement of Waltham in Essex. Harold had built a fine church to house the relic and endowed an abbey and a community of monks. The church had been consecrated by Harold in 1060 and, since then, pilgrims had flocked from all over Europe to pray to the Holy Rood. Now, a king in a dire plight was one of them. He was accompanied by Edith Swan-Neck and spent most of the afternoon praying and listening to the plainchant of the assembled community. In the evening, Abbot Aethelsinge said a private mass for them at the high altar.

Harold thanked the Abbot and asked him to pray for him and for England.

Then, in the hoary light of a full moon, he headed for London at a gallop.

Harold and Edith were in Westminster early on the morning of 7 October 1066, where the King immediately called a Council of War.

Hereward, Alphonso and Einar were there with all the captains of the King's housecarls – over fifty of England's finest, bravest men. There were at least the same number of thegns and both Harold's brothers, the Earls Gyrth and Leofwine. Hakon, the young son of Harold's dead brother, Svein, was there, making the Godwinson family complete.

Harold had invited all opinions and viewpoints.

Leofric, Abbot of Peterborough, spoke first. 'Sire, the situation is grave and news comes daily of the atrocities committed by the Normans. But I beg you to consider caution. Duke William has nowhere to go; his back is to the sea. If you take time to gather your forces, you could outnumber him on a substantial scale.'

Esegar, Sheriff of Middlesex, spoke next. 'William the Bastard's wickedness knows no bounds. He carries the Pallium of Rome, but he is despoiling it with the blood of the Saxons. Word will soon filter back to Rome and he will lose all support in Europe. He is making a noose for his own neck.'

Godric, Sheriff of Fyfield in Berkshire, suggested a more subtle tactic. 'Gather your forces on the North Downs, or at Penshurst on the Medway; send small units to harass his army and lay waste to the entire hinterland, forcing him to come north to meet you. In a month's time you could have a fully armed and prepared force of eight thousand house-carls and twice that number of fyrdmen.'

Earl Gyrth was the last to speak. 'Godric speaks well. The advice you have heard today, my noble brother and Lord King, is sound. Let me lead the raiding parties. Give me Hereward of Bourne as my second-in-command and we will make life miserable for the Normans and buy you a month to build the greatest army England has ever seen. Do not rush to battle, my brother.'

The King cast a glance at Hereward before he responded. Hereward's nod in return indicated that he concurred with what had been said. Harold rose slowly and looked around the Great Hall of Westminster before speaking. He looked into the faces of the assembled men; there were over a hundred.

Finally, he spoke.

'My lords, abbots, sheriffs, thegns of England, brothers in our common cause, I am grateful to you for your wisdom.

I have been king for barely three seasons of a year, but already I am at a crossroads in our history. We have repelled Hardrada at Stamford Bridge, but now we are to confront an even greater threat. The people of England stand on a precipice between ignominy and glory. We have had a Roman Age in this land; we have had the Age of Alfred and the West Saxons; we have had the Age of the Danes. Now we have the chance to create an era that many of my predecessors have yearned for: an English Age for all the people of these islands, be they Saxon, Dane or Celt.

'Hardrada tried to wrest that opportunity from us; but his daunting frame lies at rest in its shroud, soon to be consumed in a Viking funeral in his homeland. Now another stands in our way: William, Duke of Normandy. He wants this land, not to lead its people, not to protect them or cherish their culture and their traditions, but for himself, to feed his greed and lust for power. I have met this man and ridden into battle alongside him. This is not a man anyone would choose as their Lord. He is vain and capricious, ruthless and cruel. He will murder and maim our people, strip them of their lands, confiscate our abbeys and monasteries and abuse our women. He is an ungodly creature and every moment he spends on English soil is an abomination. We must not delay. This crossroads for our people is lit by a beacon and it lights the way to Pevensey. That is the road we must take. And we must take it without delay!'

Still heaving from the forceful delivery of his rhetoric, he looked into their eyes once more, hoping that his words had persuaded them. It was a stirring speech – his words so powerful, his conviction so firm. By its end, every man present was prepared to forego his doubts and support his King.

Loud cheers echoed around the hall, as the warriors raised their axes and beat their shields like drums of war.

The King raised his hands, appealing for a final word. 'I am not deaf to the advice given here today. Your counsel is wise, but I am responsible for every man, woman and child who, at this very moment, is being put to the sword by the Norman butchers. I will wait until dawn on the morning of the eleventh, but no longer. All men who have made it to London by then will muster on Lambeth Fields at first light and we will leave for the coast as soon as the tally is done. Any forces not assembled by then must come on as soon as they can.'

Harold had bowed a little to those who had argued for caution and decided upon a delay of five days for preparation, consolidation and the arrival of fresh men. He had done some very agonizing arithmetic: every day meant more men for his army, but every day brought more death and suffering for the people of the south coast.

His solution to the ghastly equation was five days.

Harold raised his sword in one hand and his mace of kingship in the other. 'God bless you all. For England!'

'For Harold! For England!' came the instant reply.

17. Slaughter on Senlac Ridge

At a tearful gathering on the north side of the old bridge at Westminster on the evening of 10 October, Hereward and his followers said their farewells. They had made elaborate plans for a rendezvous, whether in victory or in defeat, in Glastonbury on the eve of All Hallows, the last day of October. The following day, on the day of celebration for All Saints, they would decide their future and determine whether their destiny had been fulfilled.

Hereward took Torfida to one side to whisper his final thoughts. 'The King has been very generous; make sure you keep the silver safely hidden. There is enough for all of you for the rest of your lives. If I don't return, but the King is victorious, you will be able to live out your days here in England. If the King perishes, this land will not be worth living in. Go south; from what Alphonso tells me, Aquitaine, Castile and León are lands to explore. It will be warm there and the girls will grow strong and healthy.'

Torfida looked at Hereward as resolutely as she could, even though her eyes were full of tears. 'I don't need any more instructions; I'm not a child. Just return safely. Stay close to the King; he will need you. He is the rightful inheritor of the Talisman of Truth and a noble warrior. Everything he has done in the past nine months has had the sure touch of a wise and gracious monarch.'

The two embraced tightly.

Hereward spoke first. 'Until All Hallows Eve, my darling.'

'Until the Feast of the Dead, my brave Hereward – the feast of the Norman dead!'

Hereward, Einar and Alphonso crossed the bridge at Westminster. Martin was already in the midst of danger, scouting the Norman camps.

The other three were about to join him in a battle which would be a fight to the death for Harold and those close to him.

By nightfall on 13 October, the Saxon army had arrived at Caldbec Hill, a well-known landmark within a few miles of the south coast, which the King had specified as the ideal rendezvous point. Martin and the other scouts had made their reports and confirmed that William was well prepared, but that he had exhausted all local supplies and would soon venture beyond his bridgehead. Morale was still high in his army, despite some impatience about the delay in attacking the hinterland and in being denied the booty waiting to be seized.

William first became aware of Harold's force as it moved from Caldbec Hill at first light the next morning. Realizing that Harold held the higher ground, the Duke despatched a contingent of horsemen and archers to try and prevent the Saxon army reaching Senlac Ridge, a point just beyond Caldbec Hill which would give Harold an ideal defensive position for his shield wall. Harold was alert to the move and immediately ordered a mass advance in battle order, a manoeuvre that was successful, despite some serious losses from the lethal crossbows of Richard of Evreux. The Saxons had never seen crossbows before and some of the fyrdmen were unnerved by them. Nevertheless, Harold had the ground he wanted and slowly, over the next two hours, the armies got themselves into position.

The English line was about 750 yards long, with house-carls at the centre and fyrdmen on the outlying flanks. The Wyvern Dragon of Wessex and his own personal standard, the Fighting Man, flew from the King's command position. There were the standards of Leofwine and Gyrth, and banners and colours from burghs and shires throughout the land. Harold's uncle, Aelfwig, the Abbot of Winchester, had arrived just before dawn. He was nearly sixty years of age and had not wielded a weapon in three decades, but he was determined to fight and had brought twelve monks and a score of men. As befitted their calling, the men of the cloth carried only maces, as the spilling of blood by the sharp edge of a sword was thought inappropriate for men of God. Aelfwig's arrival meant that there were three generations of Godwins at the battle.

Horns were sounded to usher men into position; by mid-morning both sides had settled into a state of readiness.

Harold went to squadron after squadron in the shield wall, beseeching his men to give everything for the people of England.

'Remember the stories of Alfred, told by your fathers. This land has a spirit that could not be subdued by the Danes, was not broken by Hardrada and will not be humbled by this cut-throat, William the Bastard. You are gathered here from all over our land. You fight today for your families and your homes but, most of all, for your freedom. The man you face today is a cruel and vicious warlord. He will strip us of everything we live for, burn our crops, slaughter our livestock, rape our women and murder our children. We stand between him and his evil ambition. We stand together; our shield wall will never break. Men of England, stand with me until victory is ours!'

Great cheers ran along the English line as the King galloped along in front of his men. Hereward looked at the assembled army and then at the Normans massed on the lower ground below. Somehow, close to 8,000 men had made it to the English cause. Harold's heroism, resolve and generalship had inspired them to rush to the King's standard, and they would fight with the ferocity of men protecting their homes.

Over six centuries, since the end of Roman rule, the strength of the Anglo-Saxon army had been forged on the anvil of frequent battles against its ferocious Celtic and Scandinavian neighbours, building a military ethos of the highest calibre. Despite its losses at Stamford Bridge and the absence of housecarls yet to arrive, including those of the treacherous Earls Morcar and Edwin, standing with Harold on Senlac Ridge was the greater part of the finest army in northern Europe – one of the most awesome the world had ever seen.

When the King returned to his standard, Hereward offered him his own encouragement. 'Only you could have achieved this. Here stand men of Saxon, Danish and Celtic blood, bound together by their belief in you and the England that you represent.'

'Thank you, Hereward, I am proud to have you at my side. Stay close this day.' As Harold surveyed the battlefield sweeping down before him from Senlac Ridge, the opposing cavalry and its heavily armed knights were his greatest concern.

By his side, Hereward counted almost 1,500 Norman knights in full armour with lances, axes, maces and swords. He thought of his many battles, hoping to find a key to the encounter. He looked at the ground and the formation of the army, probing to see a feature that had been overlooked, or a nuance that would offer a hidden advantage, but he could see none. Five hundred cavalry hidden in the woods would have been invaluable, but they were not there. Edwin and Morcar, the two northern earls, had remained in their earldoms; a self-seeking act that denied England over 1,000 of its finest men.

Martin, who had taken a brief rest after his reconnaissance mission, rode up and joined Hereward, Alphonso and Einar in a position just behind the King, whose hearthtroop of two squadrons was fanned out in front of him. The four loyal comrades dismounted and Alphonso secured their horses to the rear. It was unlikely that they would be needed; this fight would not be about rapid pursuit or hasty withdrawal, it would be a fight for the ground they stood on – England's ground.

Hereward turned to his companions. 'If the battle goes badly, I will stand my ground with the King. If he falls, I will fall with him. Stay for as long as you can be useful to the King, then make haste to your loved ones. Take this to Torfida.' Hereward handed Einar a small purse of leather, which held a lock of his golden hair. 'God be with you, my friends.'

'God be with you, Hereward,' all three replied in unison.

Preparations in the Norman ranks were equally well advanced.

They numbered over 9,000 and were organized into three army groups: Breton allies to the left on the western side, French and Flemish supporters and mercenaries to the right on the eastern side and the bulk of the force, the Normans, in the centre. William had adopted an unusual pattern of deployment. He sent his archers forward, just out of range of the English bowmen, his infantry arranged in deep columns behind them and his squadrons of cavalry drawn up in the rear. His own command position was central to the last squadron of cavalry, identified by the papal pallium, held aloft by Pope Alexander's legate to Rouen.

Flying next to the pallium, stiffened by gusting winds from the English Channel to the south, were William's standard, the Leopard of Normandy, and the standards of all the warlords of Normandy and surrounding territories: Eustace, Count of Boulogne, an opportunist with a brutal reputation; Geoffrey, Bishop of Coutances, who led the prayers before the battle; Hugh de Grandmesnil, a warrior of great repute; Hugh de Montfort, a resolute soldier of fortune; William's half-brother, the ruthless and ambitious Odo, Bishop of Bayeux; and William's trusted henchmen who would go anywhere for a fight – Walter Gifford, William of Malet, William of Evreux, William Fitzsbern and William Warenne.

The Duke's battle cry was short and to the point. He rode out in front of his infantry, in the space between them and the archers, and above the distant din of derision from the English, bellowed in his deep, coarse voice.

'You have travelled with me on a great voyage to fight on a distant shore. You have done so in the noble tradition of our Viking ancestors. This fight was not of our making, nor was it born from the desire for naked conquest; this land was rightfully granted to me by King Edward of England, a wise and gentle king. We are here to claim what is rightfully ours. The Pope knows this and gives us his holy blessing; the rest of Europe knows this and lends its support. The richest land in northern Europe is before you. Fight to make it a Norman kingdom for your children and your grandchildren. You are the bravest of the brave.'

As the Norman roars echoed up the hill, the English hollered back, until the whole countryside was filled with the ear-splitting tumult of almost 20,000 indomitable men.

Now, there was nothing left for either army to do but fight.

On William's signal, his archers and crossbowmen advanced within range and began their fusillade at the English shield wall. As they did so, his infantry launched its first assault, making slow progress towards Senlac Ridge. They sang the 'Song of Roland' as they went, but the melody soon faded, to be replaced by the shocking clash of sword against sword and the agonizing cries of foe against foe.

After almost an hour of fighting, neither the Norman archers nor their infantry had made much impact on the English shield wall. Every time there was a minor breach, it was filled by equally formidable housecarls from the King's reinforcements. The circular shields of the English allowed them to close or open their wall at will, gave them much more freedom to brandish their battle-axes and meant that they could adopt the Roman 'testudo' – the turtle – to cover themselves against hails of arrows.

The Normans' kite-shaped shield was much better suited

to combat on horseback, where the narrow base could protect the legs of the mounted warrior. As the Normans withdrew, the ground was littered with their dead; hundreds of men had perished – almost five Normans to each Englishman.

It was time for William to launch his much-vaunted cavalry.

His powerful destriers, despite carrying 200 lbs of man and armour, managed a reasonable gallop, even up the significant gradient of Senlac Ridge. As their ground was less steep, the Bretons reached the shield wall first, but did not have enough momentum to dent it. They had to turn sideways to strike with their axes and swords, making them easy prey for the defenders. Much the same happened on the French-Flemish right. In the centre, the much more formidable elite Norman squadrons did make some breaches, but they were easily filled; Hereward and his companions rushed to any vulnerable points to reinforce the wall until replacements arrived from the rear.

Hereward was issuing vital commands in between close-quarter encounters with Norman knights who had breached the defensive line. He brought several down by scything their huge destriers from under them; others he hewed out of their saddle with a single sweep of his legendary axe. At crucial moments, Harold rode along the line, encouraging his men, but they hardly needed it. Their line was holding and the Normans were dying in droves.

William sat impassively on his destrier and waited. He knew the day was still young and that this would be a bloody battle of attrition at the cost of many lives. Eventually, in what appeared to be an English breakthrough, the Breton left reeled and retreated at a gallop. Naïvely thinking the battle won, large groups of fyrdmen on the English right broke ranks and hurried after them.

Hereward and his comrades were off at full pelt even before the King issued his urgent command: 'Stop them! Hereward, get them back into the shield wall! Hurry!'

William had also seen the English fyrdmen break ranks and immediately galloped into the fray with his Matilda Squadron. English housecarls had followed the Fyrd to try and re-establish discipline. When Hereward and his companions arrived, they organized a redoubt on a small hillock. Martin sounded his horn to summon a recall and Hereward ripped the jerkin off a dead Norman archer and waved it above his head on a spear to signal a rallying point for the fyrdman, now scattered far and wide. Within minutes, a new wall was formed on the hillock and the fyrdmen had closed ranks behind the housecarls.

Harold ordered the English archers to put up a lethal volley of arrows above William's advancing squadron just as it got within 100 yards of the redoubt. William's horse took an arrow through its neck and collapsed under him, violently throwing him to the ground. A great cry of alarm went up from the Normans, who feared their leader was dead. But the Duke quickly regained his feet and was soon on a new mount, raising his helmet to show that he was still alive. He waved his Baculus furiously, berating the fleeing Bretons and demanding that they turn and fight. His dramatic intervention worked and the Breton cavalry formed up behind his Matilda Squadron to launch another assault.

Hereward tried to keep the fyrdmen in tight formation as he ordered the housecarls to make a disciplined withdrawal back up Senlac Ridge. But when William's elite cavalry careened into the wall, many breaches were forced. Hereward had no choice but to order the shield wall to disengage and retreat en masse. Despite the valiant efforts of small groups of housecarls to defend the escaping fyrdmen by using their spears to try and slow the Norman momentum, chaos and carnage were inevitable.

William recalled his cavalry. Fortune had smiled once more on one of Harold's battles – but this time on his opponent. The headlong rush by the Fyrd was a folly which might prove to be decisive. There had been heavy casualties all along the English shield wall, so much so that when Harold ordered it to tighten its formation, a line of defence that had started at over 750 yards was now barely 500 yards long.

Hereward and his companions were among the last to get back into position, marshalling the final laggards and helping some of the wounded to get back to relative safety.

Both William and Harold looked at the sun as it moved towards the tall trees in the woods to the west. Morning had turned into afternoon. Reports were coming in that hundreds of housecarls were approaching from London and would soon reinforce Harold's position.

With the battle hanging precariously in the balance, Harold turned to Hereward.

'I need an hour less in the day, or five hundred more men. If William continues to throw his cavalry at the wall, it will break before the sun falls behind those trees.'

'Sire, if we're still holding at four hours past midday, William will have to retreat and we will have him in the morning.'

'Yes, Hereward. But I don't think we can hold for four hours; two and a half, three at the most. Let's rally the men. Somehow, they will have to buy us that hour.'

William had also done his calculations. After twenty minutes of regrouping, he ordered attack after attack: first infantry, then cavalry. Then, after a brief respite for regrouping, the onslaughts were repeated again and again. Like the English housecarls, he was battling against the hourglass as well as a ferocious enemy. The fighting was savage, with both sides taking huge losses, as William sacrificed his men to shorten Harold's shield wall.

Crucially, as it shrank to protect its own flanks, it began to turn into a crescent, allowing the Normans to reach the flat terrain of Senlac Ridge. From there, their cavalry could gain much more momentum and their infantry could fight on even ground. Nevertheless, Harold's army was still holding firm after two hours of vicious fighting. Harold and Hereward led by example; first on the left flank, then on the right. Both men were in the thick of the relentless struggle, as wave after wave of Norman destriers broke against the barricade of Englishmen. The defenders, although diminished in number, had lost none of their redoubtable spirit nor their renowned discipline. The sun was now low in the sky. The scales were tipping towards Harold; the courage of his housecarls was buying him the time he needed.

Then the Duke pulled off a masterstroke. Throughout the day he had been disappointed that his archers had been far less effective than he had hoped, so he tried a new tactic. He summoned the captains of his elite cavalry squadrons and his master bowmen and described to them a complex synchronized attack, where precise timing would be critical. He had made an important mental calculation about the speed of his cavalry and the length of time his arrows would be in the air.

If he got his arithmetic right, it could strike a mortal blow to the heart of the English line.

He ordered his archers to form up 100 yards behind his crossbowmen and for both to deploy in small units so that his cavalry squadrons could make their charge between their ranks. Next he ordered his squadrons to charge at full gallop and, as they passed his archers, they were to loose off the first of two rapid volleys high into the air against the English shield wall. By the time the cavalry reached the crossbow-men, they would be at full tilt. At that moment, the crossbowmen would shoot a single volley of bolts at a low trajectory. This would coincide with the English raising their shields in the testudo to protect them against the first hail of arrows from overhead, catching them in a withering cross-shoot of arrows and bolts. Usually, the testudo would deal with such a two-pronged attack with ease. However, with the Norman cavalry descending on them in over-whelming numbers, the testudo would have to break to allow the housecarls to deploy their spears against the destriers. If, at that exact moment, the second volley of arrows arrived from above, there would be slaughter – especially when, within seconds, the cavalry fell upon them.

William's calculations were murderously precise; the timing of the Norman archers, bowmen and cavalry was perfect and Harold's shield wall was thrown into disarray. At the vital moment in the battle, William had produced a stroke of military genius.

English reinforcements rushed forward to try and seal the devastated shield wall, exhausting Harold's reserves. For the first time, rather than reinforcing gaps, his personal hearthtroop was heavily engaged. Two Godwinsons fell within moments of one another: Earl Leofwine took an arrow in the eye and Earl Gyrth was cut down by a formidable Norman knight who caught him in open ground.

The tide had turned.

Hereward looked at the distant trees and saw that the sun had just fallen behind the tall branches of the canopy. It was perhaps four thirty in the afternoon, but dusk had not come soon enough for the English; neither would reinforcements. The King had been right: if the day had been perhaps an hour shorter, or if 500 more housecarls had arrived from London, the outcome would have been different. William's ploy would still have been effective, but almost certainly not decisive. The English would have had the numbers to regroup, leaving the Normans with no alternative but to take flight to the coast in search of their ships.

As their position worsened to the point of desperation, the English Fyrd melted away. William's strategy of attrition had taken all day, but it had worked. Many of Harold's surviving housecarls began to form a final redoubt around their King. No more than 1,000 Englishmen stood between the Normans and the greatest prize in northern Europe.

In the ever-deepening gloom, the ensuing slaughter of the Anglo-Saxon military and aristocratic elite lasted over an hour. No quarter was offered, or sought, as the protective ring around the King became smaller and smaller and the pile of corpses grew higher and higher.

Eventually, the Norman destriers were encouraged to

rake away the fallen English with their hooves, so that more could be killed. Squads were despatched by the Norman sergeants of infantry to clear the ground of dead to allow yet more carnage. Harold stood at the epicentre of it all, valiantly challenging his housecarls to even greater efforts and yet more courageous resistance. Around him were the strongest and bravest of his men, determined to make the Normans pay the highest possible price for their victory. Hereward stood beside his King, as he had promised he would, matching every blow of Harold's with one of his own, inspiring his men and writing his name into legend.

Harold remained unharmed. Hereward had been less fortunate, having taken a crossbow bolt in his thigh and one in the shoulder. He had also taken a sword slash across his chest, from which blood was seeping through his hauberk. Despite Hereward's insistence that they make their way to safety should the battle appear lost, Martin, Einar and Alphonso remained close by.

Alphonso spoke first as the circle became tighter and tighter around the King.

'Hereward, the day is lost. The English are finished. You must leave. We can regroup in the North and fight another day.'

'Not while the King stands, Alphonso. He won't leave the field and if he is to perish, then I will die by his side –'

Martin interjected. 'Let's get the King away. We and his hearthtroop can fight our way out. If needs be, Einar can carry him out!'

Einar needed no second invitation and was already making for the King. He would have readily knocked him cold and thrown him over his shoulder to ensure his safety.

'Hold!' Hereward bellowed at his friend. 'The King has chosen his ground. There is no retreat; I stand here with him.'

'Then we stand with you.'

Duke William was circling the melee from a distance of about 100 yards, his Baculus dripping crimson from the punishment it had meted out. He had been heavily involved in the fighting and was now on his third mount of the day. He summoned four of his most powerful knights: Eustace of Boulogne, Hugh of Ponthieu, Walter Gifford and Hugh de Montfort.

'The English are finished. Bring me the body of Harold, then the rest will scatter.'

The four collected discarded lances from the battlefield, raised their maces and set off at a gallop into the boiling scrum of fighting men. They made straight for the King, who was trying to seal breaches in the ring of housecarls. As the knights' destriers bludgeoned their way towards him, Hereward was alert to the danger and brought Eustace of Boulogne to the ground by scything away the front legs of his mount with the Great Axe of Göteborg. Horse and rider hit Hereward hard as they fell, pinning him to the ground. Walter Gifford grasped the opportunity and plunged his lance through the shoulder of Hereward's hauberk, a blow that exited below his collarbone and stuck firmly into the ground beneath him. Hereward, still trapped under the horse, quickly lost consciousness.

The knights made for the King. He had become completely isolated from his bodyguards as the massed Norman cavalry engulfed the English defenders.

Surrounded by four ferocious knights, three on horseback, he stood little chance.

Hereward's companions had a simple choice: to attempt to protect the King or to save their friend and mentor. They did not hesitate and were at Hereward's side in an instant. While Martin lifted and pulled Hereward's shoulders, Einar and Alphonso used their shields and spears to lever the weight of the stricken destrier, freeing him from under the animal. Mercifully, he was unconscious, so they could act without regard for pain. Einar used his great strength to break off the head of the lance and pull out its shaft, while Alphonso dragged out the arrows, tearing flesh as he did so.

The day was almost done and it was all but dark. They took their chance to escape in the gloom and the growing hysteria of the victorious Normans. Einar hauled Hereward on to his shoulder, picked up his weapons and, with Martin and Alphonso providing protection from would-be assailants, they made for the distant undergrowth, where Alphonso had tethered their horses.

Despite a prolonged and valiant resistance, his housecarls dead or facing their own demise in small pockets around the last redoubt, the four Norman assasins showed Harold no pity. After bringing him to exhaustion by their onslaught, they taunted him with their lances, piercing his flesh as a hag would stick pins in a clay effigy. They smashed his head and body with their maces, and then impaled him on their lances as if they were skewering a wild pig. Finally, while he still lived, they hacked him to pieces with their swords.

Harold's gruesome death did not have the effect anticipated by Duke William. Its savagery roused the remaining housecarls to fight even more ferociously, until none was left standing. It was a scene of mayhem. Men, crazed by killing, screamed like animals as their horses trampled over the dead and the dying. Many of the Norman knights rode off in pursuit of fleeing Englishmen in order to commit yet more acts of brutality.

The Wyvern of Wessex was ripped to shreds and Harold's personal standard, the Fighting Man, blood-spattered and torn, was handed to William, who immediately gave it to a messenger with instructions to have it delivered to the Pope in Rome.

In the murk of the autumn evening 500 housecarls drew close to the battlefield; they were the reinforcements for which Harold had prayed. Ashamed by the cowardly stance taken by the earls Edwin and Morcar, many of the younger thegns of Mercia and Northumbria had made the long march from the North. On hearing of the muster at Caldbec, they had ridden straight through London, picking up provisions as they rode.

It was an astonishing feat of endurance but, sadly for Harold and for England, they were forty-five minutes too late to save the day. When they saw the Norman knights hounding the remnants of Harold's army in headlong flight, they formed up on a ridge above a narrow valley and ambushed wave upon wave of them, until several hundred bodies filled the ravine at a place the Normans immediately christened the 'Malfosse'. Although the moment seemed sweet, the Northerners soon heard of the catastrophe at Senlac and the slaughter of the King. They had little choice but to melt away to avoid the main force of Normans.

After sounding a general recall to try and get some

discipline back into his forces, William and his high command, too exhausted to go anywhere, spent the night on the battlefield amid the bodies of the dead and dying.

Hereward's companions escaped under darkness and took his shattered body westwards across the Downs as far as they could, before descending into a wooded valley to find water and a place to camp. Hereward's breathing was shallow, his complexion ashen and his body temperature minimal. Death was near. Alphonso, the most knowledgeable about wounds and healing, faced a dilemma: should he cauterize the wounds with a hot blade to prevent infection? If he did, the shock might be too much in Hereward's weakened state.

As his leader was still unconscious, Alphonso decided to sear the wounds. With Einar and Martin holding Hereward's body, Alphonso applied a heated seax, making his leader convulse with shock. They dressed his wounds tightly and wrapped him in his warm winter cloak before carefully placing him close to the fire. Martin went off to hunt hare or rabbit, while the others took turns to stand sentry.

It was thirty-six hours before Hereward regained consciousness, and they immediately began to force food into his mouth. Alphonso's worst fears were soon realized: he was infected. It was almost certainly blood poisoning caused by arrows dipped in some form of poison or human and animal faeces. It was a well-known trick of archers to add the insult of poison to the injury of the arrowhead. They needed to find a physician – not easy at the best of times, but with the country about to dissolve into panic and chaos after a calamitous defeat, it might well be impossible.

Their first thought was Torfida at Glastonbury, but that was too far. Their second hope was Harold's manor at Bosham, but they thought it likely that William would soon despatch some men there to defile further the King's memory. They decided that Winchester would be the safest option. Although Edith, King Edward's widow, was thought to have conspired with Tostig against King Harold, she was, after all, a Godwinson and Harold's sister. Surely, after the slaughter at Senlac Ridge, she would offer Hereward the assistance of her physicians.

The three men made a stretcher from branches and tied the head end to the saddle of Hereward's horse. They then took it in turns to form a pair to carry the feet end, while the third led the horses. Hereward was over the initial shock of his injuries and the loss of blood. The first threat to his life, caused by the trauma of his wounds, had passed. But his body boiled with fever. Whenever he was conscious enough, they poured water or stew down his throat. Three times they opened his arrow wounds, cleaned them out and cauterized them again. Fortunately, the spear wound to his shoulder, although the most severe, had not become infected.

They made slow progress, taking almost a week to get to Winchester. When they arrived, the gates were closed and the sentries nervous. Only their bloodstained jerkins, easily recognizable as those worn by Harold's elite hearth-troop, earned the four of them admission to the burgh. Several fyrdmen and a few surviving housecarls had made it to Winchester, so the details of the battle were known.

Before the three weary men made any attempt to seek help, they received bad news. William's forces were on the loose, and Dover had been looted and burned. Part of the Norman army was approaching Canterbury and several squadrons were reported to be heading west towards Winchester. The old Queen had already made a hasty departure for the nunnery at Salisbury. Most of the garrison had left and were heading for Glastonbury; there would be little help for Hereward in Winchester.

Praying that Hereward would survive another long journey, his three companions bought a cart and oxen, loaded it with whatever supplies they could buy, and departed north-west for Glastonbury. They estimated they could be there by the eve of All Hallows, the agreed date set for their rendezvous. The roads and tracks were deserted, as people, paralysed by fright, ceased trading and sought refuge wherever they could find it. Winter would soon make it difficult for the Normans to rampage across the land; in the meantime, everyone hoped that they would be the fortunate ones and escape the ravenous eye of the new regime.

Torfida, Ingigerd and Maria had been sorely tempted to rush to London with their girls when news of the terrible defeat reached Glastonbury. The report said that all but a tiny handful had perished with the King. They were even more inclined to go when they heard that Earls Edwin and Morcar had belatedly arrived in London with a large contingent of housecarls. As England's only surviving senior earls, they had called a Witan at which Edgar the Atheling had been elected King in succession to the slain Harold.

However, the three women had decided to wait until the date of their agreed rendezvous had passed before making any journey. All logic suggested that their men were with Harold, lying dead on the battlefield, mutilated and stripped of anything worth stealing. Torfida was certain that Hereward would have fallen next to the King and also suffered whatever ghastly fate had befallen him.

The wisdom of their decision was confirmed only days later by the news that, two days after the Witan and the promotion of Edgar as King, Edwin and Morcar, whose treachery seemed to know no bounds, had decided that London could not be defended and had retreated to their realms in the North.

William had shown just one small mercy on Senlac Ridge.

Late in the afternoon, on the day following the slaughter, Edith Swan-Neck had arrived on the battlefield. She was accompanied by two housecarls and a monk from Bosham Abbey, Harold's private chapel. Dressed in the sombre black of mourning, her dignified beauty shone like a beacon amid the lifeless flesh of the battlefield.

Immediately recognizing her status, William nodded politely as she approached.

'How may I help you, my Lady?'

'My Lord Duke, I am Edith Swan-Neck and I have come to collect that which is rightfully mine – the body of my beloved, the King of England, Harold Godwinson.'

William's response was firm. 'You may not have him, madam. I will not have him become a martyr to his people.'

'He is already a martyr, no matter what you do with his body. I just want a Christian burial for my husband.'

'But you are not his wife. His Queen is Ealdgyth; she awaits in London.'

'She is his Queen in name only. By ancient custom, I am his wife and the mother of his children. You have no right to deny me this.' She flashed a look of defiance at the Duke, sufficient for him to vacillate.

He turned to Odo, Bishop of Bayeux. 'What is your advice?'

'It is not a spiritual issue, my brother; it is a matter of common sense. You have to rule these people from now on, so it would be wise at least to allow their dead King a Christian burial.'

William thought for some time about Edith's request. Like the English men he had just defeated on the battlefield, here was one of their womenfolk with the same stubborn resolve.

A gust of wind blew off the Channel, a breeze that had the chill of winter in it.

The Duke shivered. 'Madam, if you can find it up there, you may take the body. My trusted friend William of Malet will accompany you. Harold must be buried in an unmarked grave on the shore he so dismally failed to protect. It will be done this night, in darkness, in a secret place, so that no one may return to dig his body up and make a sacred tomb for him elsewhere. See that it is done.'

The Duke would make no further concessions.

When she reached the place where William of Malet suggested the King had fallen, Edith took off her shoes, pulled her dress up to her thighs, tied it in a knot and strode into the heap of bodies. In the fading light, aided by a single lantern, it took them nearly an hour to find Harold's body. Her mind set on her purpose, Edith paid almost no attention to the remnants of men beneath her feet. All weapons, hauberks and valuables had already been removed, so it was difficult to tell one corpse from another, but Harold bore a telltale mark that only a few had seen, an emblem that Edith knew intimately.

Without hesitation or a hint of repulsion, she pulled at the tunics of body after body to reveal their belly below the navel. At last, she found what she was looking for and sank to her knees to touch him. He was tattooed just above his pubic hair with the Wyvern, the Dragon of Wessex, and coiled around the dragon's legs was a phallic serpent, its head and protruding forked tongue pointing towards his manhood. Only the King's torso was intact; his limbs had been scattered and his head, severed from his body and bludgeoned beyond recognition, was only discernible by his distinctive mane of golden hair.

Edith was sobbing profusely, her dress and cloak covered in blood. She turned to William Malet and screamed, 'You cowardly barbarian! You bastard servants of a bastard lord, you've hacked his manhood from his body. May you and all Normans be cursed for ever!'

When William heard Edith's accusations and learned that Hugh de Montfort had committed the crime, he immediately ordered that he be banished from Normandy for a year. Then, in front of Edith, he was stripped of his weapons and armour, tethered to a horse, and ridden out of camp.

There was a strange irony in the severity of William's response. Warrior knights were expected to behave savagely in battle, but to castrate a man in death was the action of a heathen. According to a knight's code of chivalry, men fought for honour or gain, where any level of brutality was permitted, but only savages fought for barbaric prizes like an opponent's manhood.

It had begun to rain heavily as William Malet's men helped Edith Swan-Neck gather the parts of Harold's body. They were wrapped in a plain linen shroud brought specially from Bosham and transported to the shore as William had instructed. A pile of stones to mark a grave was not permitted and while the monk from Bosham read over him, King Harold of England was interred in a shallow pit in the sand just above the high-water mark. Then, by following a circuitous route in total darkness, the Normans tried hard to ensure that it would be difficult ever again to find the King's grave.

Nonetheless, Edith used every method she could think of to memorize the King's last journey.

A few months later, in the dead of a January night in 1067, Edith was able to retrace her footsteps.

With the help of four monks from his abbey at Waltham, and after many hours digging in the sand, Harold's body was retrieved. Later, in a clandestine ceremony, it was reinterred beneath the high altar of Waltham.

William and the Norman hierarchy never discovered the truth, but among the English people word soon spread about Harold's final resting place and Waltham Abbey became a place of secret pilgrimage for all Englishmen from that day forward.

John Comnenus had grown concerned about Godwin of Ely. His vivid account had extended late into another night and, as he described the gruesome encounter of Senlac Ridge, his hands had begun to shake and perspiration had dripped from his brow.

'Would you like to rest for a while?'

'You are very kind, my Prince. If I may, I will go to my shelter and spend a few hours alone.'

'Of course; take as much time as you need. Perhaps Prince Azoukh and I will walk in the mountains for a while when the sun comes up.'

After sleeping for a few hours, the two princes, accompanied by a platoon of bodyguards, stretched their legs in a leisurely circuit around Godwin's mountain-top retreat.

Both deep in thought, John Azoukh broke the mood of reflection. 'It is certainly a tale of mighty warriors, my friend. I'm glad that the likes of Harold and William lived far to the north and never threatened the gates of Constantinople.'

'My father has told me about Hardrada. People at court still talk about him with reverence, as they do Godwin of Ely. I wonder if England has benefited from the presence of men of such stature, all living at the same time? Or has it been a curse? Just imagine: the giant Hardrada, William the fearsome redheaded ogre and the two golden-haired English heroes. What times they were! The Greek poets couldn't have invented a finer cast of characters.'

'Yes, and there seems to be much more to hear.'

'I hope so'

John Azoukh looked at his friend with a hint of concern on his face. 'My friend, when you hear of the trials and tribulations of kings and rulers, does it inspire you? Or does it fill you with dread about your own succession?'

'I suppose the answer is both, in equal measure. My father has spent his life campaigning against the many enemies on our borders. When he was not doing that, he was wrestling with our enemies within. He's weary and now his reward is a slow and painful death. It seems a cruel end. On the other hand, he has had the power to protect our empire and change the lives of his people. He has won their respect and trust, and will be long remembered for it. Like Harold of England, he has done his duty.' John Comnenus paused and put his arm around his friend. 'That's my only ambition. With all the excitement and anguish it will bring, I intend to do my duty.'

The two princes smiled at one another and made their way back to Godwin's eyrie.

The old warrior was waiting for them when they returned. He was already sitting in his chosen spot with Leo of Methone helping him to get comfortable. He seemed refreshed and eager to resume his story.

'Come, my two lords of Byzantium, I thought you'd lost your way on my mountain. My tale is barely half told.'

18. A Presence in the Mist

For the survivors of Senlac Ridge, the return to Glastonbury was an occasion for tears of joy and sadness. Word
had already reached Harold's stronghold of the approach
of Hereward and his companions, so a welcome party was
waiting. As the wives and children rushed down the hill
shrieking with delight, a few sturdy veterans of Harold's
hearthtroop stood vanguard. News of Hereward's valour
had reached all corners of the land and the men snapped
to attention and looked on in awe as he passed. Rumours
about his exploits had spread, rapidly escalating into ever
more fantastic tales. It was said that it was impossible to
kill him and that his immortality was a beacon that would
summon men to his side to save England. In truth, his life
was still hanging by the slender thread that the care of his
followers had spun for him.

Torfida rushed to his side, but he barely recognized her.
She could see the poison in his bloodshot eyes and immediately started to plan his recovery. Gunnhild and Estrith
were hysterical and had to be comforted by Ingigerd and
Maria.

Early the next day, heavily armed and fully provisioned,
Einar led the group out of Glastonbury and into the
Mendip Hills to find a hiding place deep in the wildwood.
Torfida knew Hereward would not survive a winter on the
run. She also knew that William's ample purse would entice

countless spies to divulge the whereabouts of any survivors of the English nobility or of Harold's army, especially one as distinguished as Hereward.

Within forty-eight hours, a suitable camp had been established in the depths of the forest. A harsh winter would soon be upon them. Hereward's prospects were not auspicious. Injured as he was, movement was difficult, exercise impossible. It would be hard for him to fight the infection, even harder for him to keep his lungs clear of pneumonia.

Under Torfida's earnest directions, an elaborate programme began. All the adults took it in turns to lift, pull, stretch and bend him to keep his muscles supple, exercise his lungs and improve his circulation. His dressings were changed every day and his wounds cleaned. He had his own latrine next to his bed and a special diet rich in Torfida's herbal remedies. Hereward began to improve but, as he did so, Torfida began to suffer. She worked endlessly, never seemed to sleep and began to lose weight. No amount of cajoling or berating from the others would make her rest.

By March of 1067, much progress had been made. Hereward's life was no longer in danger and he was able to walk, even if his movements were laboured and painful. Perversely, to everyone's dismay, as Hereward regained his vitality, Torfida lost hers. It was as if she were transferring her own lifeblood to him. When the family expressed their concerns, she dismissed them, saying that now Hereward was healing, her own recovery would soon follow.

Martin had been back to Glastonbury several times and news had reached the camp of William's coronation on Christmas Day 1066, and the subsequent severity of his rule over south-east England. William's army had marauded across the south, forcing all the burghs to submit. Canterbury, Guildford, Winchester, Wallingford, Bedford, Cambridge, Hertford and, finally, London had all stooped to the new monarch. He had spent the winter at the abbey in Barking, in Essex, but by the time of the first spring sailings in the Channel he felt confident enough to return to Normandy. There, in a celebratory tour of his Duchy with his English hostages in tow, he was fêted as the conquering hero.

Hereward had taken the news of Harold's death with predictable anguish, especially as he had survived while his King had died, but there was no anger in his eyes, only sadness. He spent many hours staring into the distance, gazing at the tall trees of the forest. No one mentioned the Talisman; all assumed it was now a trinket in the horde of a fat Norman lord, or else lost amid the morass of human remains on Senlac Ridge. However, it soon reappeared in the lives of Hereward and Torfida.

But not as they would have wished.

It was the end of a very warm spring day. With the aid of a thick staff, Hereward had started to walk in the meadows on his own, where he would gently swing his sword through the burgeoning greenery of the forest floor. His arms were not yet sturdy enough for the Great Axe of Göteborg, but they were getting stronger by the day.

Torfida still looked worryingly thin and tired, and her hair was turning grey. Hereward was concerned about his wife and was determined to find a new life for them that would allow her some rest and peace of mind.

At first, Hereward thought he was witnessing an apparition. He had sat down at the edge of a clearing to watch the approaching sunset when, in the middle distance, striding through the glade in the mist of the early evening was what seemed to be the glistening form of a woman. She was naked, her flowing hair framing her head and shoulders like a cowl; her soft beige skin gleamed with oil, her broad hips and large breasts the focal points of a woman of astounding physical symmetry. She moved slowly, her eyes sharply focused, her jaw set.

Hereward soon knew the figure was not an apparition. It was then that he saw the Talisman cradled between the woman's breasts.

Edith Swan-Neck had pulled the Talisman from Harold's severed neck on Senlac Ridge and had vowed to return it to Hereward. She knew it had been important to Harold and that Hereward and Torfida regarded it as something of great spiritual value. Her grief for Harold was deep and genuine and at first she had no intention of seducing Hereward. However, as time passed and news of his survival reached her, her mood changed. Not only was he handsome and strong, he had become England's only chance. A new army could be built around him.

These thoughts worked on her imagination until the notion of a man formidable enough to save England in its hour of need became irresistible to her. She had found Martin on one of his visits to Glastonbury and persuaded him to take her to their camp. Her good fortune found Torfida out in the forest in search of herbs, and Hereward alone in the meadows.

Hereward swallowed hard. As Edith got closer, he could

smell the musk from the oil on her body. It invaded his senses with an aroma that pumped adrenalin through his veins and made him feel that his legendary strength had returned.

Edith did not hesitate. Parting her legs provocatively, she placed her feet either side of Hereward's prone legs, and sat on his thighs. His eyes were drawn to her pubic hair, which her body oil had coiled into tight ringlets, then to her breasts, which were only inches from his face.

He loved Torfida, but how could a man face such an enticing prospect and reject it?

'Hereward, you cannot know how much I've longed for this moment.'

Hereward did not respond. He was using all his resolve to resist the almost impossible temptation of England's most beguiling woman.

'England needs you . . . I need you. Together, we could raise an army strong enough to break the stranglehold the Normans have on this land. Their grip grows crueller by the day.'

Edith's quarry was still silent. He had closed his eyes, hoping to blind himself to her charms.

Even so, Edith could feel that he was aroused, and she continued her slow and cunning seduction. 'With me at your side, we can rule! The Witan would accept you as Regent, until the Atheling is ready. Then you would get an earldom. You could become the Earl of Wessex and Earl Marshal of England.'

Hereward was about to speak, but Edith began now to kiss him fervently, using her tongue to probe deeply into his mouth. She grabbed his head and pulled it to her breasts.

It was then that the Talisman, swinging wildly from Edith's neck, struck him on the temple.

He caught sight of its image of evil, giving him a sobering jolt and breaking the spell woven by the seductress above him. 'Edith, we must not do this. I would risk almost anything to have you here and now, but I cannot. I love Torfida. Please, stop!'

Edith ignored his plea and continued to caress him, her words calculated to break down his resistance. 'Hereward, don't think of Torfida, think of us and England! Torfida can have an estate in the country. She can pursue her destiny and, one day, her dream of designing cathedrals. I'll even let you go and serve her from time to time.'

Then to his horror, over Edith's shoulder, Hereward saw Torfida step into the glade. She had returned to the camp with her basket full of roots and herbs. Hearing from Martin that Edith had arrived with the Talisman, she had left in search of Hereward.

There was a prolonged, piercing scream of anguish when Torfida saw Edith's naked form astride her husband. She could see Edith throwing her head back and forth in delight as she caressed her husband. Hysterical, her heart full of hurt and fury, she turned and ran.

Hereward pushed Edith away and struggled to his feet. 'Torfida, wait! It is not what you think.' He repeated his plea several times, but to no avail. He was in no condition to chase after her and began stumbling back to the camp.

Edith stood up, uninhibited by her nakedness. Without speaking, she pulled the Talisman from her neck, placed it over Hereward's head and kissed him gently.

Hereward looked at her impassively. 'Please, go.'

Edith Swan-Neck, the legendary siren of England, smiled and walked away into the haze, her gait as seductive as when she had entered the glade.

Torfida ran back to the camp, her anguish turning to a steely resolve. She explained to Gunnhild and Estrith that she had to leave for a few days on urgent business for the late King, then gathered a few personal belongings and asked Ingigerd and Maria to look after the girls.

She was gone within minutes of her abrupt arrival.

Her intention was to take time to compose herself before deciding how to respond to what she had witnessed. She knew that the hurt she felt would prevent her from thinking clearly. Her dream had been shattered; her destiny with Hereward had been stolen. It would be many days before she could think clearly. She resolved not to take the girls, unwilling to burden them with the trauma of what Hereward and Edith had done to her.

She fully expected to be back with her beloved daughters after a few days of prayer and reflection. However, fate was about to deal her a cruel hand.

Hereward hobbled into the camp only minutes after Torfida's abrupt departure. Sparing no details from his friends, he explained what had transpired. He was a broken man and it took long, agonizing minutes for him to relate the scene with Edith. The men immediately went in search of Torfida, but she had taken a horse and had already outpaced them.

They searched and searched; days passed, then weeks. No sign of her was to be found. She had disappeared from their lives.

Hereward's despair at the loss of his beloved Torfida

only worsened as time passed. His girls were bewildered and hurt and desperately needed their father's love. He tortured himself with constant questions. Had Torfida returned to the life her father had lived – as a hermit of the forest – consumed by anger for what had happened? If so, why could they not find her? Had her journey been an aimless meander, without a destination? Even so, she must have left a trace somewhere, or been seen by someone. Was she still in search of herself and her destiny? But why had she abandoned everything she cared for and left everyone she loved, especially her children? Had she taken her own life? Surely, it was not possible that Torfida could have committed such a desperate act. After months of anguish, Hereward's grief turned to resentment that she had left him without a word of explanation.

Torfida had come into his life cloaked in mystery, the result of a prophecy; she left it in an unfathomable riddle.

It was only when the long days of summer began to shorten in the late autumn of 1067 that Hereward's loyal companions began to tire of his increasingly futile searches for Torfida.

A summit was called by Einar at which they challenged Hereward and, although he protested, stood their ground. Their strongest argument was the future of the children. Given that Earls Edwin and Morcar had submitted to William, Hereward was once again an outlaw and the Duke would hunt him down without mercy. They insisted that Hereward follow the advice he had so earnestly given to Torfida in the event of his death on Senlac Ridge: 'Go south, to Aquitaine, to Castile or León.'

It was a part of the world Alphonso knew well, and he gave a vivid description of the lands he loved: they were prosperous, rich of harvest, warm, both in climate and in the demeanour of their peoples, and a long way from England's trauma. Hereward offered only token resistance to the plan. In his heart, he knew Torfida had gone. He had always been able to sense her presence, even when they were apart; now there was only a void.

England was also in despair. William's grip on the country was tightening and his henchmen were building their mottes and baileys all over the land. Whenever a hint of resistance appeared, it was extinguished with a ferocity that struck fear into the hearts of Englishmen of all ranks.

After the decision to leave England had been taken, the family chose Aquitaine as their destination. There had been recent squabbles between the princes in Spain's Castile and León, so the peaceful domain of the Count of Toulouse was their considered choice. Einar took charge of the journey and Ingigerd and Maria became surrogate mothers to Gunnhild and Estrith.

Passage south was secured on a trading vessel, plying its wares between Exeter and St Brieuc in Brittany. After several more days on a Basque merchantman, the warmth of the south began enveloping them as they arrived in Bordeaux at the mouth of the Garonne, the great trading river of Aquitaine. From there, they travelled east by river barge along the ancient arteries of the Garonne and the Lot, famous for the exchange of wine, walnuts, truffles and prunes. Their route took them deep into a hinterland of forest and limestone plateaux, until they reached the city of Cahors.

Roger Guiscard had often talked about Cahors when Hereward served with him in Sicily. He had lands there and said that it was an ideal place to start a new life. An old Roman settlement on the river Lot, it was home to merchants, bankers and artisans and a city far richer than most in Europe. It sat unobtrusively amid vast areas of farmland, vineyards and forest, far removed from the anxieties of the rest of Europe.

Torfida would have approved: there were fine churches and towering bridges, wealthy residences and flourishing markets, and the climate was warm and dry. The family spent the winter in the city, in a large house rented from a banker from Lombardy, allowing them time to plan their future and decide whether Aquitaine was to their liking. By the time they agreed that it was a place where they could settle, it was early spring 1068.

England and all its turmoil and sadness were suddenly a long way away.

19. A Message from the Grave

By any standards, Hereward and his family were rich. King Harold had made generous provision for them – a legacy which might well have included an earldom, had the outcome of 14 October 1066 been different. Hereward insisted that his windfall be shared equally between the entire family, and they decided to buy a large estate several miles east of Cahors at the promontory of St Circ Lapopie. The remote settlement had many acres of vines, which produced the renowned 'black' wine of Cahors, known throughout Europe since Roman times. It had endless orchards of plums, grown for prunes, a local speciality, plantations of walnut trees, which produced much sought after nuts and oil, and truffles in abundance in its vast forests of scrub oaks. It was an idyllic setting.

News of the presence of Hereward soon reached the court of the Count of Toulouse, who was Lord of Quercy, the domain in which Cahors was located. The Count sent his Chancellor to welcome the English settlers and inform them of their feudal responsibilities, which included the payment of annual tithes. The Chancellor also brought an open invitation to attend the Count's court in Toulouse. Hereward's reply was gracious but, content just to pay their dues and avoid the trappings and intrigues of court, he never took up the invitation.

Hereward's melancholy did not improve, despite the

309

charms of their new home, but Martin and Einar took to farming and their lordly duties with great enthusiasm. Their families were healthy and growing to maturity, well away from the dangers they had previously faced in their lives. The serenity of St Circ Lapopie was beginning to have an effect and life for the migrants soon settled into a harmonious rhythm of contentment.

Only Alphonso, ever the loner, seemed restless. He and Hereward spent more and more time talking, usually about their campaigns and battles, and often went on extended hunting trips deep into the vast wilderness of the Causse de Limogne that surrounded their lands.

William had returned to England from Normandy in the summer of 1067, refreshed and ready for the enormous task of subduing the hinterland of his newly conquered realm. Although William was the anointed King and more and more Norman opportunists were arriving every day, there were still only 25,000 foreigners trying to rule an Anglo-Saxon population of close to a million. Even accounting for the slaughter on Senlac Ridge, every burgh and village was home to a body of men with extensive military training – and they did not take kindly to being oppressed by foreign rulers. Harold's sons, led by his first-born, Godwin Haroldson, had begun to raid the West Country from their base in Ireland. However, what the English lacked was organization and leadership, and they needed both quickly.

Conversely, the Normans had strong leadership and organizational skills in abundance. William had begun to campaign further and further from London, building imposing fortifications at every strategic vantage point, and he now restructured the taxation system so that wealth flowed into Norman coffers in vast quantities. His catechism of rule had only two lines of doctrine: total obedience and the severest punishments for any misdemeanour. The greater part of the English population was terrified, and William did not forego any opportunity to intensify their fear.

He campaigned throughout the autumn and winter and was still on the march in the summer of 1068. Thousands were slaughtered – women and children included – whole towns and villages were made examples of, and the scale of the atrocities cowed the people and shocked the rest of Europe.

The scale of William's brutality had not been seen since the lawlessness of the Dark Ages.

Hereward knew nothing of this. The remoteness of his idyllic bastide was a particular blessing in that it prevented him from hearing of England's agonies.

That all changed on a wet and rainy day in November 1068.

The community was preparing for winter, which, with the chilling high ground of the Massif Central only a few miles to the east, could be particularly harsh. Their bastide was high on the limestone crags above the meandering Lot, with an almost impregnable defensive position; anyone approaching on the narrow track could be seen for at least half an hour.

Alphonso saw them first and called to the others. Three of the men wore the unmistakable tunics and armour of English housecarls, a fourth was dressed like an English courtier. Behind them rode an escort of four, two abreast, who were recognizable as men from the private retinue of the Count of Toulouse. By the time the group reached the walls of the bastide, everyone had gathered to greet them. It was a warm welcome, as all were desperate for news from England, if a little apprehensive as to what it might contain.

The young courtier had been sent by Harold's Constable at Glastonbury. He had much to tell them, but Hereward insisted that his account should wait until all were seated for dinner. However, Edwin, the young envoy, who was no more than eighteen years of age and a second cousin of King Harold, announced that he had something private to share with Hereward.

Einar, sensing what Edwin's news might convey, ushered the family away.

Edwin handed Hereward a delicate silk handkerchief which carried the unmistakable aroma of Edith Swan-Neck's perfume. Hereward recognized it immediately and hesitated. He looked at the young man sternly.

The boy nodded meekly. 'Please, open the handkerchief; I'm afraid it brings bad news.'

Hereward did as he was asked, but as soon as he saw what the handkerchief contained, immediately clenched his fist around it. It was Torfida's gold ring – the one he had given her as they exchanged their vows in Kiev all those years earlier.

'How was this found?'

'Sir, it was found on a body in the forest near Hereford.'

'My wife's body?'

'So it is presumed, sir. I am sorry to be the bearer of

such news.' He paused, looking more and more uncomfortable.

'Go on, boy. You've travelled a long way to bring me this news.'

'The body was badly decomposed, but the nuns at Hereford recognized it.'

'When did this take place?'

'In the spring of this year.'

'But Torfida disappeared from our camp almost a year before that.'

'Yes, sir. Sister Magdalena, the Mother Superior at the nunnery of Hereford, wanted you to know the facts as far as she could ascertain them.'

Hereward led Edwin to a bench close to the bastide's well.

'Torfida was at Hereford for only a very short time. She had been with the nuns as a girl and arrived very distressed, seeking refuge and a place for contemplation.'

'But almost the first thing I did was send Martin to the nuns. I felt certain she would go there.'

'I know . . . Sister Magdalena sends her deepest regrets, but Torfida insisted that the nuns turn Martin away and deny all knowledge of her arrival.'

Tears welled up in Hereward's eyes, which he made no attempt to wipe away or hide from the young courtier.

'Would you like me to go on, sir?'

Hereward nodded.

'While she was there, her health deteriorated within days. The nuns were very concerned and wanted to send for you, but Torfida would not hear of it.'

Hereward's chest heaved with a shudder of emotion that

he found difficult to control. He let out a great cry of anguish. 'Torfida! I can't bear it. Why couldn't I find you?'

'She tried to treat herself, but she was very ill. Her body was plagued with swellings and she was in great pain. Mother Superior wanted you to know how brave she was, refusing all help from the nuns, asking only for their prayers. After a while, she said that she had regained some of her strength and left to return to your camp, saying that it was nearby. Mother Superior did not want her to leave, but bowed to the strength of her will.'

'What happened on her journey from Hereford to prevent her reaching us?'

'No one knows; she hadn't gone far, only ten miles or so. She took her horse, which was a good mount, and must have gone through the forest to avoid being seen by the Normans. Perhaps she had a sudden relapse and was unable to summon help. She lay undiscovered all winter. Her body was eventually found in a very remote place by charcoal-burners. Being good men, they brought her to the nuns for a Christian burial. Her horse was never found.'

Hereward looked away in despair, horrified at the thought of Torfida's lonely and painful death. He dreaded the thought that she must have known about her illness long before she disappeared, but had kept it from him for fear of hindering his own recovery. He walked away from the young emissary and began to sob, something he had not done in a very long time.

After a while, he fought back the tears and composed himself. 'Where is she buried?'

'In a quiet glade in the forest, known only to the holy sisters of Hereford, sir.'

'Good, it is a fitting place; she was a child of the forest.'

'Sir, there is something else.' Edwin pulled a small piece of brushwood from his leather pouch. 'The charcoal-burners knew that the lady was of high birth because of her ring and because she could write.'

Edwin handed the wood to Hereward, on which was etched, in barely legible scratchings, a message.

'This is in Latin; I can't read it.' He handed it back to the boy.

'I'm sorry, sir, I presumed . . .'

'You presume too much, young man.'

Edwin read the inscription almost reverentially. '*Herewarde, amuletum non pro alio fers. Id iure recepisti. Gere id cum animo* . . . Hereward, you do not carry the Talisman for another. You are the rightful recipient. Wear it with pride.'

Hereward looked at the crude scratchings on the wood. It was signed "1" and she had drawn a heart next to her name. She must have chosen Latin knowing that only a select few would be able to read it. It would have taken her hours, maybe days. He had not thought about the Talisman since Edith Swan-Neck had placed it around his neck on that fateful day in the forest. He had been sorely tempted to throw it away, and only respect for Harold's memory had persuaded him to carry on wearing it.

'This conversation is never to be repeated to anyone else – ever!'

'Of course not, sir.'

Hereward thought about the Old Man of the Wildwood, resting at peace in his forest haven. Now Torfida had her own place in the eternal cycle of England's wild places. She would be content. As her ancestors before her believed, the Wodewose had taken her. Perhaps the legend was true after all and, in her final moments, the Green Man of the forest had brought her comfort.

Hereward put Torfida's ring through the chain that held the Talisman, folded Edith's handkerchief and gave it back to Edwin. 'Please return this to Lady Edith with my compliments.'

'I will, sir.'

'Did she send you to find me?'

'She has been scouring Europe to find you. Only by chance did word reach her that an English family had settled in the domain of the Count of Toulouse. She begs you to return to England. With Edgar on the throne and you as the leader of his army, every able-bodied man would follow you in a rebellion against the Normans. Sir, if my opinion is worth anything, may I say, I agree with her.'

He paused, while Hereward came to terms with a plea he could not ignore.

After telling the others about Torfida's demise, Hereward spent the rest of the day comforting his two girls. The news had ended the awful, nagging mystery about their mother's fate. Most importantly, it established that, although racked by pain and illness, she had been trying to return to them. The circumstances of her death were harrowing, but at least they could now be comforted by the knowledge that she had not abandoned them.

Hereward would reflect on Torfida's message for the rest of his days. He hoped and prayed that it meant she had come to terms with what had happened on that fateful afternoon in the meadow. Perhaps she had forgiven him, or realized she had misunderstood what had been happening. Gradually, he drew more and more consolation from Torfida's inscription, especially the crudely scratched heart, an image he would cherish in his mind's eye for ever.

That evening the entire family were seated for dinner, while Edwin described England's ordeal at the hands of William. As Hereward listened, his mind raced, but kept coming back to the same point: Torfida's dying message meant that the love he thought had been lost when she discovered him with Edith, had endured. It would stay with him for the rest of his days. For the first time since Senlac Ridge, he began to feel whole again.

He stopped Edwin in mid-sentence and rose with a horn of wine in his hand. 'I haven't spoken Torfida's name in many months. I doubted her, for which I am ashamed. A freak circumstance drove her away, in which I played a leading part; for that, I am truly repentant. Now, with the message Edwin has brought, I feel her spirit has returned.' He paused to look around at everyone. 'To Torfida, my abiding love.'

They all raised their goblets and repeated her name. Everyone looked relieved and proud: relieved because they too had doubted her; proud because she was a remarkable woman to have known.

'Alphonso, do you think this man in Spain, Rodrigo Diaz of Bivar, who you are constantly telling me about on our hunting trips, might need some men-at-arms?'

'I'm sure he would consider modest soldiers like us.'

Edwin found sufficient pluck to speak up for his cause. 'Sir, I had hoped you would be going in the other direction. It is England that needs you.'

'Patience, young man. From the stories I hear, Rodrigo Diaz is a remarkable soldier. I want to find out more. More importantly, I was badly wounded with Harold at Senlac and I am fat and out of condition. If I am to return to England to the role suggested by Edith Swan-Neck, I must be ready for the challenge.' He turned to Martin and Einar. 'Dear friends, please stay here and protect our family and our people. We will return in the spring, when we can decide whether there is still a cause worth fighting for in England.'

They both nodded in agreement. Hereward smiled and asked Edwin to continue with his account of the trials and tribulations of England under the Norman yoke.

At the end, he turned to Edwin and thanked him. 'Stay for a couple of days to refresh yourself, then return to England with all speed. Tell Lady Edith that, all being well, we will be in England in the spring of next year. Before doing so, we will need a detailed analysis of William's forces and their deployment, and an accurate listing of all those who will rally to the English cause. In particular, we will need to know the intentions of the earls Edwin and Morcar and the morale of their Mercian and Northumbrian house-carls. Also, we must gauge the likelihood of support from the Welsh and the Scots. Finally, we must ascertain what, if anything, can be done to entice the Danes to support our cause.

'You must return to St Circ Lapopie at the beginning of March, and bring someone who is experienced in military affairs and can effectively relay this information. Alphonso and I will be here by then or, God willing, shortly after-wards.'

The others looked on with smiles of profound relief.

They had not seen Hereward exert such authority for over two years; not since the heady few days following the resounding victory at Stamford Bridge.

Two days later, Hereward and Alphonso made their way down the long winding track to the river shortly before midday.

Hereward's two girls, identical in every respect, including their beguiling beauty and stoical resolve, had kissed him goodbye. They always reminded him of Torfida, and he hoped they had inherited a little of her wisdom so that they would understand why his quest was important. He had tried to explain his actions, just as Torfida would have done.

Einar, Martin and Alphonso had stayed up late into the night with Hereward, discussing their future. Einar said that he would be happy to fight for England again, but Martin had had enough of battle and said that, as a Welsh-man, it was hard for him to continue to attach himself to the English cause now that Harold was dead. Alphonso was undecided, but was prepared to go wherever Hereward went. They all agreed that Martin's preference meant that he should stay at St Cirq Lapopie and protect their estate for the future of their women and their children. This would allow the others one final adventure together in England.

Hereward and Alphonso wanted to be in Spain quickly, so, even though winter was looming, they had decided to go over the Pyrenees. As they descended into the foothills of Aragon and into Urgel, Alphonso seemed to breathe more deeply with every mile. He had not seen his homeland in more years than he cared to remember, and he wanted to talk to all the people he met on the road. Although Spain had many languages and dialects, Alphonso could understand most of them – even a little of the strange tongues of the Basques and the Catalans. He could also speak Arabic, so the Moorish traders they met were a particularly valuable source of news regarding affairs in the lands of the Mediterranean.

After a few days, Alphonso asked Hereward a question that had been troubling him. 'Why are we here, Hereward? I am delighted to be home again but, if England's needs are so great, why waste all this time? I know you're not at your strongest, but you could get that back in a few weeks.'

'You make a good point, Alphonso. Every day, William gets stronger, I know that. But when we return to England, it will be a different kind of war. We will not be able to raise an army. We will have to work in small groups to pick away at the enemy like wolves stalking a bear – look for its weaknesses, prey on its nerves, weaken it, injure it and then strike. If we're successful, we'll attract more and more men. Our wolf pack will get larger and bolder and we can strike at bigger and bigger targets, until we confront the biggest bear of them all – the Duke.'

'Yes, I understand. But you still haven't explained this journey.'

'You are a master of this kind of indirect warfare; I saw it in Sicily in our campaigns with the Normans. You told me it's a tradition here because you had to live for hundreds of years with the Moors who conquered your lands. I have come here to learn and to listen and, if it's true what they say about Rodrigo Diaz, we will have the perfect teacher.'

Hereward paused; he looked at Alphonso, a friend with whom he had shared many things. 'Alphonso, as a comrade you will understand that I also need to renew myself. Much has happened since we met Harold in Rouen. Both he and Torfida are gone. England is defeated and, until Edwin brought me Torfida's message, I was a spent force. Now I am being asked to be England's saviour. I need this journey to find out whether I can rise to that challenge.'

Alphonso knew his friend well and understood the enormity of what was being asked of him. He did not need to say anything in reply; he merely nodded in acknowledgement, prodded his mount and moved on.

Hereward and Alphonso had sufficient status and finery to gain an audience with the Bishop of Urgel. A man of great charm, he invited them to stay with him for a couple of days to rest themselves and their horses. With Alphonso acting as translator, they told of their journeys and campaigns. The Bishop talked of Spain, the Moors and, most importantly, Rodrigo Diaz of Bivar.

His was an interesting tale, not without parallels to Hereward's story. Ferdinand I, King of Castile, León and Galicia had died at Christmas 1065, almost exactly the same time as Edward had passed away in England. Unlike Edward, who had died without heirs, Ferdinand had three sons. Almost certainly well intentioned, if a little naïve, he had divided his kingdom into three parts: to his eldest son, Sancho, he gave Castile; to his favourite son, Alphonso, he gave León; and to his youngest son, Garcia, he gave Galicia.

Rodrigo Diaz of Bivar was 'Armiger', or Champion, to Sancho, the strongest of the three brothers. As part of his father's legacy to him, Sancho had inherited tributes to

Castile from the Taifa fiefdom of Zaragoza. Sensing weakness after the death of Ferdinand, Zaragoza refused to pay, so Rodrigo was despatched to persuade them that their actions were less than prudent.

In a display of remarkable bravery, Rodrigo left his large force at the gates of the city, demanded entry and rode in alone. Then, in the central square of the city with all its knights, men-at-arms and citizens watching, he offered to release Zaragoza from its obligation to Castile if any man could unseat him from his horse. However, such was his reputation that no one dared accept his challenge and he left for Castile laden with all the city's tributes packed into chests.

In the summer of 1067, Sancho of Castile had also exerted his influence over his neighbours to the east – Aragon and Navarre. In what became known as the 'War of the Three Sanchos', Sancho of Castile campaigned against his cousins, Sancho IV of Navarre and Sancho Ramirez of Aragon, and succeeded in expanding his territories. Rodrigo was the outstanding leader of Castile's forces and, in a series of brilliant manoeuvres, he forced the Sanchos of Navarre and Aragon to recognize Sancho of Castile as their lord. This triumph, in addition to the mystique that already surrounded him following his many victories in jousts and hand-to-hand combats, made Rodrigo's reputation as a legendary warrior complete. His prowess had earned him a title by which he was known throughout Spain, 'El Cid'. It was an Arabic epithet, meaning 'The Master'.

In November 1067, Ferdinand's widow, the Dowager Queen Sancha, died. While she was alive, her three sons had maintained a grudging acceptance of their father's tripartite endowment, but as soon as she died, hostility between the brothers began to grow. This culminated in a huge battle at Llantada, on the border between Castile and León, in July 1068, when Rodrigo once more led King Sancho II's forces to victory. An uneasy truce had since held between the three of them, in which both Garcia of Galicia and Alphonso of León recognized that, with Rodrigo at his side, Sancho was the first among the triumvirate of equals.

Hereward and Alphonso's kindly host told them that Rodrigo was to be found spending the winter in the north of León, at the court of his friend Count Diego of Oviedo. It would be another long trek for the two friends, taking them even further from England.

But based on Pedro's stirring account of Rodrigo's prowess, both agreed it was a venture worth undertaking.

20. The Cid

By the time Hereward and Alphonso left Urgel, they were both impatient to meet Rodrigo Diaz. They talked about him constantly as they journeyed across ancient lands and saw places Hereward had heard of from Alphonso's stories: San Juan de la Pena with its imposing monastery, Pamplona, home to the fiercely proud Basque peoples, and Burgos and León, capital cities of the noble lands of Castile and León. Hereward liked what he saw, but the land was demanding of its inhabitants – bitingly cold in winter and searingly hot in summer. Its peoples needed to be rugged and independent. He decided there were many similarities between Spain and his own land. Just as its many kingdoms had buried their differences to fight the Moors, perhaps the Celts, Danes and Saxons would unite to defeat William.

The Bishop of Urgel's stories about The Cid had been a rude reminder of the passage of time: Hereward was now approaching his thirty-fourth birthday, whereas Bishop Pedro estimated that The Cid was only about twenty-five. Perhaps the younger man could offer Hereward some insight that would be the vital key to oust William from his palace at Westminster.

Oviedo was an impressive fortified town with an imposing cathedral. Count Diego, a rotund, jovial man with long grey whiskers, had been a staunch ally and good friend to Sancho's father, Ferdinand, and had fought many battles with him. As a pragmatic ruler and a firm believer in order and discipline, he approved of Sancho enforcing his authority over his two brothers, believing it preferable that the Christians of the north be united against the threat from the Muslims of the south. He was also blunt about the Moors. Although he thought them keenly intelligent and in possession of a wealth of knowledge from antiquity, they were not Christians. Moreover, even though he had fought both with them and against them and knew they were brave and honourable, they nevertheless worshipped a different God. For him it was straightforward: they had brought their heresy to Spain many years ago and it was time for them to go back to where they belonged.

Hereward and Alphonso arrived in the Great Hall of Count Diego in some style. They had cleaned their tunics, weapons and armour and Hereward's unmistakable hallmark, the Great Axe of Göteborg, shone like a newly forged weapon.

With Alphonso acting as translator, the Count's Chamberlain introduced the guests. 'Lord Diego, I present Hereward of Bourne, formerly in the service of Harold I, King of England. With him is his sergeant-at-arms, Alphonso of Granada.'

'Welcome to Oviedo, Hereward of Bourne.' Count Diego was polite but perplexed.

This Englishman had made a grand entrance and had the bearing and weapons of a lord, but without the title. Fearing that he had been deceived into welcoming a mercenary, he cast a look of annoyance at his Chamberlain, but the man to the Count's right, who Hereward immediately sensed must be The Cid, intervened.

'I have heard of this man, my Lord Diego. Fear not, you are right to offer him a welcome worthy of a nobleman, for that, beyond any doubt, is what he is.' The Cid looked directly at Hereward. 'Forgive me for talking across you, Hereward of Bourne, but your admirable modesty has put my good friend Count Diego at a disadvantage. May I introduce myself? I am Rodrigo Diaz of Bivar, Armiger to Sancho of Castile.'

'Alphonso and I are honoured to be given an audience by the Count of Oviedo and to meet Rodrigo of Bivar.'

Rodrigo addressed Diego, who was now looking much more relaxed. 'I hear that Hereward of Bourne has been offered many titles and refused them all. There are myriad legends that pass from traveller to traveller about his exploits.' He turned to Hereward. 'Tell me, noble Englishman, are they all true?'

'My Lord Rodrigo, I'm certain they've become embellished in the telling –'

The Count interrupted. 'You two have something in common. Rodrigo accepts no title either, so you can call one another by whatever names you choose. But may I remind you that, until I deem it otherwise, I am your Lord, Count Diego.'

Everyone laughed.

Hereward looked at Rodrigo and saw much in him that he recognized. The Castilian was not as tall, and had olive skin and hair the colour of chestnuts, but he was powerfully built and his hands were gnarled and calloused from many blows and long hours of weapons training. He wore a long ruby-coloured smock, fastened with a broad leather belt, and across his shoulders was draped a magnificent bearskin cloak fastened by a finely tooled bronze clasp. His leggings were winter riding breeches, and he had boots of the finest leather. Rodrigo's armour, which adorned a mannequin behind the high table, was comprised of a small circular shield like those of the Saracens, a straight thrusting sword, a style preferred by northern Europeans, and a small axe with a crescent-shaped blade. He also had a long lance for use in jousts and cavalry charges, and a smaller javelin, a weapon to be hurled at the enemy in an infantry encounter. His weapons were in beautiful condition, but it was obvious they had been used frequently; his mail coat, though finely worked, bore the cuts and gouges of many blows.

'May I see your axe? I have heard about this weapon. Some of my men have served the Normans in Italy and say that you are the only man alive who can wield it to any effect.'

Hereward pulled the axe from his shoulder and handed it to The Cid with one hand.

As soon as he felt its weight, Rodrigo had to use both his hands to support it. 'This is a mighty axe. I hear that you can use it with one hand?'

'I can.' Hereward hesitated. 'May I call you Rodrigo?'

'You may, if I may call you Hereward.'

'Yes, of course. This axe was made for me by a weapons-master of great skill in Göteborg in the land of the Norse. I am lucky; my arms are strong and I have learned to use either hand. In a challenge, the key is to use both hands at the beginning, as any man would, then at the vital moment revert to one hand; it surprises the opponent!'

Rodrigo tried to swing the axe with one hand but could not maintain momentum.

'Rodrigo, you are very strong. It would not take you long to acquire the technique.'

'I am not sure. We also have craftsmen skilled in the art of making weapons of war. The best of them are in the city of Toledo, a Taifa kingdom in the land of the Moors. But their speciality is the sword; they can hone an edge so fine you can trim your beard with it, yet the blade is powerful enough to split a man in two if delivered accurately.'

He handed the Great Axe back to Hereward and offered him his sword. The Englishman had heard about Toledo swords, but had never seen one. It was surprisingly light, but felt strong and well balanced. Intricate patterns and scrolls were chased in fine detail to the top of the blade, the handle and the pommel, patterns that Hereward thought were Moorish. He glanced at Rodrigo quizzically.

'Yes, the designs are Islamic. All the great swordsmiths are Moors; we learn from them all the time. Scholars, monks and apothecaries travel here from all over Europe to cross into the south in search of knowledge. There is a border area between the two parts of Spain, where both Christians and Moors mingle freely. It can be a little lawless at times, but it allows passage into Muslim Spain, the empire we call The Almoravide Dominion.'

Hereward was intrigued. He had fought Muslims in Sicily and had been close to their lands in Byzantium, but had never set foot on their soil. 'Have you been to the Dominion?'

'Yes, many times, I have good friends there. The climate is warm and their cities are splendid. Cordoba, Seville, Granada, Valencia are all wonderful places to visit.' Rodrigo stopped himself from becoming too carried away about the attractions of his homeland. 'Hereward of Bourne, famous warrior and survivor of many battles, why have you come to Castile?'

'How much do you know of the events in England?'

'A little. I know of Hardrada and Harold, and of the Duke of Normandy's victory in the great battle for the throne. Now he is King, and I presume that makes you two renegades. I see you travel with a man from Granada. A good choice; Andalucians fight well.'

Alphonso, a little shy about translating such glowing praise about himself, responded to Rodrigo in his own language, Castilian. 'Thank you, my Lord Cid. It is an honour to meet the most feared warrior in Spain.'

'The honour is mine, Alphonso of Granada. Your noble service with Hereward fills everyone in Spain with pride. We are honoured that you have travelled to the court of my Lord, Diego, but I trust you do not seek our support to win back the English throne? We have no interests beyond the Pyrenees, let alone in England.'

'It is not support we need; we search for wisdom.'

'You flatter us, Hereward.'

'Not falsely, I assure you. Allow me to explain. England is a land of Saxons in the south and east, and to the north and west of Danes and Celts. All are fiercely independent, but England has been a strong kingdom for a long time. Most of its kings have been Saxons and the majority of the earls are happy with that. The royal line of the Saxons, the Cerdicians of Wessex, goes back many hundreds of years, but the heir is just a boy, Edgar. That's why Harold, my sovereign lord, took the throne. The threat from Hardrada of Norway and William of Normandy was so great, he had no choice.

'England is a wealthy kingdom, the greatest prize in northern Europe, and envious eyes have coveted it for centuries. Now William holds the prize, but it is not yet firmly in his grasp. Harold had the finest army in Europe; thousands died on Senlac Ridge, but thousands more went back to their farms and villages. Some are fighting as mercenaries in Europe. If they could be persuaded to return and the men working their lands convinced to take up arms again, a new army could be recruited.'

'But how can we help?'

'You have lived with an occupying army for generations and learned to be patient and fight mobile campaigns using small bands of elite warriors. Let us spend time with you and your men and learn your training regimes.'

Rodrigo thought for a moment and looked at Count Diego. The Count nodded his approval.

'I have half of my lord Sancho's bodyguard with me for the winter, about a hundred and fifty men. Stay with us for as long as you like and, in return, you can teach me how to use that mighty axe.'

'We are very grateful. We will help with the training and offer you whatever we can from our own modest experience.'

The servants brought in food and, when the table was ready, the ladies of the household made their entrance. First came Diego's tall and elegant wife, Doña Viraca, with her ladies-in-waiting. She was followed by their daughter, Doña Jimena. She was tall, like her mother, with jet-black hair pulled back sharply from her face in a tight bun. She had the darkest of eyes and clear skin the colour of burnt almonds. Count Diego introduced the ladies, and the two visitors bowed. Doña Viraca nodded disdainfully, while Doña Jimena curtsied.

'Come, Jimena, sit.'

Count Diego raised his goblet of wine. 'To Jimena and her betrothed, Rodrigo, the finest match in Christendom. Also, to our visitors – may God protect you in your great challenge ahead in England.'

Doña Viraca, a woman of plain worlds, spoke bluntly. 'Are you married, Hereward of Bourne?'

'Lady Viraca, my wife died recently. Torfida was her name. I have twin daughters, Gunnhild and Estrith, who are now nine years old.'

'I see . . . I am sorry to hear of your loss. Where are your daughters now?'

'Alphonso and I are part of a family of friends who have been together for many years. We are exiled from England and now live in the lands of the Count of Toulouse, near the city of Cahors.'

'I know the Count, a silly little man of no consequence. I also know Cahors, a city of merchants and bankers with too many Jews for my liking. My family is from Carcassonne, a much more appealing city.'

'I don't know it, Lady Viraca, but I'm sure your judgement is impeccable.'

Count Diego smiled wryly. 'Oh, it is, Hereward. Doña Viraca is like the Pontiff himself – infallible in all things!' With that, he waved to the waiters to pour the wine so that the meal could begin.

Doña Jimena spoke with a soft timbre and modest demeanour. To Alphonso's relief, Doña Jimena had been taught several of the languages of France, including Occitan, Frankish and Norman French, giving Hereward a perfect excuse to talk to the beautiful young woman.

'Was your wife very beautiful, Hereward of Bourne?'

'Yes, she was, Doña Jimena. I miss her very much.'

'I am sorry you have lost her. It must be very difficult for you.'

'Thank you, I am fortunate to have a large family to take care of the girls. They are my greatest comfort; they are so like her.'

A conversation of polite conviviality ensued, during which Doña Jimena spoke more than most and brought warmth and dignity to the evening.

Rodrigo could not take his eyes off her.

The next morning, accompanied by Doña Jimena, Hereward's Castilian host took him to see the pride of Oviedo, its cathedral. Built in wood above a stone crypt, it was a sight to behold. In an atmosphere heady with incense and the smoke of countless candles, choirboys sang in plainsong. Monks busied themselves, as hundreds of visitors shuffled on their knees towards the high altar.

Doña Jimena noted Hereward's wonderment, and explained. 'These people come from Navarre, the land of the Basques, and from all over Christian Spain. Many are from lands to the north, pilgrims on the way to Santiago de Compostela. It has a shrine to mark the grave of St James the Great, one of Our Lord's apostles, who was buried there after he journeyed from the Holy Land. It is a long way to the west of us and many stay here to rest and worship our own holy relics.' Jimena changed tack, fearing she might be boring Hereward. 'Rodrigo tells me that you have been to many lands and fought even more battles than he has. He is very honoured to have you here in Oviedo, as we all are.'

'You are too kind. It is my privilege to be here with your family and enjoy your hospitality.'

Rodrigo had been admiring his beloved Jimena as she spoke with Hereward. 'Do you pray to relics and follow devotions, Hereward?'

'No, Rodrigo, I do not have much faith. Torfida, my wife, was the daughter of a seer and inherited many of his gifts. She helped me understand many things and made me ask questions to which I still seek answers. But I do carry my own relic, something that has puzzled me for years. Torfida gave it to me and said I was destined to be its carrier.'

'It is intriguing. We should talk more of this during our time together.'

'Do you think my father would let me come with you, Rodrigo? I so want to hear Hereward's stories and to learn more about Torfida.'

'Your father wouldn't dream of letting you come to our camp, neither would your mother. Besides, I will not consider it. There are some things that should be done among men alone; it is not fitting for you to be there.'

'I can ride as well as most men, and I can bring my maid to protect to me . . . Besides, who will translate for you?'

Jimena's last point made Rodrigo relent a little. 'I will speak with your father.'

'Very good. I will speak with my mother, which will get me the answer I want.'

Jimena curtsied and turned away, her cloak trailing behind, her perfume hanging in the air.

'Rodrigo Diaz of Bivar, you are a fortunate man.'

'I know, the luckiest man alive!'

With Alphonso sitting close by to translate, and men-at-arms from Rodrigo's retinue standing to attention along the nave, the two warriors sat together in one of the pews for several minutes. Hereward found the innocent devotion of the pilgrims very moving.

'You know, Rodrigo, I have been close to death more times than I care to count and I have just lost a wife who was very dear to me, but I still can't come to terms with spiritual things. As I sit here, I am stirred by all I see and hear, but it doesn't convince me that there is a life beyond our all-too-brief presence on this earth.'

'You carry a great burden. It is much easier for soldiers to do what we do if we have the certainty of salvation. For me, I am grateful that I know my God and he knows me. He has given me all my gifts and now gives me Jimena; the least I can do is to pay him homage in return.'

'I admire the clarity of your thought. I have been given a mixed blessing. My modest talents have been the making of me, but I also possess flaws. As for God, he remains a mystery to me. I think he was also for Torfida. Like her father, she became more and more interested in the power of nature and the importance of people living in harmony with one another and the land they shared.'

Rodrigo smiled at his English guest. 'I must hear more of this, but not now. Let us enjoy the choir and admire the faithful pilgrims who have travelled many miles to genuflect before the holy relics of Oviedo.'

The two warriors sat side by side, contemplating the stunning interior of the cathedral.

As they breathed in the aroma of candles and incense, and listened to the soaring sounds of the choir, they could not help but be moved by the harmony of it all.

21. The Astrolabe

Once Doña Jimena had secured her mother's support, she had few problems gaining her father's permission to travel with Rodrigo to his winter training camp. Count Diego was powerless in the face of the strategic alliance formed by his doughty wife and beguiling daughter. Jimena was accompanied by Cristina, one of Doña Viraca's ladies-in-waiting, a handsome young girl a few years older than her, with auburn hair, a fine figure and a ready wit.

Over the next few weeks, Rodrigo put his men through a gruelling regime, in which Hereward and Alphonso participated with enthusiasm. Rodrigo was a master of covert tactics. He could take fifty men through the forest and move them into position without making any sound, or giving a single spoken order. He did it with elaborate hand signals and a technique he passed on to Hereward called the 'Tally'. Every manoeuvre had a calculated distance and timescale and his men were taught to move at a constant pace and keep two counts: one of time lapsed, the other of distance travelled. The ratio between the two could put a group of men within close proximity of their objective with remarkable accuracy. Rodrigo used anything to gain an advantage in battle – fire, noise, camouflage, disguise, smoke, water, decoys – but only in addition to a foundation of basic military technique and discipline.

One evening, after a good meal and some wine, with the

campfire warming them, Hereward asked a crucial question. 'In all your manoeuvres, I've noticed that you always seem to know how to give accurate directions and know where you are at all times. How do you know so accurately? I can navigate by the stars, but I've watched you move without hesitation on a cloudy day and in the middle of a black night, with neither the stars nor the moon for guidance.'

'You are very observant, my friend. The answer is simple, but also remarkable.'

Rodrigo reached into his leather bag and removed a slim circular object, wrapped in a piece of red silk, and handed it to Hereward. He had never seen anything like it before. About the size of the span of a man's outstretched hand, it was made of bronze and riveted in the middle so that its several 'retes' (plates) sat in a 'mater' (mother case) with an 'alidade' (pointer) that could be rotated around a central pivot. The whole thing was covered in Arabic numbers and inscriptions, highly polished and lightly oiled.

Hereward was fascinated. 'It is amazing, Rodrigo. But what is it?'

'It is a Moorish astrolabe, my friend – a gift to you. I will teach you how to use it and you can take it on your campaigns against Duke William.'

'I cannot accept, Rodrigo; it is far too valuable.'

'Yes, they are rare, especially in Christendom, but your mission is worthy of it. Let me show you the things it can do.'

By deftly moving its retes and alidade around its face, Rodrigo began a detailed illustration of the intricacies of the astrolabe. 'It can plot the sun, the moon and the stars, give an accurate reading of time and the calendar,

337

and measure height and distance – if you can read the Arabic symbols.'

Hereward was intrigued, but bemused. 'I didn't follow what you did and I can't read the signs, but it looks impressive.'

'You will soon learn. Originally, they were made for astronomers and learned men, but now soldiers are using them on campaigns and they are spreading throughout Europe. I am told that a monk in Barcelona has made one with inscriptions in Latin.'

'Alphonso can read Arabic; he can help me. You are too kind. How can I thank you?'

'We have become good friends, Hereward. My life has been rewarding and successful because I am stronger than other men in battle. War is the only way someone like me can rise from being the son of a small landowner to sit at the right hand of a king. Now I have met you, whose life has been lived in parallel; such a man is worthy of sharing everything I have.'

The two men grasped each other in a warrior's embrace.

Hereward had found the inspiration he was looking for to answer the call to return to England.

The year had turned while they were in the hills above Oviedo, and their rendezvous with Edwin at St Cirq Lapopie in March was looming. Despite the chill of winter and the arduous training, they had lived well and become fit and strong. Hereward knew that it would soon be time to return to England to confront the menace of William and his Norman henchmen.

Hereward had given several displays with his Great Axe

and Rodrigo was not far off mastering it himself, even one-handed. Each had shared the other's experiences, tactics and strategies and it was time for Rodrigo to return his men to King Sancho. Enthused by Rodrigo, Hereward had regained his fitness and skills – and, most importantly, his self-belief.

The day before Rodrigo's elite troops were due to return to Oviedo, a menacing group of men arrived at his camp. They were unmistakably warriors; their sinister arsenal of weapons gave testament to that. They carried an astonishing array of war clubs, daggers, lances and Moorish scimitars and looked more like brigands who prey on pilgrims crossing the wastes of the Levant than professional soldiers.

Their leader was Hamilcar, a man with a complexion even darker than Alphonso's dusky countenance. He was also a much bigger man, standing well over six feet tall, with broad shoulders and the barrel chest of a stevedore. He was lacerated from his hairline to his chin with a gash as wide as a man's finger, an injury suffered in a knife fight with a Corsican pirate. The wounding had also taken out his left eye, the remnant of which was a crater of scar tissue that looked like it had been seared with a branding iron. Although Hamilcar's legacy from the encounter appeared severe, it was as nothing compared to the harm he had inflicted on his opponent. Other fracas had also left their marks on the man. Most of his right ear was missing, as were the two smaller fingers on his left hand and the top of the middle finger of his right. Strikingly, he possessed almost a full set of gold teeth and, hanging from those parts of him that were still intact, a king's treasure of gold chains, rings and bracelets.

Rodrigo spoke to him directly. 'Hamilcar of Tunis, my old friend. What brings you to my camp?'

'Well, my Cid. I have come to see the Englishman. I hear he is the greatest warrior in Europe and that he has joined your service as a mercenary. I have come to make him a better offer!' The big man laughed heartily, allowing the sun to illuminate his magnificent incisors in all their glory.

'Hereward of Bourne is my guest here. I will tell him that you would like to meet him; perhaps it can be arranged when we return to Oviedo.'

'Don't be inhospitable, my Cid. Where is he?'

Hereward did not need a second invitation and stepped forward. 'I am Hereward of Bourne. How may I be of service?'

'I am honoured, sir. It is said you are nearly seven feet tall – a small exaggeration, perhaps. Nevertheless, you cast a long shadow.'

'You speak excellent English, Hamilcar of Tunis.'

'Thank you. My family is descended from the Carthaginians and my faith is Islam, but my father hired Christian tutors for me and I learned many things from them, including some of their languages.'

Rodrigo intervened, beginning to lose patience at the arrival of his uninvited guest. 'You have come a long way, Hamilcar. Let us take some wine and you can tell us why we have been granted the rare honour of your presence today.'

Rodrigo's sardonic tone alerted Hereward to the need for caution with the visitor, as did the fact that Jimena had immediately withdrawn to her tent when Hamilcar's band appeared in camp.

Hamilcar was effusive in his praise for Rodrigo's wine,

but gulped it more like a man needing to slake a desperate thirst than a connoisseur of a fine vintage. 'Hereward of Bourne, I am a professional soldier. I am unsurpassed – not just in Spain, but anywhere in the Mediterranean. It is no idle boast.' He accompanied his bragging with a leering smile, behind the veneer of which was a malice that left little doubt about his claim.

Hereward, conscious of the chivalrous traditions of the Moors and Christians of Spain, remained courteous. 'Sir, I see from your signet ring that you are a man of noble birth from the Caliphate of Tunis.'

'You are very observant, my English friend.' The Moor's voice deepened and became threatening. 'My uncle is the Grand Caliph. I assume you know our seal through your service with that whelp of a Norman dog, Guiscard!'

'If you mean, my Lord, Roger Guiscard, yes, I fought with him against the Moors in Sicily.'

Hamilcar rose to his full height, drained his goblet of wine and threw the empty vessel at Hereward's feet.

Hereward remained impassive.

Rodrigo jumped to his feet and glowered at his visitor. 'You insult a guest in my camp!'

'Yes, I do! I seek revenge. This Englishman killed my brother in an ambush in the mountains above Catania. The survivors said that the leader of the attack was a golden-haired Northerner with a mighty double-headed axe.' Hamilcar bellowed at Hereward. 'You are that man!'

'Yes. I remember the encounter. Your brother was a brave man; he fought well.'

Hereward was still sitting calmly as Hamilcar leaned towards him menacingly.

341

'Let's see how well you fight and how brave you are when death offers you its eternal comforts. You need to find peace with your Christ; it is your last day on this earth,'

Rodrigo stepped between the two men. 'Hamilcar, this is my camp; Hereward of Bourne is my guest. I will have no contests here.'

'My Cid, don't jest with me, you know I have the right. This is a matter between the Englishman and me. He should never have crossed the Pyrenees. Allah himself has delivered this gift to me. He has ordained this encounter, may the Holy One be praised!'

Hereward got to his feet. 'Rodrigo, with your permission, I will accept Hamilcar's challenge. It is his right.'

Rodrigo turned to the formidable Moor. 'Very well. Hereward will need time to prepare. My men will make ready the ground; the contest will begin in one hour. Gentlemen, your chosen weapons?'

Hereward spoke first. 'Whatever Hamilcar chooses.'

'A knightly joust. If that doesn't end it, a duel – all weapons permitted.'

Hereward nodded and Hamilcar turned on his heels and left.

Rodrigo looked at Hereward with a worried expression. 'I'm not sure there is a jousting tradition in your homeland. Where did you acquire the art?'

'I haven't, my friend. I suppose now is a good time to learn!'

'Be careful. Hamilcar has never been unseated in a joust; he is very strong. Make sure to aim your lance at his midriff, just above his saddle. It is hard to deflect it from there. Follow the point of his lance with your shield; he may not aim it until the last moment, so watch carefully. Whatever happens, don't let it come down to a knife fight; he has killed many men in hand-to-hand contests.'

Rodrigo loaned Hereward one of his jousting lances and his finest war horse.

Alphonso helped him prepare. 'This man has a crazed look in his eye. Kill him quickly!'

Doña Jimena emerged from her tent as Hereward began to ride out to the improvised tilting ground. 'Be careful, Hereward. I know you are a great warrior, but this man has an evil reputation.'

'Thank you, Doña Jimena. I will be careful. I have important matters to deal with in England. That is incentive enough to meet whatever danger Hamilcar poses.'

When the two men were in position some sixty yards apart, Rodrigo signalled for the contest to begin.

Lances were lowered and the horses set off at a gallop. Both steeds were soon into their stride and closing on one another at enormous speed. Rodrigo was right about Hamilcar's threat. He was strong enough to position his lance high above and to the right of Hereward's head until the moment of impact, when he suddenly dropped it to a trajectory aimed directly at Hereward's heart. The jousting lance of a knight was far longer and significantly heavier than the battle lance with which Hereward was familiar. He tried to hold it steady, but it was not easy with his horse moving at full gallop. Jousting was a skill requiring endless practice – a training in which Hereward had little experience.

When the collision happened, Hereward had little

awareness of the detail of the impact. He hit the floor hard and his head whipped back, rendering him unconscious. Whereas his opponent's aim had been perfect and had caught Hereward square in the chest, Hamilcar had easily deflected Hereward's lance with his shield and had only taken a glancing blow. Hereward's shield had taken the impact but, even so, he had been knocked clean out of his saddle and thrown some distance from his horse.

Doña Jimena wanted to rush to Hereward's aid, but Rodrigo shook his head. Hamilcar pulled his horse round and rode back to his prone opponent, who was still motionless on the ground. The Moor catapulted himself from his mount with an athletic leap and strode towards the Great Axe of Göteborg, which was lying on the ground where it had fallen. Alphonso, realizing Hamilcar's intention, made to go to his friend's aid, until Rodrigo put a heavy hand of restraint on his shoulder.

Even though Hamilcar was a powerful man, he had difficulty lifting Hereward's huge axe and needed both hands to raise it above his head. His expression was that of a man possessed; his eyes were fixed and he moved with a slow and deliberate gait.

Hereward still had not stirred.

When he regained a vestige of consciousness, the first hazy image Hereward saw was a glint of sun on his Great Axe as Hamilcar began to propel it towards his head. His instincts came to his aid and he rolled away just as his axe embedded itself into the earth only inches from his ear. The ground was still shaking from the impact as Hamilcar struggled to pull the axe from its deep crevice. The narrow escape from his own weapon had brought Hereward to his

344

senses, and he quickly used his legs to flip his opponent on to his back.

Both men regained their footing and drew their swords at the same time. A ferocious sword duel ensued. The flashing blades cut through the air with astonishing rapidity. When they clashed, they created a harmonic percussion of steel striking steel. It was many minutes before the pair began to tire; they were gasping for air and soaked in perspiration, their muscles burning from the exertion, their concentration beginning to falter. Then came a chance occurrence that threw Hereward a crucial advantage.

Hamilcar's sword broke at the hilt, leaving him with a stub of a blade and vulnerable to Hereward's next onslaught. The Moor immediately pulled his dagger from his sheath and discarded his shield with a bravado that belied the meagre odds he faced. His weapon was a vicious implement: a saifani jambiya, handed down through his family for generations from his ancestral origins in the Yemen of ancient Arabia. Its short, curved blade was ideal for close-quarters fighting or assassination by stealth.

Hereward paused and, instead of pressing home his advantage, watched Hamilcar circle him, crouched ready to strike. The Moor, although a man of obvious malevolence, had made his challenge according to the Arab code of chivalry, a tradition that was beginning to be adopted by knights throughout Europe. Hereward decided to respect this noble tradition and, despite Rodrigo's warning to avoid a knife fight with Hamilcar at all costs, cast aside his shield and sword and drew his seax.

The Moor smiled. 'Very gracious of you, Englishman. As a reward, I will make your end quick.'

Another battle ensued, but this was much more a sparring of lunges, feints and postures than their previous brutal combat with lances and swords. Hereward knew that a knife fight was like a sword fight; the key was to avoid focusing solely on the eyes of one's opponent but also to concentrate on his weapon and his body movement. He soon realized that Hamilcar often used a rapid gesture of his right hand just before he thrust with his left. Hereward decided to gamble that the Moor would not know that, because of injuries sustained during his encounter with Thurstan's assassins many years previously, he had trained himself to be equally proficient with both his left and right hand.

He chose his moment carefully.

As Hamilcar launched another attack, he threw his seax from his right hand to his left. The Moor was surprised and distracted, giving Hereward the opportunity to grasp his adversary's wrist. At the same time, he plunged forcefully with his weapon – a mortal blow that Hamilcar only avoided at the last moment by a desperate clasp of Hereward's forearm. The two men fell backwards as Hamilcar lost his balance in defending Hereward's strike.

Now the two men were face to face, feeling one another's breath, smelling each other's sweat, sensing every strain of muscle and sinew; they were as close as two lovers in a tryst.

Hereward had the advantage; his grip was firmer than his opponent's tenuous hold on his forearm, and it was only a matter of time before he was able to wrestle free his seax. However, instead of inflicting the coup de grace, he delivered a mighty blow to the side of Hamilcar's jaw with his fist and the pommel of his seax, followed by a second equally thunderous swipe.

Hereward sheathed his seax, stood up and walked towards Rodrigo's tent, leaving the Moor dazed and motionless on the ground. He had taken only five yards when a shriek from Doña Jimena made him turn round. The saifani jambiya was only inches from his throat; he could see in detail the rubies and sapphires of its decorated hilt and the distinctive pale yellow hue of its handle. He immediately fell backwards, rolling with Hamilcar's momentum and using it to his advantage.

In their fall to the ground, Hereward was able to get both his hands around the wrist of his foe. He turned the jambiya 180 degrees, so that it now pointed directly away from him and towards the man who had come to Rodrigo's camp to kill him.

As Hamilcar fell on top of Hereward, the jambiya sank deep into his chest. He did not feel anything for a moment as the razor-sharp blade made a smooth, painless entry. It was only when the steel tip of the blade lodged between the vertebrae of his spine that he began to feel convulsions of unbearable agony. He lost all feeling in his legs, but could taste cold metal on his tongue and a searing pain. They were the last sensations he felt; within moments, he was dead.

Hereward looked at his vanquished opponent and remembered his own search for vengeance all those years earlier in Ely.

He already knew how dangerous the desire for revenge could be; this encounter with Hamilcar of Tunis was further proof that it is a craving so powerful, it can make a man as demented as a rabid dog.

22. England Beckons

It had been obvious for some time that Alphonso and the maid Cristina had become close. They were often together with Rodrigo, Jimena and Hereward – and it was evident that the two of them had found more than friendship.

As they prepared to break camp, Doña Jimena gave Cristina the evening off to spend time with Alphonso and, summoning the finest fare their winter quarters allowed, organized a final dinner for Rodrigo and Hereward.

After an excellent meal and much good humour, Rodrigo attempted to usher Jimena away to her bed. 'We are going to talk of war and the deeds of violent men, Jimena. You should go to bed.'

'Am I not betrothed to you, Rodrigo Diaz, the greatest warrior in Spain? Should I not know about war and the deeds of violent men?'

Rodrigo relented. Spending time with Jimena away from court had perhaps convinced him that she did not always want to be treated like a genteel noblewoman.

He turned to Hereward. 'When we talked in the cathedral all those weeks ago, you told me about your own personal relic. I said that one day we would talk about it.'

'You have a good memory, Rodrigo. It is something that has caused me much anguish, has led me to doubt my wife and is still something that I find difficult to understand. It could carry a message of great importance, or it could be no more than a cheap bauble. Torfida had no doubts about its worth. The only mystery for her was whether its message came from God, or whether it was a clever symbol of man's potential to solve his own riddles. Either way, she never doubted its significance.'

Hereward took the Talisman from his neck and passed it to Rodrigo, who examined it carefully.

'It is the image of Lucifer. How can this be a relic?' Rodrigo passed it to Jimena.

'How can you carry such a thing, Hereward? It is the image of the Devil; surely it's a pagan fetish?'

Hereward outlined his story, beginning with his encounter with Torfida's father, the Old Man of the Wildwood. He described how he had found her in Hereford and how she had explained the Talisman's origins. He told them about the strange reaction of Gruffydd ap Llywelyn, of Macbeth's sad demise while wearing it, and how he had been convinced that his journey as the keeper of the Talisman had ended when he passed it to Harold, King of England.

'The end of the story is a little indelicate for Jimena's tender years.'

'Fear not, Hereward, you may speak frankly in front of Jimena.'

Hereward continued quickly, to spare his own shame, as he described the Talisman's return to him by Edith Swan-Neck. He related the trauma of Torfida discovering them in the forest, her disappearance and illness and, finally, her tragic death.

As he finished his story, Jimena exclaimed, 'The thing is a curse! Give it to the Bishop of Oviedo in the morning.

He can bury it in the cathedral crypt; it will never haunt you again.'

'It is not as simple as that, Jimena. It is at least a thousand years old, and I am entrusted with its safekeeping. Besides, in her death throes, Torfida sent me a message. I keep it with me always.' He took a small, tightly wrapped linen bundle from his bag, unfolded it carefully and handed the wooden inscription to Jimena.

The young woman's Latin was perfect; she read it aloud.

Hereward's eyes filled with tears as he continued his story. 'Her death and her message helped me understand the symbolism of the Talisman. It carries five messages of abiding truth that are the key to wisdom and kingship. The first is courage – to overcome our fears and anxieties. The second is discipline – to control the darkness within us. The third is humility – to know that only God can work miracles. The fourth is sacrifice – to forfeit ourselves for God and for one another, as Christ did. The fifth is wisdom – to understand the stone, not to fear it. At first, I thought of it as a lucky charm from which the wearer would acquire the gifts it holds, but Torfida helped me understand that it is a catechism, a constant reminder of the truths it carries. It doesn't protect you, it only helps you protect yourself.'

Jimena and Rodrigo looked at one another.

Rodrigo spoke first. 'Torfida was right, you are destined to be its next recipient; no one could be more worthy.'

Jimena pressed Hereward's arm. 'They were Torfida's dying words; you must believe in the Talisman and accept her wisdom that you are the one to wear it'.

Hereward's two Castilian friends embraced him as Rodrigo placed the Talisman over his friend's head.

'I can't thank both of you enough for your friendship; it is more than I could have dreamed of. I came here knowing it was my duty to go back to England, but I also knew that I wasn't ready in mind or body. You have helped me become a soldier again – and a much better one – but, most importantly, you have helped me clear my mind and revive my spirit. I am now ready to face the task ahead of me. My eternal thanks to you both.'

They returned to the Great Hall of Count Diego for a farewell banquet. It was an evening of good humour and fine food. Count Diego, despite his stern demeanour, was a good host, and Doña Viraca brought the dignity and manners appropriate to the high table of an important city.

At dawn the next morning, Hereward and Alphonso were ready to leave. Alphonso's romance with Cristina had become serious. Within twenty-four hours of their return from the winter camp, she had gathered all her worldly possessions, obtained permission to leave from her mistress and even been granted a small dowry.

She was charming, hung on Alphonso's every word and clung to him like a leech. Cristina would be a source of great delight at St Cirq Lapopie.

Rodrigo and Jimena had risen early to bid them farewell. Jimena hugged Cristina and wished her much love and happiness and then gave Alphonso a stern reminder about his responsibilities to care for her.

She turned to Hereward and kissed him on his cheek in a fond embrace. 'God's speed to England. If Rodrigo ever forgets that one day he is supposed to marry me, I promise to come to England as a poor unfortunate spinster and throw myself on your mercy.'

Rodrigo walked with Hereward to his horse, both men contemplating all that had been said during the course of their winter together.

Hereward voiced his thoughts first. 'In truth, my mission in England has little chance of success. The English may already be a beaten people. The Saxons to the south are overrun, the Celts are mercurial and will probably only fight if William crosses into their own territory, and the Anglo-Danes, who live mainly in the northern realms of the earls Edwin and Morcar, have been badly led and failed England at the moment of its greatest need. As for foreign support, Denmark is the solitary possibility, but their only motivation will be plunder.'

'What of the remnants of Harold's army?'

'So many were killed with Harold. He does have sons, and some housecarls will rally to them. However, the true heir is Edgar of the Cerdician line. When I get back to Aquitaine, I will know if he has survived and if he has the stomach to fight for his birthright.'

'If anyone can do it, you can. I am very tempted to come with you, but my mission is here in Spain and I have Jimena to think of.'

The two men parted with one last warrior's embrace.

Hereward did not allow himself even a moment to savour the prospect of returning to England with The Cid at his side. 'We would be a formidable partnership, but you must follow the path that fate has ordained for you.'

'So must we both.'

*

In order to significantly reduce the journey time from Oviedo to Cahors, passage had been arranged on a merchant ship from the nearby port of Gigon, bound for Bordeaux. Strong winds off the Atlantic carried them along Spain's northern coast and across the Bay of Biscay at a good rate of knots.

With Alphonso's help, Hereward had mastered the astrolabe and constantly irritated the ship's captain with endless observations about their course and arrival times. Their progress up the River Garonne was much slower; sail was often no match for the strong current, and draught animals had to be used. They took a trader's barge as far as Aiguillon, where the Lot joined the Garonne, and then employed oarsmen to row them up the Lot with as much speed as their broad shoulders could generate.

When they arrived at St Cirq Lapopie there was much rejoicing, and Cristina was made welcome. Everyone could see that Hereward was in fine health and had returned to his former self. His daughters were overjoyed; their father had been restored to them.

Edwin had already arrived at St Cirq Lapopie, accompanied by a senior housecarl from Harold's hearthtroop at Glastonbury. Between them, they gave a detailed account of events in England.

With most of the Normans holed up in their mottes and baileys, the winter had been a period of relative calm for the beleaguered English. However, the harsh winter had done little for people's spirits, and the fear and despondency throughout the land had become worse. Now that spring had arrived, everyone was bracing themselves for more harsh campaigns from the Duke.

The housecarl, Edmund, a taciturn man of very solid appearance, gave Hereward a frank assessment of the current political and military situation. In the south and east, many Saxons were beginning to make money thanks to the Norman presence. Buildings were under construction at great pace and in vast numbers. Trade in the burghs was brisk, and money from the defeated Saxon aristocracy was finding its way into the pockets of merchants and artisans as the Normans disposed of their new wealth on enhancing their homes and possessions. The ports were flourishing as trade with Normandy and Europe increased at a startling rate. Farmers were prospering – at least, those close to Norman strongholds.

The losers were the provinces and the poorer parts of the community. Most of the hinterland was still not under direct Norman control. There, the people were living in a vacuum of destitution, with neither trade nor security. The peasants of the south, left to their miserable existence, continued to toil for scant reward as they always had. The Saxon aristocracy and the ecclesiastical elite, whose lands and possessions were all but gone, were dispirited and dejected and many had gone into hiding.

Finally, Edmund described the status of England's surviving professional soldiers. Some had returned to their homes and hidden their weapons. Others, determined to fight the Normans in any way they could, had formed small bands of irregulars. Many had left England to find a life elsewhere.

Hereward interrupted Edmund's account. 'Is no one gathering the men together and organizing them?'

'We are trying, but it is difficult. We lack a leader. Sir, we need you back in England.'

Edmund finished by describing Edith's attempts to form a coherent group to begin a rebellion. Edwin and Morcar had pledged Northumbrian and Mercian forces to the cause. Harold's sons had a few hundred men in Ireland and would sail as soon as summoned. She had an agreement with the Danes that they would set sail if an English rebellion began, but there had been no commitment from the Scots or the Welsh.

'What of the men of the southern earldoms – how many housecarls could be mustered?'

'It is difficult to estimate. Another winter has passed and skirmishes go on all the time where men die. William has ordered searches for weapons and armour. If any are found, all men of military age in that household or village are executed. Hundreds must be in hiding, but we don't know exactly how many.'

'How many men are at Glastonbury, or could be available upon our return?'

Edmund, not wanting to be the bearer of bad news, gulped a little. 'Five, maybe seven hundred.'

Everyone was shocked.

Hereward tried to hide his disappointment. 'Not an army of biblical proportions!' He paced around in circles, deep in thought. 'If that is the number in the south, those in Ireland make it a thousand. Edwin and Morcar should be able to muster two thousand more. If we can attract a few sturdy men back from their mercenary endeavours overseas, we have the beginnings of an army. It depends on their quality and whether they have the stomach for the fight. Remember, things went against us on Senlac Ridge by only a few minutes and a few hundred men.'

'You are right, sir. If you will return and lead us, we have a chance.'

'Thank you, Edmund. Worry not, I intend to return and fight. England is too precious to me; I cannot grow old and fat here as her lifeblood drains away.' He paused, deep in thought. 'Would it be possible to raise the Fyrd – or, at least, some of them?'

'Some would come but, I think, in small numbers. Besides, if many came, we wouldn't have the resources and organization to look after them, or use them effectively; they might be more trouble than they're worth.'

'You're right. Thank you for your excellent and candid report. Stay close to me over the next few months; I'm going to need men like you.'

'I am yours to command, sir.'

'What about you, young Edwin?'

'I'm going to fight with you, sir . . . if you'll have me.'

'I will. Stay close to Alphonso and Einar; watch what they do, and follow their orders to the letter. Do you understand?'

'Yes, sir.'

Hereward took a deep breath. 'From what we've heard, we must make for the North of England. It is beyond William's immediate reach and is Edwin and Morcar's stronghold. We can sail around the south-west coast and meet Harold's sons in Ireland on the way. The North is also a good place to meet representatives of the Danes. Einar, that is your homeland – what do you think?'

'It is a good plan. Most of the wealth is east of the Pennines, but William may well have York under his heel by now. The same might be true of Chester, although you could make contact with the Welsh from there. Lancaster may be too far north, but there is a settlement at a place called Preston, near the mouth of the River Ribble. Although it is isolated, it is on the westerly route to Scotland. York is due east, accessible by an ancient track through the Pennines via a hamlet called Skipton. It is a place I know well; it is where I was born.'

'There could be no finer recommendation, Einar. We will make landfall in England at Preston on the Ribble, in the earldom of Northumbria. Edmund and Edwin, return to England as quickly as you can. We have much to do here, but we will follow as soon as we can and rendezvous in exactly one month. Tell Edith Swan-Neck to stay where she is; there are too many spies around and we don't want to alert William. Bring only two hundred men to Preston, but be sure they are the best available; all must be trained housecarls, fit and eager to fight. We must have a small and mobile baggage train; no wives, children, camp followers of any kind.

'Finally, and this is important, tell no one where they are going; just tell them that they are to meet me in the North to form a new army. They should expect to be away until the autumn harvest at the earliest, but that is all you can tell them. Is that clear?'

'It is, sir.'

Much needed to be done at St Cirq Lapopie before the departure for England.

To Hereward's surprise, not only did Martin change his mind about staying, so did the rest of the family. At an emotional gathering, Martin led the discussion and all agreed that, having been through so much, they should face this final challenge together. Even when Hereward gave them his truthful assessment of the odds against success, they were not discouraged.

Only Cristina said anything negative – and that was about the English weather, which Alphonso had told her would chill her blood.

The bastide of St Cirq Lapopie was entrusted to the care of an estate manager, and a feast was prepared to mark the departure to England. It was a gathering tinged with doubts on both sides. The local Quercynoise feared their landlords would never return, leaving the estate to face an uncertain future, while Hereward and his family knew they were leaving behind a tranquil and happy existence to face a perilous destiny.

As they loaded their weapons and belongings on to the barge of a Lot trader to begin their journey to England, Hereward checked his astrolabe and made his calculations.

It was 8 March 1069.

Blowing from the cool heartland of Europe, a freshening gale from the Massif Central hastened them on their way. Everyone huddled together and turned their backs to the piercing gusts. High above them, flurries of snow swirled around the crags of St Cirq Lapopie as birds of prey rode the currents in search of food. Their occasional screech and the incessant chop of the water against the boat were the only sounds to be heard above the howling elements.

Hereward knew that the next birds of prey they saw would be high above the fells of northern England.

23. The Rising Begins

Hereward and his devoted followers were once more on the move and yet again journeying by sea, but this was a particularly extended excursion. They needed to avoid Normandy, so decided not to make landfall between Bordeaux and Plymouth.

After anchoring off Plymouth Sound to take on water and provisions, they were soon at sea again, on course for Dublin. There, if all went well, they would be able to plan a strategy with Harold's sons and their supporters. As they sailed towards Ireland, Hereward thought back to the first time he had crossed the Western Sea. He and Torfida had just become lovers and, as they stood together on deck, she had given him the Talisman.

It had been the beginning of their odyssey.

Soon he would be in England once more – this time without Torfida. The pain of her absence had barely diminished over time. On occasions like this, the sharp stab of her tragic loss cut into him. He had but one comfort – his children and extended family. And just one distraction – plotting to topple William from the throne of England.

The first part of the plan did not go well. Diarmaid, Lord of Dublin, was sheltering Harold's sons. Edith Swan-Neck had sent word that Hereward was returning to lead a rebellion. However, to Hereward's fury, only Godwin Haroldson was there to greet him; the other two, Magnus and Edmund, had gone hunting. To make matters worse, Godwin was less than enthusiastic about Hereward's plans. He did not agree that Edgar the Atheling should be King, arguing that the boy had relinquished his right to the throne when Harold became monarch.

Godwin regarded himself as the rightful heir to the throne of England.

The young pretender exclaimed that his priority was Wessex, that he had many loyal supporters in Devon, Cornwall and the South West, and that Exeter would be his bridgehead into his father's earldom. He expressed little affection for the North and suggested that it should lie in the bed it had made for itself.

Hereward, scarcely able to contain his anger, begged to be allowed to speak directly to Godwin's housecarls, but he steadfastly refused. Finally, when Hereward asked if they could at least coordinate the timings of Godwin's raids in the West Country so that William could be put under pressure on two fronts, he replied, haughtily, that he would consider it at the time. Hereward's blood boiled and he stormed out, bellowing at Godwin's callousness and stupidity.

They were at sea again on the next tide and, with only a brief stop on the Island of the Manx, were soon sailing up the Ribble to their rendezvous at Preston.

None of them had thought they would ever see England again – especially Hereward – and they were greeted by a bright, fresh spring day. Cristina smiled at Alphonso; her first sight of England was a very pleasant surprise compared with the dreary prospect that her beloved had described.

In the distance they could see the dark mounds of the

Pennines, brooding and hostile. Few people ever went there, and only tiny isolated communities were to be found along the narrow routes that snaked into the deep valleys. Above the treeline were desolate moors where no one ventured. It was a bleak world without landmarks where, in moments, a dank mist could envelop the unwary and make them disappear without trace.

As their vessel rose on to the north bank of the Ribble at Preston's old Roman bridge and the party disembarked, Edwin and Edmund were there waiting for them. Hereward's mood improved dramatically when he saw the contingent of men they had with them. The housecarls were assembled in squadrons of twenty and stood smartly to attention with their mounts tethered in orderly lines.

They were still the finest body of fighting men Hereward had ever seen.

'Sir, you asked for two hundred of the best. Here they are, and our baggage train is trim, just as you wanted it. Also, sir, twenty-three thegns of England have come to join your cause. You will know many of them.' Edmund waved towards the trees in the middle distance.

As he did so, a squadron of thegns emerged from their hiding place, knightly leaders of England's army. They were men from backgrounds like his own; the backbone of England. He recognised many he assumed would be dead: Wulnar the Black, Starelf, Hogor, Gaenoch, Ylard, Toste of Rothwell, his brother Godwin, Broher the Brave, Alutas Grugan, Wenotus, Wulfric the White. With men like these, he could storm the walls of Constantinople.

Hereward addressed the beginnings of his new army. 'Men, it is good to see you.' He jumped on to a wagon so that he could be seen and so that he could look into the eyes of all the noble men who had rallied to his cause. 'That I am here today is a miracle – a miracle worked by my friends who fought with me on Senlac Ridge, and by Torfida, my beloved wife, who nursed me from the brink of death. Sadly, she is not here to share this day with us, but she is here in spirit, an inspiration to us all in her abiding love for England.

'I have heard the accounts from Edmund and Edwin of what life in England has been like under the heel of Duke William. I know this monster; I have witnessed his depravity. He has blighted our land and we must rid ourselves of him and his henchmen. He uses only one tactic – the slaughter of anyone who gets in his way. He knows only one strategy – unyielding terror towards his opponents. But our ruthlessness will be greater than his, our desire for victory more powerful, our determination to triumph more overwhelming, until we rid our land of this evil tyrant.'

A great cheer rose from everyone present. Hereward's presence was a glimmer of hope after nearly three years of oppression and brutality.

'At the request of Edith Swan-Neck and the surviving members of the Witan, I have returned to give leadership to a revolt on behalf of Edgar the Atheling, who, by right of blood, is the true heir to King Harold's throne.'

Another roar rang out from the assembly.

'The Duke and his Norman lackeys have started to build mottes and baileys for their protection. That is wise; they are going to need them! But we will burn the Norman towers to the ground and slay those hiding inside like the cowardly vermin they are!'

Hereward lifted the Great Axe of Göteborg and raised it high above his head.

'For Harold, for Edgar, for England! Our quest begins!'

Within the hour Hereward summoned all the thegns and senior housecarls to a meeting, at which everyone was assigned their tasks. The thegns were given squadrons to command and Einar was made Captain of Hereward's personal hearthtroop, a corps of twenty who would be selected on merit. Alphonso was made responsible for all covert operations and training. Edmund was to be constantly at Hereward's side, as his standard-bearer, and Edwin would be his aide-de-camp. As always, Martin Lightfoot would act as leader of a corps of messengers.

Hereward then asked Edmund of Kent to update them on the latest military situation.

'Sir, matters are not as positive as when we spoke in Aquitaine.'

'Don't worry, Edmund, our course is now set and our destiny is in our own hands. Tell us what we need to hear.'

'Edith Swan-Neck is angry with her sons. They defy her and continue their sporadic raids in Devon. Their men are ill disciplined and they are squandering the inheritance from their father on too many Danish and Irish mercenaries who seek only plunder. The people of Exeter have risen to support them once, and paid dearly for it, when Duke William sent a squadron to punish them. Many were executed; they are unlikely to support them again.'

Hereward interrupted Edmund to ask about the Scots.

'King Malcolm of Scotland lends support to Edgar the Atheling, and to anyone else who needs a safe haven north of the border. He did send a large force down the west coast from Carlisle but, when they reached Penrith, they turned west and started to burn and pillage in Cumberland. We have learned not to rely on his men. There is good news in Mercia, especially Shropshire and Herefordshire, and Chester is strong in its support for us. Their leader is a thegn, Eadric the Wild. He attacks from the Welsh Mountains where he is being aided by Bleddyn, Prince of Gwynedd, and his brother Rhiwallon, Prince of Powys.'

Hereward had another question. 'What are these men like?'

'They fight well enough and have helped Eadric become a sharp thorn in William's side. They destroyed a half-finished Norman motte and bailey at Hereford and now hold the borders, more or less unopposed. William's heavy cavalry are no match for them on high ground.'

'Do you think they would venture beyond the borders and move east to attack Nottingham, Warwick, or even Lincoln?'

'It is doubtful whether the Welsh would support Eadric that far from their homeland.'

'And what of the Danes?'

'Many messages have been sent. Their king, Svein Estrithson, says he will come when the time is right.'

Hereward spent a few moments pondering Edmund's answer before commenting. 'We have to think about the Danes carefully. They will demand a great deal in return for their support – perhaps the whole kingdom! There is little point in removing a Norman, only to replace him with a Dane. But it is good to know he will come. If his army has to be bought, what do we have?'

'I have brought all of King Harold's remaining treasury with me. Half his wealth went with his three sons to Ireland, some went to his daughters in exile in Flanders, and Edith Swan-Neck has enough for herself. What remains is sufficient to support this small force plus the men I've dispersed around the earldoms.'

'But nothing left to entice the Danes?'

'I'm afraid not, sir. Our resources are very limited, especially compared to the plundered gold and silver available to the Duke.'

Hereward left until last the vital question about the most important of England's surviving forces. 'What of the Earls of Mercia and Northumbria, Edwin and Morcar?'

'I'm afraid that is the worst news of all, both have submitted to William and are at his court at Winchester.'

Hereward's blood rose. 'Absent on Senlac Ridge, and now they sup with the Devil!'

'They bring shame to all of us, sir.'

'What of their housecarls?'

'Some, the loyal ones from Northumbria, are with us. Some of Edwin's Mercians are with Eadric the Wild, but most have gone to ground.'

'These are the men we have to recruit; then we will be much more powerful. So, Edmund, after that gloomy account, I hope you can offer me at least a tiny morsel to nibble on. Tell us some good news.'

'Well, sir, your judgement to land here in the North has been vindicated. There is good news from Northumbria, and it may be the spark we need. At the turn of the year, William elevated a Norman brigand called Robert de Commines to be Earl of Northumbria. He arrived with an escort of five hundred men and installed himself in the house of the Bishop of Durham. He and his men then went on the rampage, murdering anyone who stood in their way. Now the whole area has risen against him. Scouts arrived two days ago with news that de Commines and his entire garrison have been put to the sword by a large force, led by the Northumbrian thegns, some of Morcar's housecarls and a vigilante group formed by the people of Durham. There is now no Norman presence in the North beyond York. What's more, York is for the taking, as few Normans are within its walls.'

'Excellent. That will feed our hunger, but we must act quickly.' Hereward was galvanized. The adrenalin started to rush as he barked his orders. 'Martin, you must organize your messengers. Their instructions need to be very precise and everyone must act in unison.'

'How many men?'

'At least ten. They must be able to ride like the wind and be swift of foot, as they may need to abandon their horses. Have them ready at dawn tomorrow. Edmund, is the Atheling with King Malcolm in Scotland?'

'Yes, sir.'

'Good. He must come south, proclaiming that he is the rightful King and that his army is on the march under my command. He must gather all the support he can in Durham and continue south to York. York will be our stronghold and, for the time being, our capital city. The Archbishop can crown Edgar as King.'

'Sir, I'm afraid Archbishop Ealdred has sworn allegiance to William.'

Hereward's enthusiasm turned to anger. 'How many traitors do we have in this kingdom?'

'Too many, sir. Far too many.'

'Ealdred is clearly a coward, and cowards can be easily persuaded. Martin, word must be sent to our supporters in York that we will approach across the Pennines, and that Edgar will enter from Durham. Emphasize that our arrival is imminent. Convey my congratulations to Eadric the Wild for his brave resistance in Mercia. Tell him that now would be the ideal time to mount another attack on any burgh or city he feels appropriate. Finally, when our base in York is secure, he should be prepared to join us on a full-scale march to the South. Please stress that his Welsh comrades, the Princes Bleddyn and Rhiwallon, are more than welcome as part of his force. A message must go to King Harold's sons in Dublin, encouraging them to accelerate their raids in Wessex.

'Next, the Danes. Edwin, this is a task for you. Your blood is sufficiently noble to look King Svein in the eye and say that I would be grateful for his regal presence in England. Tell him that the spoils will be great, but that he must accept Edgar's sovereignty of England. Edmund, where is Edith Swan-Neck?'

'She is with the nuns at Lincoln, sir.'

'She must know of our plans. Her presence in York in support of Edgar would be invaluable. Finally, Edmund, send for the remainder of our men and tell them to bring provisions, blacksmiths, carpenters and cooks. A general rallying call must be sent via your network of scouts for all loyal men to join any of the forces we've mentioned, or to instigate actions in their own areas to add momentum to our cause. Now is the time to act swiftly and decisively. All Norman soldiers are targets; all Norman merchants are to be attacked; all Norman goods are to be plundered. Are there any questions, gentlemen?'

There was no response, only a look of steely determination in the eyes of all present.

'Very good, let's rest. Tomorrow we set out to regain a kingdom.'

As Hereward walked away, he took the Talisman from under his smock and looked at it. He remembered Torfida's words and knew that her spirit was with him.

His sternest test, as leader of the great English rebellion against William and the Normans, had begun.

By midday the next day, the messengers were long gone and Hereward's force was on the march.

At Einar's recommendation, it had been agreed that the family, protected by a small group of housecarls under the command of the thegn Hogor, would camp at a place called Clitheroe Hill, an isolated knoll with commanding views over the heavily wooded valley of the Ribble. It would serve as the rear encampment for the approach to York, with a forward camp further into the Pennines at Einar's birthplace, the fortified hilltop settlement at Skipton, only two days' ride from York. The baggage train, supplies and treasury would remain on Clitheroe Hill, from where, should things not go well at York, a speedy retreat was possible into the surrounding fells.

As they made their way eastwards, the ground rose and became more remote. Other than a small settlement of monks and peasants at the Abbey of Whalley, they saw no one between Preston and Clitheroe. The only significant presence was the great cowl of Pen Hill, which glowered at them whenever there was a clearing in the forest. Einar said it was a place of worship for those who still followed the old religion and that Druid sacrifices to the old gods were made from its summit. Hereward paid little attention to the stories, but thought the presence of the massive hill might be propitious. He also knew it was a perfect lookout, should a tactical retreat be needed in the next few weeks.

The parting at Clitheroe was a heart-rending affair. Martin and Einar warmly embraced Ingigerd and Maria, while Gwyneth and Wulfhild, in floods of tears, tugged at their tunics imploring them not to go. To Alphonso's great embarrassment, Cristina too burst into tears. Hereward picked up his girls, one on each arm. Their beauty and boisterous personalities reminded everyone of Torfida.

Hereward smiled at his precious offspring. 'Kiss your father goodbye; the men are waiting. I love you both very much.'

The girls spoke in unison and in perfect harmony. 'We love you too.'

Both girls kissed their father and then joined the others. Hereward mounted his horse, rode up to the head of the column and signalled for it to move off. Edmund unfurled Hereward's standard: in black, on a gold background, was the twin-bladed Great Axe of Göteborg. Below, in crimson, over the shaft of the axe, was the circular shield of a Saxon housecarl, crossed by two black swords. Each squadron leader carried pennons on their lances in the new colours – gold, crimson and black – the colours of the Talisman and of Hereward's own battle-shield. As the wind blew from the Pennines, the standard of Hereward of Bourne flew proudly in the cool air of a fresh March day.

Ahead of them was York, the city that Hereward hoped would soon be the new capital of a resurgent England.

When they arrived in the city, the streets of York reverberated with wild rejoicing. Hereward's clarion call had been heard and the city was full to bursting with people celebrating as if a thrilling victory had been snatched from the jaws of a tragic defeat. There were camps in the woods and fields around the city, men slept in the streets, and the taverns began to run short of mead and beer. The celebrations went on for days.

Edgar the Atheling, who had arrived from Scotland, as requested, with several hundred of King Malcolm's Scottish warriors, was paraded around the streets to wild cheering. It was remarkable that a Cerdician atheling was being greeted with such enthusiasm in Anglo-Danish Northumbria, the most Scandinavian of all England's settlements.

Cospatrick, the Earl of Bamburgh, had arrived with a force of over 500 men; Maerlesvein, the Sheriff of Lincoln, brought 300; Earl Waltheof, a senior earl from the East Midlands, brought 200; and Siward Bjorn, a wealthy thegn from Nottingham, contributed 100 to the growing ranks. Eadric the Steersman and Aelfwold of St Benet at Holme, both men from East Anglia, brought 100 men between them. Not counting the fickle Scots, Hereward estimated that, including his own men, the English force was now 1,600 strong; not enough to meet William head-on, but it was a beginning. If they could consolidate in York, a march south could swell their ranks to many thousands.

In his private thoughts, Hereward estimated that he

needed 6,000 men to meet William in a full-scale battle. He presumed that William could not muster many more than that in one place, for fear of losing strongholds that he had already established. Disappointingly, Edith Swan-Neck had not appeared. William's men were watching her closely and, following the rising at Durham, she had not dared to travel north.

In any case, events in York were certainly worthy of celebration.

English morale had been given a vital boost.

Hereward called a Council of War and insisted that Edgar, as heir apparent, preside.

Bowing to Edgar, Hereward began. 'Sire, your presence here is the vital piece in our game of chess with William. Our war with William has not yet begun – and must not, until we are stronger.'

'On whose authority do you speak here, Hereward of Bourne?'

Shaken by this unexpected dissent from Cospatrick, Earl of Bamburgh, Hereward hesitated for a moment before continuing. 'Well, my Lord of Bamburgh, I was asked by Edith Swan-Neck to lead a revolt on behalf of Edgar the Atheling, heir to the throne of England.'

'Edith Swan-Neck does not have authority here in Northumbria.'

'No, but I do!' Macrlesvein spoke with barely concealed fury. 'When Earl Morcar was defeated at Gate Fulford by Hardrada, King Harold appointed me Governor of Northumbria until he could speak to Morcar about the earldom. As Harold is now dead, my authority here still stands. So, with Prince Edgar's permission, I give Hereward authority to lead this Council.'

Edgar nodded his approval and Hereward continued.

'Thank you, Maerlesvein of Lincoln.' He turned to Cospatrick. 'My Lord Earl, now is not the time for us to argue. Do I have your support?'

'Yes, but let us be clear – neither I nor my men will go scurrying south in the futile hope of removing William from the throne of Westminster. The Saxon earls have lost that battle. Wessex, Kent, East Anglia – those earldoms have gone to the Normans. Don't expect the Northumbrians to get them back for you. What we will fight for is a kingdom here in York. I'm not sure Prince Edgar is the right choice to rule here but, if he has the support of the Danes and Malcolm Canmore, then I suppose that's who it must be.'

'Allow me to thank my Lord Bamburgh for such a heartfelt endorsement,' the young Prince interjected.

His sarcasm lessened the tension a little, but it did not thwart Waltheof, Earl of the East Midlands.

'The Earl of Bamburgh is a fool! What's more, he's always been a fool. He's got a nerve to stand here and talk to us about Saxon defeats. First of all, after the Northumbrians and Mercians had been taught a lesson by Hardrada's Norwegians at Gate Fulford, it was King Harold's army, largely composed of housecarls from the earldoms of the South, which routed the Norse at Stamford Bridge!'

Men shouted at one another as the Council split between North and South, each faction accusing the other of cowardice and treachery.

Earl Waltheof raised his voice above the din, despite

Hereward's attempts to stop him. 'My Lords, consider who was missing from Senlac Ridge! Cospatrick for one . . .'

The Council began to resemble a riot.

Waltheof, his blood up, screamed, '. . . And those other cowards – Edwin and Morcar – who are, at this very minute, licking the fat arse of William the Bastard!'

Swords were drawn and axes raised as men closed in on one another. The gathering was in danger of turning into a civil war rather than a council of war, when, with a deafening crack, Hereward slammed the Great Axe of Göteborg into the middle of the high table. The rapidly advancing factions stopped in their tracks and silence replaced the mayhem.

Hereward took two breaths, then spoke with the strained voice of a man struggling to control his rage. 'You have until noon tomorrow. Any man still in the city by then will, by his presence, recognize Prince Edgar as the future King of England and accept my authority over all the forces loyal to the Atheling. If any man still here does not so recognize and accept, I will split him asunder with this axe, so help me God! Now go, all of you!'

Hereward wrenched the Great Axe from the table and held it out in front of him. He glared at Cospatrick, willing him to challenge him there and then, but the Earl turned and left. The Council emptied slowly and in silence. Hereward grasped the Talisman and sighed.

He tried to summon up Torfida's image; he needed her blessing if he was to face what lay ahead.

The council gathered again at midday the next day and, to everyone's relief, all were present, including Cospatrick and Waltheof.

Hereward stood and addressed the Council once more. 'Prince Edgar, with your permission.'

The Aetheling signalled his approval.

'My Lords, I thank you all for returning here today. Edmund of Kent, standard-bearer of my hearthtroop, has some news that will gladden your hearts and quicken your pulses. My Lords, news has arrived from Martin Lightfoot's corps of messengers. Eadric the Wild sends his greetings to all here and lends his unqualified support to me as leader of England's vanguard. His attacks continue throughout Mercia and will go on until our objective is achieved. He has over a thousand men under his command, including five hundred Welsh supporters from the Princes of Powys and Gwynedd, and he looks forward to joining us whenever we choose. Prince Godwin, son of King Harold, will set sail for the South West from Dublin within the week. He promises sixty ships and three thousand men.

'Finally, Edwin has returned from Denmark. We have an answer from Svein Estrithson, King of the Danes: he will set sail as soon as his fleet can be assembled, probably by August. Led by his brother, Osbjorn, a fine warrior of great repute, he will send two hundred and fifty ships and seven thousand men.'

There was an astonished silence around the room as men looked at one another in disbelief at so much good news from all quarters. Hereward had known since dawn, when Edmund and Edwin had woken him with the reports. His fury at the discord of the night before had had its effect. Now, all factions listened intently, waiting to hear what his next move would be.

Suddenly, without warning, the door of the hall was thrown open.

A breathless sergeant-at-arms called out to Hereward. 'Forgive me, sir, a messenger has just arrived at the gates of the city. Duke William is on the march and has been for three days. He moves with great speed and is already at Nottingham with three thousand cavalry.'

'Thank you, Sergeant.' Hereward was impressed at the speed of William's response, and had to think quickly. 'Gentlemen, we are not in a position to stand against the Normans. We need more men and more time. We must conserve our strength. Martin, send for your messengers. Thank everyone for their noble support and summon all forces loyal to Edgar to assemble in the Forest of Arden on Midsummer's Day for an attack on Nottingham. There we will wait for the Danes before we advance on London and the South. Until the agreed rendezvous, we will become like the men of the forest: unseen and unheard to all but ourselves.'

It was Edgar the Atheling who asked the obvious question. 'But what of William's advancing army?'

'Let him advance; we will be long gone by the time he gets here.'

Unable to contain himself, Cospatrick bellowed at Hereward. 'Gone! But what of the people of York?'

'I am sorry, my Lord Cospatrick, but we have no choice. If we face William and three thousand of his heavy cavalry, he will destroy us. It will be the end for our cause.'

'But left to the Bastard's mercy, it could mean death for thousands in York.'

'What else would you have me do, my Lord?'

Cospatrick stared at Hereward forlornly, reluctant to accept his decision, but knowing that he was right.

'I suggest that we are all gone by midday tomorrow. The people of the city and its surroundings must be warned and all who can leave should do so; for the rest, we can only pray for them. Return to your strongholds. I will send regular messages to all of you.

'Until we meet again in Mercia on Midsummer's Day, have faith in our cause, stay strong and keep your resolve.'

24. Midsummer Madness

Led by William himself and several of his most able lieutenants, including William Fitzbern, Gilbert of Ghent and William Malet, the Norman army arrived in York only forty-eight hours after the English rebels had dispersed. Furious to find that his opponents had vanished, he immediately sent out squadrons to hunt them down and began to build a towering motte to impose his will on the population. However, on this occasion, he refrained from meting out his usual draconian punishments to the people of the city.

Cospatrick was not so fortunate. Having not met anyone as rapacious as William before, his force dawdled on its route back to Durham and was caught in the open near Thirsk by several Norman squadrons. Cospatrick got away, but most of his men were ruthlessly cut down, their heads brought back to York in baskets and hurled into the streets as a warning to the inhabitants.

Two days later, a similar fate befell a large group of King Malcolm's Scots. They had meandered into the Vale of Pickering in search of plunder and were set upon in their camp at dawn. Most of them were killed and their severed heads were added to the morbid collection of English skulls littering York's thoroughfares. When, a few days later, the Normans granted permission, the monks and nuns of York collected more than 1,000 heads for burial. Fortunately,

Waltheof, Siward Bjorn and the other Saxon earls from the South had accompanied Edgar the Atheling and the remaining Scots on a more direct route northwards and had made it to Durham safely.

'Stupid! Utterly stupid!' Hereward paced up and down in rage and disbelief when news reached him of the shambles of the withdrawal from York. 'I told them to melt away! It's a disaster – a stupid, reckless disaster. No man will ever cross me again; no man will ever countermand my order, or ignore my instructions. No one!'

A decision was made to break the forward camp at Skipton and return to Clitheroe. Einar was commanded to send some men up Pen Hill. Hereward's instructions were clear: 'Make sure they have good eyes and are not afraid of whatever spirits you say live up there. Tell them that they must return immediately if there are any signs of Norman movement. If the danger is imminent, they must light a beacon.'

During the days that followed, Hereward called another meeting of his senior warriors. A messenger had arrived from York with news that the city was calm. Malet, Ghent and Fitzsbern remained, but the Duke had returned to Winchester for his Easter crown-wearing.

Hereward opened the meeting with a bold change of plan. 'Gentlemen, William's audacity has surprised us once again. This, combined with the ill-discipline of our forces, leads me to conclude that a different strategy is required. We will stay here for the time being and begin an exhaustive training regime. If we are to be let down by our comrades again, we must have an elite force here. Contrary to what was agreed at the Council, we are going to split our attacks. The squabbles between us in York made it clear that, for the time being, acting as one army is going to be well-nigh impossible.

'I think we can rely on Eadric the Wild, and we can certainly depend on Waltheof and Siward Bjorn and the other Saxon earls, so the Atheling must stay with them. Send word to Waltheof of our plans and be adamant that, when he next comes south, he must insist that the Scots stay at home – unless he can rely on them totally. The rendezvous in the Forest of Arden is cancelled. Our new strategy is to wait for news of the Danes. When they are sighted, Waltheof, Siward and the others are to come south to York with the Atheling. We will go south to meet Eadric at Chester. At the same time, we will encourage Harold's sons to launch another challenge in the South West. We will then be in effective control of the North, with William being harassed in the South West. If Edgar then joins forces with the Danes and declares himself King at York, that will entice William to attack. Edgar and the Danes will be ready for him and, with Eadric's help, we will move quickly across Mercia to block the Duke's retreat south. Your comments, gentlemen.'

Everyone agreed that, under the circumstances, it was a clever plan, typical of Hereward's burgeoning leadership.

'Edwin, you must make another trip to King Svein's court in Denmark. Take some of Martin's messengers with you, so that I know every move the Danes make. They must do two things. Firstly, their fleet must appear in the South, near the Thames Estuary, or in Kent. It must look like they are trying to find a place to launch an invasion, and they must send out raiding parties to harass the local Normans. That will persuade William to despatch men eastwards and southwards, and fewer men will be available for his northern expedition. The second task for the Danes is to destroy the Norman fleet. In every port from the Isle of Wight to Shoeburyness, they must burn and sink all Norman vessels they find. This will cut the Normans off from their homeland, which is vital if we're to have any success in moving on the South.'

Everyone looked at Hereward in admiration. He had formulated an audacious new strategy that, if all went well and everyone played their part, could have William on the run and unable to escape to Normandy.

If the English then rose en masse, William would be finished.

Einar spoke for all of them. 'It is daring and it is cunning. Congratulations, Hereward.'

'Thank you, Einar. Call the men together. Alphonso, the training becomes your responsibility. We start tomorrow; make us suffer, make us think and make us ruthless.'

The days passed quickly. Alphonso was a master of intelligent regimes; he organized weapons competitions, assault courses, tests of navigation and horsemanship. He believed that irregular warfare should be undertaken by small groups of equals and insisted that all join in, regardless of status. When in training, there were no ranks and everyone spoke to one another by first name.

The routine of training was interrupted only once, at the end of June, when a messenger appeared with sad news for everyone close to England's cause.

Edith Swan-Neck had been given permission by William to return to her family home at Nazeing in Essex. She went under heavy guard and called at Waltham Abbey to pray. But by the time she reached Nazeing, she was ill with a fever. Only two days later, she was dead. Her family was convinced she had been poisoned on orders from the Duke. Fearing that the Normans might realize Harold was interred there, the family chose not to bury her next to him at Waltham, but in the family plot at Nazeing Church.

Training resumed early the next morning, as usual. Hereward had ridden off with Einar well before dawn to survey from Pen Hill the vast forested landscape of the western Pennines. Over 1,800 feet above sea level, there was a remarkable view from its summit. The great expanse of Bowland Forest lay to the north and beyond that was Lancaster, the last major English bastion before the northern wilderness and the lawless Scottish borders. To the west, the land fell away to the Irish Sea, just visible in the distance. To the south and east, rising above the forests, stretched the endless rolling moorland of the Pennines. Local folklore claimed that, when York was burned to the ground during the Viking invasions many years earlier, the glow could be seen from Pen Hill.

Just after midday, Ingigerd and Maria appeared, clambering up the steep track towards the summit. They had decided to bring food for the men. But, more than that, they had been concerned about Hereward. It was Midsummer's Eve, a special day in the old religion and, aware that news of Edith's death had arrived at such a symbolic time, they wondered how much it had disturbed him. Often, they had discussed whether he secretly yearned for a consort with whom to share the burden of leadership. Could Edith have fulfilled that role? They would have made an extraordinary

couple as England's Regent and Consort, despite the oppro-
brium of those who might have resented their humble
origins.

After they had eaten, Einar, guessing what the women
were up to, took the sentries off to patrol around the
summit.

Ingigerd spoke first. 'Hereward, why don't you take a
woman?'

He smiled at them both. As a soldier, he admired their
strategy – a full-frontal assault, no initial skirmishes, no
feints.

'Do you think I'm in need of one?'

Maria's tone was softer but her approach was just as
direct. 'It is a long time since Torfida died, and you carry
such a huge burden for all of us and for England. Wouldn't
it be a comfort to have someone to confide in and open
your heart to?'

Before Hereward could respond, Ingigerd resumed.
'Aren't you lonely?'

'My dearest friends, you are very thoughtful and I appreciate your kindness. The truth is, there have been only two
women in my life that I wanted to spend the rest of my
days with – and both are dead. When I was no more than
a boy, Gythin was my first love. Her death in terrible
circumstances was the catalyst that began the extraordinary
events that have shaped my life. Then there was Torfida,
the amazing, beautiful Torfida we all loved. She was my one
true love; no one could fill Torfida's place in my heart.'

They both put their arms around him.

Maria had tears in her eyes. 'But, Hereward, what of the
future? When all this is over, what will become of you?'

'I don't know what will become of any of us. England is in a perilous state and we are facing almost insurmountable odds. We will need great good fortune to be successful.'

'Will we ever see St Cirq Lapopie again?'

'I sincerely hope so. My greatest wish is to make England secure, oversee Edgar's ascendency to the throne and then retire to France to watch Gunnhild and Estrith grow into women and produce grandchildren for me to spoil.'

'And will you live out those days with a beloved you can call your own?'

'Who knows? First, let me deal with the small matter of England's future.'

Ingigerd and Maria realized that Hereward was focused on one thing only. He was a man of remarkable conviction and strength. He had always had a warrior's spirit but, since recovering from Torfida's death, and following his journey to meet Rodrigo Diaz, he had also added profound wisdom to his many other qualities.

Hereward brought their discussion to a close. 'Let's find Einar and go back to camp to see the girls.'

The four of them began the steep descent to their waiting horses. As they did so, they caught sight of a small plume of smoke rising from the tiny hamlet of Downham, nestling in the shadow of Pen Hill.

'Einar, in all the time we've been here, not a single local man has come to us and asked to join our cause. They must know of the peril that is only two days' ride away in York?'

'Yes, they know, but they pray it won't come their way. York is another world for them; so is Lancaster. As for Winchester, it could be in the Holy Roman Empire for all they know. You can't expect them to rush to our side when they don't have the strength to wield a weapon properly. Don't judge them too harshly; it's not so very different throughout much of England. Remember all the earls, merchants and burghers who have already bowed to the Duke.'

'That's our problem. The Normans have ambition and a steely resolve, made stronger by the riches of conquest. Most of the English, be they Saxon, Dane, or Celt, already have the look of a beaten people and are resigned to their fate.'

'Hereward, how do you keep going with such grave doubts?'

Before answering, Hereward reflected for a while, touching the Talisman as he did so. 'My good friend, I have come to understand that all a man can do is follow his own path. Whatever his destiny, he will only find it by being brave in the choices he makes. Somehow, at the end of all this, there is an outcome that will be determined by circumstances playing themselves out like a gigantic game of chess. We are only four hundred men and there are perhaps no more than a few thousand we can rely on in the whole of England. But the game is not William's yet; there will be weaknesses in the Norman position, and we have to find them. I don't know how many Normans hold this land – perhaps fifteen or twenty thousand – but they rule only with the support of many Englishmen. That will change if William makes an error of judgement. Tactically, I'd say we've lost too many pieces, especially our pawns and knights. Now our Queen has gone, but our King still lives – Edgar, our rightful heir. Our defence is still solid in our wild northern stronghold. If we keep our nerve, William may yet make a mistake, and those who have submitted to him will think again. Our four thousand will quickly become forty thousand; then it will be a different endgame.'

'Hereward, you have become a wise man as well as a great warrior. You are England's last hope, and we are proud to follow you.'

Hereward did not respond. He put his hand on Einar's shoulder, then hurried away down the slope, once again deep in thought, leaving his friends to follow in his wake.

The summer of arduous training at Clitheroe Hill continued for many weeks without interruption. No word came from the lookouts on Pen Hill, and the warning beacon was never lit.

The news everyone had been praying for finally arrived on a gloriously sunny day in the third week of August 1069.

A messenger from Edwin reported that the Danish fleet had left Jutland and sailed through the Skagerrak at the end of July. By early August, it had begun marauding along the south coast of England, just as Hereward had asked. Raiding parties had attacked Dover, Sandwich, Norwich and Ipswich; the Norman fleet was being systematically destroyed. As King Svein had promised, there were nearly 250 ships in a fleet commanded by his brother, Osbjorn, and two of his sons, Harold and Cnut. Christian, the Bishop of Aarhus, was present to make the cause a holy one, and the war party included opportunists and mercenaries from the Baltic and most of northern Europe.

It was a genuine invasion force. Hereward could not have hoped for more.

The new strategy swung into action immediately. Guarded by Hogor, the family remained at the camp on Clitheroe Hill as all twenty squadrons moved south to Chester to join forces with Eadric the Wild. By the time they arrived at the banks of the Dee, men were on the march everywhere and an upsurge of confidence was gaining momentum.

Harold's sons had arrived from Ireland with 3,000 men in more than 60 ships. They had sailed up the river Tavy and made their headquarters at Tavistock. There had been a general rebellion throughout the whole of Cornwall and Devon, which was spreading to Dorset and Somerset. The latest reports said that Montacute castle, seat of the powerful Norman lord Robert of Mortain, was besieged. Hereward sent an urgent message of congratulations to Godwin Haroldson and asked him to hold the ground he already had, but to wait for a signal to advance on Winchester.

Edgar the Atheling, Earl Waltheof, Siward Bjorn and a large force had arrived from the North and were ready to attack York. The Danes had sailed up the Humber and lay in wait to the south of the city. Hereward ordered an immediate attack on the Norman garrison in the city.

His own rendezvous with Eadric the Wild had gone well; the two men found an immediate rapport and shared a common desire to rid England of the Normans. Eadric's contingent of 300 included only 100 men from Bleddyn, Prince of Gwynedd – far fewer than Hereward had anticipated. Bleddyn's brother, Rhiwallon, Prince of Powys, had been killed in a skirmish and his men had gone home to Wales in mourning. Nevertheless, despite the absence of

Rhiwallon's men, the combined force now under Hereward's command was over 700, a sufficient number to ruffle the feathers of a few Normans.

Hereward planned to attack Shrewsbury before turning east to challenge Stafford and Nottingham. By then, he hoped William would be well to the north, busily engaging Edgar's force and Osbjorn's Danes, and effectively cut off from his stronghold in the South. That would be the time for Harold's sons to march on Winchester, leading to a general rising in the South and leaving William outflanked and isolated.

As they made camp outside Shrewsbury, Hereward consulted his astrolabe. The date was 24 August 1069, one month short of the third anniversary of the eve of the Battle of Stamford Bridge, a coincidence he thought very auspicious.

The Norman fortification at Shrewsbury was formidable. The perimeter of the bailey was protected by a ditch, overlooked by a tall wooden palisade, and the motte was a mound of earth of considerable height, topped by a tall wooden tower. No such structures had been seen in England prior to William's conquest and the English had no strategy for dealing with them. Hereward knew that, short of a prolonged siege for which he had neither the time nor the resources, a costly full-scale frontal assault was the only option. The Norman lord of Shrewsbury was Roger of Montgomery, an experienced soldier who had prepared well and whose initial defensive position was drawn up at the walls of his outer bailey.

Hereward's and Eadric's men suffered many casualties in more than half a dozen assaults before retreating to regroup. Norman casualties were only light, but they used a pause in the English attack to abandon their bailey and move into the even more secure tower on top of the motte. To mount an attack on this stronghold involved crossing the open ground of the bailey before clambering up the steep slope. Only then would they reach the fortification itself, an edifice nearly seventy feet high.

Nevertheless, the rebels launched three ferocious attacks, but failed to weaken the Norman position. As the English casualty toll mounted from the arrows, stones, hot oil and spears cascading from the battlements, they shot burning arrows to try to ignite the wooden structure and hurled bales of blazing straw in an attempt to set fire to its base, but the defenders were able to extinguish the flames before they caught hold. Then, as Hereward led a testudo of housecarls towards the base of the Norman motte, parts of the burgh of Shrewsbury caught light from incendiary arrows deliberately aimed at the houses by the Norman archers. Hereward called an immediate halt to the assault. The Normans cared nothing for the local population. If the fires were not put out quickly, Shrewsbury would be lost – and with it the support of the local people, many of whom were of Celtic descent. His men helped the populace douse the flames that threatened their homes before a general withdrawal was ordered.

Hereward decided to move on to Stafford, having prepared all kinds of subversive techniques, but the local Norman warlord had taken hostages into his bailey and threatened to burn them alive if the attacks continued. They made one more attempt at Tutbury, almost halfway to Nottingham, but, once again, their attacks could not breach the Norman defences without endangering the local population. They were left with no choice but to slip away to lick their wounds in the safe haven of the lower Pennines.

Once encamped, Eadric could offer little consolation for Hereward. 'I'm afraid that we have no answer to these Norman towers.'

'My good friend, there is always an answer. If we had ballista or siege engines, we could pound them into submission or we could starve them out. We don't have the time or the resources to organize and protect the local people, and our numbers have fallen to a little more than five hundred. We need a new plan. Take the remainder of your men and go with Bleddyn and his Welshmen. I will give you four squadrons of mine. Retrace our route; keep the Normans locked in their towers, while I go north to see what is happening in York. Let's hope that ours is the only part of the strategy that has not gone well. Our main hope now is the Danes.'

By the time Hereward's force reached Tadcaster, they had received news that lifted their spirits once more. It was brought by Edwin, who, breathless with excitement, blurted out the details. When Edgar and the Danes attacked in overwhelming numbers, they had been able to scale the tower at York and achieve total success. The only Norman survivors were William Malet and Gilbert of Ghent and their families. It had been a fierce and bloody battle. Earl Waltheof had distinguished himself by killing dozens of Normans single-handedly, beheading them as they tried to escape through the gate of their tower.

However, there was one significant and disturbing piece of news, which Edwin saved for the end. 'I'm afraid the city is in ruins, burned to the ground. The Normans torched everything before they scurried to their tower.'

'So the city is ours, but nothing remains!'

'I'm sorry, sir.'

'And what of the Norman tower?'

'Gone, sir. We burned that down.'

'Where are Malet and Gilbert of Ghent?'

'With the Danes – they have taken them to their ships on the Humber. They intend to ransom them.'

'And Edgar and his forces?'

'Outside York, waiting for a response from you.'

Hereward shook off his despondency and replaced it with a look of defiance.

'Then let's give them one. Martin, send a messenger to the Atheling. Tell him to wait outside York; we will arrive as quickly as we can. We will then go to the Danes to prepare for a major battle with William on ground of our choosing. Edwin, who is Bishop of Durham?'

'Aethelwine, sir.'

'Is he loyal?'

'Yes, sir, he is now. Initially, after the coronation, he spoke for William, saying that he was the anointed King. However, he changed his view because of the behaviour of the Normans, especially when Robert de Commines threw him out of the Bishop's Palace!'

'Send word to him; he will anoint Edgar as King. If York Minster is in ashes, we can take Edgar to Durham. It is an important enough bishopric to persuade Rome that the hand of God is supporting Edgar's crown.'

Hereward and his force hurried to meet the triumphant Prince Edgar at Selby on the Ouse, a few miles south of

York. It was a joyous meeting and Hereward reserved a particularly warm welcome for Waltheof to acknowledge his heroic deeds at the Norman tower. Edgar declared that a great banquet should be held and hunters were sent out to provide the fare. It mattered little that their dining hall was a clearing beside the old road to York; a grand celebratory feast was enjoyed that very evening. Later that night, in the midst of the gorging, more news came to gladden their hearts.

Hereward stood to make the formal announcement. 'Men of England, following your great victory at York, the heroics of the sons of King Harold in the South West and the courageous stand of Eadric the Wild and his Welsh allies in Mercia, Aethelwine, Bishop of Durham, has agreed to crown Prince Edgar in what remains of York as the rightful and proper King of England. He has already left Durham for the coronation and will be here in a couple of days.'

A cry of joy rose from everyone assembled.

'Tomorrow, we will travel to meet Prince Osbjorn, commander of the Danish army, to plan our attack on the Normans.'

Another, even louder cry echoed around the clearing.

'Eat and drink your fill. Enjoy your great and noble victory!'

At noon the next day, Hereward and a small group were ready to leave the camp to meet the Danes on the Humber.

Suddenly, the calm was disturbed by the noise of sentries announcing that a messenger approached. The herald, a boy of only nineteen who had the physique of a hunting dog, jumped from his horse gasping for air.

Sir . . .' He could not speak.

'Get him water. Take your time . . .'

Einar came to Hereward's aid. 'It's Uhtred, sir.'

'Uhtred, compose yourself. Your message can wait until you get your breath.'

After a few moments, the messenger was able to deliver his report. 'Sir, it's not good news. Duke William is at Tadcaster. Arkil the Fair has stayed behind to keep watch, but he told me to come here as quickly as possible.'

'He is almost on top of us; how can this be? How can he have got here so quickly?'

'His good fortune, and our bad luck, sir. He was hunting in the Forest of Dean on the Welsh border. His army was on a tour of Mercia in a show of strength to intimidate the locals. He summoned his army and was on the move as soon as he heard the Danes had entered the Humber.'

'How does Arkil know this?'

'Sir, it makes me sick to say this, but many Englishmen are cooperating with the Normans. It is easy to hear of the Normans' plans, because so many Englishmen are part of them.'

'It is hard to believe!' Hereward kicked at the ground in frustration. 'Please, carry on with your report.'

'Yes, sir. The Normans have split their force at Tadcaster. The Duke has sent two of his most senior men to York. They are to re-garrison the city, help the locals rebuild their houses and businesses and erect a new Norman stronghold. William has gone east to the Humber to negotiate with the Danes.' Uhtred had lowered his voice for the final sentence.

'He's done what? My God, he must have passed within a couple of miles of us.'

'Sir, he moves so quickly, it is impossible to keep pace with him.'

Hereward turned away in fury. 'Will he never give us breathing space? Will he never make a mistake? He outflanks us, out-thinks us, outpaces us. And now he's ambushing us by going to parley with our own allies! Damn him! Damn him to Hell!'

He started to pace up and down silently, then barked at Uhtred. 'How many men?'

'Arkil thinks two thousand on their way to York and another two thousand with the Duke. All heavy cavalry, in full armour, with plenty of provisions. We counted at least a dozen lords with gonfalons and more than a hundred knights' pennons.'

'Thank you, Uhtred, for an excellent report – and well ridden. Go and get some rest.'

'Thank you, sir. I'm sorry it's not better news.'

Einar waited for a moment before addressing Hereward, who had his head thrown back in exasperation and was inhaling deeply.

'There is still a chance to talk to the Danes; they have no love for the Normans.'

'I know, but then we should take Prince Edgar with us. Osbjorn is brother to a king. If he's going to ask his men to put their lives at risk on foreign soil, the covenant has to be between Edgar and Osbjorn.'

Prince Edgar spoke without hesitation. 'Hereward, I am happy to go, whatever the risk.'

'Thank you, my Lord Prince, but I must insist that you don't. It's not safe. William will have set a trap.'

Einar spoke much more forcefully than usual. 'Then you

and I will go, with Edwin. You are Regent in all but name; they will listen to you.'

'No, we would go to our certain deaths. I don't trust the Danes. It is obvious now why they returned to their ships and took William Malet and Gilbert of Ghent as hostages. They never had any intention of standing with us against William's army.'

Einar waited patiently, giving his friend time to think.

Eventually, Hereward spoke. 'We wait. We wait to hear the outcome of William's parley with the Danes. Double the sentries and post men all the way to York. At the first hint of any Normans moving towards us, we must know immediately so that we can be ready to move before they snare us like Cospatrick's men. Keep everyone busy and alert.'

Einar and the others then left Hereward alone to ponder their fate.

No matter how brilliant Hereward's strategy, William responded in equal measure; no matter how carefully he prepared, misfortune seemed to dog every fleeting success.

Even more disheartening was the ever more evident reality that the great majority of the English simply lacked the will to resist the Norman occupation.

25. The Harrying of the North

The news Hereward feared most arrived just three days after Uhtred's report of William's march north and his audacious plan to negotiate with Osbjorn of Denmark.

The young messenger spoke clearly and without emotion. 'Duke William and the Danes have come to an agreement. A major part of the Danish army will spend the winter on the Humber, on the Isle of Axholme. They will be allowed to hunt and forage within a radius of fifty miles of their camp and the Normans will send them additional supplies from York and Lincoln if needed. William Malet and Gilbert of Ghent and their families have been released. In addition, a Danegeld has been paid and sent to Denmark on this morning's tide. It is an amount so large that it took three hours to load the chests of silver and gold on to the Danish longships. But the treasure represents only half of the levy; an equal amount will be paid in the spring of next year, when the remaining Danes sail home.'

Hereward questioned the messenger further. 'What of William and his army, will they return to Winchester?'

'No, sir. The Duke has sent to Winchester for his crown and regalia. He is to celebrate his Christmas crown-wearing at York in his new motte and bailey.'

'Yes – and, at the same time, keep an eye on the Danes of course!' Hereward observed. He was becoming hardened to misfortune and reversals.

This time, Prince Edgar was the first to ask what their new plan would be.

Hereward was succinct in his reply. 'It will soon be October. The Danes will not fight, but will sit on their ill-gotten gains and grow fat in their winter camp. William will light fires and eat Yorkshire's game in his Great Hall and parade around in his crown, thinking he is Charlemagne. As for us, we must lie low once more. Don't go to Malcolm – I don't trust him not to be seduced by William's riches and hand you over to the Normans. Go north, high into the Pennines, and make a secure winter camp there. Wait for news from me; we will launch a new campaign in the spring.'

'Do you still have the heart for this, my brave Hereward?'

'As long as the Normans plunder this land, I have the heart for it.'

The Prince thanked Hereward warmly, while Einar gave Edgar advice about where he should go.

'My Lord, go to the head of the valley of the Swale; no one will find you there. There is some good pasture, and the valley is deep and will protect you from the winter gales. I know the area well. We can reach you from our camp without having to leave the sanctuary of the Pennines. There is an old housecarl who lives in the Swale. His name is Osulf – I served with him for Aelfgar, Earl of Northumbria. He will be invaluable to you. Winters can be very hard there.'

'Thank you, Einar. What will you do, Hereward?'

'We will return to our base on Clitheroe Hill for the winter. It is better if our forces are spread far and wide; it will keep William guessing. I will send for news of Eadric in Mercia, and of the forces of Godwin Haroldson in the South West, and pass it on to you.'

'Be careful, my good and loyal friend.'

'I will, my Prince. God's speed to your safe haven.'

Edgar's force rode off at a gallop. He took many good men with him, including Waltheof and Siward Bjorn.

Hereward wondered if he would ever see any of them again.

Within a few hours of the Atheling's departure, Hereward had made a decision.

'Einar, lead the men back across the Pennines to Clitheroe Hill. Edwin, Edmund and I are going to see a Danish prince.'

The Danish camp at Axholme was a flurry of activity. A significant wooden palisade was being built on what was, in effect, an island. The ground was being cleared for wooden barracks and a massive centre post was being driven into the ground for Prince Osbjorn's Great Hall.

The Englishmen were given a warm welcome. Osbjorn was tall, but lacking the heavy build of a typical Danish warrior, and more resembled a diplomat or a cleric. Paradoxically, the cleric standing to Osbjorn's right – Christian, the Bishop of Aarhus – had both the build and demeanour of a housecarl. Harold and Cnut, King Svein's sons, were imposing men who looked more than capable of leading an army into battle. Osbjorn introduced several senior Danish nobles and magnates from Poland, Saxony and Lithuania, all of whom would be taking home significant shares of the bounty from William's treasury.

'Prince Osbjorn, thank you for seeing us. I am Hereward

of Bourne, commander of the forces of Edgar the Atheling, rightful heir to the throne of England. You have met Edwin before, my aide-de-camp. This is Edmund of Kent, my standard-bearer.'

'Gentlemen, please sit and eat with us. We are roasting some fine English mutton.'

'Thank you, sire.'

'Hereward of Bourne, we are honoured to have you in our camp. Your reputation goes before you. Edwin we know well. He is a fine young soldier. We were delighted to have him at our court in Aarhus.'

'Prince Osbjorn, I will come to the point.'

'Of course.'

'William, Duke of Normandy has been here.'

'He has. I am amused that you still refer to him as the "Duke of Normandy". I thought he had ruled here as King for almost three years.'

'Only by force of arms.'

'Many kings win their throne by force of arms.'

'That is true. But many kings are also unseated by force of arms, and that will be William's fate. Isn't that why you came here – to help us do that?'

Prince Osbjorn was a man of palpable intelligence and cunning and did not take offence at the bluntness of Hereward's question. 'Following your pleas, conveyed by Edwin, I was asked to lead our forces by my brother, King Svein. Our objective was to bring a large enough army to help the English in their campaign against King William – the "Duke", as you call him. We destroyed his navy, as you asked. We caused disruption along the east coast, as you asked. And then, with Prince Edgar and his men, we

stormed the gates of York and put the Normans to flight
. . . as you asked.'

'Yes, you did all that we asked of you, and for that we
are grateful. But the final piece of the strategy was to rout
William in the North with an attack on his main force,
after which we would sweep south together and claim the
Kingdom.'

'Yes, we know.'

'But then you parleyed with him and filled your longships
with gold and silver!' Hereward's voice was rising in anger.
'Why?'

'Let me do some reckoning for you. We are close to six
thousand; William has four thousand heavy cavalry and
more could be summoned at any time. How many men
could you have brought to the field?'

'Several thousand, Prince Osbjorn.'

'Our estimate is two thousand at best. And your cavalry
is light cavalry; you don't have heavy Norman horses.'

'It would have been enough, sire.'

'Forgive me, it would not. Six thousand Danes . . . two
thousand Englishmen . . . Should it not have been the other
way round? Aren't we on English soil, fighting for an
English crown? If the circumstances were reversed, and
we were in Denmark, we would be able to put twenty-five
thousand men into the fray.'

Prince Osbjorn's blunt analysis was difficult to accept,
but Hereward knew it was accurate. 'So, you've taken
William's geld instead.'

'Of course! We have an army to feed and many supporters to reward.'

The pragmatic summary delivered by the Prince was the

only logical position that the Danes could have taken. Nevertheless, it made Hereward angry – angry that only two thousand Englishmen could be mustered to stand with the Danes.

'I am sorry, Hereward of Bourne. We respect William's heavy cavalry. Our view is that, without cavalry, we would need to have an advantage of at least two to one for our shield wall to hold. Remember what your cavalry did to Hardrada at Stamford Bridge, and bear in mind that Harold's mighty shield wall eventually gave way to the destriers at Senlac Ridge.'

Hereward, angry and saddened, rose to leave, resigned to the brutal reality that Osbjorn had described. 'My Lord Prince, I thank you for your candour. Many a man would have engaged in platitudes and tried to exact an advantage from us.'

The Prince beckoned Hereward to one side, away from everyone's hearing, and spoke in a hushed voice. 'Let me tell you frankly our position. William is no lover of the sea and has no skills as commander of a fleet. Therefore, as it has been for centuries, England's east coast will be vulnerable to us for a long time to come. Malcolm, King of the Scots, is our ally and a serious threat to England. Then there is Edgar and your English rebellion; there is much we can exploit here and William is rich. We will take William's money for as long as he's prepared to offer it. As for you, we will stand with you only if you can muster six or seven thousand housecarls and at least four thousand men on war horses.'

'And your price, my Lord?'

'A new Danelaw: Lincoln, Nottingham, Gloucester and

everything to their north would be Danish. Our capital would be at York. The South would be English.'

'That is a high price, even for a Dane!'

'Yes, it is half your kingdom – and we Danes would say it's the better half! But when you have found ten thousand men, we can haggle about the price. As you know, we have decided to stay for the winter. We thought there would be a few more twists in this tale before it ran its course. Come back and talk in the spring; you will always be welcome here.'

'Thank you. But you must realize that if I had ten thousand men, I wouldn't need the support of the Danes.'

'Perhaps, but William is an awesome opponent. Never underestimate him.'

'I've learned not to. Winter well here in Axholme.'

'Thank you. Good luck in your noble attempts to rouse your English comrades.'

The two men parted far more amicably than at first seemed possible. At least Hereward now knew the full extent of the dilemma he faced.

It was going to be a long hard winter of reflection in his Pennine eyrie.

Clitheroe Hill, his family and his girls were an uplifting sight as Hereward approached the camp – a home that was beginning to have an air of permanence about it. Gohor's men had built a wooden hall with a stone hearth for the family, and his men were building longhouses to replace their canvas tents and pelt lean-tos; the Pennines was not a place to be huddled in a makeshift shelter through the long winter months.

Hereward's band had become smaller. Some men were ill, some had injuries or wounds that refused to heal, and some had asked to go, weary of the fight. When the four squadrons which had been campaigning with Eadric returned, the 80 men who had gone with him had dwindled to 56. A roll-call was taken. Only 268 Englishmen remained at Hereward's side.

The winter of 1069 was particularly hard. Pen Hill was enveloped by deep snow from mid-November onwards, and the camp was engulfed by several heavy blizzards. At the turn of the year, although it did not seem possible, the weather worsened. Hunting became difficult, even dangerous; nights were long and black; firewood became sparse and spring seemed a long way off. The only comfort was that the dead of winter made England subdued. Few men stirred, offering at least a chimera of peace and tranquillity.

That falsehood was rudely exposed on the Sabbath of the second week of January.

Hereward had sent a scout to York to reconnoitre the disposition of William's forces and assess the progress of the building of the new Norman city and fortifications. To the scout's astonishment, within hours of his arrival, he watched as William rode out of the city with a force of nearly 2,000 men. A return to Winchester, in the depths of a winter as fierce as this one, would have been an intrepid move, but Winchester was not his destination; when he passed the new gates of the city, instead of turning south, he turned north.

The scout galloped back to Clitheroe Hill as quickly as his mount would carry him, eager to give his report.

Hereward looked at him in disbelief. 'How long has it taken you to get back here?'

'Less than a day, sir.'

Alphonso spoke before Hereward. 'That is an outstanding ride. Well done!'

'Thank you, sir.'

Hereward's mind was racing, realizing what the implications of William's move might be. 'That can only mean he's looking for Edgar and is a day ahead of us. He must have heard that he is not with the Scots and realized that he is in hiding in the North. By the time we're ready, we'll have lost another day. Then we have a day's riding east or west before we turn north; that means he's got three days on us –'

Einar interrupted. 'We can get to him in time if we're a small enough group and don't mind a bit of snow and hard toil. There is a route up the watershed of the Pennines. There are some high traverses, but it's not impossible.'

'How many men?'

'Twenty, no more. Two horses each, no baggage.'

'Not many of us if we stumble across two thousand Normans!'

'The Normans won't be able to go where we're going.'

'We must make haste. Alphonso, you take charge of the camp, organize a series of wide-ranging patrols. I don't care how bad the weather is, they're to go as far east as Skipton, west to Preston, south around Pen Hill to the valleys beyond and the settlement at Burnlea, and north over Bowland Trough to the old road at Lancaster. If any Normans come close to Clitheroe Hill, break camp immediately and go north, high into the Pennines, taking only what a horse will carry. Send word of your final destination; we will come and find you. There's much to do. Let's get moving.'

Einar led the small troop of men on his hazardous path through the heart of the Pennines. The route went due north; the snow was deep, the rivers icily cold and the wind piercing. Conditions were even worse at a gallop, when faces ached from the chill of the cold air.

It took them four and a half days before, on a bitterly cold but clear day, they crested the summit of their last high traverse and descended into the head of the valley of the Swale. The sky was sapphire blue and cloudless. But rising from the horizon, about twenty-five miles to the east, was a plume of darkness.

'Richmond.' It was all Einar needed to say.

Hereward turned to his men. 'We must hurry.'

As they cantered down the fell, they could see below the tiny specks of a column of men moving along the north bank of the river.

'Let's hope that is Prince Edgar and his men, retreating from the Norman advance. Martin, you have the sharpest eyes here, how many men?'

'No more than fifty.'

'If it is Edgar, he has lost many comrades.'

It took them nearly an hour to reach the retreating column. They were shocked by the condition of Edgar's men: they no longer had the bearing of an elite escort for a king-in-waiting. Winter had obviously taken its toll on them; they were dirty, their weapons and horses neglected, and they had the vacant stare of men who were cold and hungry.

Hereward immediately sent a patrol down the valley of the Swale to determine the Normans' progress. He ordered fires to be lit, hot food prepared and instigated the familiar routines of soldiers. With the wintry sun offering a little warmth, Edgar and his men were made to take a quick plunge in the Swale, cut their hair and beards, clean their armour, sharpen their weapons, and feed and groom their horses. Only then were they allowed to relax by the fires while Hereward and his troop fed them bowls of broth and bread.

When they had eaten, Hereward gave them a short but inspiring speech. It ended with a simple rallying cry: 'Your responsibility is the greatest of all. You ride with England's only hope – Edgar, the rightful King. Keep him safe. Do this for me. Do this for our people!'

Prince Edgar then told Hereward the grim tale of his winter in Upper Swaledale.

'It has been awful here. Usulf, the man Einar spoke of, died a couple of years ago and when we arrived, the locals fled, taking everything with them. There isn't much game up here in the middle of winter and we were reluctant to venture too far down the valley, so we had to scavenge for whatever we could find. The men became restless; many deserted, some in broad daylight. Then, about a month ago, one of Cospatrick's spies in York heard a rumour that William was planning a major campaign for the New Year.'

'So it is true? William is looking for you?'

'Only in part. The word is that he spent every night before Christmas getting blind drunk, bellowing that he was going to rid England of its vermin once and for all, burn every house and slaughter every animal. As soon as they heard the spy's story, Cospatrick and Waltheof left for their earldoms to protect their communities.'

'And Siward Bjorn?'

'He had left earlier, to go on a recruiting mission for more men. He said he was embarrassed that so few Englishmen had joined the revolt. What do you think we should do now?'

'You have to go to King Malcolm. With William on the rampage like this, Scotland is the only safe place for you. I've never known anyone like him; he's totally ruthless and utterly relentless. If he's prepared to maraude through the Pennines in the middle of winter and massacre his subjects on the supposition that a few of them might be rebels, then nowhere in England is safe for you.'

'But I'd prefer to come with you.'

'That is not a good idea. I have my own plan, which will put you in harm's way. I've had enough of avoiding William until the time is right; I'm going to confront him directly, not in a pitched battle, but close enough so that he knows it's me. That will infuriate him and make him come after me. And when he does, I'll be able to choose my ground and stand and face him.'

'Then I should be at your side.'

'No, my prospects are not great in such a challenge. You have to survive, albeit in exile in Scotland, Flanders, or wherever you choose, but you must live. You are the only legitimate heir England has. Can you rely on your men to get you to Scotland?'

'Yes, I think so, now that you have reminded them of their discipline.'

'Good, then our cause is not lost. We go on.'

'Do you think William knows you lead the revolt?'

'I'm sure he does. He must know by now that I was on Senlac Ridge. When we meet again, it will be quite a reckoning.'

Prince Edgar, the Saxon Atheling to the English throne, left within the hour. The patrol Hereward had despatched returned shortly afterwards and confirmed that the reports from York were true: William had split his force into several smaller groups, which were fanning out into every habitable part of Northumbria, hell bent on finding all the English rebels and exterminating them. The patrol had met dozens of people trying to escape from Richmond. Disorientated, hungry and tired, there was little hope for them; if the Normans failed to ensnare them, then winter and starvation would do its worst.

Whole villages were being put to the sword and entire families burned alive in their homes.

It was a massacre of the innocents.

26. The Ambush

When Hereward and his men returned to Clitheroe Hill from Upper Swaledale, all was well. There had been no sightings of William's forces, not even at Skipton, and everything was calm. Hereward called a gathering of his entire contingent and related the gruesome details of what was happening east of the Pennines.

The stories were heard in silence, in a mood of disbelief and anger.

Hereward paused, before outlining yet another strategy. 'For the time being, we hold what we have. William is sweeping north; I suspect he will go to Durham, then perhaps as far as the Tweed. He knows that Edgar was not in Scotland for the winter, but let's pray that he doesn't discover that he soon will be. He is punishing the people east of the Pennines for opposing him by turning it into a wasteland. He will soon turn towards the west, to the fertile plains along the coast, and to Chester, the stronghold of our ally, Eadric the Wild.

'Einar says there are only two logical places where William can cross the Pennines. If he goes much further north than Durham, he will cross through Alston to Penrith and then south. If Durham is his furthest point north, then he will turn and go south through Ripon and Harrogate, before turning west through the Pennines to Skipton, right under our noses. Let's hope he chooses the Skipton route.

If he doesn't, we will have to intercept him at Preston. Whichever way he chooses, we're going to provoke him, in the hope that he might make the mistake we need. He's now on our ground, close to our camp; he has split his forces and, because none of the innocent victims of his killing spree has been able to fight back, his guard might be down. Alphonso, we need a rota of men to watch the approaches to Skipton, and a party to climb Bowland Fell to watch the road from Lancaster. See to it.'

'It will be done.'

'Martin, send someone to York. We need to hear the latest news of William's movements and of any other Normans on the rampage.'

'He will leave immediately.'

'The rest of us will sit tight here.'

On the last day of January 1070 word arrived from York and a patrol returned from the east. William had chosen the southerly option to cross the Pennines and was moving quickly towards Skipton. After the months they had spent there, they knew all the contours of the fells, and they also knew William would not expect anything untoward in such a remote location. Hereward ordered the lookouts on Bowland Fell to be recalled and gathered his entire contingent together to announce that he intended to ambush the Duke.

'Men of England, today our struggle adopts a new guise. William comes to us and into the jaws of a trap we will set for him. This is the last time we will see Clitheroe Hill. It has been a good home to us, but today we move on. From now on, we move only on horseback and take only what each of us can carry. The Duke will soon pass through our valley. I intend to get close to him; close enough to kill him.'

Later that day, Hereward's force left Clitheroe Hill for the final time and moved north-east towards Skipton. Gohor and his small group continued to protect the family, who were under strict orders to stay close to Hereward's hearthtroop. The women and girls had cut their hair, dressed in men's clothes and put a seax into their belts; they too were now at war.

With his hearthtroop taking the central position, Hereward split his squadrons into six groups and ordered each to camp at one-mile intervals along the valley. In the shadow of the mighty Pen Hill, Hereward's squadrons waited.

They were concealed in the trees of Piked Acre Wood, above Chat's Burn, a ford on Hey's Brook, a small tributary of the nearby Ribble just north of the settlement of Downham. They knew that William's force would be following an old Roman road that had become dilapidated and overgrown, and would cross the brook at this point. The ford was two parallel pairs of clapper stones, supported by a central pier, just wide enough for a cart. The column would have to cross at no more than two abreast.

When the Norman column was halfway across the ford, the two forward squadrons would attack, cutting William's force in two. The other squadrons would then confront the entire length of the column. The English cavalry would emerge from the trees in compact groups of forty, while the Normans would be strung out along a thin and vulnerable line. The rear squadrons would try to destroy William's baggage train, disperse his spare horses and make off with his supplies. Hereward and his men would attack William's Matilda Squadron head-on.

In different circumstances, the scene of the ambush could not have been more picturesque. Nature had painted the valley in shades of black and white, its blanket of snow dissected by the inky silhouettes of the trees and by the burnt umber of the winding brook.

Two hours later the weather was atrocious, with snow falling heavily, driven by a powerful westerly wind that would lash the faces of the oncoming Normans. Their cloaks would be drawn across their mouths and noses, and their heads would be bowed into the teeth of the blizzard. Few would be casting glances to the sides of the valley. The conditions were ideal for a surprise attack; for once, circumstances favoured the English.

The Normans came on slowly. Hereward could see the Duke clearly; he had become fat and now bore only a passing resemblance to the fearsome figure he remembered from Rouen. Only the men of his Matilda Squadron were watchful, riding upright, scanning the trees for danger.

On Hereward's signal, his squadrons swept down through the trees and scythed into the Norman column. The ambush worked perfectly and the Normans had no time to form up. When William's herald signalled full gallop and the column tried to ride out of trouble, the track soon became congested. Most riders dispersed anywhere they could through the forest.

Hereward got within ten yards of William and their eyes met for the first time in six years. In the Englishman's was fiery determination; in the Norman's, boiling anger. Repeatedly, Hereward rode into the Duke's finest cavalry, cutting them down in droves in his attempt to bring down his prey. Every time he cleared a path, more of the Matilda Squadron closed around their leader. At one point, Martin handed him a lance, which he hurled at his quarry with immense force. It missed William by only a foot and thudded into the chest of his standard-bearer with such venom that it took him clean off his horse.

Hereward could see the Duke fervently directing his men and issuing orders. At one point he could hear William bellowing threats of revenge but, try as he might, the ranks of defenders were too deep for Hereward to get any closer; there was just too much equine and human flesh between him and his enemy.

William escaped at a gallop into the trees and out of sight, and Hereward ordered his squadrons to return to their original positions. Short of impaling William on a lance, the ambush had been a great success: Hereward had lost over 30 men and a few more had serious injuries, but there were over 250 Norman dead and William's entire baggage train had been captured.

There were a dozen or so Norman soldiers from the battle who had not been able to flee the carnage. Hereward learned from these prisoners that many of their fellow soldiers were appalled at what had been happening in recent weeks, but that William was constantly in a rage and would listen to no one, not even his senior lieutenants. William had split his force into four as it left York. One group had gone north-east towards the coast, a second had made for Lincoln and the South, and a third had moved south-west towards Wakefield and Doncaster. William's group, about 500 strong including his own Matilda Squadron, had travelled as far as

Durham, which had been put to the sword in an orgy of killing. None of the local people was spared, no building was left standing, nothing edible was left alive, and all food stores and smokehouses were destroyed. The group was now bound for Chester.

The Duke's regime was almost unbearable. He made his men ride for twelve hours every day; it was pitch black when they broke camp in the mornings and just as dark when they made camp in the evenings. When they were ordered to leave York in the winter, there was significant discontent in the ranks, but when it was discovered that they were to go through the Pennines to Chester, murmurs of mutiny began. When hints of this reached William, he had the ringleaders singled-out and flogged in front of all his squadrons. The talk stopped, but the resentment grew deeper.

Hereward had heard enough. The morale of William's men was clearly at a low ebb, and disgruntled men do not fight well. In addition, William was obviously in a constant rage, and men in ferment make mistakes; perhaps he would soon present Hereward with the opportunity he prayed for.

Alphonso asked Hereward what should be done with the Norman prisoners.

'Let them go. Tell them to help their wounded, but they must fend for themselves.'

'We should kill them. They've been slaughtering the innocent – women and children. Besides, when they are found, they'll tell William everything they've seen and heard here.'

'Let the Normans do the cold-blooded killing. We will have plenty of opportunity to kill them in battle. As for what they reveal about us, William will know all our secrets long before we see these men again.'

Hereward looked back on the scene of the ambush.

The wind had relented, allowing the snow to fall gently on the fells. The valley was no longer the light and dark of a winter idyll. Chat's Burn had turned crimson; the chestnut flanks of the fallen horses glistened in the snow amid the bloodied shapes of the dead.

In a series of lightning strikes from horseback and night-time guerrilla attacks, Hereward harassed William all the way to Chester.

None of the encounters was on the same scale as Chat's Burn, but they were effective. At long last, the Normans were on the run. By the time they reached Chester, William's force had dwindled to less than half the strength he had when he left York.

On several occasions, their eyes met and they came close to one another, but Hereward's force was too small to do anything other than harry and withdraw. William also seemed to retain his good fortune: well-aimed arrows and lances missed him by inches or struck men close to him. He was never isolated from his elite defenders, and he was always able to find an escape route from any trap Hereward had designed for him. Even so, it was a disconcerting and embarrassing experience for the Duke.

However, Hereward soon had to face yet more disappointment.

Eadric, his English rebels and their Welsh allies had abandoned Chester and fled to the relative safety of Wales as soon as they heard that William's murderous campaign had turned westwards. The Normans were able to ride into the burgh unopposed, depriving Hereward of any more opportunities to snipe at them. William licked his wounds and sent for reinforcements. Hereward moved inland, towards Stafford, and found a remote place to camp and plan his next move. It also provided an opportunity to make a tally of the significant booty he had taken from William at Chat's Burn. It was a major windfall: there was a considerable amount of money, enough to keep his campaign going for some time, although not enough to entice the Danes into more action. There was also a plentiful supply of food, armour and clothes, plus over sixty horses, including nearly thirty cavalry destriers.

To celebrate, Hereward declared two nights of feasting and the entire contingent was given a pouch of silver each, enough to keep a family for the best part of a year. But the celebrations were short-lived. Within days, more bad news arrived – and continued in a steady stream over the ensuing weeks.

When they had reached the safety of their homeland, the Welsh had told Eadric the Wild that, having witnessed William's unrelenting determination and gruesome tactics, they were gravely concerned about their future security and would not be returning to England to continue the rebellion. Eadric's daughters had been taken hostage to persuade him to submit, and he had returned to Chester to bow to William.

In the South West, Count Brian the Breton, the new Lord of Cornwall, had driven Harold's sons back to Ireland. Their siege of Montacute had failed, and the defenders had been relieved by the Norman lord Geoffrey of Coutances, at the head of a large force that included a significant number of Englishmen from London, Winchester and Salisbury.

Disastrous news also came from the North. Of the brave men who had fought so well at York, only Siward Bjorn was prepared to continue the rebellion. Cospatrick, cowed by William's merciless slaughter of the people of the North, was not prepared to leave the safety of Scotland and had been made Earl of Dunbar by King Malcolm. Worst of all, Earl Waltheof, horrified by the slaying of thousands of innocents in the North, had thrown himself at the mercy of William, who forgave him, and had become betrothed to William's niece, Lady Judith.

Finally, finding that he had few honourable companions left and unable to persuade King Malcolm to do any more than offer a safe haven, Edgar the Atheling had become dispirited and was preparing to go to the court of Philip of France, to raise support for an attack on Normandy from the south.

Hereward found the depressing reports hard to take, especially the news of brave Eadric's submission and that of the courageous Waltheof, who had decapitated Normans at York as if they were daisies in a field.

Hereward's men were stood down and given leave until the autumn. They were to return at the beginning of October, after the harvest. The rendezvous would be at a ford over the Great Ouse just outside Huntingdon, a place all soldiers knew well. Standing the men down was a huge risk, as many might not return, but Hereward had no choice. He had no more speeches to give and no more rallying calls to issue. He had not given up, but he did not know how to continue.

His senior retinue stayed with him. Edwin had no family left, as his father and brothers had died on Senlac Ridge.

Although Edmund had a family in Kent, he refused to go, perhaps fearful of what he might find. As for Gohor, he let his men go, but he decided to stay; he had adopted the womenfolk in his care, just as they had adopted him, and he now felt part of the family.

Now, as a renegade band of just fourteen souls, they travelled through England's heartland in an arc from the Avon and the Thames to the Stour and the Trent. They kept on the move, stayed away from villages and burghs, and spoke only to the poor people of the land in their isolated communities. From a distance, they watched the Normans build their mottes and baileys and saw their soldiers scurrying about their duties.

Hereward avoided the subject of the rebellion and would not be drawn on his thoughts or his state of mind.

Accompanied only by his daughters, Gunnhild and Estrith, he made a private pilgrimage to the holy sisters at Hereford, and from there to visit Torfida's grave. On his return, he offered few details of the trip, except to say that the nuns had taken her to a wonderful resting place in a clearing she often talked about, deep in the forest and close to the summit of Pennard Hill near Glastonbury.

There were commanding views across the water meadows below that were not unlike the fens of his own home. Glastonbury Tor stood proudly in the distance, a towering symbol of Harold, of Wessex and of England. The grave had been marked by an oak sapling, reared from an acorn gathered from the place where she had died. The nuns had called the clearing 'Torfida's Glade' and made pilgrimages there to pray.

Hereward was content that it was an idyllic resting place for his wife, where her soul could mingle with the heritage of the wildwood.

27. The Brotherhood

In the middle of August 1070, Hereward announced that he would like to undertake another pilgrimage. It would be to Bourne, his Lincolnshire home, a place he had not visited in a very long time and somewhere his girls had never seen. This journey would not be a private one; he wanted his companions to see the enigmatic Fens and his unremarkable birthplace.

In the turmoil of a conquered England, he had no idea if his family would still be there. He had often thought about them and had vowed that, when the time was right, he would return.

Several days later, they could see in the distance the small bronze cross above the unassuming wooden church of Bourne. Little seemed to have changed as they moved through ever-widening clearings of the Bruneswald to reveal fenlands stretching far into the distance. The Fens were just as challenging as the Pennines, but the trials were different. The most ominous presence was the ground itself, often an impenetrable melange of water and earth, matted by centuries of the decay and renewal of reeds, moss and sedge. There were many rivers and streams, but their courses were concealed by undergrowth so dense, it made them unnavigable.

To the north-east was The Wash and the beginnings of the North Sea, but where land ended and sea began was impossible to chart and constantly changing. There were few landmarks or vantage points and the ground was so unpredictable, it would bear the weight of a man in one moment, but become a deep bog in the next. The few settlements that did exist stood on higher ground, often no more than a few feet above the vast quagmire.

Bourne was on the western periphery of fenland, on the old Roman route north, with the giant Bruneswald to the west, and the morass of the wetlands to the east. Before they got to the village, Hereward made a private excursion to Gythin's cottage nearby. It had become an overgrown ruin, but he found the small mound, marked by a pile of stones, where his father and his men had buried her pitiful remains seventeen years ago. He stayed and reflected for over an hour, evoking memories of his wayward youth and the needless tragedy that had befallen a harmless woman.

Later, when he had regained his small band of followers and they were within a mile of the village, Alphonso noticed something about twenty yards off the track. It looked like a pile of discarded clothes in the thick undergrowth.

Martin's equally sharp vision recognized the bundle immediately. 'It's a child.' He rushed over, picked up the lifeless little heap and brought it to Hereward.

It was indeed a child, a little boy, filthy and cold to the touch and barely breathing.

Hereward sensed danger. 'The fact that he's here could mean that all is not well in Bourne. Alphonso, go and see what's happening. Let's move into the trees and get some nourishment into this boy.'

Alphonso was soon back with a shocked look on his face. He pulled Hereward away from the others and sat him on the trunk of a fallen tree. 'The Normans are there; they are inside the longhouse. I counted nine horses.'

Hereward made to get up, thinking the village was in imminent danger.

Putting a heavy hand on his shoulder, Alphonso shook his head. 'I'm sorry, we're too late. There are bodies all over the village and all the houses are burned to the ground except the longhouse and the church.' He then hesitated for a moment and swallowed hard. 'There are three heads on lances outside the church. I think one is the priest; the others are an elderly man and woman.' He paused again, knowing that Hereward would have realized what the news implied. 'This boy must be the only one who got away.'

Hereward lowered his head and grasped it firmly in his hands. Alphonso walked away to join the others. By the time he had reached them, Hereward was on his feet, marching with purposeful strides towards Bourne.

'Martin, stay here and keep everybody safe. Watch the trees and the road; there are Normans around. Alphonso, Einar, follow me. When I go into my father's house, wait outside. If any Normans try to leave, cut them down.'

Hereward's companions were used to taking his orders and acting on them precisely, so they stood and watched as their leader pushed open the door of his parents' longhouse. They could see the three heads impaled on lances next to the church, their expressions strangely calm, their eyes closed, as if in repose. One of the men had the tonsured scalp of a monk, leading to the obvious conclusion that the grisly heads were those of the village priest and the thegn and his wife, Hereward's parents.

The scene that confronted Hereward as he walked into

the house in which he had been born more resembled a brothel than a family home. Food and drink were strewn across the table and floor, half-naked men dozed around the embers of the fire and the room stank of stale sweat, urine and vomit. Huddled together and cowering in the corner were three young village girls, perhaps fourteen or fifteen years old. They looked terrified and pulled the rug they were hiding behind tightly to their chins.

Hereward gestured to them to stay quiet, but two of the Normans stirred.

One of them spoke. 'What do you want?'

Hereward did not answer.

The largest man, who seemed senior to the others, focused his eyes and realized that standing before him was a fully armed warrior, dressed like someone of high rank. 'Who are you, Englishman?'

'I am Hereward of Bourne and, now that my father has been murdered, I am Thegn of this village.'

'Well, Hereward of Bourne, there isn't much of a village left for you to be "Thegn" of.' He leered cruelly. 'Except these young wenches, who have been kind enough to keep us entertained.'

The other Normans had roused themselves and were looking around for their weapons. They were not unduly alarmed, as Hereward was but one Englishman in a room of nine, highly trained Norman soldiers.

Hereward remained calm. 'I would like to have your name, sir.'

One of the Normans peered out of the window to see if more Englishmen lay in wait. He could see no one and turned to his leader with a reassuring shake of his head.

'I am Ogier the Breton. These are my men and we serve William, King of England and Duke of Normandy. By his authority, I am now Lord of Bourne and all its lands. King William granted me this privilege in recognition of my service to him. Following your repeated attacks on him in the North, about which he is greatly vexed, he told me to punish the entire village and spare no one. I was also to make it abundantly clear to all before they died that it was the treasonable behaviour of Hereward of Bourne that had led to their suffering.'

Again, Hereward chose not to reply. Instead, he drew his sword and pulled the Great Axe of Göteborg from his shoulder.

The Normans scattered in every direction, but Hereward was at them like a whirlwind. He cut two men down to his left with his sword, then with his axe cleaved the Breton almost in two from his left shoulder to his midriff. The girls screamed in horror and hid their eyes while the remaining Normans shouted at one another in blind panic. Two more were dead before either of them could find a weapon, while another one threw a lance that Hereward easily deflected with his shield. He kicked one of the remaining quartet into the corner, while another clambered out of the window, only to be met by Einar's deadly axe. A third rushed through the door, to be grabbed by Alphonso, who calmly slit his throat from ear to ear. The last Norman offering any resistance was impaled through the midriff by Hereward's sword and pinned to the wall like a hog on a spit. Finally, he turned and brought his axe down on to the man cowering in the corner, creating a spew of blood and a deafening shriek of agony.

Einar and Alphonso appeared in the doorway to check that Hereward's vengeance was done.

'Einar, please go and get Maria, Ingigerd and Cristina; these girls need their help. Nobody else must see this. We leave as soon as we've buried the dead. Alphonso, make sure these pigs are dead too.'

Hereward looked around the house and saw no possessions that were important to him. He then went to the Normans' horses and retrieved his father's sword and the money and jewellery stolen from his parents. Finally, without hesitating, he set fire to his home with a log from his own hearth and watched it burn to the ground, consuming the Normans within.

A large communal grave was dug next to the church and all the bodies of the villagers were placed in it. Hereward retrieved the three heads and carefully put them in their rightful place with their bodies, a gruesome but necessary task. A simple cross was made and, when all evidence of the terrible carnage that had been visited on this tiny village had been removed, Hereward's small band of followers joined him in a short ceremony.

In failing light, which added an appropriately sombre pall to the occasion, Hereward pushed the small cross into the ground at the head of the mass grave, stepped back and spoke solemnly. 'Let us pray for the souls of these people of Bourne, who, like so many throughout England, have done nothing to deserve their cruel fate. May they rest in peace.'

He then closed the door of Bourne church, locked it and put the key on his belt.

He would never return.

Hereward and his extended family, now numbering eighteen with the addition of the four survivors of Bourne, spent the next few weeks well away from conflict of any kind.

They had much to reflect on, especially the young orphans from the village. Hereward spent many hours with Gunnhild and Estrith, talking to them, telling and retelling stories about their mother and teaching them as much as he knew about anything and everything. It became a special time for all of them. Only occasionally were there moments of tension, and always about the same subject: when could they return to St Cirq Lapopie? Hereward was often sorely tempted to agree to go at a day's notice, but would only ever give the same answer: 'Soon, one day soon.'

No matter how painful and threatening it was to those closest to him, he had unfinished business in England; the events in Bourne had only added to his resolve.

William had stood down his army and returned to Winchester, confident that the English rebellion was over. His only minor concerns were that the Danes had not yet left Humberside and that Hereward had disappeared from view. The Danish garrison had suffered badly over the harsh winter and William had not kept his word to keep them well supplied. However, he had sent the second instalment of their Danegeld and, assuming that they would not relish another winter far from home, William felt the continuing Danish presence did not warrant a further expedition to the North.

When the first flurries of snow appeared over the downs of southern England in the autumn of 1070, and the Danes had still not departed, William grew more concerned. News then arrived at Winchester that the charred remains of Ogier the Breton and his men had been found in the ruins of the longhouse at Bourne. He knew at once who was responsible and, as usual, his rage was unbounded.

The first sharp bite of winter had also prodded Hereward into action. The period of calm he had deliberately created after the events of Bourne had given him time to clear his head. Now it was time for one final clarion call. When he arrived at the agreed rendezvous on the Great Ouse in October, to his great joy almost three-quarters of his men had returned. They knew that the last few moves of Hereward's game of chess with William were about to be made, and they had resigned themselves to whatever ending those moves would create.

Hereward now gathered together the 200 valiant souls who still followed him and asked them to sit on the ground in a relaxed, informal group; this was going to be a different kind of address.

'Men of England, let me speak to you of things we all know to be true, but are reluctant to accept. We fought and lost in the North; we were too few in number and outmanoeuvred by a formidable opponent.' He paused and looked around at the faces of those assembled. He was grateful to them for still being at his side after all the setbacks they had suffered and he admired their great courage when so many others had slunk away. 'It is four years since Senlac Ridge. William has won this land.'

His men began to shake their heads and mutter.

'It is true; an unbearable truth, but true all the same. He is relentless, vicious and cunning and a master of tactics and planning. He is also lucky; fortune has favoured him all along, especially on Senlac Ridge. The gods have smiled on the Normans: they were blessed in the Channel, when the wind didn't blow; they were fortunate that we had to fight at Stamford Bridge before facing their onslaught; and they were lucky on the day of the battle, when the outcome could so easily have been different. To have to face Hardrada and the Norwegians in the North and then William and the Normans in the South, all within the space of a few days, was a cruel hand that fate dealt our noble King Harold. In his case, fortune didn't favour the brave.' He hesitated, reluctant to utter the words. 'Now, his England, our England, has gone. It has gone for ever.'

The men shifted uncomfortably in the face of this barrage of unpalatable truths, but all knew in their hearts that Hereward was right.

'It took many generations of war, struggle and nego-tiation to fuse England into a whole from its many parts. Now there must be a new England.' He paused again, catching as many eyes as he could, trying to gauge whether these men would accept a new vision of their homeland. 'We can make it happen. By your presence here, you are saying that you are not prepared to accept that England has become a province of Normandy, nor that we English have to think and act like Normans. I have a proposition for you. We will make a final redoubt, as we did on Senlac Ridge; one last stand to remind the world that England will not die easily. We will convince William that he has to recognize our collective will, just as we have had to bend to his. We will make the Normans realize that to rule here, they will have to acknowledge our ways, as we have to recognize theirs.'

Hereward paused again, relieved to see a brightening in the eyes of his men as he offered them new hope.

He started to raise his voice. 'England will never die; it will live on in our customs, our language and our traditions. For now, we are conquered, but we will stand up to these Normans, make them appreciate us. And when they respect us, England will be England once more.'

The entire assembly rose as one; this time, not with a massive roar of approval, but more solemnly, like men preparing to stand together in battle.

'From this moment, we will no longer call him William the Bastard; we will refer to him as William, King of England.'

There were many shouts of 'No!' from the men.

'Yes, King of England, William the First! It is not a crown he wears by right, but one he has won in battle. He is now our King. It is a fact, and we must accept it. Even so, we retain the right to challenge any oppressive ruler. So our final redoubt is a stand we make to press our claim to be ruled justly, in the true tradition of England.'

Hereward clasped the Talisman. 'I offer you a brotherhood of men. We will ride to Ely, to the tomb of the virgin martyr, St Etheldreda, where each of us will take this ancient amulet, the Talisman of Truth, and swear an oath affirming our rights as Englishmen. There we will stay until the King comes to us.

'The Isle of Ely is my territory, close to my home, it is easily defended and its treacherous marshes and waterways will keep the King's army at bay. Perhaps then he will listen to us. The people of England will hear of our stand; it will lift their spirits and gladden their hearts.' Once more he raised the Great Axe of Göteborg. 'To Ely, to form our Brotherhood and to make our last redoubt. Long live England!'

Every man present raised his battle-axe in solemn concord, followed by the cry 'Long live England!'

Martin Lighfoot and Edmund of Kent sent word all over the land, proclaiming that an Oath of Brotherhood was to be taken at Ely and that any man willing to swear to defend the rights of England and the English should journey there.

Hereward deliberately chose a wide circular route to Ely. Everywhere they went, they sought out Normans. They spared lowly ones, giving them only a simple message: 'We will be ruled fairly and justly, or not at all.' But for Norman lords and knights the encounter meant death by axe and sword.

In a series of bloody encounters, the Brotherhood ambushed and killed a long list of prominent Normans: Ivo Tallebois, Sheriff of Lincolnshire; Frederick of Ostergele-Scheldewindeke, the brother-in-law of William Warenne; the Earl of Surrey; Gilbert of Ghent; Richard Fitzgilbert of Clare; and the biggest prize of all, William Malet, Sheriff of Yorkshire. Hereward was in the vanguard of all the attacks. He was the avenging angel, not driven by personal emnity, nor by a warrior's duty, but by his faith in the cause of the Brotherhood – a devotion to a new England, the England Harold had dreamed of, a land where the fraternity of the people is far more important than the ambition of kings.

The slayings sent William into a rage that lasted all winter, causing Matilda and her children to return to Rouen. He drank and swore continually, barked orders at the top of his voice and threw things at anyone who got in his way. He became fatter by the day, sores broke out on his face and he suffered increasingly from gout and piles.

Neither the King's health nor his mood were ameliorated by the sudden influx of pleas and representations about the harshness of his regime. They came not only from the English who had submitted to him, but also from many Normans. Hereward's change of stance had struck a chord in English hearts and even in some sympathetic Norman ones.

William's mood became even darker when, early in the spring of 1071, he heard that not only were the Danes still in Yorkshire, but that Svein Estrithson, the Danish King, had arrived in the Humber with a substantial fleet. William immediately prepared to ride north with his army.

Hereward was camped near Rockingham, on his way to Ely, when he heard the news of the arrival of the Danish King and of William's march north. He immediately despatched Edwin to find out the reasons for Svein's unexpected arrival.

Meanwhile, Martin's scouts were ordered to track William's every move.

28. Homage to a Virgin Martyr

Hereward and his Brotherhood rode into Ely in March 1071, more than seventeen years after he had crossed the burgh's ancient causeway seeking vengeance on Gythin's assassins and their paymaster, Thurstan, Bishop of Ely. It was a similar day, with a threatening sky and a bitterly cold wind. For his first fateful visit, the surrounding waterways had been an expanse of ice, but this time the wind was whipping the water of the Fens' countless meres into frenzied plumes of spray. Not only had Hereward's life come full circle to England, he was now back at the very place where his juvenile pursuit of retribution had led to his banishment and the beginning of his remarkable odyssey.

The Brotherhood made camp in the grounds of Ely Abbey. As the men busied themselves with their duties, Hereward paid a courtesy call. Although there had been an interregnum when King Edward removed him, having lost patience with Thurstan's corrupt behaviour, he was still the Abbot of Ely after being reinstated by King Harold. As in their previous encounter, Hereward went alone. There were numerous monks in the cloisters and refectories, but the abbey looked shabby, not a hive of activity like other ecclesiastical establishments.

As Hereward approached the door of the Abbot's Great Hall, an armed monk stepped towards him. 'Do you have business with Abbot Thurstan, sir?'

'I do.'

Hereward brushed past him and, for the second time in his life, pushed open the heavy oak door of the hall. The timbers of the roof were still charred, the large table he had clambered on to all those years ago was still in the same place, and Thurstan was once again sitting at its head. But gone was the air of opulence surrounding him. He wore a plain black cassock, which looked worn and dirty, and absent from his neck was the ornate gold chain and crucifix. He was hunched over his food, his back arched and misshapen, and his hair was thin and grey and grew in sparse tufts. His eyes were sunken and his skin had the jaundiced pallor of a man in poor health.

He did not look up but, as if reliving their previous encounter, repeated the same phrase. 'Do close the door; Ely's winter chills me to the bone.'

Hereward, also in a reprise of their first meeting, did not respond.

Thurstan began to move, but struggled to raise his head. Whatever was afflicting his spine – something, no doubt, resulting from the injury Hereward had inflicted on him – he could not lift his chin much beyond his chest. Hereward could see that Thurstan's chair still had the deep gash of the axe that had almost taken off his head all those years ago.

With the help of two young monks, the Abott hobbled over to the fire and sat on a bench close to the hearth. 'I suppose you have come here to kill me?'

'Nothing could be further from my mind. I am only interested in killing Normans, until they respect justice and the law.'

Thurstan's face contorted into a sneer. 'I see, vengeance used to be your hallmark, now it is self-righteousness.'

'Thurstan, I have had to live with the consequences of my actions, just as you have had to live with yours. It seems I am coping with the legacy of my deeds somewhat better than you are handling yours.'

Thurstan's face turned to fury. 'What do you want in my abbey?'

'Tomorrow, we go to the tomb of the virgin martyr, St Etheldreda, to swear an Oath to our Brotherhood of Englishmen and assert our rights as subjects of King William.'

'Have you not learned your lesson by now? Senlac Ridge was lost, Harold is dead, England is William's; he will do with it as he sees fit.'

'All those things are beyond dispute, except the last. We mean to convince him that kings should rule with wisdom.' Hereward clasped the Talisman, which he now wore openly outside his armour.

'Ah yes, I've heard about this magic amulet you wear. You have become the hero of legend: a saviour, protected by a magic spell woven by a sorcerer from the forest and his enchantress of a daughter. So what do you expect from me?'

'I expect nothing from you. We will stay outside the cloisters, which come under your jurisdiction, except for the right of passage to visit St Etheldreda's tomb. However, if, as an Englishman, you feel you should take the Oath of the Brotherhood, that is for your conscience to consider. I intend to fortify Ely against an onslaught by William and no one will come or go without my direct authority. Other than that, just stay out of my way.'

'And what of our reckoning – surely you must seek a resolution?'

'I do not. God will punish you for your actions and, from the look of you, the fires of Hell already begin to burn brightly within you. As for me, your evil deed set me on a course which has brought me a life few have been fortunate enough to experience.' He paused for a second and looked Thurstan in the eye. 'Don't misunderstand me. If you cross me in any way, take any action, or say anything that undermines the cause our Brotherhood has proclaimed, I will kill you in the blink of an eye.'

Hereward turned and left, his heavy steps once more echoing around the cloisters of Ely Abbey.

Built to hold her remains, and to allow pilgrims to make their devotions to her, St Etheldreda's vault stood in a small chapel on the northern side of the cloisters of the abbey. Except for her hands, clasped in prayer and standing proudly from it, the stone slab of her tomb had her elaborately carved life-size outline cut into it. Laid across her hands by the nuns was a beautiful rosary in pearl and ruby beads, culminating in a delicate silver cross on which was chased the figure of the crucified Christ.

The daughter of a seventh-century East Anglian king, she had taken holy orders rather than relinquish her virginity in an arranged marriage imposed on her by her father, and was the foundress of the Abbey of Ely. She had become revered for her generosity, piety and wisdom and lived the rest of her life in poverty, bearing the constant pain of a large tumour on her neck, an infliction that she regarded as appropriate punishment for all the fine jewellery she had worn as a child. St Etheldreda was the perfect patron for the Brotherhood's cause.

The entire burgh of Ely looked on as the Brotherhood filed into the chapel to take their Oath. Hereward stood at the head of the sepulchre as each man placed his weapons on Etheldreda's image and rested his left hand on her rosary. He then placed the Talisman of Truth over their head as they pressed the clenched fist of their right hand to their chest and recited the Oath.

On the holy remains of the martyr, St Etheldreda, and in the sight of God, I swear to assert the rights of all Englishmen to live in peace and justice.

By wearing this amulet of the ancients, I attest to my belief in truth and wisdom.

By this salute, I enter the Brotherhood of St Etheldreda and do solemnly commit my life to it and its noble cause.

So help me God.

Hereward's family were the last to take the Oath. As they finished, Thurstan appeared with the entire community of Ely Abbey, all of whom asked to take the Oath.

When it came to Thurstan's turn, he was helped to the tomb. 'Hereward of Bourne, I humbly offer myself to your cause. I am one of the many who has submitted to the King, but there is no contradiction in submitting to a rightful king and seeking to be governed with fairness and equanimity. Thus, I will happily take the Oath of the Brotherhood.' He turned to Hereward and addressed him in a voice loud enough to be heard way beyond the confines of the chapel. 'Your fellowship needs a chaplain. I offer myself to you as its priest and confessor.'

Hereward suspected evil intent in Thurstan's conversion, but knew that he could hardly refuse his gesture. 'Your offer is accepted, Abbot Thurstan.'

Hereward placed the Talisman over Thurstan's head. For reasons only the Abbot knew, the Talisman did not sit well with him. As he took the Oath, he seemed very agitated by it, his eyes darting around in their sockets and his face twitching even more than usual.

Finally, Hereward took the Oath himself. As he did so, the monks formed into a choir around the cloisters and raised their voices in a majestic canticle of celebration. Every Christian soul present hoped and prayed that the Brotherhood would find favour with God and the King.

Thus the Brotherhood of St Etheldreda was sworn; its deeds would soon become legend.

Hereward immediately set about reinforcing the fortifications of the burgh. Paying well for them, he commandeered all the boats in the area, built watchtowers around Ely's walls and posted sentries around the perimeter of the island.

Within a couple of days, the Danes arrived. Their entire fleet had made its way from the Humber to Wisbech, where it anchored. King Svein Estrithson, his brother Prince Osbjorn, his three sons and Christian, Bishop of Aarhus, travelled to Ely in ceremonial style. The King was accompanied by his hearthtroop and was heralded by the Danes' distinctive hunting horns and the measured beat of their war drums. Flying his royal standard, the Eagle of the Skagerrak, and wearing his heavy bearskin cloak, he was the epitome of his renowned Viking ancestors.

As he had no Great Hall to accommodate the royal delegation, Hereward had benches brought from St Etheldreda's chapel and met the King in the open.

After the usual formalities, Svein Estrithson began. 'I hear you have become like the slave Spartacus – a man who fights against the tyranny of his rulers?'

'Yes, my Lord King, I fight for the freedom to live in peace and with justice.'

'So you reject the rule of kings?'

'I do not, sire. I simply ask that they rule with wisdom and fairness.'

'And who decides that?'

Beginning to resent the tone of Svein's questions, Hereward bristled. 'The people do.'

Estrithson continued to goad. 'I'm sure King William will think that he should decide what is wise and fair.'

'Sire, that is his prerogative; it is ours to disagree with him.'

'An interesting philosophy.'

Estrithson looked around at his companions, the elite of the Danish aristocracy. 'But I'm not sure it's an idea we would embrace in Denmark.'

The King's companions began to snigger, except for Osbjorn, who was watching the exchange intently.

Hereward had had enough of the teasing, even from a king. 'You are not in Denmark; you are in England, in the presence of the Brotherhood of St Etheldreda. You have come here for a purpose, King Svein of Denmark.'

The King stiffened in anger.

Prince Osbjorn quickly intervened. 'My brother, Hereward is a man I respect. He responds tersely because he is a man of principle. Besides, I suspect he no longer needs our support; what he fights for now needs faith, not an army.'

'That doesn't excuse an insult to me!'

Hereward stepped forward. 'Svein, King of the Danes, you are welcome in Ely. The Brotherhood and I are honoured by the presence of a great warrior and a noble king.'

Hereward's conciliatory tone defused the King's anger.

Prince Osbjorn continued the discussion. 'By not keeping his word, King William owes us a debt – not the Danegeld that he duly paid, but compensation for the harm he has done to us and the insult of his indifference. Winter was harsh on the Isle of Axholme and the supplies he promised did not arrive. We suffered badly; disease spread throughout the camp, and those who were fit enough to hunt found their quarry gone to ground. We lost many men and we mean to extract recompense from the King's Exchequer.'

'I am sorry to hear of the hardship your men have suffered. How can we help?'

'There is an agreement we could reach. William is robbing the English earls of their titles and lands and emptying the abbeys and monasteries of their treasures. Is this not so?'

'It is, my Lord Prince.'

'We intend to raid Peterborough Abbey and remove all its treasures. It is one of the richest in England and would yield fair compensation for William's dishonour. We are told that a new Norman abbot, Thurold, has been installed and that he has recruited a force of a hundred and sixty men so that he can strip bare the abbey's treasures to pay William for his appointment.'

'And you want us to help in this?'

'Yes, we presume that it makes no difference to you whether the treasures of Peterborough fall into Danish hands or Norman. Our offer is simple: if we attack, there will be resistance, especially from the monks, and there will be bloodshed on both sides. If you help us and explain our purpose to the people of the burgh and the monks of the abbey, the resistance will be much less.'

'And what do we get out of this?'

'William will think it is another rising and that we are supporting you. Also, we will leave you with as many weapons as you need. We have a great surplus from our dead comrades on Axholme and my brother, our noble King, offers them to you in support of your campaign, a cause he doesn't agree with but thinks is honourable. He will also order his sappers and boatswains to help you prepare the defence of Ely. After the raid, William will come for you and you will have the confrontation you seek.'

'And you?'

'We will continue to give the appearance of being prepared to fight for you, and William will negotiate with us again. He will pay us another large Danegeld, which, after protracted negotiation to maximize its worth, we will accept as sufficient and set sail for Denmark!'

Hereward had to smile at the Dane's cunning. 'So we face the onslaught of King William, and you sail off to Denmark with yet more geld and the riches of one of the great abbeys of England.'

King Svein broke his silence. 'If you choose not to help us, we will attack anyway, burn the abbey to the ground and kill anyone who gets in our way.'

Hereward looked at the King; he knew the Dane's threat was no bluff. He had little choice in the matter. His own force was too small to stop the Danes, and William was too far away to prevent an attack. Although they had their original Danegeld from the previous year, King Svein must have put another severe strain on his coffers by making a second crossing and would not contemplate going home without further booty.

Hereward thought about a compromise. 'There are some conditions: no one is to be harmed; you may take all the gold and silver and any of the treasures which have monetary value, but the relics of saints may only be taken under the custody of Christian, Bishop of Aarhus. They must be accompanied by several monks of the abbey and kept under their protection as curators until such time as they can be returned to Peterborough. Finally, you must forego five one-hundredth parts of the geld, which will be distributed among the Chapter of the Abbey, who will receive one hundredth, and the local people, who will receive four hundreths.'

The Danes looked at one another. After some murmuring, Svein turned to Prince Osbjorn.

The Prince nodded his agreement, before turning to Hereward with a broad smile lighting up his face. 'Like Spartacus, you are truly a man of the people. It is agreed; we have an understanding, Hereward of Bourne.'

'We have, Lord Osbjorn.'

The sack of Peterborough was executed as planned. The monks and the retiring Abbot reluctantly accepted Hereward's negotiation. As they said they would, the Danes then retreated to Wisbech to count their riches, leaving a corps of engineers to help with the defences of Ely.

When William heard of Hereward's support for the sack of Peterborough, it had the desired effect. Fearing the beginnings of another rising, he made haste to East Anglia. In due course, William asked to parley with King Svein at Bytham, a Norman fortification on the River Nene, where, after much haggling, William paid a sizeable geld. A month later, after their sappers and boatswains had retuned from their work at Ely, the Danes sailed home, laden with a substantial part of William's treasury.

A few days after the Danes had left, Hereward's intuition that Prince Osbjorn was a man of honour was confirmed. A small chest arrived containing two handfuls of English gold – a significant sum of money, sufficient for a knight to live comfortably for the rest of his life.

It also contained a message in Latin:

Accept this gift to your cause. May it serve as my personal Oath to your Brotherhood.

Osbjorn, Prince of Denmark

Hereward drew great strength from the Prince's message. Even though he and the Brotherhood were alone on a small island, isolated in a remote corner of a land where few were prepared to rally to his cause, Osbjorn's testamonial reinforced his belief in the justice of his crusade.

The Brotherhood continued to send its bulletin to all England's earldoms, monasteries and burghs: peace and justice for all under a wise and fair King.

With the defences of Ely well under way, Hereward met with Martin, Einar and Alphonso to discuss what to do about the women and girls. First of all, they decided that the orphans of Bourne should be recognized as full members of the family, meaning that there were now eleven non-combatants to worry about. Secondly, after much soul-searching, it was agreed that the women and children must escape to Aquitaine as soon as the situation in Ely became untenable.

A boat would be secreted away on the north side of the isle, in a place known only to them. It would be fully provisioned and checked regularly. At any time from when William's attacks began, they would be ready to leave at only a moment's notice. At the last minute, Edmund, Edwin and Gohor would be told of the plan and ordered to join them. Einar, Martin and Alphonso would execute the escape as soon as they feared the family was in imminent danger.

When the strategy was explained to the girls, it was Gunnhild who asked her father the obvious question. 'But, Father, what about you?'

Then Estrith. 'It sounds like you're staying, no matter what.'

They both started to shed tears of exasperation, exhausted by the endless fight their father was engaged in.

'You said we would go home soon.'

'Very soon, you said.'

Hereward was at a loss to know how to answer his girls,

hoping to avoid the conclusion they had already arrived at. 'You are going home soon, just as I promised.'

They shouted their response in unison. 'But you're not coming with us!'

'I'm sorry, but I must do this; for you, for your mother and for all good people everywhere.'

Maria and Ingigerd took the girls away to try to comfort them.

Hereward turned to the three men. 'When the time comes, get them away. Don't hesitate, and don't look back; think only of them and your own children.'

Einar spoke for the three of them. 'Nobody else has to die to prove the justice of our cause; it is undeniable. This damned crusade must have driven you insane if you can even think about letting the girls go while you remain here.'

His loyal friends looked at Hereward, each knowing in his own heart that Hereward's mind was made up and that nothing would deflect him from his course of action.

29. The Siege of Ely

Over the next few weeks, and as Easter of 1071 approached, something remarkable began to happen on the Isle of Ely.

First, entirely alone in the middle of a bleak, cold afternoon and with no personal belongings to speak of, a man appeared on the causeway who could easily have been the father of most of the defenders and the grandfather of many. He had no military experience, but carried a battle-axe that had belonged to his father, a former housecarl with the old Danish King, Harold Harefoot. He said he had heard the call to join the Brotherhood and had walked from Essex to take the Oath. Two brothers from Mercia came three days later. Next came a group eight fearsome-looking men from Richmond and the valley of the Swale, who had escaped from William's cull of the North. They had heard that Hereward and his men had rescued Edgar the Atheling from his plight in Swaledale and felt it was their duty to join his cause.

At first it was a trickle of men, then it became a constant flow and by May it was a deluge rushing to join the Brotherhood. They came with and without weapons; some came on horseback, but many walked; some brought money, but most came with only what they wore or carried. The majority were trained soldiers, a few had land and wealth and an important number were artisans: carpenters, blacksmiths, chandlers and shipwrights. As each man took the Oath, his name was added to the Roll of Honour of the Brotherhood.

In addition to the survivors of the original contingent that Hereward had met on the River Ribble almost two years earlier – men like Gohor, Brohor the Brave and Wulfric the White – were added the names of new followers: Leofric the Black, Alveriz, the son of a mason from Spain, Azecier, a good friend of Alveriz, Matelgar, Alsinus, Wulric, Ailward the White, and Hugo, a Norman priest born in Rouen but with a parish near Winchester.

Soon there were 2,500 members of the Brotherhood on the Isle of Ely. If that were not remarkable enough, early one morning, emerging through the mist of the distant horizon, an even more unlikely group of men appeared. Hereward had been woken before dawn to be told that a large column of men was approaching from the west. At first, the scouts assumed it was a contingent of Normans, but then realized that they were English.

As they came into view across Ely's causeway, Hereward recognized at once that the two men at the head of the column were England's most senior surviving nobles, Edwin and Morcar, the Earls of Mercia and Northumbria.

Accompanying them was a substantial phalanx of housecarls and several senior members of England's gentry, including landowners, clerics and thegns. They included Thorkill of Harringworth, a wealthy thegn from the East Midlands; Siward of Maldon, a rich merchant who was a major benefactor of Ely Abbey; Ordgar, Sheriff of Ramsey Abbey; Godric of Corby; Tostig of Davenesse; and Acore 'the Hard' of Lincoln. The last man to cross the causeway was Siward Bjorn, the only

English magnate from the attack on York not to have submitted to William. True to the promise he had made to the Atheling in the Swale, he brought yet more men – over 150, a contingent he had been recruiting ever since he left Edgar over a year earlier.

Siward also brought news from the Atheling. The Prince was effusive in his praise for the Brotherhood, but asked to be excused from its stand at Ely. He was in Europe encouraging opposition to William and spending time with Philip of France, trying to persuade him of the threat posed by William to all men of decency and honour. Also, as he still regarded himself as the rightful heir and had ambitions to claim the crown for himself, he could not acknowledge William as King, even though he understood Hereward's new position and admired the principles it represented. He sent the Brotherhood his full support and looked forward to the day when it would form his honour guard at his coronation at Westminster.

Siward was accompanied by a notable companion, Aethelwine, Bishop of Durham, who was to have crowned Edgar as King at York. Aethelwine was not originally a supporter of the rising, but the actions of William in the North had appalled and frightened him. He had been initially intimidated by the King's ruthlessness, but when he heard of the Brotherhood at Ely, he found new heart and resolved to join him.

Edwin and Morcar, being of Danish descent, had found it difficult to accept the Cerdician domination of England. Both would have preferred a separate kingdom in the North and had been reluctant members of a federal England. However, after their ignominious defeat at Gate

Fulford at the hands of Hardrada, their ambitions had been compromised. In defence of their absence at Senlac Ridge, they argued that it would have been impossible for them to get there in time. They felt it would have been much wiser for Harold to have waited, built a bigger army and then asked for their help, which they said they would have readily given.

Nevertheless, they admitted that they had not rushed to join his cause, something they deeply regretted. Their submission to William was another act that now filled them with remorse. Having, at his insistence, been at court with him and seen and heard what he was doing to England, their distaste for him had grown immeasurably, as had their shame at their own capitulation.

After their exhaustive and emotional account, they both stood and made a formal address to all present.

Earl Edwin spoke first. 'For anything we have done or not done that has put our homeland in jeopardy, or added to its pain, we beg forgiveness.'

Earl Morcar continued. 'We join the Brotherhood of St Etheldreda willingly and pledge our support wholeheartedly.'

They both raised their drinking horns. 'To the Brotherhood!'

Their toast was immediately echoed by the assembly. 'To the Brotherhood!'

It took a week and a half for all the new arrivals to be added to the Roll of Honour. When it was done, the Brotherhood had well over 3,000 members.

They all knew that there was little or no chance of inflicting any kind of significant military defeat on King

William. Even so, they had chosen to stand on principle. Although 3,000 men was not an army strong enough to defeat the King, it was more than sufficient to make a din so loud it would be heard the length and breadth of the land and across Europe. At long last, the spirit of England, those proud traditions of Saxon, Celt and Dane, had emerged from the humiliation of defeat. William was attempting to make a people cower by butchering anyone who dared utter a sound in opposition. Now, a few good men were speaking out, despite the price they knew they would eventually have to pay.

When the warmer days arrived, Hereward ordered that the causeway, Ely's lifeline, be destroyed. Ely would, like England itself, become an island again.

Once more, as he had in 1066, William would confront a military challenge across an expanse of water.

Throughout the early summer of 1071, the Norman army gathered around Ely and William's newly commissioned ships sailed into fenland waters.

The fleet consisted of standard longships carrying butescarls, smaller, flat-bottomed boats to navigate shallow waterways, and vessels adapted to carry catapults and ballisti. There was also a flotilla stationed in the Wash to act as supply ships and to prevent any naval ambush by Danish or Scottish allies of the Brotherhood.

On land, William ordered permanent camps to be prepared on the solid ground around the Isle of Ely and assembled a formidable show of strength. There were 4,000 infantry, 40 squadrons of cavalry, 500 archers and crossbowmen, and an array of blacksmiths, sappers and shipwrights. He had thought carefully about the assault; his planning, as always, was scrupulous. He intended to use catapults on any surrounding hillocks and islands that were within range of Ely and build tall towers for ballisti that could hurl stones, fire and boiling oil at the defenders. Finally, and most significantly, he intended to use pontoons to construct a new causeway for a final assault on the island.

When all the King's forces were in position, the Brotherhood was heavily outnumbered. Just 3,000 defenders faced an amphibious Norman assault force of almost 8,000. Crucially, William was able to bring in more men, equipment and materiel to an all but limitless extent.

The first assault would come from ground to the southeast of the island. While archers and crossbowmen loosed hails of arrows, and catapults launched their projectiles on to the Isle, Norman sappers would build a new causeway to the island. It would be a floating pontoon to span a stretch of water almost 800 yards across. The causeway would have to fall short of the island by about 200 yards because of the threat from the arrows of the defenders, but William estimated that his horses could cope with the shallow water at that point and reach the island. When it was completed, William planned to mount a cavalry attack with infantry in support.

Hereward's defence on the landfall side was a high peat bank and ditch. However, to prevent him massing too many defenders behind the bank, William planned simultaneous amphibious attacks all around the island, thinly stretching Hereward's forces around Ely's twenty-mile perimeter. Communications would be vital for the defenders, and

Martin Lightfoot's messengers would have one of the most difficult tasks.

When, several weeks later, the pontoon was ready, William's first cavalry attack, early on a clear June morning, was heralded by a single arrow shot high into the sky. Dawn had brought an amber glow to the water and the distant clouds were framed by golden sunbursts. There was silence, the meres and waterways of the Fens still, but the calm was soon interrupted by the rumble of heavy cavalry. As the riders began to cross the causeway, three abreast in tight formation, their horses' hooves clattering on the timber of the new bridge sent a chilling echo around the Isle.

The attack was a hopeless failure.

William had to put a large body of cavalry on to the causeway for the attack to have any momentum, but the structure appeared unable to support such a volume of men and horses, especially in the middle where it crossed the much deeper course of the River Cam. The pontoon began to give way after about 250 yards, and the charge lost its discipline. The lead horses panicked and, within minutes, hundreds of men and their steeds were floundering in the murky waters and deep mud.

Few got out alive.

William ordered his senior engineer to be executed on the spot and twenty of his sappers were flogged in front of the entire army.

Although the design of the pontoon was flawed, what William did not know was that its imperfections were significantly exacerbated by Hereward's cunning. Night after night, Alphonso and Hereward and their squads of saboteurs had slipped into the cold waters of the Great

Fen to partially sever the structure's ropes and timbers beneath the waterline. Thanks to their handy work, the pontoon was doomed.

William rarely made mistakes, so to have made two in one day was unprecedented. Not only had he built an inadequate causeway, he had also failed to realize the significance of the day chosen for the attack. If he had owned an astrolabe, he would have known that it was the twenty-third day of June.

Hereward knew the date, because he had used his precious gift from Rodrigo of Bivar to calculate it. He had made plans for a religious service, followed by the roasting of an ox, because 23 June was the feast day of St Etheldreda, the virgin martyr of Ely and patron saint of the Brotherhood. When William belatedly heard of the coincidence, his fury knew no bounds. He dismissed his seers, sending them back to Normandy bound hand and foot and dressed as harlequins complete with foolscaps. He stormed around his camp in a drunken rage, berating everyone in sight.

William ordered a new, much more substantial causeway, to be built. It would begin opposite Aldreth, on the southern tip of the island at the furthest point from the Burgh of Ely. Norman soldiers were despatched far and wide to round up hundreds of English peasants to provide the forced labour to construct it. The new structure would be much longer, almost a mile, and would be solid and permanent. It would be based on piles formed by stone gabions, topped by sheepskins of sand and covered by heavy timbers of elm and oak.

Protected by towers and sentry posts and wide enough

for cavalry six abreast, it would form an important part of the fortifications being built all over England to ensure that the kingdom remained under Norman rule for generations to come.

William would not repeat his earlier mistakes.

As July and August came and went, Hereward watched the new causeway grow. He knew that he needed to buy some extra time, to allow winter to come to the aid of the Brotherhood.

He organized raiding parties, large and small, all of which he led himself, to harass the Normans. Using small boats along the hidden waterways and streams of the Fens, he ambushed Norman patrols, burned their supplies and scattered their horses and livestock. On one of these punitive raids, Edwin, Earl of Mercia, was caught trying to cross a mere by a troop of Norman cavalry and cut down. His body was later recovered and, presided over by Bishop Aethelwine, he was given a funeral befitting an earl of England. His death meant that Morcar, Earl of Northumbria, became the last English earl not under the heel of the Normans.

In the middle of September, Hereward returned to Ely from a three-day raid on one of William's supply camps on the road to Cambridge, to face disturbing news.

Bishop Aethelwine, Siward Bjorn, Earl Morcar and Martin Lightfoot came to see him with a report that, although morale remained high, Abbot Thurstan's monks had been fomenting dissent within the Brotherhood. Earl Morcar had discovered that Thurstan was sending messages to William and that a deal had been done between them for the end of the siege.

In return for encouraging opposition within Ely, William would grant significant new lands to Thurstan and endow Ely Abbey with a considerable sum from his treasury at Winchester. Several monks were very tempted by this and, with Thurstan's encouragement, had started a whispering campaign to spread doubt through the ranks. The monks were also talking seditiously to the townspeople, some of whom, especially the wealthier ones, had no real sympathy for the Brotherhood's cause and would much prefer to trade with the wealthy Normans.

Hereward gave swift instructions to convene a court of fifty randomly-selected members of the Brotherhood in the cloisters of the abbey. Thurstan was summoned to appear before it. Earl Morcar presided and conducted an elaborate trial with witnesses and formal statements.

Thurstan spoke eloquently in his own defence, arguing that the 'messages' in question had all come from William and that none had gone the other way. He also claimed that it was the duty of monks to listen to all God's children, to hear their concerns and to offer advice; that was all his clerics had been doing. Where previously there seemed to be certainty about his guilt, Thurstan's clever arguments and subtle oratory were creating a sense of doubt within the court.

Then, a young monk, one of Thurstan's men, rose from the back of the cloisters. 'My Lord . . .'

The entire court turned to see where the faint voice came from.

The boy breathed deeply and spoke more loudly, trying to suppress his nervousness. '. . . Abbot Thurstan has been plotting for many weeks to undermine the Brotherhood and reach a settlement with the King for the future of the abbey. He cares nothing for our Oath and thinks only of himself.' The boy sat down, relieved to have found the courage to speak, but still fearful of the consequences of his words.

Earl Morcar addressed him directly. 'What is your name, young monk?'

'Rahere, my Lord.'

'Thank you, Rahere. Thank you for your faith in the Brotherhood.'

Thurstan seethed with anger at Rahere's denunciation. He sat and rocked like a child, his face contorted in rage. 'The boy lies! How dare he impune my name!'

Earl Morcar shouted Thurstan down and stood to address the court. 'Members of the Brotherhood, Thurstan, Abbot of Ely and twelve of his monks stand before you. They are accused of dishonouring our Brotherhood, defaming our Oath and undermining our cause in an insidious negotiation with the King. How do you judge them? Guilty or not guilty?'

A great cry of 'guilty' rang around the cloisters.

The Earl then turned to Hereward. 'Hereward of Bourne, founder of our noble Brotherhood, what would you have us do with them?'

'Execute them!' was the cry from many throats. 'Execute them! Execute them!' The cries grew louder.

Hereward rose. 'Like you, I am sorely tempted to have them cut down here and now. Indeed, there is much history between Abbot Thurstan and me, a past so grievous it would warrant a bloody end to our relationship. We now know he did not take the Oath honestly, but out of expediency, to protect his own interests. He and his monks have wronged us, and now we are entitled to punish them. But our Oath does not mention vengeance, it talks only of justice. Our purpose here in Ely is to foster tolerance and forgiveness. Therefore, let us abide by our Oath and expel them from our midst. Let that be their punishment.'

Earl Morcar looked around. Most of the men nodded their heads in agreement, and Morcar declared that Hereward's suggestion had been accepted.

Edmund of Kent was delegated to expel the guilty clerics. He summoned three small rowing boats and, stripped to their loincloths, the traitors were bundled into the craft.

Thurstan was a pathetic sight: hunched, disfigured and pale as a ghost, he cowered in the bottom of the last boat to leave as the disgraced monks rowed themselves to the Norman positions.

By the time the autumn gales of October arrived, King William's second causeway was almost complete. Hereward's subversive tactics had stalled the King's plans, but not enough to allow winter to bring respite to the defenders of Ely. He needed just a fraction more time – a salvation that would be denied to him, as it had been to England's stricken King on Senlac Ridge.

Now it was only a matter of days before England's final redoubt would face the second Norman onslaught.

Under the guardianship of Bishop Aethelwine, who had become the new Chaplain to the Brotherhood, Hereward issued orders that all the non-combatants of the burgh be given refuge in the abbey. A third of his defenders would mass behind the ditch and bank at Aldreth, the landing point for the King's causeway, while the remaining two-thirds would be dispersed around the island to repel any waterborne attacks by William's butescarls. If any of their positions were overrun, they were to fall back inside the walls of the burgh to make a final stand.

William's logistical task was much more complicated. Not only had he to synchronize the massed attack along the causeway with the simultaneous amphibious attacks from the Fens, he also had to manage the complex positioning of the catapults and ballisti and coordinate the supply of projectiles for them. Hereward watched for over a week as the Normans manoeuvred themselves into position and William displayed his skills as a master of the art of military planning.

In the second week of October, the bustle of Norman activity had all but ceased and they were poised to attack. Hereward was convinced that hostilities would commence the next morning.

He called the Brotherhood together to address them.

'Tomorrow we will stand together to face the King. We do so willingly, as free men. We have sent a message to him, to all Normans and to the whole of Europe, saying that we will not be intimidated by an unjust and cruel regime. Most importantly, we have sent a message to our fellow Englishmen – a message that will live in their memories and those of generations to come – that on this October day, in the year 1071 on the Isle of Ely, three thousand Englishmen stood and fought for justice. By our Oath, we stand together for our Brotherhood and for England!'

An immense roar resounded across the Fens, heard by William and every Norman for miles around.

That evening, Hereward's family gathered. They went over the escape plan several times to ensure that everyone knew it by heart. Hereward then walked to the walls of Ely and looked out over the Fens.

The night was black with menacing clouds, and the wind blew with a piercing chill. There was nothing left to do, other than allow the circumstances he had set in motion months earlier to come to their conclusion. In the protracted game of chess he had been playing with William, he had been put into check for the last time.

William's demeanour had not softened; the many pleas to him to loosen the vicious grip he had on the neck of England had been to no avail. His cruelty still knew no bounds and there was no hint of compassion in his heart. Nevertheless, Hereward believed it had been worth the struggle. Even if the King remained unmoved, what was happening on the Isle of Ely had lit a powerful beacon to signal that men do have rights and that they are entitled to defend them, even against their sovereign lord. The message of the Talisman of Truth was clear: no evil is so great that it cannot be overcome, not even that of the Devil.

Hereward was about to return to try to get some sleep, when Gunnhild and Estrith appeared.

As usual, they spoke as a duet. 'We do understand what you are trying to do, Father; it's just that we don't want to lose you . . . We have lost our mother . . . We don't want to lose our father as well.'

He knelt down to look them in the eye. 'One day you will have children of your own and will understand that sometimes things have to be done that are not concerned with the needs of the present, but the well-being of future generations. Everything that has happened here – the Brotherhood, our Oath, and the fight against the King's cruelty – has a single aim: to make sure that those terrible things that happened in Bourne, to your grandmother and grandfather and all the others, never happen again. Our deeds are also a tribute to your mother's memory. Torfida shared this burden with me from the very beginning, and her wisdom still guides me in my thoughts and helps me in my moments of doubt.'

'We know, Father.' They held him tightly.

After a while, he carried them back to their tent and put them to bed. As they kissed him goodnight, he could see the anxiety in their eyes; if ever there was a moment to abandon his cause, this was it.

Just then, in unison, they smiled at him. 'We love you.'

'I love you too.'

They closed their eyes and he bent down to kiss them. With tears rolling down his cheeks, he sat with them until long after they had fallen asleep.

It was the most difficult thing he had ever had to do.

30. Denouement

Everyone was in position long before dawn – defenders and attackers alike. Edmund proudly unfurled Hereward's standard, the Great Axe of Göteborg, and those who had fought with him in the North flew his gold, crimson and black pennons.

Hereward checked his astrolabe; the date was 14 October 1071, five years to the day from the momentous events of Senlac Ridge.

Earl Morcar was in command to the north, Siward Bjorn to the west, Thorkill of Harringworth to the east, while Hereward took charge of the all-important southern defences at Aldreth. Everything was ready, all preparations made, every detail attended to.

Now it was time to fight.

The sky was threatening and the wind howling, drowning any sounds except, carried from afar, the snorting and stomping of the Norman destriers. Hereward grasped the Talisman just as William gave the signal to attack.

This time, the causeway held as a relentless stream of Norman cavalry hurtled towards Aldreth. The defenders launched a fusillade of arrows and javelins, inflicting heavy casualties on the front ranks of the Norman squadrons. When the cavalry reached the end of the causeway, they were able to fan out across the shallow water. Some became trapped in the cloying mud, lost to a lingering death, but most got a firm footing and started to assail the Brother-hood's bank and ditch. The defenders at the top adopted the tactics of the shield wall of the English army, placing their shields on the parapet and using their spears above and swords between. A cacophony of yells and screams, clanging armour and straining horses filled the air.

Initially, the bank held, with many Normans floundering in the ditch, but eventually the number of squadrons pour-ing across the causeway became overwhelming. Following in their wake were massed ranks of infantry, with water-borne assaults and aerial bombardments around Ely's entire perimeter. Hereward, realizing that Ely's outer defences would soon be breached, ordered a general retreat to the burgh's walls. To cover the withdrawal, he led a counter-attack, using his hearthtroop in a mounted charge against the advancing Norman cavalry.

Hereward's charge led to a ferocious clash of mounted warriors, which lasted for over two hours and cost him many men, some of whom had been with him from the beginning. They had been in the charge against the Norwe-gians at Stamford Bridge, had stood their ground on Senlac Ridge and then fought against William in the campaigns in the North. He watched as they fell all around him – England's finest, the bravest of men, almost the last of Harold's legendary housecarls.

Eventually, when all the defenders were within reach of the walls of Ely, Hereward ordered the withdrawal of his cavalry. Of the 600 men who had charged into the Norman destriers, only 200 galloped back to Ely. When the last man had ridden through the gates, they were closed behind him.

Morcar, Bjorn and Harringworth had also withdrawn

and positioned their men inside the walls. They too had taken heavy casualties. In all, the Brotherhood had lost more than a third of its men.

Hereward looked around. Einar was close to him and unharmed; Martin had been slashed across the arm by a sword, but his wound was superficial; Alphonso had a deep gouge on his forehead and was covered in blood, but nodded at Hereward to say that he could still fight; Edmund of Kent and Edwin were where they always were, right behind their leader.

Hereward quickly dismounted and climbed to the shooting platform behind Ely's wooden ramparts. He looked at the encroaching horde of Norman infantry battalions, the menacing catapults and ballisti being wheeled along Aldreth causeway and the swarm of butescarls coming ashore from boats on the Great Fen. Their cavalry was regrouping in neat lines and he could see scaling ladders being carried by sappers for the final assault on Ely's walls. Then, in the distance approaching the causeway, he saw William at the head of his Matilda Squadron.

He hurried down to his loyal companions. 'We must put the escape plan into operation. If we wait any longer, the family will not get out alive; the noose is tightening. Martin, Einar, Alphonso, you must go.'

Each of them refused.

'This is madness. We have to get the women and children off the island.'

In exasperation, Hereward gave Einar a direct order to lead Alphonso, Martin and the family off the island. 'Do it. Do it now!'

The big Northumbrian nodded reluctantly and pulled

Martin and Alphonso away. Hereward pushed Edwin towards them, and Einar included him in his corral. When Hereward tried to do the same with Edmund, he shook his head in defiance.

In a parting gesture, the four men turned to Hereward and placed a clenched fist over their heart, the salute of the Brotherhood.

Hereward's defensive strategy had been well rehearsed and, after little more than an hour, the civilians were safely inside the abbey precincts and Ely's walls were well manned.

Hereward quickly gathered his senior command together to agree on the positions each would take, before returning to the ramparts, where he had left Edmund holding the gold, crimson and black of his standard. However, as he approached, he noticed not just one figure standing beneath his colours, but four.

They all stood erect and motionless, silhouetted against the sky like sentinels.

Hereward stopped for a second, thinking he must be mistaken, but there, standing beside Edmund, were Einar, Martin and Alphonso.

'What's happened, where are the girls?'

Einar answered for all of them. 'They all got away safely. Edwin has been put in charge and Gohor is a fine soldier. They will take care of them.'

'But what about when they get to France?'

Martin then answered. 'I don't know about you, but I've got every intention of fighting my way out of here and joining them at St Cirq Lapopie.' He moved towards Hereward. 'The girls knew we had to stay. We've been through too much together to miss this fight. When I'm old and I'm telling the famous story of Hereward Great Axe, I can't say that, when it came to the final battle, his three loyal companions went home!'

Alphonso made a similar point. 'In Spain, we sing songs about heroes, but not about men who go home before the last battle!'

'Are you all sure? This is a battle where the odds suggest our only victory will be a moral one.'

Einar responded. 'With the three of us behind you, the odds are better than you think.'

There were embraces all round, before each chose his position for the onslaught.

William's final attack on Ely's ramparts, a masterclass of military coordination, was launched thirty-six hours later. It began with a hail of stone missiles and a torrent of boiling oil, followed by wave after wave of arrows shot high into the air. The stones inflicted terrible injuries on the defenders and massive damage to Ely's buildings. The oil, delivered in clay pots which shattered on impact, burned people and homes far and wide. The arrows landed with a deadly cadence, and killed or maimed the defenders in droves. It was a lethal bombardment, against which there was no protection.

Then came a pause in the barrage, as King William ordered his infantry to advance. Men in the front ranks carried scaling ladders, and row upon row of archers and crossbowmen followed behind the solid phalanx of foot soldiers. As the front line reached a point about 100 yards from the walls, the bowmen knelt and shot rapid bursts of bolts directly at the defenders on the ramparts, to murderous effect. Then, while the deadly cascade continued, the infantry surged forward at a run and flung their ladders at the walls.

The battle for the ramparts took nearly four hours. Hundreds of William's assault troops were killed and the piles of corpses beneath the ladders grew and grew. However, the men of the Brotherhood had no means of protecting themselves against the torrent of arrows and bolts which, slowly but surely, whittled away at their numbers. It was simply a matter of arithmetic: if William was prepared to send enough men up the scaling ladders, no matter how many were killed, they would eventually overwhelm the defenders.

With his companions constantly at his side, his standard always flying proudly as a beacon to the Brotherhood, Hereward ran along the thin ribbon of defenders. Wherever there was the prospect of a breach, he would stop to lend support. The Great Axe was not effective so close to his own men, but his sword meted out terrible retribution to any Norman foolish enough to clamber over the ramparts within his reach.

By the late afternoon, there was nothing more that Hereward and the defenders could do. The Normans had driven the Brotherhood from the ramparts along most of Ely's walls and were swarming down the inside stairways. Hereward ordered a shield wall to be formed in front of the abbey; it would be the Brotherhood's final redoubt.

It was then that Alphonso fell, hit between the shoulder blades by a lance thrown from the ramparts. Much as he tried, he could not get up. Blood poured from the deep wound in his back and, within moments, there was no movement at all.

Alphonso was the finest soldier Hereward had ever known. He could adapt to any conditions, fight on any terrain and use any kind of weapon. He was at his best on his own, or in a small group, and Hereward had learned more from him about the art of warfare than anyone – including William of Normandy, Harold of Wessex and Rodrigo of Bivar.

Now he was dead, killed by an aimless weapon thrown at random by an enemy he never saw.

The Brotherhood's shield wall held for over an hour, but there were too many Normans and too few Englishmen. As quickly as an English battle-axe cut down a Norman adversary, another replaced him, until the wall was unable to steady itself against the weight of overwhelming numbers. The carnage was horrendous. Men were being hacked to pieces in a flailing mass of swords, axes and spears. Hereward stalked the redoubt with Martin and Einar, constantly moving up and down the line to reinforce weak points.

He was powerless to prevent the blow that killed Einar. He had rushed to a hole in the shield wall and had managed to close it when a spear was thrust between two shields, impaling him below the ribs. He fell to the ground on his knees, clutching at his chest and trying to stem the flow of blood, but it was futile. Hereward managed to get Einar to his feet, but he was losing consciousness. Martin and Edmund came to help; they pulled him away from the melee and laid him down.

He tried to speak, but was fighting for breath. Blood spluttered from his mouth as his chest filled and his lungs were swamped. There was nothing they could do, other than hold him as he fought for air. He looked at Hereward and, despite the pain of his wound and the terror of suffocation, managed to grasp his hand and summon a brief smile. Then he was still. Hereward gently placed his head on the ground, carefully wiped the blood from his face and beard and placed his weapons on his chest. Despite the mayhem just an arm's length away, Hereward took his time, making sure the mighty Northumbrian met his death in the manner of a noble warrior.

Einar had been proud of his Viking blood, loyal to his English homeland, and a true friend.

By the time Hereward, Martin and Edmund got back to the shield wall it was in disarray. Earl Morcar was frantically trying to encourage the left flank, Thorkill of Harringworth was nowhere to be seen and had presumably perished, but Siward Bjorn still stood on the right, vigorously trying to keep his part of the wall in one piece.

Hereward did a quick count; there were barely 500 of the Brotherhood still fighting.

William summoned his cavalry. With the Matilda Squadron in the centre, the Normans formed up just beyond the walls of the burgh and streamed through the gates in a charge. The Norman infantry parted, to give their cavalry a corridor along which to attack, and they came on at full gallop.

Hereward rushed forward and took a solitary position in front of the shield wall. He ordered the remaining Brotherhood to close ranks behind him, raise their shields and spears and follow him to meet the Norman cavalry head-on. At the final moment, Hereward signalled to his men to fix their spears firmly in the ground and close their shields. Now it was time to deploy the Great Axe of Göteborg.

An irresistible force met an immovable object. Destriers reared and were impaled on spears; men were flung from their mounts and put to death on the ground by battle-axes; knights and sergeants barked encouragement; the fallen cried out in their death throes. Beyond the shield wall stood Hereward, the only man with space around him. Wielding his Great Axe in huge arcs, he fashioned a circle of death, despatching anyone who ventured into it.

He was used to fighting with armies of well-trained soldiers who fought with the steel of professionals, but now he was leading a band of zealots who fought with relentless vigour behind him. Their faith inspired him, multiplying his already prodigious strength, so that he cut swathes through the ranks of Norman cavalry. As he did so, the last of the Brotherhood followed him, wreaking havoc in the Norman ranks. The death toll rose inexorably.

Hereward continued routing all around him, advancing into the Norman lines, until he sank to his knees in utter exhaustion. He tried to raise his shield and axe to parry the blows he knew were about to rain down on him, but he could not; his arms were numb with fatigue and, not wanting to see his slayers, he bowed his head.

The blows did not come. The mayhem ceased. Where, moments ago, there had been the hideous din of battle, there was now silence. Hereward slowly raised his head. He was surrounded by Norman cavalry, its men and horses breathing deeply, clouds of perspiration rising from their bodies. Mounted in the middle of them, red with rage, was William, King of England.

The Norman cavalry parted to allow the King to see the remnants of the Brotherhood. Fewer than a hundred men were clustered in a small group, some on their knees, some trying to get to their feet. The pile of bodies around them was twenty yards wide and in places as high as a man. Hereward could see Edmund, who still held his standard. Next to him was Earl Morcar, covered in blood from head to foot, his chest heaving from the titanic struggle. Martin was on the ground next to Earl Morcar, propping himself up on his elbows, trying to get his breath. He too was drenched in blood, but not his own.

Hereward was relieved to see them, but so many good men were dead. He could see the young monk Rahere lying in a lifeless heap. The bodies of the two young men of Spanish descent, Azecier and Alveriz, were nearby and next to them were the still forms of the two friends Matelgar and Alsinus.

The King ordered that all the survivors be bound and led away. He dismounted to approach Hereward and, as he did so, saw Martin Lightfoot being dragged away.

'Bring that little Welsh brigand over here. We will deal with him before we devote our attention to the man who thought he could teach a king how to govern his people.'

Martin was made to kneel in front of William and his hands were tied behind his back. Four knights approached Hereward and held him while his hands were also bound. He had further bindings tied around his elbows, knees and ankles. A noose was put around his neck and pulled, forcing his head backwards and his chin in the air. Then the noose was tied to his ankle bindings, leaving him with no freedom of movement.

William lifted his Baculus high into the air and, with a guttural cry, struck a fearsome blow to the side of Martin's head. He died instantly, keeling over without making a sound, blood pouring from his ears, mouth and nostrils.

Hereward let out a cry of anguish and tried to free himself, but to no avail. He looked at William with loathing.

William was coldly impassive. 'Before you also receive my justice, the justice you have been at pains to recommend I should exercise wisely, I have a surprise for you.'

At a signal from William, Hereward was pulled up on to his knees. Then, from between a gap in the circle of cavalry, a bedraggled line of humanity appeared, wet and dirty and shivering from cold. It was his family, with a badly beaten Edwin beside them.

'You should have killed me when you had the chance.' It was Thurstan's voice. The Abbot spoke sneeringly as he threw a bloodstained tunic on to the ground, which Hereward presumed was Gohor's. 'My monks knew exactly where your boat was hidden. They have lived on this Isle all their lives and know its every nook and cranny. They followed as your happy band refreshed it with provisions. When the boat pulled away, we simply let it disappear out of sight, before the Norman butescarls took it in tow and brought your loved ones to face their King's judgement.'

Hereward felt a burning hatred that knew no limit. Thurstan was right; he should have killed him when he had the chance. Hereward again strained at his bindings, but even his great strength was unable to make any impression on them.

The King began to speak, but Edmund of Kent, who had not yet been manacled by his captors, grabbed the reins of

469

a knight's horse, pulled a lance from his grasp and hurled it at Thurstan. It struck the crippled abbot squarely in the chest, knocking him on to his back. He grabbed the lance with both hands in a futile attempt to pull it from his ribs, but it was embedded too deeply. He was dead within seconds.

William bellowed to his knights and Edmund was cut down.

Hereward cried out in desperation. 'Stop! Stop this killing! It is me you want, my Lord King. You are right, I have spoken for the justice of kings, and I am now ready to receive it. Kill me now; let it be an end to it. Spare the others, spare my family, I beg you, William, King of England, Duke of Normandy, I beseech you.'

'So it is true, you do acknowledge my sovereignty of this land.'

'I do, sire, I did many months ago. What we fought for here was the right to be fairly treated as Englishmen.'

'How could I have failed to hear? You made such a din about it all over my kingdom! It is good that you now beg before your King, because I intend to make you pay for your conceit.' William turned to his knights. 'Have him lashed!'

Hereward was held down while his bindings were removed and he was stripped of his armour and clothes. His hands and elbows were tied again, and he was strapped to a post where he was flogged repeatedly.

His family screamed and begged the King to show mercy. He ignored them, not even glancing in their direction. Hereward did not cry out; his only sounds were deep intakes of breath to counter the searing pain of each blow. Eventually, he lost consciousness.

A pail of cold water brought Hereward back to consciousness with a shudder.

Odo, Bishop of Bayeux, then barked a question at him. 'What say you now about the King's justice, Hereward of Bourne?'

Hereward answered with difficulty. 'I say the King has the right to administer justice as our sovereign lord. But he also has the responsibility to administer that justice according to the dictates of his own conscience. I would ask him this: is his justice compassionate?'

William rose in a fury, picked up his Baculus and strode towards Hereward.

As he lifted the huge mace, Hereward made himself as upright as he could and looked William in the eye. 'Strike well for England, my Lord King. Do what you think is right.'

William took aim but, as he did so, a flicker of light from the many torches that had been brought to the ever-darkening scene was reflected in the Talisman that still hung from Hereward's neck.

William saw the face of the Devil.

He stopped, suddenly intimidated, remembering the stories he had heard about the charm that the English leader carried around his neck. The Baculus hovered above Hereward's head for several moments before the King let it fall to his side.

'Lock up the women and children. Leave Hereward of Bourne where he is – no food, no water, no fire. He is to be guarded at all times. We shall see how defiant he is in the morning.'

*

471

By dawn the next day, Hereward was a pitiful sight; still naked and deathly pale, he shivered uncontrollably. Although the lacerations on his back had dried, early morning rain had moistened them and they stung sharply from the salt of his perspiration.

King William appeared with his retinue about an hour after dawn. Hereward's family members were once again brought forward. They were calmer than the night before, but only through exhaustion. So that he could fully comprehend what he was about to witness, Hereward was roused by ice-cold water and a few well-aimed kicks.

Loaded on to carts, the survivors of the final redoubt of the Brotherhood were paraded before their stricken leader. Earl Morcar was shackled hand and foot, gagged and blindfolded, but he was the only man still whole. All the others had been tortured and brutalized. Some had had their eyes gouged out, others had lost hands, tongues, ears, or feet; all had been whipped and beaten. Hereward recognized almost all of them: Siward Bjorn, Bruhar the Brave, Wolnatius, Siward the Blond – ninety men, England's finest, now mutilated such that few had much chance of survival.

'So, Hereward of Bourne, this is what has become of your "Brotherhood". This is what happens to men who dare to challenge me in my own domain.'

Hereward's words came slowly from the edge of consciousness. 'You can't kill all Englishmen. Eventually, you will have to accept that strong kingdoms are those that are ruled with the goodwill of their subjects.'

William turned ever more puce. He walked over to Hereward and bellowed at him. 'Is there no limit to your defiance?'

'Sire, I beg you. I beg for compassion for the people of England.' Hereward slumped against the post to which he was still bound.

'Drag him into the cloisters! Bring the family!'

William led the procession into the broad cloisters of Ely Abbey, long since deserted by the citizens of Ely. Still under the care of Bishop Aethelwine, they had dispersed to their homes around the burgh – safe, for the time being, from the King's wrath.

Hereward was on the threshold of death as he was dragged into the Chapel of St Etheldreda and thrown at the base of her tomb. Gunnhild and Estrith were pulled from the others, dragged into the chapel and spreadeagled over the image of the virgin martyr. Once more, Hereward was revived. This time, cold water was not sufficient and they had to use hot torches on his feet until he regained consciousness sufficiently to hear the King's enraged voice.

'Will you, Hereward of Bourne, sacrifice your children for the Oath of the Brotherhood?'

Hereward failed to respond and the King bellowed more loudly.

'Will you sacrifice your brood for the Oath of the Brotherhood?'

As Hereward raised his head, he could see two of William's henchmen, each with a sword to the throat of his girls.

'They will die here and now on the Virgin's tomb unless you renounce the Oath of the Brotherhood.'

William was shaking and sweating, his voice tremulous with rage. Estrith and Gunnhild screamed as he shouted his demands; their cries echoed around the abbey.

Hereward summoned enough strength to speak. 'I will not renounce the Oath! Too many have died for our cause for me to reject it now. Spare my children. They are innocent of any crime; they have not offended you in any way.'

The King stepped forward and placed a gold piece on the breast of St Etheldreda. He grabbed the Talisman from Hereward's neck and placed it over the rosary beads on her hands. One of his knights brought him the Great Axe of Göteborg and William clasped it firmly in both hands.

'With this offering to St Etheldreda, I, William, King of England, Duke of Normandy, strike down this traitor and his kith and kin. In so doing, I bring to an end this Brotherhood and all it stands for. So help me God.'

William raised the Great Axe of Göteborg above his head and aimed it at Hereward's neck. His two knights pulled back their swords, ready to strike at the throats of Gunnhild and Estrith, who screamed in horror.

'My Lord King, spare my girls. Strike me down, but spare them.'

'Renounce the Oath!'

'I cannot! Saying the words to save my children will not negate the Oath. You cannot deny truth with an act of violence. And I cannot reject it with an act of expediency.'

'So be it.' William flexed the Great Axe, ready to swing it.

At that moment, a shaft of sunlight burst through the window, caught a reflection from the Great Axe and illuminated the opposite wall. The chapel shone with an amber glow. The light reflected on the crucifix of St Etheldreda's rosary, casting a beam through the Talisman that lay on her hands. William looked at the amulet and saw the crimson flash across the face of the Devil. He was horrified, but transfixed by it, unable to turn away until, after several moments, he blinked and shook his head, trying to gather his senses. As he did so, he was blinded by the dazzling sunbeams now pouring in through the windows, filling the chapel with light.

Suddenly panic-stricken, the King dropped the Great Axe, sending it crashing to the stone floor with a deafening clang that reverberated around Ely like a bell ringing in Hell. The knights who were about to strike the girls dropped their swords, multiplying the discordant clash of steel on stone. All the King's men took flight and spilled out into the cloisters, leaving William alone.

Moments later, he staggered breathlessly from the chapel, his ruddy, blotchy countenance suddenly deathly white. He felt a vice-like pain tightening around his chest, jagged jolts running down his arms and, no more than five yards from the chapel, he collapsed to the ground, uttering just one sentence before slipping into unconsciousness.

'Seal the chapel; no one goes in or out.'

31. The Reckoning

Gunnhild and Estrith were locked in the virgin martyr's chapel with their stricken father. They soon gathered their composure and began to think about how to cope with their confinement. Outside, the Normans ran around in disarray, convinced their King had been struck down by a holy visitation wrought by St Etheldreda.

William was hurried away to his headquarters on Belsar's Hill, where his physicians attended him. Guards were posted outside the chapel, while, inside, the girls began to care for their father. They covered his nakedness with the altar cloth and kept him warm by cutting a hole in the thatch above and starting a fire, using candles as kindling and benches as firewood. They cleaned his wounds with communion wine, prepared a crude vegetable soup from the harvest offerings at the foot of the martyr's tomb and washed him with water from the baptismal font.

Gradually Hereward gained some strength; not so, William.

The King was only fit to leave his bed over a week after the mysterious events in St Etheldreda's Chapel. Dressed in full armour, he donned his royal regalia and rode into Ely in great pomp. However, he entered St Etheldreda's Chapel cautiously, with only Robert, Count of Mortain, his half-brother and most trusted lieutenant, for company.

Gunnhild and Estrith, who sat either side of their father, moved closer to him as the King appeared. William was still pale and vapid. Hereward, however, looked alert and tolerably comfortable. His daughters had done a remarkable job in keeping him alive.

The King looked around nervously and beckoned to Robert of Mortain to take the girls outside. Looking back anxiously, they struggled and screamed, but had no choice.

The Talisman still lay across St Etheldreda's praying hands. The gold piece was still on the virgin's breast, and the rosary still decorated her clasped fingers.

'You have put a spell on this place, Hereward of Bourne. The hand of the Devil is at work in this chapel.'

'There are no devils here; there is only goodness in this place.'

'You conjured a trick to deceive me. Your wife was a sorceress; her girls have inherited her proficiency in the black arts.'

'This has nothing to do with the black arts. It is about truth and justice.'

William inhaled a deep sigh, sat down on a bench and stared at St Etheldreda's tomb. He suddenly seemed vulnerable. 'I was born the son of a duke, but my mother was a tanner's daughter from Falaise. I have had to fight all my life to be recognized as the rightful heir to the Dukedom of Normandy. Now I am a king but, again, I have to fight to be accepted. Why won't the English recognize me? Why?'

'Sire, Normandy is used to being ruled with an iron fist. England is a different land, with a diversity of people, languages and customs. England has always been ruled according to ancient traditions: that its rulers can be challenged; that oppression is to be resisted; and that independence is to be cherished. This is the land you have won in battle; it is very different from Normandy. You must understand that.'

'Would you have let your daughters die when I challenged you?'

'I had no choice, sire. I could not renounce a sacred oath under pain of death – either theirs or mine. I hope Gunnhild and Estrith, young as they are, understand that. It is a terrible thing for a father to place his daughters in mortal danger, but that peril was wrought by you, not by me.'

The King stood. 'Something happened to me in this chapel. Whether it was visited upon me by God, the Devil, St Etheldreda or the Talisman, I do not know, but it was real. I saw a vision of Christ's blood and a blinding light. I felt pain, like a giant hand gripping my chest. I couldn't breathe; I believe the Hand of God was telling me to stop.'

'Then listen to it, sire.'

The King walked towards the window of the chapel. 'Hereward of Bourne, I acknowledge the hand that stayed my arm. Although you may be surprised to hear this, I have considered what you have said to me. The resistance of the English has made me think. They surprised me at Senlac Ridge, and the defence of Ely by your Brotherhood has been beyond my comprehension. You are an exceptional man. I have never regarded anyone as my equal. When I was a child, I feared everyone, because of the endless plots to kill me and take my dukedom. When I became a man, I had the strength and desire to make other men bend to my will; there was no room for respect, let alone for the recognition of an equal. But I respect you, Hereward of Bourne. You are the only man I have met who shares my determination and resilience.'

The King paused. There was a glimmer of compassion in him as he looked at Hereward.

'I will not change – I am too old for that – but I will acknowledge that the English are worthy of my respect. There are things about them that I have come to admire. I will not forget; my fellow Normans will not forget.'

Hereward sighed. At long last, at the cost of thousands of lives, including those of his loyal comrades and closest friends, the King had relented. It might have been divine intervention, the mystical influence of Torfida and her father, or simply a stroke of good fortune created by nature; regardless, the King had conceded.

Hereward thought about the Old Man of the Wildwood and his long journey with Torfida and the Talisman. Now, it all made sense.

'I am going to spare you, Hereward of Bourne.'

'But, sire, I cannot live when all around me have died. I will happily face execution. My journey is at an end.'

'You have no choice; I have made my decision. You will not die here and become the focus of more English resistance. If there are more risings, I will have to suppress them as ruthlessly as I have suppressed this one; you cannot want that. You must leave this land, never to return, your whereabouts always an enigma. Hereward of Bourne must fade away as mysteriously as he, his wife and their infernal amulet appeared. In exchange, I will spare you and your family. Most importantly, and this is my real concession to you, I will endeavour to understand this land and its people.'

Hereward was torn between two wildly contrasting emotions: elation at the King's words, which were at least the beginnings of justice and compassion, and ignominy that he would live when so many had died.

'Sire, I am ashamed at the prospect of survival amid so much death.'

'Why feel shame? Isn't it what you fought for?'

William summoned Robert of Mortain and told him to take the girls away. Hereward begged to be allowed to see them, but the King was adamant.

'Your girls will stay in England as guarantors of your future conduct. You have my word that they will live and prosper for as long as you remain beyond England's shores and well away from its affairs.'

Hereward could hear Gunnhild and Estrith's howls of protest as they were taken away. They were harrowing sounds that he would hear for the rest of his life.

'Sire, you have my word as to my conduct, but please let the girls go to their home in Aquitaine with the others.'

'I believe you now, but circumstances change over the years. The presence of your children here will ensure that you are never tempted to change your mind. They will be well treated at Mortain's court; he is a good man. They will be given a dowry and allowed to marry by choice; husbands will not be forced on them.'

'And what of my other family, sire?'

'They will be given a safe escort to Aquitaine with the young English knight, Edwin. They may take their money with them, but they must know nothing of your fate, or your whereabouts; neither must your daughters. It will be for the best if they come to accept that you are dead. They will all leave Ely today, your girls with Count Robert to live in Cornwall, the rest of the family on a ship to Normandy. You will stay hidden in this chapel under guard until you are fit enough to travel.

'When you are ready, you will be spirited away to Normandy's border with France. From there, you can go anywhere you choose, on condition that no one knows your true identity and that your destination is far from England and Normandy. Nobody must know what has been said in this chapel. Your fate will become a mystery and your deeds the stuff of legend; you should be content with that.'

Without another word or parting gesture, William turned and left.

St Etheldreda's Chapel was sealed, except for one of the King's physicians who came and went under cover of darkness.

After ten days of treatment and healing, Hereward and all his belongings were packed on to a cart. A month later, he was in Paris, recovering from his ordeal; he would never see England again.

Hereward's struggle and the resistance of the people of England were over.

The events surrounding the end of the Siege of Ely were soon woven into legend. Some stories suggested that Hereward had escaped into the Bruneswald to fight another day; others said he had died under torture at William's own hand and that his body had been taken for burial at nearby Crowland Abbey.

The most fanciful tale claimed that he had died from his

wounds, but that his soul would never leave his body until England was free and that on dark nights his spectre could be seen high above Ely Abbey, hovering over the Great Fen like a beacon.

Epilogue

The sun had been up for an hour over the western Peloponnese by the time Godwin of Ely came to the end of his story, a story that had been almost three days in the telling.

Godwin of Ely and Hereward of Bourne were one and the same man. Godwin, the old recluse, who had lived for years in his lonely eyrie, was indeed the guardian of the Talisman and the leader of the English resistance to the Norman Conquest.

Only three men had heard his account of the life and times of the Lincolnshire thegn, Hereward of Bourne: Prince John Comnenus, the son of Alexius I, the Emperor of Byzantium; Prince John Azoukh, close friend and lifelong companion to John Comnenus; and Leo of Methone, priest of this remote valley in Hellas.

Godwin was exhausted. He was very pale and was lying heavily in his padded resting place amid the rocks of his mountain hermitage. Prince John Comnenus ordered the fire to be built up and told his stewards to prepare food. But when hot soup was served, the old warrior was too weak to raise the bowl to his mouth and refused it.

Godwin looked very frail, so much so that John Comnenus became concerned. 'Godwin of Ely, we must take you down the mountain so that we can take care of you properly.'

'No thank you, sire. I will spend my remaining time here in my home. I have been here for many years; I've grown very fond of it.'

'How can we make you more comfortable?'

'I am fine; the morning sun will refresh me.'

483

John Comnenus realized that Godwin would not be persuaded to move. Although he looked feeble, he seemed content.

'Then, if you will permit me, I have one final question for you. How did my father come to wear the Talisman?'

Godwin took a deep breath, as if summoning the last of his strength and resolve. 'After a long period of recovery and reflection, Hereward of Bourne became reconciled to never seeing his country or his family again. He found modest contentment in knowing that he had made some impact on the brutality of William's rule. He was sure that the King would keep his word about his daughters, who had a good chance of a happy life, and that the survivors of his loyal family would live out their days in safety at St Cirq Lapopie.

'As for England, he was relieved to hear that, as the years passed, the cruelty diminished and Norman rule became more bearable. He travelled to Constantinople and joined the Varangian Guard of the Byzantine Emperor, and served with distinction for many years. When your father became Emperor in 1081, Hereward, who had by then created a new name for himself, rose through the ranks to become Captain of the Guard, of what we now call the Old Order. They campaigned together until Hereward was well over fifty years of age, when he retired with Alexius' blessing. Despite repeated pleadings, Hereward would take no title nor accept a gratuity of estates or wealth, asking only for anonymity, which your father gladly gave him.

'Hereward asked your father if he would accept the Talisman, which, knowing its significance for Hereward, Alexius agreed to. So Hereward withdrew to a remote part of the Empire, the whereabouts of which were known only to the Emperor and a few men he trusted. He has been there for over twenty years and is now a very old man.'

'That is quite a story, Godwin of Ely. I am grateful to you for sharing it with me. Now that my father has entrusted me with the

Talisman, I wonder if you would return it to Hereward of Bourne for me?'

'But I am sure he would want you to wear it, my Prince.'

'I am flattered, but I don't think it is necessary. Your story has taught me all I need to know about kingship. I think I understand the Talisman's message.' Prince John Comnenus placed his hand on Godwin of Ely's shoulder. 'I hope I can live my life as bravely and nobly as Hereward of Bourne did.'

'You have made a good beginning, my Prince. Your father is a great Emperor and an even better man. You seem to have many of his qualities. Follow his advice, live by his example, and you will become a worthy successor. Byzantium will flourish under your reign and you will leave a legacy that will be remembered for generations to come. But remember, you are only a man; even emperors are mortal. Lives, even great ones, soon become memories. Learn from the past, but live your life in the present and hope that the future will benefit from what you do on earth.' The old man leaned over and grabbed the Prince's arm. 'Remember, once your time is over, it has gone for ever.'

As the Old Man of the Wildwood had become wise beyond the grasp of ordinary men, so the Old Man of the Mountain had acquired extraordinary intuition and insight. Now he was able to guide the young prince, as his mentor had once guided him.

Prince John Comnenus, deep in thought, looked to the east towards his home in Constantinople. He realized that the story of Hereward, Thegn of Bourne, would always be with him. He hoped that when his reign as Emperor came to be judged by history, his deeds would stand comparison with those of Hereward, England's last and finest warrior.

Leo of Methone abruptly interrupted his contemplation. 'My Lord Prince!'

485

John Comnenus turned back towards Godwin of Ely. His eyes were closed and he seemed very still.

The three men rushed to his side to rouse him, but the drama of his long life was finally over.

Godwin was facing north-west, towards England, and looked content. As he died, he would have been remembering those he loved. The faithful Edwin, the young envoy; Ingigerd and Maria, the family's heart and soul, and their lovely daughters, Gwyneth and Wulfhild; Edmund of Kent, who finally committed Abbot Thurstan to the fate that he deserved; mighty Einar, his loyal second-in-command; Alphonso of Granada, the finest soldier he had ever known; Martin Lightfoot, a mercurial companion who could sing as well as he could fight, and whose stories filled their lives with humour; and his delightful daughters, Gunnhild and Estrith, whose love and understanding nursed him through the terrible ending of the Siege of Ely.

Finally, he would have thought of Torfida, the remarkable woman whose life had shaped his own. The prediction made by the Old Man of the Wildwood had come to pass; she did indeed become his guide and his inspiration, and it was her destiny to help him find his.

He would also have been contemplating his homeland; a realm he must have assumed had already forgotten him. In truth, he had changed it more than he could have imagined. His legacy would be generations in the making, but would be part of a new England, where the storytellers would one day call Hereward of Bourne 'The Last of the English'.

In fact, he was not the last of his kind; he was the foremost. He was 'The First of the English'.

John Comnenus organized an honour guard for the funeral. A soft piece of ground was chosen, not far from where they had spent the long days and nights of storytelling, and Godwin of Ely – for that was now his name – was buried facing England.

Men of the Varangian Guard dug a deep grave, so that he would never be disturbed, and so that they could place in it all his precious belongings.

Leo blessed each one as it was arranged around his body: the neatly wrapped robe of a Captain of the Varangian Guard of the Old Order; an awesome arsenal of weapons, including his English battle-shield in ash, his Byzantine bronze shield and his father's sword; his personal standard in gold, crimson and black; and his astrolabe, a gift from Rodrigo of Bivar and the lodestone that he always carried.

The Great Axe of Göteborg was positioned on his chest, resting under his chin, and smaller items were laid either side of it: the Order of the Cotentin, given to him in Sicily; an array of medals awarded by the Emperor Alexius; the old iron key to Bourne Church; and his mother's jewels, a few simple stones set in bronze.

A single gold piece from the reign of King Cnut, which King William had placed on the tomb of St Etheldreda, was put carefully into the palm of one hand. And in the other was placed a handful of bullion from the reign of Edward the Confessor, wrapped in a scroll from Osbjorn, Prince of Denmark. Finally, the Virgin Martyr's rosary was draped over them.

The most precious items were arranged in a fine inlaid chest, a gift from John Comnenus, and placed above his head: the Roll of Honour of the Brotherhood of St Etheldreda; Torfida's wooden inscription, his beloved's last and most important message to him; her wedding ring of Russian gold; and her valued personal possession – a parchment map of the world.

Last of all, the Talisman of Truth, the ancient amulet that had given meaning to his life, was placed around his neck for the final time.

At the last, Prince John hesitated. He signalled to the funeral party to pause. The heir to the Purple of Byzantium then fell to his knees

487

and reached into the grave to retrieve the Talisman from the neck of Godwin of Ely.

He turned to John Azoukh. 'He sacrificed so much in its cause; I don't think he would have wanted the Talisman to lie in his grave for eternity. After all, he was only its guardian. We will take it back to Constantinople; perhaps one day we'll have need of it.'

Each of the Varangians present then took it in turns to cover the body of Godwin of Ely with the parched earth of the Peloponnese. Afterwards, Prince John ordered that everything on the hilltop be destroyed so that, in keeping with his oath to King William, no trace of his final resting place would ever be found.

Leo of Methone read an epitaph. 'Here lies Godwin of Ely, known in a previous life as Hereward of Bourne. No nobler man has ever lived. May he rest in peace.'

John Azoukh placed a simple wreath of olive leaves on the grave.

Prince John Comnenus looked towards the north-west. 'I would like to go to England one day. They are an interesting people; I feel certain we will hear more of them . . . I wonder if the domain of the Wodewose of England's wildwoods extends all the way to the Peloponnese?

'But I don't suppose it matters – I'm sure he will welcome back the Old Man of the Mountain to the earth that gave him life.'

Postscript

In the year 1118, following the death of his father, Alexius I, John Comnenus became the Emperor of Constantinople. His reign was the high point of a Comneni dynasty noted for the wisdom and justice of its rule. Despite his less than handsome features, his own tenure as Emperor was so highly regarded that he became known as 'John the Beautiful'.

The Norman dynasty prospered in England long after William's death, and there were no more risings by the English people. A revolt of the earls in 1075 was little more than a dispute about levels of taxation within the feudal aristocracy. The wild reaches of Wales were soon subdued and King Malcolm of Scotland had to bow to William by the Treaty of Abernathy in 1072.

Harald Hardrada was the last of the great Viking warriors as Scandinavian power in the world began to decline. Prince Olaf, the son of Hardrada and the only senior Norwegian aristocrat to survive Stamford Bridge, became known as Olaf the Quiet and ruled over a peaceful Norway for twenty-five years.

Prince Osbjorn never became King of Denmark. Upon the death of his brother, Svein Estrithson, in 1076, the King was succeeded by five of his many sons in turn: Harald, Cnut, Olaf, Eric and Niels. Svein Estrithson had so many children, all of them illegitimate, that chroniclers lost count of the total.

William 'the Conqueror', as he became known, died near Rouen on 9 September 9 1087. He had become so fat that he ruptured his stomach on the pommel of his horse as it stumbled, and never recovered from the injury. Awful scenes followed his death as those around him scrambled to claim his possessions. At his funeral, as they tried to force his body into its stone sarcophagus, it burst open, causing an unbearable stench. His tomb was later defiled four times so that, by 1793, only a single thighbone remained.

Pope Nicholas II was succeeded in 1061 by Alexander II, who was Pope until 1073. However, in 1075 Father Hildebrand became Pope Gregory VII. During the ten years of his papacy, he became widely respected for his wisdom and kindness.

Rodrigo of Bivar continued his military prowess and became Lord of the Taifa of Valencia. He died peacefully in his bed in July 1099. Doña Jimena outlived him and died a few years later.

In 1074 Edgar the Atheling led a force against Normandy from his base in Montreuil-sur-Mer, but it failed when a storm destroyed most of his ships. He finally submitted to William, and was reconciled with him. He became a friend of Robert Curthose, William's son, fought with the Normans in Apulia and accompanied Robert on the First Crusade in 1100, leading the English contingent. He returned to England and lived into the reign of Henry I. He died in 1125, becoming the only one of Hereward's contemporaries to outlive him.

Earl Morcar remained imprisoned by William, who, in a moment of remorse on his deathbed, ordered his release.

Unfortunately, William 'Rufus', the King's second son and successor, had him rearrested and he died in prison sometime after 1090.

Even though he is now known as Hereward 'the Wake', Hereward of Bourne was not given the suffix 'Wake' until many years after his death. The term is thought to come from the Old French 'wac' dog, as in wake-dog, the name for dogs used to warn of intruders.

Nothing is known about the fate of any of the survivors of Hereward's extended family. However, through his daughters, Gunnhild and Estrith, there are intriguing claims linking several modern-day families to Hereward of Bourne. In particular, a family of ancient origin from Courteenhall, Northamptonshire, claims that the present baronet, the fourteenth Sir Hereward Wake, is directly descended from one of Hereward's twin daughters. The present-day Wakes of Courteenhall are certainly directly descended from a Geoffrey Wac, who died in 1150. His son, Hugh Wac, who died in 1172, married Emma, the daughter of Baldwin Fitzgilbert and his unnamed wife. That wife, it is claimed, was the granddaughter of either Gunnhild or Estrith in the female line from Hereward and Torfida. It is suggested that the woman's mother had married Richard de Rulos and that her grandmother had married Hugh de Evermur, a Norman knight in the service of King William. It is a tenuous link, but an intriguing possibility.

There are also other claimants to the lineage of Hereward the Wake, including the Harvard family (the founders of Harvard University) and the Howard family (the Dukes of Norfolk and Earls Marshal of England).

The cruelty of Norman rule diminished in the years following the Conquest and although hardly benign in its outlook, England settled into a long period of relative calm and growth. England was never invaded again, but Normandy ultimately fell to the French and was ruled from Paris. Ironically, therefore, the long-term heritage of the Normans became better exemplified in England than in Normandy itself. But England's future was not entirely cast in the Norman image. The invaders gradually adopted English ways and the English language and although the Norman system of government remained paramount, English culture gradually regained its status.

William's fourth son, Henry I, became the third Norman King of England in the year 1100. He had married Edith (who took the name Matilda), the daughter of St Margaret of Scotland and her husband Malcolm Canmore. Fittingly, Margaret was the granddaughter of Edmund II (Ironside), King of England in 1016, and could claim fourteen generations of Cerdician royal blood. The *Anglo-Saxon Chronicle* rejoiced that the new Queen was of 'the right royal race of England'.

Henry and Matilda's firstborn son was named William, in honour of his grandfather, 'the Conqueror', but also 'Atheling' in honour of his Cerdician blood. Thus, less than forty years after Hastings, English pedigree was once more embodied in the monarchy. In the reign of King John, William's great-great-grandson, much of what Hereward and the Brotherhood fought for at Ely was enshrined in Magna Carta. The 'Great Charter' was signed by the King in a meadow at Runnymede on 15 June 1215 and became the first milestone on the road to modern democracy.

The legends of Wodewose, the Green Man, and the ancient beliefs of the peoples of the British Isles in the harmony of the natural world, did survive the coming of the Normans. The Old Man of the Wildwood would be content to know that throughout the length and breadth of England and its Celtic neighbours, the folk memories of the distant past remain enshrined in legends, never to be forgotten. Just as they did centuries ago, they remain part of the art, literature and customs of these islands and help define its unique identity and that of its peoples.

The Harrying of the North, 1070

The true scale of the atrocities committed by King William in northern England in 1070 will never be known, but the brutality of the crimes shocked the whole of Europe. Even scribes writing under Norman rule could not hide their contempt for what had been done.

Within a lifetime of the events, the Anglo-Norman chronicler Orderic Vitalis wrote the following account. He described the event in the first person, thus emphasizing William's personal responsibility.

I fell upon the English of the Northern shires like a ravening lion. I commanded their houses and corn and all their chattels to be burnt without distinction and large herds of cattle and beasts of burden to be butchered wherever they were found. It was then I took revenge on multitudes of both sexes. I became so barbarous a murderer of many thousands, both young and old. Having there-

493

fore made my way to the throne of that kingdom by so many crimes, I dare not to leave it to anyone but God.

Orderic Vitalis' estimate of the number of English dead in the Harrying of the North was 100,000. This figure was also reported in other chronicles of the time.

Acknowledgements

To the wonderful friends and outstanding professionals who have helped me transform a vague idea and a very amateurish transcript into a moderately decent story, my eternal thanks and gratitude.

Genealogies

The Lineage of the Cerdician Kings of Wessex and England from the Ninth Century to Edward the Confessor

The Lineage of Harold Godwinson, Earl of Wessex and King of England

The Lineage of William the Bastard, Duke of Normandy and King of England

The Lineage of Harold Hardrada, King of Norway

The Descendants of Hereward of Bourne and Torfida (conjectural)

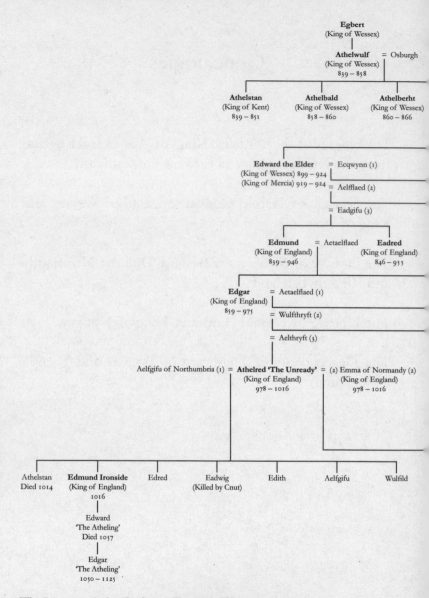

The Lineage of the Cerdician Kings of Wessex and England from the Ninth Century to Edward the Confessor

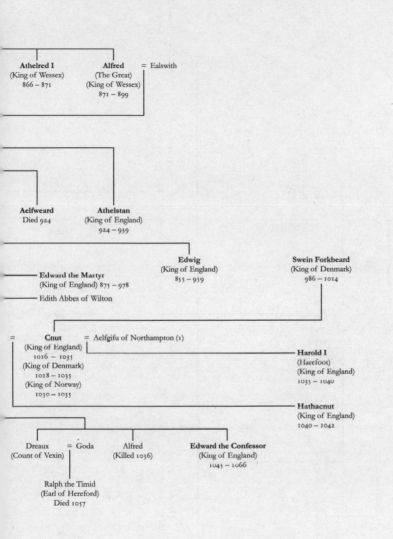

Athelred I
(King of Wessex)
866 – 871

Alfred
(The Great)
(King of Wessex)
871 – 899

= Ealswith

Aelfweard
Died 924

Athelstan
(King of England)
924 – 939

Edwig
(King of England)
855 – 959

Swein Forkbeard
(King of Denmark)
986 – 1014

Edward the Martyr
(King of England) 875 – 978

Edith Abbes of Wilton

= **Cnut**
(King of England)
1016 – 1035
(King of Denmark)
1018 – 1035
(King of Norway)
1030 – 1035

= Aelfgifu of Northampton (1)

Harold I
(Harefoot)
(King of England)
1035 – 1040

Hathacnut
(King of England)
1040 – 1042

Dreaux
(Count of Vexin)

= Goda

Alfred
(Killed 1036)

Edward the Confessor
(King of England)
1045 – 1066

Ralph the Timid
(Earl of Hereford)
Died 1057

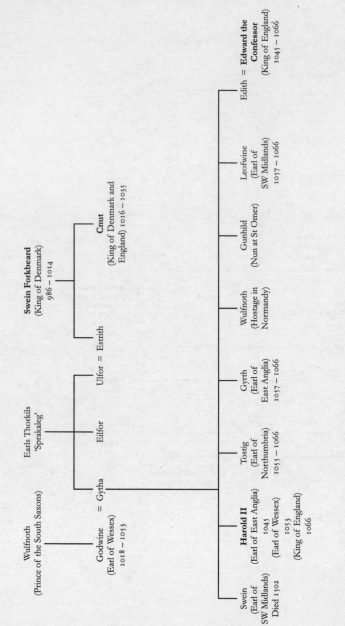

The Lineage of Harold Godwinson, Earl of Wessex and King of England

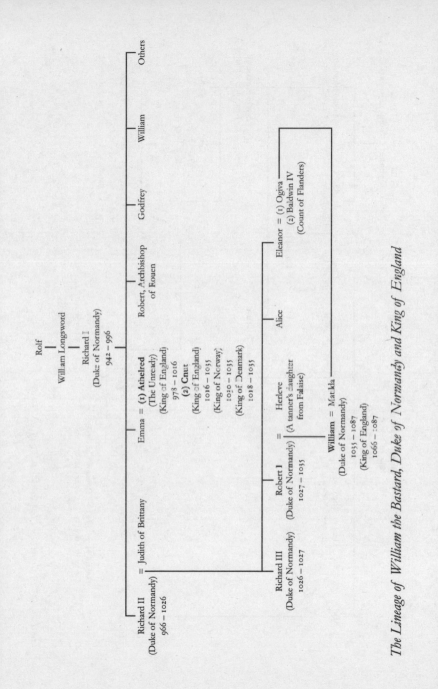

Rolf
|
William Longsword
|
Richard I
(Duke of Normandy)
942–996

Richard II = Judith of Brittany
(Duke of Normandy)
966–1026

Emma = (1) Athelred
(The Unready)
(King of England)
978–1016
(2) Cnut
(King of England)
1016–1035
(King of Norway)
1020–1035
(King of Denmark)
1018–1035

Robert, Archbishop
of Rouen

Godfrey

William

Others

Richard III
(Duke of Normandy)
1026–1027

Robert I = Herleve
(Duke of Normandy) (A tanner's daughter
1027–1035 from Falaise)

Alice

Eleanor = (1) Ogiva
(2) Baldwin IV
(Count of Flanders)

William = Matilda
(Duke of Normandy)
1035–1087
(King of England)
1066–1087

The Lineage of William the Bastard, Duke of Normandy and King of England

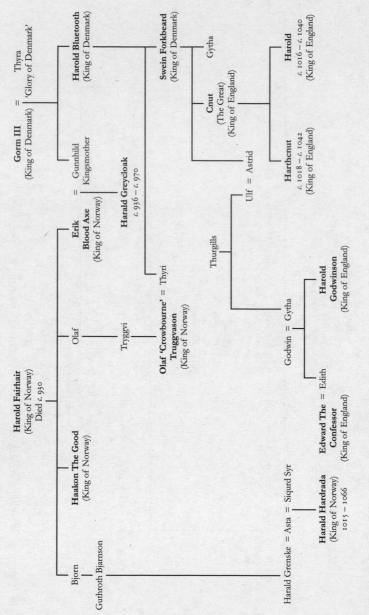

The Lineage of Harald Hardrada, King of Norway

The Descendants of Hereward of Bourne and Torfida (conjectural)

Hereward = Torfida
1035–1118 | 1039–1067

Daughter = Hugh de Evermur

Daughter = Richard de Rulos

Daughter = Baldwin Fitzgilbert

Emma = Hugh de Wac
Died 1172

Geoffrey Wac
Died 1150

This conjectural genealogy, through a succession of marriages to Norman nobles, would confirm that the Wake family of Courtenhall, Northamptonshire, England may have claim to descendancy from Hereward and Torfida. The present Baronet, Sir Hereward Wake, BT, MC, DL, is a direct descendant of Geoffrey Wac

'Hereward the Wake'

Hereward of Bourne is better known as Hereward the Wake, especially after the publication in 1871 of Charles Kingsley's popular novel of that title. However, the name 'Wake' is not contemporary with Hereward of Bourne, who has also been called 'Hereward of the Fens', 'Hereward the Saxon' and 'Hereward, Last of the English'

The name'Hereward the Wake' was first used by John of Peterborough in his chronicle, completed in 1368. Its meaning is obscure but is likely to refer to Hereward's persistence in 'disturbing' the Normans; his attacks meant that they were constantly kept awake. There is support for this in the accounts of Fulk, Count of Anjou, who was at war with Count Herbert of Maine (1015 – 1036). The latter was so persistent in his night attacks that even the dogs were kept awake by his frequent sallies and Fulk's men-at-arms got no sleep. So, Count Herbert was called the 'Wake' or 'Wake-dog'

Maps

N

Norway

Kristiansand · · Sweden
Göteborg

Scotland
· Lymphanan

Iona

Ireland
Dublin · · Preston

Wales
England

Holy Roman
Empire

Rouen · Paris
Normandy

France

Geneva ·

Bordeaux ·
Oveido · · St Cirq Lapopie
León Toulouse · Pisa ·
León · · Burgos
Castile
Zaragoza · · Urgell Rome ·

Almoravids
(Moslem)

→ The First Great Journey, 1059–1064
--→ The Journey to Spain, 1067–1069

The Great Journey and the Journey to Spain

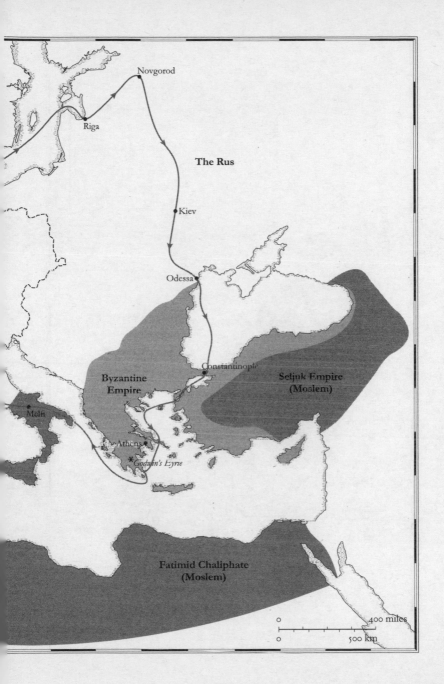

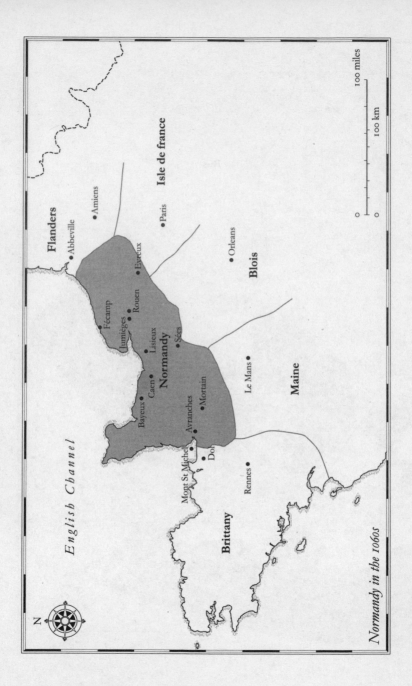

Normandy in the 1060s

English Channel

Flanders

Isle de france

Blois

Maine

Brittany

N

100 miles

100 km

Abbeville •
Amiens •
Fécamp •
Jumièges •
Rouen •
Evreux •
Lisieux •
Caen •
Bayeux •
Avranches •
Mont St Michel •
Dol •
Séez •
Mortain •
Le Mans •
Rennes •
Paris •
Orleans •

Normandy

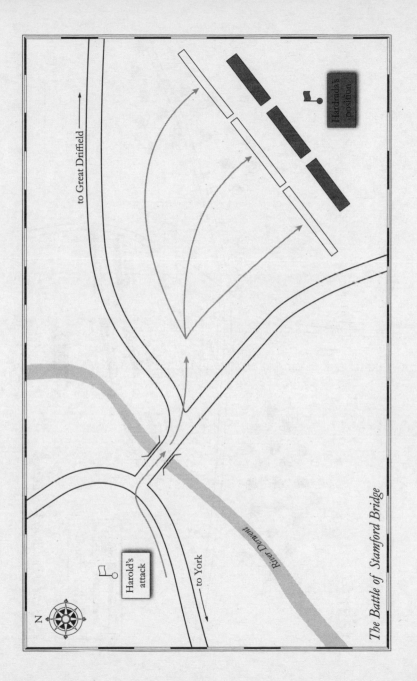

The Battle of Stamford Bridge

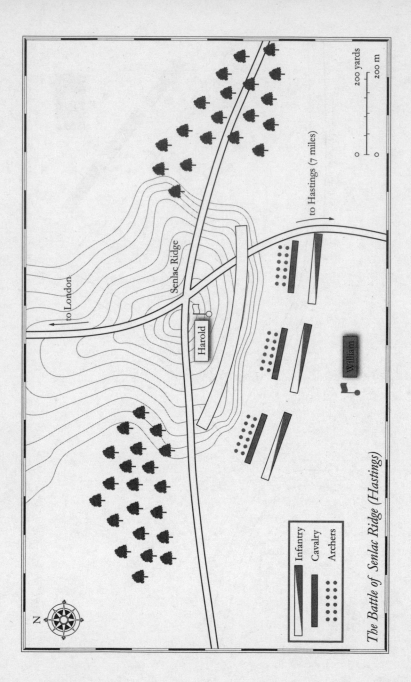

N

Infantry
Cavalry
Archers

Harold

William

Senlac Ridge

to London

to Hastings (7 miles)

200 yards
200 m

The Battle of Senlac Ridge (Hastings)

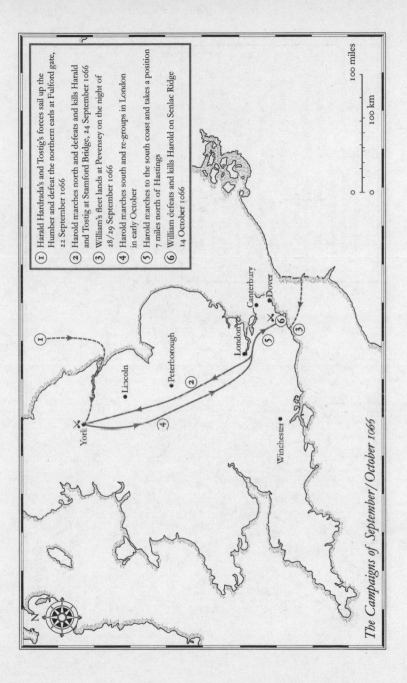

① Harald Hardrada's and Tostig's forces sail up the Humber and defeat the northern earls at Fulford gate, 22 September 1066

② Harold marches north and defeats and kills Harald and Tostig at Stamford Bridge, 24 September 1066

③ William's fleet lands at Pevensey on the night of 28/29 September 1066

④ Harold marches south and re-groups in London in early October

⑤ Harold marches to the south coast and takes a position 7 miles north of Hastings

⑥ William defeats and kills Harold on Senlac Ridge 14 October 1066

The Campaigns of September/October 1066

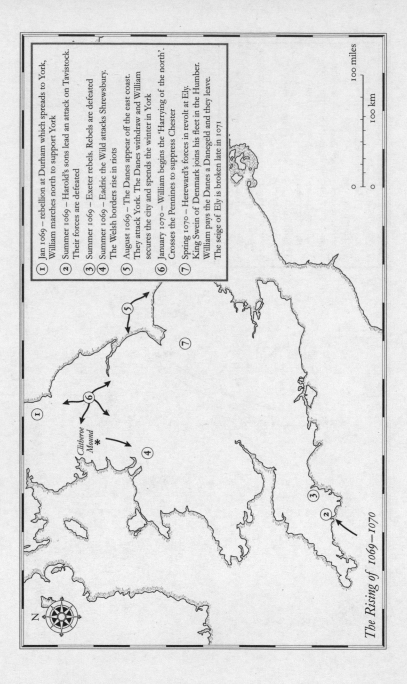

1. Jan 1069 – rebellion at Durham which spreads to York, William marches north to support York

2. Summer 1069 – Harold's sons lead an attack on Tavistock. Their forces are defeated

3. Summer 1069 – Exeter rebels. Rebels are defeated

4. Summer 1069 – Eadric the Wild attacks Shrewsbury. The Welsh borders rise in riots

5. August 1069 – The Danes appear off the east coast. They attack York. The Danes withdraw and William secures the city and spends the winter in York

6. January 1070 – William begins the 'Harrying of the north'. Crosses the Pennines to suppress Chester

7. Spring 1070 – Hereward's forces in revolt at Ely. King Swein of Denmark joins his fleet in the Humber. William pays the Danes a Danegeld and they leave. The seige of Ely is broken late in 1071

Clitheroe Mound

N

0   100 miles
0   100 km

The Rising of 1069–1070

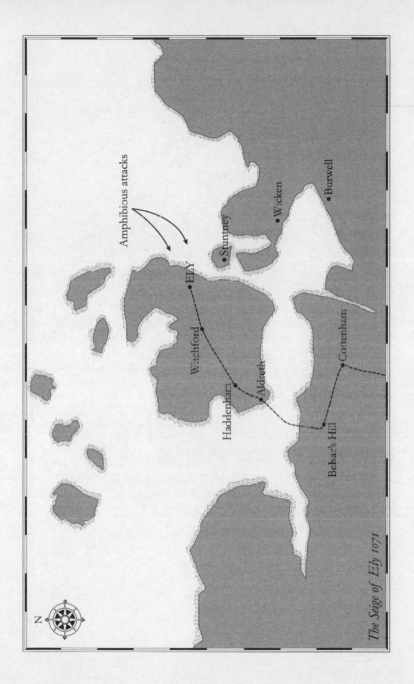

The Seige of Ely 1071